TRAGEDY DAY

DOCTOR WHO – THE NEW ADVENTURES

Also available:

THE NEW
DOCTOR WHO
ADVENTURES

TRAGEDY DAY

Gareth Roberts

First published in Great Britain in 1994 by
Doctor Who Books
an imprint of Virgin Publishing Ltd
332 Ladbroke Grove
London W10 5AH

Copyright © Gareth Roberts 1994

'Doctor Who' series copyright © British Broadcasting
Corporation 1994

ISBN 0 42620410 7

Cover illustration by Jeff Cummins

Phototypeset by Intype, London
Printed and bound in Great Britain by
Cox & Wyman Ltd, Reading, Berks

For my chums, without whom . . .

Prologue:

The Curse

1

Sarul opened her palm, offering the grain. Three birds swooped down, formed a line on her forearm and began to peck. She winced as their tiny beaks nipped at the skin beneath the seed.

'Give them some more, Linn,' she asked the slim, dark-eyed boy at her side a little nervously. He laughed and scooped handfuls of the seed from the wool pouch at his waist. The birds cawed happily and flapped over to collect it. They were soon joined by another ten.

Sarul adjusted her clothes and stood looking about at the steep green sides of the valley they had been walking through. 'How,' she asked, 'do the gulls always know to come here?'

Linn shrugged. More birds had been attracted by the grain and he looked in danger of toppling over as they settled along his arms and shoulders. 'How do the suns know when to shine? It isn't important.'

Sarul didn't agree but she didn't want to start an argument. She glanced back over her shoulder. Through a break in the far side of the gorge she saw the business of late morning continuing back in the village. Excited cries came from the harbour, beyond the small grey houses. The first boats of the day had returned, their nets ready to be sliced open. Sarul turned her head to the other side of the valley and the sea that lapped around the curve of the bay. The wind was stronger than it had been at dawn and the sky was clouding over. 'It'll be winter soon.'

Linn shook himself and shooed away the birds. 'Don't be silly, summer's barely started.' He walked over, holding out his arms in a familiar gesture he knew she would respond to. She entered his embrace and their lips brushed wetly.

Sarul broke the kiss. 'It's such a depressing day,' she said. 'Listen to the wind.'

'Sarul,' Linn said impatiently.

She walked away, climbing over to a knoll where she made herself comfortable. 'Tell me an old, sad story.'

'I don't want to.'

She patted the grass at her side. 'You know all the old tales. Go on, tell me . . .' She thought over the legends. 'I know, tell me the story of the black tree and the silver spear.'

He sat. 'I don't want to, it's boring.'

She placed a hand on his thigh. 'It's the one I like best. Go on.'

He brushed her away. 'Well, I prefer the legend of the curse of the red glass.'

'If you must, then.' Sarul leant back and closed her eyes. When he told one of the stories, Linn's voice lost its natural adolescent wheedle. It became the voice of his father, a man twenty years in the fields with another ten hunting in the forests before that. Sarul thought that Linn's father would have been much more attractive at his son's age. It was typical of her mate to have chosen a strange, fantastic story over the simple, straightforward tale of the black tree and the silver spear.

He began. His initial reluctance soon gave way, as she had known it would, to an enlivening enthusiasm that punctuated his delivery with significant pauses.

'In the time between the storms but before the land shook, the people were feasting. The night was lit well by a full north moon and they danced between the houses, meat juices dribbling down their chins. The harvest had been a good one, with more than enough food for all, and the old ones were pleased. They lit pipes and passed them about to celebrate.

2

'The day had been clear and fine. Yet over the roar of the feast they heard the low note of an oncoming storm. The sea splashed over as far as the outer houses. It ran along the gutters and into the channels. The old ones were troubled and called a meeting in the street. They forbade fishing for one week and warned the curious away from the shore.

'The feast went on but the people were uneasy. Some gathered in small groups and spoke of their fears. One man believed that a mighty stone had been hurled into the water, another that a great bird had dropped one of its eggs from a nest in the tree at the top of the world. But they respected the words of the old ones and despite their worries they retired that night and slept well.

'A few days passed and nothing further occurred. Then one morning a group of children disobeyed their parents and left for the shore to play. In a cove on the far side of the bay they found a giant grey house that had been smashed into pieces by the rocks. Lying beside it was a man, taller than any in the village. His arms and legs were thicker and his head was more square. The children could see that he was close to death, but they were still afraid. He passed them a small piece of jagged red glass. Then he smiled and died.

'The children returned to the village. They decided to say nothing of their discovery, knowing they would be punished for going against the orders of the old ones. They wrapped the red glass in barjorum leaves and concealed it in the forest.'

Linn paused a second. In spite of herself, Sarul saw the events clearly in her mind.

'And then one of the group, a tiny girl, slipped when playing in the trees and was killed, her pretty head split against a rock. Soon after, the father of another of the children, a good hunter of many years, lost his way in the woods and was killed by a bear. Added to this, many of the boats came back with dead black fish in their nets.

'Somehow, the old ones knew what had happened. They confronted the eldest of the troublesome children and

3

demanded the truth. He led them to the red glass and they took it to their hut. They tried to break it and could not. One suggested that they throw it to the sea but the others reminded her that to pass on a curse is to invite its effects seven times over. Instead, they placed it inside a lattice of herbs and hid it. The body of the stranger and the grey house were set alight until not one hair of his head remained, and the stench from the pyre was terrible.'

Linn smiled and sat back. He slipped an eager arm around Sarul's neck but now it was she who pushed him away. 'That's not the end,' she prompted. 'The old man and the girl.'

'I thought you didn't like this story.'

'Finish it. Go on.' Sarul's eyes remained closed.

'Very well,' Linn said begrudgingly. 'Years passed and the crops started to fail. Several men died of a long, wasting sickness. The people despaired. Then one day, an old man and a young girl walked out from a new rock that had appeared on the shore. They offered their friendship and the situation was explained to them. The old man was very wise. He called the blight "radiation". He brought blue powder from the new rock and spread it over the fields from a chalice. Soon the crops started to grow again and they have remained plentiful ever since. The fish bred swiftly and the waters were again full.'

'And the red glass?' Sarul prompted.

'The old ones were grateful to the old man and offered him a pipe. He declined, saying that he had one of his own. He requested the red glass, which fascinated him. He would not listen to the warnings of the old ones and said that the red glass was not connected to the sickness called radiation. He took the red glass back to the new rock and it disappeared. The people were contented.'

'And were freed of the curse,' Sarul concluded for him. 'Because the old man had taken the red glass willingly.'

'Yes,' Linn confirmed. 'But there are many who say that the curse of the red glass still haunts our people and our land. And that only if it returns will the spell be broken. It is better, perhaps, not to think of that.' •

4

Sarul opened her eyes. 'You may kiss me now,' she said.

Linn smirked. 'Don't you want to hear the story of the black tree and the silver spear?'

She pulled his head down to hers and placed a finger over his lips.

2

Barbara knocked on the door of Susan's room. 'Come in,' the girl answered.

'The Doctor says the co-ordinates are matching up. We'll be landing soon,' she began, then broke off as she noticed that Susan's hair was dishevelled. She was sitting bolt upright in her bed. 'Susan, what's the matter?'

The girl smiled weakly. 'Just a stupid nightmare, that's all. Nothing important.'

Barbara sat on the bed and took Susan's hand in hers. 'You look white as a sheet. I didn't think you had nightmares.'

'Not normally. I can't even remember . . .' Her voice trailed away.

'Never mind,' Barbara said, getting to her feet. 'You'd better get dressed, anyway. You wouldn't want to keep your grandfather waiting. He's in a bad enough mood as it is.'

'Yes!' Susan cried suddenly, not even listening. 'Yes, I can remember!'

'Do you want to talk about it?' Barbara asked, disturbed by Susan's reaction to what was, after all, only a dream.

'Oh, it was about a place that Grandfather and I visited a while before we met you and Ian. There was a small village by the sea, made entirely of a sort of mud. The people were friendly, they didn't want for anything. Grandfather said they had been living the same way for centuries.'

'It sounds wonderful,' Barbara commented. 'A lot better than the places we've seen recently.'

Susan wriggled herself under her sheets, making herself

comfortable. 'But there was something wrong there. Their crops refused to grow and the stores were running out. Grandfather took samples and carried out some tests. There was a high level of radiation. It was coming from the engine of a spaceship that had crashed there.'

'What happened then?' asked Barbara.

'Well, Grandfather mixed up some powder from chemicals in the Ship and spread it over the land. He thought it would give the growth cycle a shock, get it going again. And it worked and we went on our way.'

Barbara was puzzled. 'I don't understand you, Susan. Why did you have a nightmare about a wonderful place like that?'

Susan shivered. 'The people there believed that they'd been cursed by a piece of red glass. It had been brought to their planet by the pilot of the spaceship. He'd passed it on and died. Grandfather told them that was superstitious nonsense and it was the ship's reactor that had caused all the problems. So we brought the red glass back to the Ship with us.'

'And what exactly was it?'

'He couldn't tell,' Susan said. 'He spent weeks just trying to scratch it. Whatever it was made of was indestructible. Anyway, eventually he lost interest and put it away somewhere.'

She climbed out of her bed and walked slowly over to her locker, yawning. 'You see, sometimes I think that those people on that planet were right and that one day, because of that glass or whatever it is, something terrible is going to happen to us.'

Barbara smiled. Sometimes Susan was so easy to understand, full of exaggerated adolescent fears like any other girl of her age. 'Well, the answer's easy,' she said. 'We'll throw it out next time we land.'

'I'm afraid it's not as simple as that,' Susan replied. 'You see, Grandfather can't remember where he put it.'

3

My dearest Marsha,

I was pleased to receive your letter and to read of the progress of our little soldier. Your touching story of his antics with the clowns in the town square made my troopers laugh when I related it to them over breakfast yesterday.

As you can imagine, with all the hard work to be done, there is little time for mirth here. Nevertheless, the men's spirits are high, their hearts filled with devotion to the Truth and Light of Luminus.

You will see from the heading of this letter that the Leader has decided to name this beautiful planet in honour of Marshal Olleril and that a new metric calendar has been established. The eugenic streaming operation is now almost complete. We were appalled by the nature of the natives here; a small, feckless people with dark skin and eyes. Their puny limbs were unsuited to toil and our boys could find no satisfactory women among them. The Leader decided it would be best to stream them down by seven-eighths. They offered no resistance. In fact, their spineless acceptance of death is irritating. Even when we broke the bones of their old women (their leaders!), they displayed only fear. Yesterday we drove a small group of them into a swamp by firing at their feet. You should have seen them, jumping about like baboons at the fair!

Tell your friends at the nursery that work is progressing swiftly and morale is high. The plans for the city to be built on this spot were approved by the Leader this morning and they fill my heart with pride. To take such an important place in history!

Yet there is something unsettling. I impart this in confidence, my love. Last night two of our men drowned and today the communicators broke down for over an hour. A

*feeling of unease surrounds us. Earlier, I executed one
of the men. He had been spreading unease with some
crackbrained tale told to him by one of the natives, of a
red glass that had cursed the planet and any upon it.*

Kiss our son for me,
General Stillmun

4

*Extract from Empire City Quality News, Fennestry 17,
Year 597*

CONSPIRACY WEARY

Richard Nemmun on current affairs

My college days, like many others of my generation I'm
sure, were spent in the main outside official buildings,
protesting about this and that. These were the early days
of decade six, when liberalism held out hope and anything
seemed possible. When we tired of shouting and crashing,
we'd sit and talk politics for hours on end. One member
of our group, a tall, shock-haired boy who I'm told now
works in the financial sector, attributed all our problems,
from the eight-hour day to the hydronics failures of '67,
to a conspiracy; a grand order that controlled our entire
world. At the heart of it all, of course, were the Luminuns.
We'd argue that for a secret society they couldn't be much
cop if humble humanities undergraduates could uncover
their clandestine influences. 'Ah,' he'd reply archly, 'but
what if that's what we're *supposed* to think?'

I note without particular surprise that, following in the
wake of the turbulent international events of the last few
months, this theory is coming back into fashion. If last
year the glossier mags seemed obsessively concerned with
the 'rigged' Vijjan elections, this year's craze is very definitely the cult of Luminus. Facts seem to have been thrown
out of the window, wrapped in a bundle of sloppy journal-

ism. Luminus, let us remind ourselves, had almost collapsed even before its minions could complete the settlement of this world and the horrific extermination of its natives. Six hundred years later, it seems incredible that there are those who still apportion blame for our troubles on them, claiming that Luminus somehow survived.

Why, though, this need for conspiracies? Can Empire City, all that is left of our once-proud nation, with its cordon and access laws, its homelessness and lawlessness, bear to face itself and its failings? Should we not confront the underlying issues that have created these flaws?

Could it be that we would rather shirk the responsibility and sit back idly to read concealed Luminun messages in everything from the *Martha and Arthur* reruns to the Tragedy Day lottery numbers?

The star was a red giant, a colossal sphere that had burned for millennia, throwing out light for years around. Its density teetered on the point of collapse, a calamity held back only by the labouring wills of the civilization its energies supported. It glowed at the exact and indivisible centre of the galaxy of Pangloss.

Two hundred and thirty-five million miles away the first of the planets spun unhurriedly. It was a hot, steaming, heaving pit of a world. The flame fields, scorching vistas of coke, slag and tar, covered nine-tenths of the land mass. The workers toiled under the rufous sky, shovels and forks clattering and clinking as they stoked the furnaces. Their bodies were blistered under rough sacking. Clouds of thick smoke clogged their lungs and blackened their faces. The remainder of the planet's pock-marked surface was covered by gushing torrents of white-hot lava.

The workers' hovels were huddled together inside a worked-out mountain of petrified soot. Towering above them at the peak was the shrine, where the Union of Three kept vigil over their dominion. The Friars controlled the strange frictions that bound the galaxy of Pangloss together in eternal suffering. The workers in the flame fields believed that the Friars had always existed. The Friars were too old to remember.

The Immortal Heart of the shrine was decorated in glinting red crystal. One of the crystals was missing from the series. A distinctive jagged outline marked where it should have been. No other piece of red glass could fill the space.

The Friars stood before the three hundred and thirty-seven Bibles of Pangloss, which were ranged along one wall. The books balanced on a shelf made from timber carted from the far distant groves of Knassos. The enormous faces of the Friars were concealed beneath red cowls. Waves of psychic energy pulsed about them invisibly. The air vibrated under the combined power of their concentration. Their minds were tuning in to the forty-ninth plane.

The signs were unmistakable. After fourteen centuries, the moment was approaching. They sensed the strands of Time weaving the circumstance that would allow them to reclaim what was theirs.

'I sense his return,' boomed Caphymus, 'at last.'

'He is passing back through the vastness of ages and the infinity of stars,' said Anonius.

Portellus gasped and the cowl covering his head slipped back. A human would have died instantly at the sight of the face.

'The TARDIS machine shall be ours,' he gasped. 'The red glass of the curse shall be redeemed. And he that took it must die.

'The Time Lord . . . must . . . die.'

1

The Refugees

The lowest clouds of the night sky met the highest spires of Empire City; two thousand square kilometres of weathered concrete, granite and plastic that had, in the six centuries since the settlement of Olleril, spread upwards, outwards and downwards as the influence of Empirica, its mother nation, had waxed and waned. Big War Four had left the outlands of the country empty and blasted. Almost all that was left was the city.

Gentle rain began to patter over the dirty streets of the South Side. At three in the morning, only a fool would have walked down the intersection of 433 and 705 alone. George Lipton was not a fool. He was only drunk and lost.

His night had been spent in the bar at Spindizzy's, a chrome parlour virtually in the shadow of the media compound, way over in central zone one of the city. After clearing his desk, George had walked straight over and ordered a double rakki, the first of many. Well-meaning acquaintances had sashayed through the double doors after a hard day in the office or on the studio floor to find him slouched over the bar, a line of empty glasses before him. The whispers had begun soon after, floating around the balding heads of these florid-shirted media types.

'Yes, it's true!' he had shouted suddenly, raising his head. The bar shushed immediately, silent apart from the backbeat of Fancy That's latest hit. 'Devor has sacked me! Captain Scumming Millennium has fired his producer!'

He had burst into tears and was consoled by drinks, sympathy and more drinks.

Several hours and a blurred subcar ride later and he was on the South Side, stumbling down streets with no lights or names. George had only been to the South Side once before, to record a few location scenes for a crime drama. He hadn't liked it then, in daylight. The dim crescent of the north moon had failed to pierce the grimy clouds and he could hardly see. He had to find an access point. That was the problem with the cordon. It was easy to get out of Central, but very difficult, if you overshot, to get back in.

He stopped to urinate on a corner and noted changing patterns of light reflecting off his steaming yellow stream. He shook, tidied himself away and staggered over to a gridded shop window. Eleven third-hand television screens flickered erratically through the mesh.

'Hey!' Lipton laughed. 'That's one of my shows!' The fourth screen from the left was showing one of the third season *Martha and Arthur*s, probably the best run. It was the segment where Arthur got locked in the toilet during an important business meeting.

George reminisced happily as Arthur's hazy monochrome image struggled with the lock. He could almost hear the laughter track. In that small moment his troubles were almost forgotten. But then the camera cut and they came rolling back. Devor, his runty, freckly ten-year-old features already formed into a superior Captain Millennium sneer, was cracking one of his smart-alec jokes to Martha in the kitchen set.

George pulled his eyes away and glanced over at the other screens. At this time of night there were only commercials, cartoons, city news or all three in quick succession. The screen on the far right was tuned to Empire TV Drama, which was saving money by rerunning shows from the previous day. And there he was again, Howard scumsucking crustball Devor, raygun poised to save the universe from destruction. Again.

'I gave my life to that show!' George screamed. He

rattled the mesh. Two tramps and a dog looked up from their places on the next shopfront along, shrugged and went back to sleep. 'I spent my life setting you up, Devor! Captain Millennium books, Captain Millennium underpants, Captain Millennium glow-in-the-crudding-dark pessaries . . . You owe me, you crustball scum!'

George's voice cracked and he started to cry. His legs buckled and he slid to the ground. All of this because he had refused to allow Devor another vacation in the recording block of this season. It would have been so easy to have agreed. A memo to his department head, a word with contracts and another 'Gee, do you remember when . . .?' script and he would have walked into his trailer tomorrow as secure as ever. What were things coming to when an actor could fire a producer?

Slowly, George pulled himself up from the pavement. His head was spinning and he realized he was going to be sick. He walked into a fire hydrant, doubled up and vomited. The muscles across his chest spasmed as he retched again and again. Images of the cheap fillers and educational videos of the producer's graveyard filled his mind, increasing the bitterness of his bile.

A white van pulled up alongside him, its side almost touching his lolling, outstretched arm. George looked up blearily, wiping flecks of vomit from his chin with his shirt-sleeve. The side of the vehicle had been sprayed with explicitly pictographic graffiti that left him in no doubt that those inside were considered by their detractors to be sexually deviant pigs.

He heard the back doors of the van being slammed open. Steel-capped boots dropped onto the cracked tarmac of the road.

'Officer,' George drooled, struggling to his feet once again. 'Officer, I'd like directions to an access point.' After all, he thought, police are police wherever you go, even on the South Side.

He rounded the corner of the van and his stomach met an armoured fist that reversed the previous year's costly and time-consuming paunch reduction op in seconds and for free. A second blow cracked him over the head. Blood flowed freely from his nose and lacerated lip.

'Up!' a voice ordered from the shadows. George's assailants hauled him upright by the arms. His head flopped back limply. The face of the police officer appeared before him, lit by the television screens. It was a face that George could tell it wasn't worth trying to reason with. Angular, unshaven, small drugged eyes. The tattoo of his gang, a broken dagger, stretched across his neck.

'It's him,' the officer said. 'Load him aboard.'

George was pulled forward and thrown head-first into the police wagon. His three attackers leapt in behind him. The doors slammed. One of the three rapped sharply on the divider and the wagon started off.

'Why . . .' George groaned. 'Why?'

'Shut him up,' ordered the officer.

George was kicked into unconsciousness. The pain of the blows got less and less sharp until he felt almost massaged by the pummelling. It was quite unlike the violence he was accustomed to in the studio. No incidental music, no sharp editing, no sudden rescue. No point.

He closed his eyes at last, but not before he'd noticed that all three policemen were wearing Tragedy Day buttons. The glistening black teardrop.

That was odd. They hardly seemed the caring sort.

Not far away was a large office block. The people who lived in the neighbourhood believed it to be the headquarters of the Toplex Sanitation company. None of them had had reason to question this assumption. They sometimes wondered why Toplex Sanitation needed such large offices all to itself, and why they had rented out all the warehouse space for miles around to store, it was claimed, spare parts. Only a few had been bothered enough to investigate and none of them had lived to tell the truth. The Toplex Sanitation company was the front for the Empire City base of Luminus, the organization that controlled the planet.

The largest office had been converted into a scanner

16

room. Operatives uniformed in the traditional aprons of Luminus sat before scanner screens that covered every area of the city. It was their task to make sure that the control program was functioning perfectly. And, as ever, it was.

At the centre of the scanner room sat a tall man called Forke. He was reviewing the events of the day and preparing a report for his superior. Everything in the city was proceeding smoothly. This would bode well, he thought, for his standing with the Supreme One.

A call came through on one of the top security frequencies. 'Accept,' he told his communicator.

'Sergeant Felder,' the caller identified himself. 'We've got the man you wanted.'

Forke smiled. 'George Lipton?'

'That's the one.'

'Very well. You know your orders. Carry them out. Your payment will be mailed tonight.'

'Fifteen thou?'

'Fifteen thou.' Forke broke the connection and stared at his reflection in the screen he was using to write his report. It was time to activate the processor. He reached for the communicator again.

In his apartment, Howard Devor was sticking his tongue down the throat of one of his fans. She was a bit skinny for his tastes and her breath smelled but he was too drunk to care.

The phone rang. Howard pushed her aside for a moment and picked up the receiver. 'Accept.'

'It's Mr Forke here, sir,'

'Yeah, whaddya want?'

'I thought you'd like to know we've dealt with Mr Lipton for you, as requested.'

Howard smiled. At last the geek was out of his hair. 'That's cool, Mr Forke,' he mumbled happily. 'That's just fine.'

'And I wondered,' asked Forke, 'how is the implant?'

Howard traced the tiny scar on his forehead. 'A bit sore

at first, all right now. Er, I have to go, I've got business to attend to. Er, convey my thanks to the Supreme One, okay?'

'Of course, Mr Devor.'

Howard returned to the task in hand, but he was finding it hard to concentrate. George Lipton was out of his life. He was free to do things his way. Since his initiation into Luminus, his life kept getting better and better. His rise to greatness had been pretty inevitable, though, he decided.

'All right,' Forke ordered. 'Bring the processor implant on line.'

The operative who was watching Howard Devor's apartment pressed a switch on the console before him. On the screen, Howard jumped.

'What's wrong, Howie?' asked the fan.

Howard shook his head. 'Nothing, er, nothing.'

Forke smiled as a bank of lights on the console lit up and started to flash erratically. 'Excellent.'

The next morning, not far away, an unearthly trumpeting noise broke out in a small metal compartment. A blue beacon began to flash illogically in mid-air. Seconds later, the police box shell of the TARDIS had solidified from transparency.

A few minutes later, the battered blue door of the time-space craft creaked open and the Doctor and his two travelling companions, Bernice and Ace, stepped out curiously and looked around. They were not impressed.

They had recently endured nightmarish experiences that had tested their wits, strength and loyalties to the utmost. Their relief at the ultimate defeat of the vengeful Mortimus had brought home how much they needed each other's trust, support and friendship. The women were particularly pleased to see the Doctor more cheerful and contented. With a new spring in his step, he had promised them a mystery tour and allowed the TARDIS to select their next port of call at random.

He stuck his hands in his pockets and humphed. 'Perhaps this is why I don't usually let the TARDIS go it alone. I must have forgotten to reset the linear spools of her curiosity circuits.'

Ace ran her hand along the facing wall of the compartment. 'Space station, I reckon. Perhaps a cargo hold.'

Bernice sniffed affectionately. 'Don't be so unimaginative. Besides, the gravity reading was planetary, remember?'

The Doctor tapped his fingers against his lips. 'Let's find out, shall we? Air is coming in, so there must be a way out of here.' He tapped the facing wall of the compartment and to his surprise a small panel whirred open at knee height. He shrugged and squeezed through the hole.

'Open doors,' said Bernice. 'Always trouble, never less than completely irresistible.'

Ace grinned and crouched down in order to peer through the hole in the wall. It took her only a second to recognize what was going on outside. A glimpse was enough. She stood. 'Hell, Benny,' she said. 'It's a prison camp or something.'

'Wait a second,' Bernice suggested. 'Don't you think we should . . .' But Ace was through the panel before she could complete the sentence. Bernice sighed and followed her.

There seemed to be no border to the camp. Wherever Bernice turned she was confronted by more and more emaciated people, their bones pushing through their skin. Although a good head higher than most of them, her superior vantage point allowed her only a vision of a sea of shaven heads, blurring into the distance. There must, she thought, be another wall at the far side of the camp.

Or perhaps it never stopped.

The Doctor and Ace were easy to find in the crowd. They were clean, fully clothed and healthy. Bernice pushed past a man whose face was covered with running sores and joined them.

They did not talk for a few seconds. Somewhere nearby somebody was screaming horribly.

'Put anything in a cage,' the Doctor said, 'and it will start to behave like an animal.'

'I can't believe this,' said Bernice, staring at her shoes. The awfulness of her surroundings was beginning to affect her. 'Get us away from here, Doctor.'

Ace turned to the Doctor. 'The TARDIS really mucked up this one. We're still on Earth somewhere, aren't we?'

He sighed and put a hand to his head. 'No, no, Ace, that's quite impossible. For one thing, the ambient radiation is of a completely different kind.'

'And for another two,' put in Bernice, pointing upwards. Ace looked up and saw two small suns, very close to each other, at an angle that suggested early morning or early evening.

Ace nodded. 'Well, what is going on here?'

The Doctor waved a hand about vaguely. 'I'm not sure, but I think these people can speak for themselves.'

'You're right,' Ace said. 'I'll be back in ten minutes.' She squared her shoulders and walked away, head lowered.

Bernice's lower lip juddered. 'Doctor, I said let's leave. This place is too much for me.'

He slid an arm around her shoulder. 'You can go back to the TARDIS if you like. Ace and I will join you later.'

She held him about the waist and rested her head on his shoulder. 'No, I can't go back alone. We'll wait for Ace.'

Ace pushed her way through the unresisting crowd, memorizing her route carefully. She wondered if these people had been drugged. Their only reaction to her was to stare.

Up ahead, two kids were standing over the dead body of a woman. Their eyes and their bellies were huge. Ace looked away. This was going to be a difficult one to get over. She was surprised at how guilty she felt at their plight. Somehow, she felt she was responsible for their imprisonment. The guilt made her feel anger, too, but she had learnt how to counter that with logic and planning.

She wondered what kind of people had set the place up. It was one of the sickest places she'd ever seen.

An engine droned above. She ducked down as a small, boxed-off aircar hovered over. Its exhausts belched only a few feet above the heads of the crowd. Small packages of wheat were tossed over the sides of the open-topped vehicle. Hands stretched up eagerly to receive their gifts.

Ace was afraid that the people in the aircar, the evil oppressors or whatever, were going to notice her clean face and long hair. She sneaked a glance up at them. They were kitted out in standard issue not-very-secret police uniforms with visors. Their movements were careless and casual. They were not interested in the starving mob. The aircar turned and sped off, trailing fumes that clotted the lungs of those caught in its slipstream.

Ace decided that she'd seen enough and began to retrace her steps. As she walked she saw tiny skeletal hands passing the food to kids. She knew that she had to do something about this place or she would never be able to relax again.

A folk harmony reached her ears, the last thing she expected to hear. She stopped to listen, closed her eyes and concentrated.

The narrative line of the song was simple. It told of a beautiful country, Vijja, which was the last refuge of the natives of the planet. Vijja had been torn apart by a conflict called Small War Fifteen. The villages had been burnt by soldiers and the people had fled across the wide ocean to find a new life in the bountiful nation of Empirica. They were expecting to be welcomed by the free citizens of Empire, the great city, but found themselves imprisoned and threatened with repatriation. To return home would mean certain death. Worst of all, some of them were being taken away from the camp at random.

A klaxon sounded. Another aircar hovered over, even lower this time. The refugees reacted for the first time. Their unity, so much in evidence only moments before, broke up. They struggled frantically to get away from the aircar, pushing and scuffling in all directions at once and getting nowhere. Ace was caught up in the crush and forced to her knees. She pushed upwards angrily. The aircar was hovering back directly above her.

Something splashed across her face. Those around her had also been branded with a liquid that resembled purple paint. It didn't sting or scald Ace's face, but its other victims cried out in terror. With difficulty, Ace freed her left arm from the struggle and scrubbed at her nose. Whatever the stuff was, it had dried instantly.

A voice, gruff and male, spoke from speakers mounted somewhere nearby. 'Purple section to Area D for relocation. Repeat, purple section to Area D for relocation.'

Ace could tell that the Vijjans had about as much idea of where Area D was as her. Not that they, without her gift of instant translation via the Doctor, could have understood the command from the speakers. She didn't like the sound of relocation much, either.

More aircars arrived. The guards inside leaned over the edges and began to prod members of the crowd with long metal spikes that sparked on contact with flesh. The purple-splattered group were herded in a particular direction. This process, obviously another familiar routine, took effect in seconds.

The crowd were jostled to a huge, inward-curving concrete wall. A section of it was sliding upwards on hydraulic hinges. Ace swallowed and tried to keep a level head. The crowd lurched forward again, crying out as it was poked and prodded along. The unmarked refugees backed away from them as if they were contaminated. Ace's feet were lifted off the ground. This was a ruck gone mad. There were no weapons to hand, nothing to fight back with. She heard herself calling for the Doctor and Bernice. Some hope.

There was no getting out of this one.

A hand clasped hers. She held out her other and another stranger received it desperately.

The first hand was thin and twisted. The second was pudgy and smoother than her own. The first belonged to a dark-haired woman whose face was crumpled with a kind of weary agony. The second belonged to a short balding man dressed in what had once been an expensive suit. He was screaming over and over again. He was at least ten times as terrified as Ace.

The child Bernice was tending to was terrified of her. She had learnt to reset bones years ago, but the process depended on the patient remaining still and the kid was punching and kicking her. She let the child go and he limped away into the crowd.

She turned to the Doctor, who was staring intently into the distance, a deeply troubled look on his kind face. 'Doctor. We can bring out some food from the TARDIS.'

The Doctor looked about at the refugees and shook his head. 'I think, Bernice,' he said, 'that these people at least deserve the dignity of being allowed to find their own food again.'

She nodded. 'Fine. But we must do something, yes?'

'Other people's problems,' he said. 'Always trouble, never less than completely irresistible. My nosiness is obviously contagious.'

He smiled and turned back to the compartment where the TARDIS had materialized. The block sprouted from one of the camp perimeters, an inward-curving wall that stretched up further than Bernice could see. The Doctor walked over to a sturdy scaffolding tower that ran parallel to the wall and hooked the handle of his umbrella over the lowest rung. 'Going up,' he said and started to climb.

'Are you sure it's safe?' Bernice called after him.

'No.'

'Somebody might see you.'

'Yes,' he said mischievously to himself. 'Somebody might.'

Bernice bit her lip and kicked the wall next to her. The Doctor had already begun to respond to events in his usual way. Her heart fluttered with the combination of exciting and frightening feelings she always associated with him. Already she could hear some sort of commotion in the distance.

She leant against the tower and looked up. The soles of the Doctor's shoes had receded into an indistinct blur of struts and girders.

The Doctor climbed upwards, hands, feet and umbrella working together almost unconsciously. He stopped to catch his breath for a second and looked down. Hundreds of heads were huddled below. Hundreds of lives that he was about to change if he could. But first, he had to find out more.

He went on until he reached the top of the tower. A rusty observation box was built into the framework. Carefully, he swung himself over and kicked at the door. It opened more easily than he had anticipated and he threw himself in.

The box, a relic of more prestigious days for this place, contained an old chair with ripped foam seating and a couple of dusty magazines. A rectangular opening looked out over the view. The Doctor squinted over at the far side of the camp, about half a mile away. Beyond the high wall opposite he saw a thick overground tunnel and a scattering of long, low outbuildings. Still further he glimpsed the ocean, made murky by the thick clouds which were moving in to obscure the two suns.

His scouting mission accomplished, the Doctor was about to climb down when he registered a disturbance below, in the camp. A ripple passed in all directions through the refugees. An alarm sounded distantly.

Intrigued, he brought a brass stick from his jacket pocket and snapped it open to form a telescope. He raised it to his eye and scanned the crowd, noting the passage of small aircars above them. The black-uniformed guards inside were using electric spikes to herd a large group of about two hundred refugees towards the far wall.

He turned up the magnification on the telescope and looked again at the tunnel, more closely this time. It ran forward for about four hundred metres, then forked. The left fork led to the guards' quarters. The right sloped over

24

to a large launch pad that he had not noticed before. A craft was touching down.

Angrily, the Doctor returned his attention to the pushing, shoving crowd. He saw something and cursed. Among them, her face and hair splattered purple, was Ace.

2

The Celebrities

Robert Clifton examined himself carefully in the filthy mirror. His handsome features, framed by his immaculately lacquered steel-grey hair, returned his penetratingly direct stare through layers of dirt. He always liked to check his appearance before going on camera and he'd not been disappointed yet. Even in this insanitary cubicle, he thought, my natural gorgeousness shines through like an incandescent supernova.

He made for the door, then cursed as he remembered that he wasn't wearing his Tragedy Day button. He produced it from the pocket of his suit and moved to affix it proudly to his lapel. Tragedy Day was, after all, the only reason for his unfortunately necessary visit to this crustawful hole.

Damn! The pin on the button pierced the skin of his forefinger. Thinking quickly as always, he took out the neatly folded handkerchief from his breast pocket and wrapped it around his injured digit. Thankfully, there was no blood. He shook his hand a couple of times and replaced the handkerchief. He checked both hands again and left the toilet.

As he passed along the narrow, dimly lit corridor back to the blockhouse he made a mental note to ask Ed to book him a manicure. It was in Robert's nature to be prepared, to plan well ahead. Oddly, he couldn't remember his last manicure. Or his last haircut, come to that. Then again, anybody with a lifestyle as exciting as his would have difficulty remembering the little things.

He turned into the main security control room, which

bristled with screens and scanners. One corner was lit brightly. Ed, the producer, and Sal, the camera girl, had set up the shot and were now fussing over a young Vijjan woman. She had been picked for the broadcast because she was exotically pretty and she could speak a little Empirican. There were a line of bruises across her forehead. They weren't too disgusting, unlike some of the others they'd auditioned. This insert might be going out while people were eating, after all.

His wife Wendy stepped forward, pristine as ever in her sensible salmon suit and shoulderpads. God, how beautiful she still looked. He thought back to the day they'd met . . . Only it wasn't there in his memory. Odd.

Yes, of course. They'd met in the offices of Empire TV News back in '78. It had said so in the publicity brochure for their last series. He remembered knowing that, anyway.

'There's a problem, love,' Wendy said, smiling.

'What's that exactly, Wendy?' asked Robert, lifting an eyebrow. It was the kind of direct, thrusting questioning that he knew millions of viewers adored.

'They've had some sort of security alert in there,' Wendy replied, gesturing vaguely in the direction of the camp. 'Somebody was climbing one of the old observation towers. I suppose it might be a protestor.'

'That's a possibility, Wendy,' Robert said, nodding emphatically. He hoped they wouldn't be held up for too long here. Today's schedule had been particularly busy and they had to pick the kids up at five.

The kids? Where were they again? At school, wasn't it? Yes, at school. Weren't they? These memory lapses were rather disturbing. He'd have to do something about it, get Ed to book him in with a therapist, maybe.

Hang on. Hadn't he decided to do that yesterday?

There was a commotion at the other end of the blockhouse. The far door burst open and two oddly dressed people, a man and a woman, were dragged in by a group of guards. Robert summed the intruders up at a glance. The man, with his offensively awful clothes, looked like a fairly typical example of a woolly-minded bleeding-heart liberal. Perpetual student. The woman was younger – perhaps his daughter? She was dressed in a tassled suede jacket, similar to those worn centuries before by the native Ollerines. She probably thought she was making a statement by wearing it. That was the trouble with these sort of people, always making statements. What was the point? Couldn't they just get on with their lives?

One of the visored guards, his striped collar marking him out as an officer, cracked the man over the neck with his electro-truncheon. 'What were you doing up the tower?' he barked. Robert put his hands to his ears. He didn't like it when people raised their voices.

'Well,' the intruder replied, 'as towers go, I find it fascinating. All that bracket welding, functional and yet somehow decorative . . .'

'I'm only going to ask you once more,' the guard shouted viciously, saliva shooting from his mouth. He held up the spiked truncheon. 'This thing has eleven settings. At the mo – '

'At the moment,' the little man snapped irritably, 'it's on level three, rhubarb, rhubarb.'

Robert was surprised by the ferocity of the officer's reaction to the stranger's flippancy. He stepped up the setting on the truncheon and struck the man's side, felling him with a shower of sparks. The woman struggled free from the guards holding her and rushed to his side.

'I'll ask again, shall I?' said the guard. 'What were you doing climbing the tower?'

The man gasped. 'I keep telling you why, I wanted to get to the top . . .'

'You could have killed him, moron,' the woman said.

'Fragile little scug, is he?' sneered the guard. He lifted the man up and threw him roughly into a nearby chair. 'He'll live.' He turned to his men. 'Turn out their pockets.'

They obeyed. Robert watched as the officer lifted off his visor. The circle of face revealed by the balaclava beneath was thin, moustached, younger than he'd expected. While the intruders were searched, the officer poured himself a glass of water from a tap that protruded from a nearby desk. Then he sat in the chair opposite the male intruder, crossed one of his rubber-booted feet over the other and sighed.

'Sir,' called one of the troopers. 'There's nothing.' He held up an amazing jumble of junk taken from the man's pockets.

'Any ID?'

The guard shrugged. 'Doesn't look like it, sir. Could be Vijjan sympathizers.'

The officer grunted. Robert guessed that an organization like the Vijjan Liberation League would not encourage its members to carry identification with them. All that the woman carried was a small book in a language he didn't recognize. It was always the same with these poncy pseudo-intellectuals.

'Let me tell you something,' said the officer. He stood and crossed over to them. His voice was quieter now, thick with menace. 'I don't really care how you got in here or why you went up that tower. But remember this. The next time any VLL get in here they won't be thrown out. They'll be shot.'

He gripped the man's jaw in his huge hand and jerked it upwards. Blood dribbled from the little man's mouth.

'Scum!' the woman screamed and lashed out with one of her long legs, winding the officer. Guards hurried to subdue her.

The officer wiped his mouth, breathing heavily. 'Get them both out of here!' he screamed. 'Before I get angry!'

The intruders were taken out, the woman still struggling and kicking furiously. The officer straightened himself up and addressed the television people. 'Sorry about that,' he said. 'I didn't need that. That's the fourth intrusion in a fortnight.'

He pulled off the balaclava, revealing a shiny bald head. A large bird in flight was tattooed above one ear. It was good, thought Robert, that some of the kids in gangs were given the chance to prove themselves in responsible jobs on the right side of the law.

'Don't worry about it,' said Wendy brightly. 'We're used to delays. Live television and all that.'

'I can't understand,' Robert added, never one to withhold his opinion on anything, 'why, in a democratic society, people can't air their grievances in a responsible, democratic way.'

The officer stared at him strangely, as if he had said something stupid. Robert looked away, embarrassed. He was used to receiving looks like that from some of the people he interviewed. He had put it down to them not understanding the cleverness of what he was asking.

He asked Wendy for his notes for the broadcast and wondered what she would prepare for the evening meal. Perhaps they could go out somewhere. They hadn't dined in a restaurant for a long time. So long ago he couldn't remember when.

A few minutes later, the security breach had been all but forgotten. Ed and Sal had ironed out all the technical problems and pancaked over a few of the Vijjan woman's blacker bruises. She was brought forward. Robert noted that although she was pretty, her eyes were dumb, like the rest of her people. They ought to feel glad that Empiricans felt sorry for them and tried to help out now and then. It wasn't as if they'd made a success of things on Olleril before the colonists arrived, what with their backward way of life.

'So,' he asked, 'here we have,' he consulted his notes, 'Frinna, one of the many sultry young Vijjan girls to have fled their nation for the bright lights and glittering excitement of Empire City. Frinna, let me ask you, first impressions and all that, how are you enjoying it so far?'

An unmarked, open-topped truck drove up to the main blockhouse. The Doctor and Bernice were hustled into the back and it drove off, away from the camp.

The Doctor dabbed at his mouth with his handkerchief. 'I lost my brolly in that scrap.' He put a hand to his head. 'And my hat.'

'You left it in the TARDIS. How are you?' asked Bernice. She didn't like to see the Doctor injured.

Before he could reply, alarms sounded, signalling the end of the day shift at the camp. Guards emerged from the rows of identical buildings. To one side a large launch pad played host to a dirty grey sub-atmospheric freighter. Windows on its blunt nose showed a small crew preparing for flight. Beyond the pad Bernice glimpsed the ocean.

'I suppose Ace will be able to get back to the TARDIS, anyway,' she said. The Doctor said nothing. She looked over at him suspiciously. 'What's happened?'

'Ace isn't in the camp any more,' he said. 'She's been taken out to that freighter with a large group of the refugees.'

Bernice turned her head and watched the launch pad recede into the distance. Even if they overpowered their driver, a rescue attempt stood little chance of success. 'So Ace is off to, what did they say, Vijja?'

The Doctor nodded. 'It would appear so.' He looked up at the sky and tutted. 'So much for the TARDIS without the captain at the helm.'

The truck passed through the security checkpoint at the perimeter of the camp outbuildings and turned onto the streets. It continued along rows of boarded-up terraces that were lined with drooping trees, cracked mailboxes and fallen masonry. Bernice guessed that this had once been an exclusive area. Many of the houses displayed mock-Georgian façades that whispered of long forgotten terrestrial influences. There were no people or animals or vehicles in the streets at all. Bernice guessed that this area formed part of an exclusion zone around the camp. On the thick murky ribbon of the river she saw freighters and trawlers following them upstream, presumably to the centre of habitation.

They looked up at the sound of a low-flying aircraft. The blunt-nosed freighter from the camp had taken off and was flying away from the city. The Doctor and Bernice looked at each other. 'She'll be all right,' said the Doctor. 'I'm sure of it.'

The truck turned a corner and came to a halt at the end of a long bridge that straddled the murky river. For the first time the Doctor and Bernice saw the towers of Empire City, spread out before them as if in a picture postcard. The faded charm of the abandoned quarter was nowhere in evidence. The city was tall, grey and ugly. Its buildings had been thrown together by a thousand architects, each with his own aesthetic axe to grind. No block complemented its neighbour. Over the basic framework was stretched a pattern of bright lights, blinking on as afternoon began to give way to dusk.

Their driver conversed briefly with a scruffy-looking official at the bridge and they were allowed through. More of the city came into relief as they crossed the bridge. Puffs of smog were tinged a mellow orange by the setting first sun. Cars crowded the wide streets. People darted about, heading home from work. Illuminated billboards displayed advertisements for deodorants and chocolate and benefit payments. It should have been a city like any other.

Bernice had always felt as comfortable in a large city as anywhere else. Even in the roughest areas there were reassuringly human activities. Laughter, music, kids playing. She could see all of those things at the end of the bridge in Empire. But something was wrong, so wrong that she had to stop herself from crying out. There was a frightening strangeness, an artificiality about the place. Nothing she could have pointed to, but it was there.

She looked across at the Doctor. He was staring at the city and fiddling with the knot of his cravat. He muttered under his breath, something that sounded like, 'That can't be right, it's too exact . . .'

The truck reached the end of the bridge. The driver ordered them out. They clambered down and he drove off.

They had been put down on one side of a wide road with four lanes. Occasionally a car or a lorry flashed past.

The Doctor took Bernice's hand and they ran over. Up ahead was a crowded concourse, where a scrap-iron market was being taken noisily down. A crowd of dirty people were sat grouped in a circle nearby around a fire. They looked curiously over at the approaching strangers.

'Now,' said the Doctor, walking straight past them, 'let's see the sights.'

Bernice stopped. 'You're treating this as a holiday? Despite what's happened to Ace?'

'Because of it,' he replied, 'it's even more important that I do.'

3

The Night

Forgwyn returned from his evening run, his two guards trailing behind him. The small ring of tents that formed the centre of the settlement was still busy with tribespeople going about their business. One group sharpened spears while others wove huge nets.

Three days had passed since he'd staggered into the tribe and he still couldn't raise the nerve to tell them that he wasn't a god, he couldn't protect them and that spears and nets might be useful for catching fish but weren't going to be much good against another shower of compression grenades. They seemed to overreact to everything that he said, good or bad, and he was worried that telling the truth would result in painful retribution on their part. Worse, they wouldn't let him go on alone, saying that this would bring certain death. Whichever way he looked at it, the situation was a bad one. When the next attack came he would be as unprepared as the tribe. All his gear was back in the ship. And, of course, there was Meredith to think about. She'd smiled and laughed bravely as she'd packed him off to fetch help but he knew she'd been worried about the baby.

Laude emerged from his tent to greet Forgwyn. The leader of the tribe, he was almost seven feet tall. His face was tanned and bearded, brutally handsome. Like Forgwyn, he wore only a cloth about his waist. The rest of his enormous, muscular body was displayed openly as a gesture of strength. Forgwyn always felt self-conscious when his own slight frame was next to Laude. There was really no comparison.

'Forgwyn,' Laude said, shaking the boy's shoulders, 'uggerah chomball iri kapernokk . . .'

'Hold on, hold on,' Forgwyn said slowly. 'I haven't got my interpreter on.' He gestured to his ears.

Laude laughed and smote himself across the forehead. He followed Forgwyn into the tent that had been specially prepared for the boy. It was wide and tall, with a patch cut open in the roof to allow the light of the suns to shine through. A hammock was strung up between two poles, under which Forgwyn's own clothes were neatly folded.

'Wait a second,' said the boy. He knelt under the hammock, pulled out the interpreter unit from his jacket pocket and popped in the earpieces. 'Go on.'

'The gods of victory are truly with us,' said Laude with a smile that looked ridiculous spread across his massive face. 'An aircraft has been sighted nearing the place of strangers. We have been granted new strength against the Unseen.'

'An aircraft?' exclaimed Forgwyn. 'Where is it?'

'It is at the place of strangers, on the far side of the island,' Laude told him. 'We will gather our warriors at dawn to greet the newcomers.'

Forgwyn frowned. In his three days with the tribe he had learnt that they were a mongrel bunch. For every man that was killed in one of the attacks another would appear as part of a consignment dropped off regularly. Most of the new arrivals of late, he had been told, were half-starved refugees from a country called Vijja. The Unseen, as the tribe called them, were whoever had planted small, electrified spy cameras around the island.

He said, 'You said, didn't you, Laude, that every time strangers arrive, there's an attack soon after?'

The tribal leader grinned. 'It is so. But this time,' he grabbed Forgwyn by the shoulders again, 'our god will protect us!'

'Yes, of course I will,' the boy replied uncomfortably.

'Make ready for victory!' Laude clasped his hands together over his head in a gesture of triumph and strode from the tent, growling with pleasure.

35

As soon as he had gone, Forgwyn detached the interpreter and hurled it angrily across the tent. What a way to die, alone and helpless on the island that time forgot. Cannon fodder. He should have gone out blazing with some act of selfless heroism, like Auntie Doris. According to Meredith, she'd taken seventeen Rutans with her. By the tribe's account he'd be lucky even to see the enemy.

He gathered together some clothes and walked out to the shower hut. He shed his loincloth and pulled down the wooden handle. Cool water ran over his body, washing the sand from between his toes. He tossed his fringe back and stared up at the clear blue sky and the setting suns. It seemed impossible that death could strike in a place like this.

But he'd seen the bones of Laude's tribe piled high just outside the settlement and recognized traces of cellular displacement. There were some bad people on this planet and they were on their way.

Nobody in Empire City had looked up at the stars for over seventy years. Nobody could. The twin pulsars at Rexel, the crimson binaries of lonely Quique and the fringes of distant, forbidding Pangloss had all been blotted out by a profusion of upward-shining groundlights. The old City Council had decided it was for the best, for reasons of personal safety. People needed to feel secure in the streets. And there were public planetaria for the kids, even in the poorer areas. Well, there had been in those days.

Seventy years on, another starless night crept over the towers of the South Side. On the intersection of 209 and 357 a man was shot dead and his new shoes taken. Outside the diner on 511, a street-corner band played old hits from decade six to an enthusiastic audience. In Daisycombe Park, a woman's head was being beaten to pulp. Tom Jakovv and Elena Salcha, lovers since street-sweeping college, got drunk and made love on a waterbed in the smashed window of Tyack's Fittings. A fire broke out in the tenements of the Parsloe estate and ninety-one people died. A couple of million VCRs clunked on automatically as the news gave way to *Captain Millennium*.

This Tuesday was different to any other before it, however. People wandering the streets in search of faceless encounters hugged themselves against a chill that seemed to come as much from within as without. Dogs howled up at the flat golden sky, their eyes darting from side to side, as if they expected to see something up there. Children turned uneasily in their tiny beds, their dreams filled with giant, grotesque faces.

Bernice walked confidently down 507. Her expensive clothing, filed under the TARDIS' eccentric wardrobe coding as 'Apache', marked her out as a visitor. She'd had to deal with two attempted muggings already. The first had happened shortly after she'd stopped to buy a soggy samosa from a stall using money the Doctor had obtained by selling his telescope. She had been set upon by two kids on bikes. The second had occurred as she went to help an old woman who had tripped. A wild-eyed boy in leathers had leapt at her from the shadows. The family resemblance was astonishing. She'd cracked their heads together, thrown her own back, looked straight ahead and walked on briskly.

The Doctor was there at the end of the street, as arranged. He was leaning against a post that supported a crackling, flashing lamp. He grinned as she approached. 'Impressions?' he asked her.

'A standard late-capitalist rat-hole,' she replied. 'But there's something else. I can't put it into words. Say a sort of tangible unease.'

He nodded and offered her a potato crisp from a brightly coloured bag. 'I know. Like a scratch you can't itch.'

'You mean an itch you can't scratch.'

He sighed and crunched a crisp. 'That's what I just said.'

'What do you think about this place, anyway?' she asked.

The Doctor put his crisps away and took her arm. They crossed the road and continued walking. Up ahead a billboard glowed LOWER 500 SHOPPING.

'I bought this earlier,' he said and produced a tattered pocket guide. 'Would you like a potted history of the planet?'

'Please.'

The Doctor cleared his throat and began his précis. 'Olleril was settled very nearly six centuries ago by Luminus, an evil bunch with a wicked philosophy behind them. They exterminated much of the native population, and what was left became the Vijjans. Luminus was overthrown shortly after the occupation, but not before the foundations of this city had been built.'

'So we're walking over a mass grave,' Bernice remarked.

'Now,' the Doctor went on, 'the colonists spread over the planet, forming a complex international community of independent states. In three generations this country, Empirica, had risen to become the largest and most powerful. Forty years ago it finally polished off its major rival, a communist nation that there isn't much left of. It also possesses an economy linked in small part to offworld markets, although visitors are rare. Vijja, where Ace has gone, is very small and poor. There's been a civil war there for years.'

'Anything else I should know?' asked Bernice.

'Oh, yes,' the Doctor said, returning the guide to his pocket. 'But you can see it with your own eyes, I'm sure. Anachronisms. How's your Comparative Technology, Bernice?'

She pulled a sour face. 'Er, no good.'

The Doctor indicated several items as they walked on. 'Two-dimensional television and light powered underground railways. Petrol pumps and laser keys. And most telling of all . . .'

'Yes?'

'During our interrogation back at the camp,' he said, 'did you notice that well-dressed couple in the corner?'

Bernice nodded. 'They looked a bit out of place, yes, but hardly anachronistic.'

The Doctor stopped and looked around once again, comparing this to that. 'I'd agree,' he said, his brow creased with concerned curiosity. 'Yes, if they'd been human I'd agree with you.'

Bernice waited a second before she said, 'Bomb dropped. Direct hit.' And then, 'Sorry?'

'Robots,' growled the Doctor. 'Their stillness was too precise for human beings. And the woman's head was angled all wrong. Her neckbone would have to be made of plasticine.'

'I would have noticed,' said Bernice.

'You might have, but at the time you were rather more concerned with me.'

'Don't mention it.'

They had now reached a small metal bridge that led to the shopping mall. Bernice sat on a railing and swung her feet, thinking. 'This is a level three society, more or less. Grotski's theory of cultural retrenchment could account for a few level four artefacts about. But sophisticated facsimiles like that point at least to late level five, early six. There must have been recent cross-cultural intervention.'

'There is another possibility you don't appear to have considered,' said the Doctor.

'Tell me.'

'Later,' he said. 'We've got things to do.'

Before he could explain, something very large was overturned in the darkness of the mall ahead of them. They were showered with tiny slivers of glass. Bernice grabbed the Doctor and dragged him behind a line of stinking dustbins at the side of the bridge. The streetlamps around them snapped out one by one.

A blue light flashed from the direction of the mall. Low animal growls came from human throats. There were shouts and cries, the stomp of booted feet. Shots were fired. Steel blades glinted in the flashing blue. The mob was coming closer. A second wave followed on motorbikes. Three white wagons trundled along at the rear.

Bernice could smell her own fear over the rotting fish in the bins. She looked across at the Doctor. He was absolutely still. A slight pressure on her wrist advised her to remain the same.

A stampede broke out from the sky. About fifty people powered by rocket packs slung across their shoulders flew down onto the bridge. Bernice wondered if they were masked super-vigilantes. Then she saw that some carried guns, others flaming torches. They broke out machine-rifles, crossbows and baseball bats in what was obviously a well-rehearsed routine, and charged to meet their oncoming opponents.

The two groups met. Bones cracked, blood spilled. Bodies were pushed over the bridge to be smashed open on the concrete below. Automatic gunfire rattled over shots and screams. Somebody caught fire, producing a blaze that extended an arc of flame close to the Doctor and Bernice's hiding place.

They ran out, keeping low and heading for safety the way they had come. Fortunately, the gangs were now too occupied with fighting each other to notice them.

At the end of the bridge, Bernice looked back at the battle. The participants included older men and women. She turned to the Doctor. 'Shouldn't we call the police?'

'I hate to disillusion you,' he said, 'but I think that they are the police.'

Harry Landis had owned the bar on the corner of 525 and 578 for six years. He'd changed the name from Hazard's to Yumm's shortly after taking up the lease. Since Urma had taken sick two years ago his time had been divided between looking after her and keeping the bar running. The doctor had told him on his last visit that what she needed more than anything was plenty of relaxing sleep. That had made Harry laugh, because nobody on the 500 streets had got a good night's sleep for years.

Things weren't too bad, though. He'd managed to keep the price of his ales and his rooms down, despite increases in property charges, personal charges, business charges, criminal extortion and police extortion. The punters were happy, too. It wasn't enough nowadays to serve up only drinks. What they wanted was entertainment, variety, and Harry had hit upon a winning formula. Stripper on Monday, stripper on Tuesday, drag on Wednesday, stripper on Thursday, stripper on Friday, music and stripper on Saturday and stripper on Sunday.

Tonight had been an odd one. Somebody had been glassed and then half an hour later another fight had broken out. There was an awful draught blowing in from somewhere, too, although he'd checked all the windows and doors were closed. The act had been a right pain as well, making it even more obvious than usual that she was just going through the motions. They'd had an argument afterwards, about the cordon. The act was from central zone three, slumming her way through university. She said that the cordon was a bad thing because it allowed the rich to ignore the poor. Harry reminded her that *he'd* been born and raised on the South Side and that the cordon was the best thing that could have happened to the area, may the red glass curse his soul if it weren't.

Well, he used to think that. He liked people to think he still did. It wasn't good to back down in public. But it was a while now since they'd put the thing up and he had to admit that things didn't seem to be getting any better. The police had got much worse, what with all their territorial disputes. He remembered the papers saying that soon it would be safe to walk the streets again.

Of course, it was still nice over in Central. The folks there, like him, remained respectful of the law and kept their neighbourhoods smart and reasonably crime-free. He hadn't been over there for a while. The last time he'd tried, the barrier at the subcar station, stupid thing, had spat out his access wafer. He'd written off to the admin company and seven weeks later got back a small piece of photocopied paper. It said that his access grading had been reviewed and downgraded. Bureaucrats. They were just as bad as the government had been. He'd written off again to point out their error, reminding them that he only had three offences recorded against him, very minor ones. He still hadn't heard anything back, despite having left several messages on their answerphone. His letters to the Complainants' Charter company went unanswered. He'd even contacted that consumer programme on the telly about it. The woman on the phone had said she was sorry, but there were lots of cases like his and they didn't make very interesting television. 'They've got me every way, haven't they, love?' he'd joked. She'd laughed and said she had to ring off because a kiddie had been murdered and she had to sort out music for the reconstruction in Sunday's programme. Nice girl.

Still, he had a lot to thank the people in Central for. Without their generosity last Tragedy Day, he wouldn't have been able to fix up that doctor for Urma.

The door buzzer rang. Harry checked the exterior camera and signalled the bouncers to open the door.

A strangely dressed man and a youngish woman entered and walked up to the bar. 'Good evening,' said the woman. 'A pint of your best ale and a glass of water, no ice, please.'

Harry served them their drinks and watched as they settled down over by the pool table. They were an odd couple, for sure.

'So, Doctor,' Bernice shouted over the roar of the jukebox. 'What's the plan?'

He sipped at his water and frowned. 'I want to be treading the corridors of power. We're going to have to get into the central area of the city.'

'Why not go over there tonight?'

He wagged a finger at her and showed her a map of the city in the guide. The centre, about a third of the total area, was shaded a different colour. 'I said get into, not go over to. The area we're in now is separated from the centre by a most efficient security system.'

Bernice grimaced. 'How can the people here stand for that?'

'Well,' said the Doctor, 'most of them are too busy

struggling to stay alive. It's a textbook example of rule and divide.'

'You mean divide and rule.'

He thumped his glass on the table. 'That's what I just said. Anyway, I think we'll sleep on the problem and think about it tomorrow. We do have one advantage over the people here.'

'What's that?'

The Doctor rubbed the fingers of one hand together in a meaningful gesture. 'Money. That telescope fetched me quite a profit at the scrap auction.'

Bernice's attention was taken by a large TV screen suspended above the Doctor's head. She clutched his arm and pointed up. 'Look, it's those robots.'

The couple they had seen at the camp were on the screen, sitting comfortably in swivel chairs. Bernice recognized the signs of a talk show. The male robot introduced the first guest but his words were lost to them under the music in the bar.

A tall, dark-haired and very handsome man in his mid thirties walked onto the pastel-shaded set. His jaw was large and almost comically square and he was dressed in an expensive-looking suit that was perfectly tailored. Bernice saw heads in the bar turning to face the screen. The public were obviously very familiar with this person. The interview continued for a couple of minutes. Bernice noted the unnatural precision of the female robot's hand movements.

The jukebox quietened, bereft of attention. The sound from the TV screen was revealed to them.

'. . . and then we took the coach over to Funland and the kids had a smashing time,' the guest was saying. 'And they'd all like to say thank you to all of you who put your hands in your pockets last year. It was all thanks to you.'

The studio audience applauded heartily. The guest smiled, indicated them and started clapping too. The female robot leant forward. 'So, Howard, with this year's Tragedy Day only, what, three days away now, and apart from saving the universe, what are your plans?'

'I'm glad you asked that, Wendy,' said the guest. Bernice shuddered at the transparent falseness of the set-up. 'Because on Friday, I'll be . . .'

The jukebox returned with a boppy anthem about everybody working together to help the homeless and save Olleril from environmental devastation. Bernice groaned and leant across the table.

'Doctor,' she shouted. 'What's Tragedy Day?'

The operative assigned to observe Howard Devor had tuned his screen to news and the Cliftons' talk show. The audience were clapping Devor again. The operative registered Mr Forke's presence.

'How's it going?' asked Forke.

The operative pointed to the flashing lights on the console. 'There you are, sir. The processor is functioning perfectly.'

Forke grinned. 'Good. Continue your observations.'

Ace's final visit to the dentist had been on a rainy day when she was nine years old. She'd woken from the anaesthetic with a puffed-up mouth that tasted of blood, an Abba album for being a brave girl, and a determination never to go back even if all her teeth fell out.

The gas had smelled exactly the same, pouring out at them from concealed nozzles in the pitch black of the tunnel. The hands she had grasped slackened. Then nothing. Until now.

The engine noise hurt her ears. It sounded like an aircraft. She opened her eyes, almost expecting to find herself on a runway. About two hundred of the painted people were with her. They were packed close in a high-ceilinged concrete chamber. Most of them were still asleep. Outside, a bird was twittering exotically.

Ace pulled herself up on her elbows. She didn't even know the name of this planet. She let her spinning head fall back.

Well done, Doctor, she thought. Another classic cock-up.

Reluctantly, she looked up. Might as well get on with it, Ace, she told herself. Too much thinking only gets you jumpy.

The man in the tattered suit she'd seen earlier was stumbling about. Beneath the dye he was covered in bruises. His left eye was torn across and had been left untreated. He saw her and tottered over.

'You're ...' he began, and broke off coughing. 'You're Empirican. Not a Vijjan.'

'I'm neither,' she replied. Her voice echoed strangely in the chamber.

He collapsed in front of her, broken and helpless. Ace saw that some of his fingers were hanging loosely from their sockets. 'What's happened to us?' he wailed in a cracked voice. 'I haven't done anything.'

Ace laid a hand on his shoulder awkwardly. 'It's okay,' she said confidently. 'We can get out of this if we all work together.'

'But where are we?' he cried. 'Vijja? Why have they done this to us?' He began to weep.

She extended a hand. 'I'm Ace,' she said. 'I'm tough enough for both of us, so cease the whining and tell me about it.'

He held her hand as tightly as he could and irritatingly did not let go. With his other hand he wiped at his streaming eyes, smudging the dye and the blood. 'George Lipton,' he said. 'I've got to speak to somebody in authority. There's been a terrible mistake.'

'Yeah?'

'You've seen *Captain Millennium*?'

It was the last thing she'd expected. 'Who's he?'

'The serial. About the space policeman. With Howard Devor,' he prompted her.

Ace clicked. 'Er, no, I travel around a lot, don't get much time for TV. What's that got to do with it, anyway?'

'Well, I'm the producer,' Lipton spluttered petulantly. 'I've never committed an offence in my life. My wafer is clean. I have access to all areas.' He shuddered. 'What has happened to me? I don't understand it.'

45

Their heads turned as the wall of the chamber slid up smoothly.

The fine white sand of the beach outside was untouched. The air was the freshest Ace's lungs had ever drawn on. The water was so blue it almost hurt to look at it. Twin moons clung close in a sky full of stars. 'Brochure city,' muttered Ace.

Lipton got to his feet and stared out. He turned to Ace, confused. 'Have we died? I mean, this is paradise.' He walked out. Encouraged by his example and invigorated by the cool sea breeze and warm night air, many of the healthier Vijjans raised themselves up and followed.

Ace stopped at the edge of the chamber and watched the Vijjans as they began to smile. They danced falteringly, stretching out their arms to feel the emptiness around them. They chattered excitedly. One ran into the water and was joined by others. Lipton walked in slowly, still dazed.

Ace almost stopped to treasure the scene before her, but logic warned her against accepting it at face value. She looked suspiciously about. There was a high cliff face behind them, into which the chamber had been built. She reasoned that a tunnel inside the cliff led up to a landing pad. None of this made any sense. Was this Vijja?

She slid down against the edge of the chamber. Her foot nudged something and she shifted about to get more comfortable. She looked down. Embedded in the sand was a human head, almost decomposed enough to be called a skull.

4

The Clearance

*Visitors to Empire City are often attracted by the famous
yearly festival known since 559 as Tragedy Day. Crowds
take eagerly to the streets in a celebration of the generosity
of individuals towards the less fortunate people of Olleril.
A wide variety of fund-raising events and wide media
coverage ensures that a fun time is had by all in the pursuit
of many worthy causes. The festival stands as a beacon of
hope in the modern world; for whatever the tragedy, the
citizens of Empire are united in their compassion on
Tragedy Day.*

From **Corry's Guides: Empire City**

The sky was white over Empire City. At first light, the
slight figure of the Doctor emerged from the door of
Yumm's, where he and Bernice had rented rooms. He
looked up and down 525 and started to walk briskly along.
His hands clasped and unclasped anxiously, missing his
umbrella. The streets were almost empty and he was left
undisturbed to think things out, which he always did best
when he was alone and on the move and not being
hurried. He skirted around a small tree that was cased in
a dome of shatterproof plastic. An enormous placard next
to it read;

REFLOWERING THE SOUTH SIDE
*This shrub donated by citizens of Central Four
in association with Riftet Insurance
Tragedy Day 595*

As he walked and thought, the Doctor looked about curiously, studying every detail of his new environment. His theory about Olleril was reinforced.

A few minutes later he had come to some important conclusions and formulated a plan. He turned about and made to return to Yumm's and Bernice.

Bernice had slept in her clothes on an uncomfortable bed. Her fears for Ace were compounded by a lullaby of gunshots that rattled not far away. A woman in the next room had been whimpering in pain all night. There were no other guests signed in to Yumm's so she presumed this was the wife of the proprietor.

Sunlight poked its way through the holes in the tattered curtains of her small room. She leapt up and went to find the Doctor in the hope that his confidence and good humour would lift her spirits.

When she found his room empty, Bernice sat down on the bed and buried her face in her hands. She was well used to the Doctor's arbitrary ways, but there was something about this dismal, drooping city that whispered to her that this time he wasn't coming back. Perhaps he'd been mugged and was lying dead in a gutter. Still only half awake, she didn't register the creaking tread moving up the stairs until it was too late.

The door burst open and the Doctor burst in. He was singing loudly and discordantly: 'Oh, for the wings, for the wings of a dove . . .'

Bernice leapt up from the bed, clapping her hands to her ears. 'What do you think you're doing?' she screeched.

'Practising my singing,' he replied.

'I wouldn't bother. You can't.'

The Doctor shrugged. 'You should hear me play the piano.' He noted her shocked expression. 'Bernice, what's wrong?'

She sighed, crossed over to the window and pulled the curtains. Grey light seeped in. 'Did you have to come charging in like that? I thought you were a drug-crazed madman.'

'But I'm not,' he stated with alacrity. 'I am the Doctor, one of your best friends, and I've brought you some breakfast.' He tossed her a pastry obtained from a street vendor. She eyed it warily. 'Don't worry. It's not poisoned.'

Bernice smirked and started eating. 'Cheers. Doctor, to use an old Earth expression, something about this place really gets on my wick.'

The Doctor joined her at the window and they looked over at the tenement opposite. An elderly woman with a shock of dyed red hair was pushing a trolley twice her own size down the stairs of the fire escape. They wondered how she intended getting it back up again.

'Yes. My theory,' the Doctor announced importantly. 'Would you like to hear it?'

'At last,' said Bernice. 'Go ahead. And I'm warning you, I'm expecting to be impressed.'

'Six centuries,' he began, 'after the settlement of this planet, rumours persist that the cult of Luminus still exists here. It's all over the papers.'

Bernice finished eating and licked her fingers. 'So the overthrow of Luminus was staged and they control Olleril from behind the scenes. Sorry, Doctor, I'm not impressed. Where's your evidence? Like I said last night, there are plenty of places like this about.'

The Doctor nodded. 'And as I replied, this particular rat-hole contains certain rather interesting anachronisms and anomalies.' He nodded to the window. 'What's more, as I'm sure you'll agree, this city is uncannily similar to Western cities of late twentieth-century Earth.'

Bernice whistled and sat down on the bed. 'Social engineering on that scale is unbelievable. The resources involved, the cost, the planning . . .'

'Think of the robots,' he reminded her. 'Products of a technology that's centuries ahead of the ordinary people here. And there could be hundreds of them. Cultural figures, politicians. Every one planted in an ideal position to shape ideas, shape a society. Impressed now?'

Bernice wiggled her fingers. 'Semi. I'll buy it as a theory, anyway. It appeals to my sense of the ridiculous at least.

I don't suppose it stretches to why the cult of Luminus would want to do such a peculiar thing?'

The Doctor smiled. 'I'm afraid not. I think it's time we found out, though.'

'You do?'

'Yes,' he said and took her by the arm. 'Professor Summerfield, I am your wayward father; a hopeless drunk and a lousy singer.'

'Brothers!' boomed Laude, clasping his great arms above his head. 'We have waited for many years! Since the day our forefathers were brought here and abandoned, we have fought and died for the pleasure of the Unseen. Deadly metal eyes in the sand have watched our suffering. But now, with new might from the place of strangers and the god child revealed to us, victory will be ours at last!'

'Victory! Victory!' cried the tribesmen gathered around him. They rattled their spears up at their leader, who was standing on the high rock on the edge of the settlement which was the traditional point of public address.

Forgwyn gulped. He had hardly slept for fear of what daylight might bring. He had emerged from his tent at dawn to find the tribe preparing to greet the strangers in strength. He had decided to tell Laude that he was not a god.

Now that the tribe had been whipped into such a frenzy again his resolve slumped. If they suspected any weakness they'd probably kill him. At least cellular displacement was quick, in the vids anyway, if messy. Tribes were into torture and splitting skulls and ritual disembowelments, weren't they?

'We must go to the place of strangers,' Laude continued, 'and greet our new warriors. And then we will be ready to attack!'

'Attack! Attack!' the tribe agreed, rattling their spears again.

Attack what, wondered Forgwyn. If he got out of this, he decided, he would write a lengthy treatise on the correlation between excessive spear-rattling and lack of conceptual understanding.

Laude clambered down from the rock. His men gathered about him, clapping him about his massive shoulders. 'Boy Forgwyn,' he called over, 'when we return from the place of strangers, we will feast well to give us fire in our blood! You will join us in our revels!'

Forgwyn forced a smile. 'Oh. Thanks, Laude.'

An enormous elbow jabbed him in the ribs. 'And you shall join us in the enjoyment of our young women! Which of them will be yours for sport, eh?'

'Well, if it's all the same to you, Laude, I'd rather not,' mumbled Forgwyn, red-faced.

Laude eyed him suspiciously, then grinned. 'Ah, I see. You wish to remain pure as a god should be, yes?'

'Something like that,' Forgwyn said quickly. 'Are we off, then?'

'You thirst for victory,' cried Laude. 'It is good. Victory! Victory!'

The tribe took up Laude's cry and surged forward. Forgwyn found himself being lifted off the rock and carried on the shoulders of one of the men.

The women of the tribe watched as the men swarmed away from the settlement towards the place of strangers. Many of them did not share in their leader's confidence and feared that the god child would bring only disaster to their people. This could be another trick by the Unseen, those with metal eyes.

It would have given them little comfort to know that Forgwyn himself was entertaining similar fears.

The fish that swam in the waters around the island were startled when an enormous shape passed by. The shape was a submarine called the *Gargantuan*. Its side was emblazoned with the symbol of a silver apple. Its mighty engines roared as it ploughed through the depths. Operatives of Luminus moved dutifully through its many corridors.

In a room on the lowest level of the craft, the Supreme

One switched on his video set. Rows of screens brightened. Reception this far from the Empirican mainland was still hazy, despite the booster buoys he'd had floated out. The final few seconds of *Whittaker's Harbour* were being transmitted by Empire TV Drama. He could understand why so many of the citizens of the nation were ardent viewers of this particular programme. It was so undemanding. The pressures and strains of millions of lives were alleviated by a twice-daily visit to the fictional marina. The Supreme One, who considered himself vastly superior in intellect and purpose to any other being on Olleril, gave a tolerant smile.

'Zach, when I said we could give our relationship another try, I wasn't expecting you to run out and tell the whole of the harbour!' protested Lophie.

'What am I expected to do?' replied Zach. 'People here still think I'm a cag. You dumping me, on top of being fired from the surf store . . .'

Lophie sneered. 'If your shavving job was more important to you than us, I don't think we have any future together!'

'But, Lophie . . .'

Close-up. 'Forget it, Zach, I've heard it all before. We might as well be finished!'

The image froze. A cymbal rippled and a menacing chord was struck on the piano. The closing credits rolled.

The Supreme One selected another channel, one that was not available to any other viewer. The reception was much improved. This was unsurprising as the source was much nearer. A group of about two hundred emaciated Vijjans were gathered uncertainly outside the reception point on the far side of the island. A few of the healthier ones were wading in the sea. The Supreme One had never learnt to swim, and secretly he envied the confidence with which the weak, thin bodies were moving through the water. A quick glance was enough to confirm that all was normal at the reception point. The clearance was about to begin.

He called up another camera. This showed the tribe of

Avax pouring loudly from their settlement. They looked as defiant as ever. The Supreme One liked the tribe. It was a part of the system developed on the island that their small society was never allowed to develop to any creative level. They were too occupied with survival. This gave them a refreshing vivacity that endeared them to him. It was almost a shame that they had to die.

The Supreme One sat back in his chair. His large head fitted snugly into the specially moulded rest. Something unusual had been promised by the research team for the clearance. They were always saying that, though. The last test, a bombardment of compression grenades, had been impressive but only routinely entertaining.

A voice came from a speaker in the console at the base of the video unit. 'This is research to the sanctum. Requesting authorization for weapons test 343, dated 5.9.597.'

The Supreme One extended a bony white finger and keyed in his assent. The test would begin in a few minutes. A new gas, research had said. He hoped it would be interesting.

Ace had spent the night exploring the island. She had walked inland for about two miles and found a line of twisted rocks that she knew would be almost impossible to cross alone. She'd made some important discoveries and decided to turn back. She had slept soundly for a few hours under some tropical palms. Dawn came and after a breakfast of thick-skinned fruit she made her way back to the beach and those who had been brought with her.

She picked her way down the cliffside carefully and walked over to Lipton. He was lying half in, half out of the water, allowing it to wash over his broken body.

'Mister Producer,' she called. 'Don't get too comfy.'

He opened a nervous, weary eye. 'What do you want? I need to sleep.'

She knelt down and held up a battered metal cylinder to his line of sight. 'Know what this is, do you?'

'No.'

'It's a spent compression grenade. There's a tidy pile of them at the foot of the cliff. The design's new on me but I recognise the principle.'

Lipton dragged himself up painfully. 'What's happening?' he babbled. 'Are we in danger here? What are we going to do?'

Ace sighed. The last thing she needed was a panicked civvy. 'Keep your hair on,' she advised. 'There's no immediate threat. Best thing would be to move. So stand up and get ready.'

She walked away. Lipton watched her talking to the Vijjans in their own language. She held up the grenade for them to see and some of them began to wail and take the hands of others. He thought of his apartment in Central Zone five. It occupied the entire basement of a luxury block. It contained a deep pile carpet, a surround entertainment unit, three bedrooms, a study, a utility room, and quarters for his two Vijjan domestic staff. He stirred the sand with his hands. Why was he here? He had never done anything apart from make television programmes. Some of them had been fairly bad, admittedly, but that was hardly reason enough to exile him with refugees. There must have been some terrible mistake. Surely somebody in the city would notice soon and do something about it.

He let his head drop back again and stared at the sky. It was no longer empty. A small grey shape was descending gradually through the blue. Perhaps it was a rescue craft. He got to his feet and waved his hands above his head.

'Hello!' he cried. 'Hello! Hello!'

Ace turned from instructing the Vijjans on a plan of action. She raced across the beach. 'What are you doing, slughead?'

Lipton pointed skywards. 'Look!' he shouted. 'It's a rescue ship!'

Ace, with her years of combat training, summed up the situation instantly. The craft was an automatic carrier similar to those she'd seen employed in a border conflict on the planet Eferun. It had already let loose a cargo of shiny silver spheres. The objects, which were about the size of footballs, floated down dreamily.

'Move!' she cried. She grabbed Lipton by the arm and dragged him away along the beach. The Vijjans screamed and started to run in all directions, seeking cover. There was no cover.

The first sphere settled on the sand. The impact of landing triggered a tiny nozzle set into its surface. White vapour streamed out, forming a large cloud that billowed into the path of a small group of fleeing Vijjans. They fell to their knees, choking and clawing at their throats. They were dead in seconds. It was one of the fastest-acting gases Ace had seen. More Vijjans fell screaming and gasping as the gas reached them. She remembered the hope of the refugees as they had run out onto the beach the night before.

More of the spheres were landing. Ace turned about frantically. Every way she looked clouds of gas were seeping out. The startled yelps and splutters of the dying surrounded her.

Lipton broke free from her grip and ran back stupidly. He waved up at the departing carrier. 'Stop it! Stop it! I'm an Empirican citiz – '

The gas caught at his throat. He gurgled horribly. His eyes opened wide and he fell on his face. His career was over.

Ace had not stopped to watch. She ran between the hissing spheres in her path, hoping to reach the rocks at the far side of the beach. She lost her footing and tumbled over. Her head caught on a stone and she blacked out.

The gas had almost done its work. It lifted from the few survivors and began to dissipate harmlessly.

The Supreme One nodded his approval. This new gas was most effective. There were some small wars in the northern hemisphere where it might prove useful, perhaps to soften up the guerillas in Yuvador.

The second part of the clearance was about to begin. The carrier was moving back into position. On his screen, the Supreme One noted the arrival of the tribe at the reception point, at exactly the time predicted.

'No!' cried Laude. 'Our victory has been taken from us! The Unseen have already attacked!' The beach was strewn with dead bodies. Only seven or eight strangers remained. They were huddled in a small weeping circle. The leader raised his huge axe and whirled it over his head. He moaned in anger. Many of his tribesmen did the same.

Forgwyn shuffled uneasily. He felt sure that somebody was going to remark on his lack of success in leading the tribe to victory. And then it would be goodbye extremities.

Before anybody could, a large silver box dropped onto the beach with a thud. It came to rest a few feet away from the tribe. Some of the warriors muttered fearfully, but Laude strode towards it bravely. He raised his axe and brought it down on the lid with a hefty blow. The gleaming surface was not even dented.

'Aarrggh, what is this evil trickery!' he screamed. He raised the axe again.

Forgwyn had noticed something. 'Wait, Laude!' he ordered. The leader eyed him suspiciously for a couple of seconds, then lowered the axe and waved the boy forward.

'Is this the means of our deliverance?' he asked.

'It might be,' Forgwyn replied. He felt for the simple lock at the side of the unit and swung the lid open. The box contained a moulded plastic base, into which had been packed three rows of protective respirator masks. Griddled filter devices covered the eye and mouth apertures of each. Forgwyn reached for one. He held it out to Laude. 'Quick, get this on.'

Laude took it from him. 'What is this demon's face?'

Forgwyn demonstrated, clamping a mask to his head and securing the clasp at the back. Laude stood still and glared at him. He raised the mask in his own hand and snarled at it.

'Quick, put them on,' urged Forgwyn. He produced more masks from the box and made to distribute them around the tribe.

Laude smacked them from his hand and raised his axe. 'You think we are fools,' he boomed. 'You think we are like the women who wear demon's faces to drive out spirits from old stories.'

'Er, no, I don't,' Forgwyn mumbled feebly, backing away. The tip of the axe swung inches from his face. Dried blood on its edge showed that Laude had been angry before.

'You promised victory,' accused Laude, moving forward. 'You have given us nothing!'

'Nothing!' chorused the tribe, rattling their spears, which was a bad sign.

'Actually, you assumed it,' Forgwyn protested, but his words went unheard.

'You are not the god child but a weakling idiot,' Laude continued. He lunged forward suddenly and twisted Forgwyn about, clasping him around the neck. 'We will peel away your skin and leave your bones to rot under the suns! Your Unseen masters shall have their amusement!'

Forgwyn writhed in Laude's grip. The muscles of his former worshipper tightened around his neck. He kicked and struggled frantically. He could feel himself losing control of his body as the pressure increased. He thought of Meredith back at the ship. If she survived, would she discover his fate?

Laude dropped him suddenly. Forgwyn, senses reeling, looked up to see the man lurching drunkenly as a cloud of gas enveloped him. He gave a final frustrated roar as the vapour took its effect and then sunk to the earth like a felled oak.

The dispirited remainder of the tribe fled from the second wave of silver spheres which were dropping from the sky. Many of them ran straight into pockets of gas.

Forgwyn pulled himself up. He was half conscious and his only concern was to get away from the beach. He could smell the pungent chemicals through the mask. The stench alone was almost enough to overpower him. He staggered on through the bodies towards the rocks at the edge of the bay.

Another body lay among them, different to those of the other strangers. Forgwyn guessed the woman to be in her mid-twenties. She had long dark hair pulled back from a pleasantly angular face. Although she was taller and better-fed than the others, it was her clothes that marked her out. She was wearing machine-woven garments.

He looked back. The attack appeared to be over and the gas was rising. Not one member of the tribe and none of the strangers had survived. He was alone with the dead.

Curious, he clambered over the rocks towards the woman. He leant down and brushed the hair from her face. There was a large bruise on her forehead and blood trickled from a cut on her lip. There were no pockets in her clothes so it was unlikely he'd find any identification.

He stood up and removed his mask tentatively. There was no sound apart from the waves breaking. The rising suns shone warm rays on his undraped body. He supposed he'd have to go back to the settlement, make up some story to convince the women to let him pass, get back to the ship if he could . . .

A hand gripped his shoulder. Terrified, he whirled around. The odd woman stood before him, looking very alive.

There was a knock at the door of the sanctum. 'Come,' ordered the Supreme One. The door slid open slowly with a low hum and Streel, leader of the research team, a thin, middle-aged man dressed in grey coveralls, shuffled in nervously. He swallowed a couple of times, unwilling to address the Supreme One without being invited to speak. The high-backed chair of his master was swivelled to face the banks of screens on the far wall of the dank, dripping chamber.

'Streel,' the Supreme One said at last. His voice was high-pitched and nasal, and as calm as ever. 'This new gas, it appears, has been rather too successful. Every able-bodied male of the tribe has been killed before the second stage of the clearance can begin. And I was very much looking forward to it.'

'It was not foreseen, Commander,' stammered Streel. 'The psych unit predicted that the tribesmen would reason how to use the masks after seeing the bodies of the Vijjans, but . . .'

His voice trailed off as the chair turned on its base. For the first time he saw the face of the occupant, a privilege reserved for the Supreme One's closest advisors and personal guards only. He stammered with surprise and terror. 'They were supposed to . . .'

The large eyes of the Supreme One were still and watery green. They betrayed no expression. 'But they did not. Their deaths mean that the results of the final test will be unreliable. The efficiency of the new equipment may be in some doubt.'

Streel wrung his hands. 'Commander, I did not intend to . . .'

'You cannot excuse your mistakes, Streel,' his superior interrupted. 'You have failed me. And you know what happens to those who fail me.'

The scientist fell to his knees before the chair. 'No, Commander, no! I have served Luminus faithfully for many years!'

'I will not tolerate incompetents on my payroll,' said the Supreme One. He pressed a button on the remote control unit that he gripped tightly in his left hand. Two of his personal guards marched in and stood to attention.

'Gentlemen,' he greeted them politely. 'Would you kindly escort Mr Streel to chute seventeen? Thank you.'

The guards grabbed Streel and pulled him to his feet. He made one last attempt to appease the Supreme One. 'Please, I beg of you, not the Slaags, please . . .'

'Dismissed,' said the Supreme One lightly.

The guards dragged the protesting Streel from the sanctum. The door closed behind them.

The Supreme One licked his lips. He had been waiting for this moment for a long time. The loss of the tribesmen was a disappointment. A struggle between them and his creations would have been most entertaining. He pressed a button on the console before him.

'Research team, Gortlock speaking,' said a voice.

'This is the Supreme One,' he said. 'I have important news for you, Mr Gortlock. You are the new head of research.'

'Oh,' said the voice. 'Oh. Thank you, sir.'

'Here is your first opportunity to shine,' his master went on. 'It's a simple order. After all these years, the time has come for the final clearance. Release the Slaags.'

5

The Slaags

Ace walked slowly around the dead bodies on the beach
and shook her head. They hadn't been given a chance.
Her hands clasped and unclasped anxiously, missing her
weapons.

The boy who had introduced himself as Forgwyn laid a
tentative hand on her shoulder. 'I don't mean to sound
callous,' he said, 'but shouldn't we get away from here?'

Ace shook him off. She was disturbed by the coolness
of his reaction. 'These were your people!'

He shook his head. 'No, they weren't. I'm offworld,
same as you.'

She frowned. 'How d'you make that out, then?'

'Nobody here wears clothes like that,' he pointed out,
gesturing to her outfit.

Ace, almost unable to control her aggression, lunged
forward and grabbed his jaw in her hand. 'Did you have
anything to do with this, squit?'

'No,' he shouted. 'I was trying to save them.' He wres-
tled himself from her grip and dangled the respirator
mask in front of her. 'Somebody is killing this lot off like
animals. So I think,' he continued, reaching down to scoop
up another mask, 'we ought to get out of here.'

He tossed her the mask and strode off, back to the
concealed channel between two rocks through which
the tribe had entered the beach. Ace turned the mask
over in her hand and watched his departing back. Of
course she had no choice. And he was absolutely right.
She thought of herself at that age. *Let me at them, Professor! I'll kill them! How could they do that?*

The boy was too cool to be true, she decided. He was too young to think like that. To think like a professional.

The fish that swam in the waters around the island of Avax were generally a happy bunch. The tribe's attempts to reduce their numbers had not been at all successful. Without boats they were at a severe disadvantage and they were so noisy that the fish were often well away before they had even cast their nets.

The other humans that swam about in their big machine didn't bother them, and the predators they shared the waters with stayed within their natural limits. All in all, they were perhaps the most well-adjusted fish on the planet Olleril. All this was about to change.

A panel on one side of the big machine slid open and the Slaags came out. Twenty minutes later there were no fish in the waters around the island of Avax. But the Slaags were still hungry.

The cordon that protected the law-abiding citizens of Central from the supposed depravity of the outer city had taken two years to construct. Most of the work had been carried out by offenders from one of the detention centres run by the security company. Their hire had brought costs down considerably, although their lack of training had resulted in a few problems and there had been a couple of escapes. Twenty-five years on the cordon remained, strong and high. Empty streets bordered it on both sides. Properties in Central with a view of the cordon had been swiftly abandoned as estate agents produced a downward spiral of lower and lower quotes. Properties on the South Side with a view of the cordon had become squats, until the police gangs had gone in with guns and knives.

It was a depressing place to work, but Anna was used to it. She'd been with Cordon Customer Care for fifteen years and promotion had at least taken her away from checkpoint duty. Now she had her own office with filing cabinets and curtains that slid open and shut when you pressed a button. She kept them shut in the main. Her job nowadays was mostly concerned with disputes over access. She had ten big piles of letters from complainants on the South Side, all of them asking for a review of their downgraded status. She was putting off going to the piles by attending to other tasks such as picking fluff from her toenails or watching television. Nobody at the company really seemed to mind. At a public relations do recently, she'd met one of her peers at another access point, on the North Side, and he had thirty big piles of letters.

Anna was picking at a particularly stubborn piece of fluff when her communicator bleeped. She slipped her shoe on, arranged a few papers in what she hoped was a busy-looking way on her desk, picked up a pen and accepted the call.

'Hassle at the main gate,' snapped the duty guard. 'Situation forty-four. Won't go away.'

'Very well,' Anna said sternly. 'I'll come over.' She broke the link and threw her pen across the room. The elegant hands of the company wall clock indicated to her that only three minutes remained before the second episode of *Whittaker's Harbour*. She wasn't going to let any vagrant prevent her from finding out whether Lophie would get back with Zach. He deserved a second chance, even after stealing from the surf store.

The access point was a drab metal corridor built into the concrete of the cordon. At the far end was a line of electronic barriers; they had ticket readers built into them. QUERIES was written above a plastic shutter set into one wall.

The Doctor was overdoing it, thought Bernice. Since arriving at the access point he had tottered about, singing and belching. She had gone over to the queries shutter, fluttered her eyelids and said, oh, she was ever so sorry, but she'd come to pick up her poor old Dad from the South Side and left her pass papers at home. The man behind the grille had nodded and moved off. They had been waiting for a response for five minutes.

The door next to the shutter was unlocked and a short, fat, middle-aged woman waddled in. 'Yes?' she said.

'Oh, I'm sorry,' Benny gushed, horribly aware that fluttering eyelashes were unlikely to sway this formidable opponent. 'It's my poor old Dad, see. He will wander off and I get so worried. It took me ages to find him and, see, we've lost our pass papers . . .'

'I'm forever blowing bubbles,' the Doctor sang tunelessly, bumping into a brightly coloured chart that displayed a league table of Cordon Customer Care's success rate over the last year.

'Dad,' Bernice called reprovingly and shrugged to the woman.

The woman shook her head and hissed. 'This is the worst I've ever seen. Pass papers were rescinded seven years ago. If you're going to try again, love, and I wouldn't bother, it's access wafers nowadays.' She waddled back through the inner door.

The Doctor, suddenly sober, said, 'Well, it was a good idea.'

Bernice took the guide from her pocket and tossed it to him. 'I wonder what else this isn't telling us.'

'We'll just have to try another access point,' the Doctor said resolutely. Bernice looked at her shoes and said nothing. 'You did think I was good?' he asked her.

She raised her eyebrow. 'Honestly or not honestly?'

'Honestly.'

'Stick to the day job, Doctor.'

A cackling laugh came from a bundle of rags in a corner. The Doctor and Benny looked at each other in surprise. The bundle of rags rearranged itself, revealing at its centre a dirty, bearded and wrinkled face that was creased with merriment. 'Pass papers!' he wheezed, tears of laughter trickling down his cheek. 'Pass papers!'

'Definitely a critical failure,' remarked Bernice.

The Doctor knelt down and addressed the old man. 'You would advise a different approach?'

'There's no way through there for the likes of you and

me, mate,' the old man replied. 'They're not letting no one in any more.'

The Doctor glanced up at Bernice. She handed their wad of money to him and he passed a note to the old man. A grimy hand reached out for it suspiciously. 'You're obviously familiar with this place. What more can you tell us?'

The old man smiled. 'You're offworlders, aren't you?' he said happily. 'I haven't seen offworlders in years. What are you doing over this side?'

'Please,' said Bernice, 'can you tell us how to reach Central?'

'Depends, really,' said the man, 'how much more money you've got.'

The Doctor proferred more notes. The old man laughed again and waved his hand aside. 'I didn't mean that, mate, although I'll have it if you're offering. What you want is to see Madam Guralza.'

'Who is?' prompted Bernice, who was beginning to feel like a detective from an old film.

'You'll find her on 722. The gangs take their cut and let her be. I should watch yourself, though, she's mad as an old snake.' The old man took the notes from the Doctor's hand and shuffled himself back into his rags. 'Pass papers,' he said and chuckled again.

'722,' said the Doctor, consulting the guidebook. 'That isn't too far away. Let's go.'

'Well, I'm a tourist,' Ace, not in the mood for lengthy explanations, was telling Forgwyn. 'I got caught up with those refugees when they were brought back here.'

Forgwyn shook his head. 'This isn't Vijja,' he said. 'It's an island two thousand miles from Empirica. It's in a sort of artificial tropical weather belt.'

'Oh. Great. Brilliant,' said Ace, who couldn't think of anything else to say. 'So what's going on here?'

They had stopped to rest between the huge oddly shaped formations of rock that separated the beach from the settlement. Ace lay slumped against one, dangling a spear she had taken from one of the dead tribesmen, while Forgwyn scooped up water in his cupped hands from a small pool that ran amongst the rocks. He drank eagerly, licked his lips and looked up. 'No idea,' he said simply.

Ace studied him again. He reminded her of somebody and she couldn't think who. Somebody from years back, pre-Doctor. Paul Wilkinson, that was it, from the year above her at school. She'd gone out with him a couple of times and they'd snogged behind the generator at the fair. She had completely forgotten him.

'So much for me. How did you get here? And where's home?' she asked.

Forgwyn smiled. Ace considered the smile a pleasant one. Too boyish and too girlish for her taste, though. Perhaps in a few years time.

'I was born in hyperspace, aboard a ship called *Ganymede*,' he said, speaking matter-of-factly as if used to giving an account of himself, 'at galactic co-ordinates four five zero four by nine eight one five. Makes me an authentic hyperbaby. I haven't stayed in one place for longer than five months, so home is nowhere. I've been in warp stretch so many times I don't even know how old I am but I guess I'm about seventeen. And I came to Olleril because my mother didn't give me much choice.'

Ace frowned. This was getting more bizarre by the minute. 'Your mother?'

'Yes, she's been hired to do a job here,' he stated pleasantly. Ace could tell he was enjoying her confusion. 'Only our ship fell out of orbit at the wrong place. And I mean dropped like a stone. We've got a crash cushion but the ship's not going anywhere again. I left to look for help and ran into the tribe. I think this place is some sort of weapons-testing centre.'

Ace nodded. 'Yeah. I found some spent c-grenades on the beach. Couldn't make out any specification but it looked like they had some sort of internal power source, something like neutrino acceleration. And that gas, well, the vapour must have contained something like Gumm's reagent to disperse so quickly. I've seen droid troopers felled by corrosive agents as quick, but never humans. And the masks, they were dropped as part of a psych test. So I think you're right.'

She realized that Forgwyn was looking at her with a troubled expression. 'You know a lot about weapons, don't you?' he said smoothly and walked on.

Ace followed. Grief, she thought, I was *boring* him. I really must be getting old. I am a weaponry bore.

Forgwyn stopped suddenly and turned with an alarmed expression. 'What's that noise?'

Ace listened. Something nearby was making a ferocious clicking and scraping noise. She looked about for the source. To their left was a large and almost vertical spur of rock, part of the jagged series they were moving around. 'It's coming from over there,' she said and began to climb up for a look.

Forgwyn looked up anxiously. 'Do we really want to see?' She ignored him, scrambled to the top of the rock and peered over the edge.

On the other side was a drop into another small pool that was fortunately surrounded by high rocks. The noise was being made by a creature that was splashing about on the near side in an attempt to climb up. Ace had never seen an animal like it. Its basic shape and size brought back more pre-Doctor memories, of space-hoppers and Christmas puddings, although its skin was leathery, tough and a glistening pea green. Two antennae bulged from the top half of its bulbous, scaly body and she caught a glimpse of a pair of unwieldy flippers beneath with which it was attempting to manoeuvre itself upwards. But what alarmed and disgusted her most about the creature, and what was making that ferocious clicking and scraping noise, was an enormous round mouth that contained two adjacent sets of dagger-sharp teeth.

Ace extended the spear and prodded the flailing beast. Its reaction was sudden. Its teeth clamped around the sharp end of the spear. It munched through the wood enthusiastically and slithered its way up the shaft. Three seconds later it had devoured half of the spear. Ace dropped her end in alarm. The creature splashed back into the water. It completed its meal of the spear and then resumed its attempts to climb out of the pool.

Ace thought fast. The thing was obviously an amphibious carnivore but its capacity for feeding did not tally with the flourishing community of small animals she had seen moving peaceably about the island. It had an unnatural look to it that she had learnt to recognize from products of genetic experimentation. This island was a weapons-testing range. The conclusions she drew from those thoughts was not a comforting one.

'What is it? Ace?' called Forgwyn.

Ace bit her lip and climbed down carefully. 'Just some kind of animal,' she said. 'It looks nasty, but there's only the one and it can't get out of the water.'

'Let's get on, then,' Forgwyn said nervously and started off again. 'I've got to get back to the ship soon.' He led the way forward once more.

Ace looked up at the rock behind which the creature was still gnashing and grinding its teeth. She shuddered and followed him.

After a long wait for a bus that didn't arrive and another long wait for a subcar that didn't arrive, the Doctor and Benny had decided to make their way to 722 and Madam Guralza by foot. A half-hour walk brought them to a street that looked almost exactly similar in its griminess and deprivation to every other they had seen on the South Side. Benny used some of their money to buy information from a passer-by, who took it gladly and gave her directions.

'She's a forger, it would seem,' she told the Doctor as they walked along. 'Local benefactor, runs soup kitchens and that sort of thing. And a bit of a celebrity. Used to be in the movies.'

The Doctor raised an eyebrow and followed her along the street to a high wall at the end. A large metal door was set into the wall, with an ornately decorated and well-polished brass bell push next to it. Favouring the direct approach as ever, the Doctor rang for attention. Seconds later a small hatch in the door slid open and a beady pair of eyes peered out suspiciously.

'Hello, I wonder if you can help me,' the Doctor said brightly. 'I'm looking for a lady by the name of Madam Guralza.'

'Have you got an appointment?' queried the owner of the eyes in cultured tones.

'Unfortunately we didn't realize that one was necessary,' Bernice said. 'But we're prepared to wait.'

The owner of the eyes gave them an eighth of what Bernice was sure was a withering expression of contempt and slammed the hatch shut.

'We can't keep on like this,' Bernice protested wearily. 'I'm beginning to appreciate what it feels like to be a Jehovah's Witness.'

The Doctor stepped back from the door and looked up at the high wall it was set into. It continued both left and right for a considerable distance. 'Wherever you go in the galaxy,' he said, 'places like this always have a tradesman's entrance.'

Bernice followed as he scurried along the street, all the while looking up, muttering and shaking his head at the tall spikes deterring intruders. At last he stopped at a blank face of wall and pointed upwards. 'Tradesman's entrance,' he said and formed a step with his hands.

'Tradesperson,' corrected Bernice, stepping up. In a few moments they were both up and over the wall.

The huge walled garden seemed to belong on a completely different planet to the South Side. An intriguing variety of exotic plants were in bountiful bloom, countering the smoggy air with a pleasant combination of scents. The lawns between had been expertly tended and were divided by an asphalt pathway of garnet, a sparkling fountain and a small ornamental bridge that led to a bright yellow summer-house. The picture was completed by rows of hedges that had been sculpted into simple animal shapes. In the distance stood a large white house.

The Doctor hurried over to a clump of white flowers. 'Frashels,' he said happily and knelt to smell one. 'I haven't seen one of these in centuries. And look at those lovely begonias . . .'

Bernice gripped his arm. 'Doctor, over there. Spy cameras.'

He looked around, confused. 'I don't think I've ever heard of those, are they . . . oh.' Two large black cameras, concealed in a hedge, were swinging their lenses about to face them. Before either of the travellers could react, a whistle blew in the distance and they heard hurrying footsteps. An armed young man in a black uniform and peaked cap sprang suddenly from the hedgerow. Surprising herself, Bernice kicked the gun from his hand and knocked him out with a couple of well-aimed blows.

'That was good,' she said breathlessly. 'That was quite good. I'm quite pleased with myself about that.'

The Doctor darted forward and scooped up the gun. He fumbled it nervously in his hands and finally passed it to Bernice. 'Would you look after this, please? I'm afraid I'm rather scared of them.'

'Oh, thanks,' she found herself saying as she accepted it. The footsteps were coming closer. 'Shouldn't we get out of here?'

The Doctor raised a hand. 'Just a moment.' He knelt down to examine the prostrate body of the guard. Tucked into the waistband of his uniform were a large pair of shears. The Doctor withdrew them and scissored the air gleefully. 'Ingenious. Guards that are gardeners. Or gardeners that are guards. This takes me back. Do you know, it's been years since I . . .'

Bernice grabbed him by the arm and angrily pulled him away. 'Doctor, come on!' They set off at a run across the bridge towards the summer-house. More of the black-uniformed men broke from cover at the far end of the garden and hurried after them.

Bernice threw the Doctor into the summer-house, turned, and fired three warning shots at the approaching guards. They scattered and returned her fire. She cursed

70

her jumpiness and tumbled back into the summer-house, landing almost on top of the Doctor.

'Watch yourself,' he told her, brandishing his shears. 'There's a sharp point on these, you know.'

Further shots rang out and bullets whizzed over their heads. 'Doctor, I've just realized something,' Bernice gasped.

'Oh? What's that?' he asked politely.

'You're insane. And we, who have risked our lives against evil from the darkest corners of the universe, are about to be shot for climbing over someone's garden wall! The indignity of it all!'

The Doctor nodded over her shoulder. 'Or perhaps not.'

Bernice turned. The guards were gathered outside the summer-house, their guns pointed down at them. She got to her feet slowly, threw down her gun and raised her hands. The Doctor stood next to her, still smiling.

The guard leader stepped forward. 'I ought to kill you now,' he barked, beads of sweat glistening on his forehead. 'What are you doing in here?'

Bernice extended a hand and said with resignation, 'Hello, we're members of a religious order. Would you like one of our leaflets?'

6

The Actress

Much exertion brought the Slaags to the settlement of the tribe at last. The scurrying movements of the women at work had alerted the antennae of the carnivorous beasts long before they had finished feasting on the bodies of the dead at the reception point. The prospect of a living feast filled them with glee and they bounced eagerly along, the majority sensibly taking the longer route and avoiding the ring of rocks that would only have delayed them. Their usual diet consisted of meat dropped down into their crowded tank. In the two years since their origin, they had craved the excitement of biting into living human flesh. The occasional living human they had been provided with was often dead before they could start to rip away his skin.

They fell on the tribe. Many of the humans were resting and were woken as they were eaten. The blood tasted fresh and strong and good. The flesh was tasty and filling. The bone and gristle was savoury and sharpened their teeth.

But it was still not enough. Somewhere they knew there was more living flesh on Avax and they wanted it. In their frustration they ate the tents and the wooden poles that supported them and then licked the brown, drying blood from the sand.

Still not sated, they quietened and concentrated. There was silence for a few minutes as they turned together slowly, antennae twitching. Excited clicks and scrapes burst from their mouths as they sensed the presence of a few more humans on the surface. Behind and ahead. They decided to move forward and return for the others later.

As they left the area that had once been the settlement, the Slaags excreted a sticky coating of waste matter to show what they thought of the species that had given them form and doomed them to a life of anger, blindness and insatiable hunger.

The house had been built in the style of the Frestan classic period, the main building surrounded by a cluster of lower kitchens and servants' quarters. The exception was the courtyard at the centre. High stone arches festooned with curling creepers supported an incongruous glass dome that intensified the heat of the two suns. A fountain babbled happily as small birds chirped about it. The air was pure.

Madam Guralza sprawled over a *chaise longue*, savouring the last few moments of her weekly foot massage. Gerd, her masseur, flexed her left foot for the last time and stood.

'It is always good to see you,' she told him. 'Until next week. Collect your payment from the gate as usual.' The masseur nodded and left.

The woman, now alone, sat up, yawned and slid her tiny pink feet into tiny red slippers. The large ornamental sunsdial facing her warned her that the movie matinee was about to begin on the nostalgia channel. She had only begun to watch her old pictures recently. Many of them she had never seen before. This afternoon they were showing *They Met On A Surface Car*. She'd co-starred with Richud Danner in that. He used to hold the shooting up by entertaining one of the grips in his trailer. She had to kiss him straight afterwards when his breath smelt of sweat. And people thought the movies were glamorous. One day, she thought, I'll publish my diaries. Or, more likely, I shall die and have them published for me.

The service bell tinkled. Guralza sighed and called, 'Oh, come in, Jalone.'

Her staff leader, formal in his black uniform and cap,

entered the courtyard and bowed. 'Intruders in the grounds, Madam. Do we have your permission to hand them over to Sergeant Felder's gang?'

His mistress' nostrils flared with indignation and she threw her head back. 'To Felder? Oh no, Jalone, I am not a savage. I will see them and decide then.'

'With respect, Madam,' Jalone said, shifting uncomfortably, 'these are not autograph hunters. They were shooting at your groundsmen.'

Guralza raised a heavily pencilled eyebrow and pondered. 'Really?' she said as she lit the cigarette at the end of a long holder. 'I would like to meet these people. Nerve is not something one sees in the young nowadays so much.'

She flounced famously from the courtyard. Jalone followed.

The armed gardeners stood over the Doctor and Bernice, who were sat together on a bench in a colonnade of hedgerow that led out from the garden to the vast front lawn of the impressive house.

'This is all wrong,' the Doctor said suddenly.

'You've noticed,' replied Bernice. 'It hasn't been one of my most successful days either.'

But the Doctor was obviously not listening to her. 'This area ruins the symmetry of the entire garden. It's not as if the rest of the arrangement is in any way either pleasantly routine or intriguingly abstract to the extreme.'

'I'm more worried about the guns, actually,' Bernice said, to no apparent effect.

'No, this pathway has no place here. A flowering column, perhaps, at each end might improve things . . .'

'I suppose you're an expert gardener, then?' Bernice was warming to what she assumed were the Doctor's attempts either to calm her fears or distract the guards before they made to escape.

The Doctor smiled and rested his head on his hands. 'Although I never met him personally,' he said, 'without me, Henry the Eighth might have written *Greenfly* instead of *Greensleeves*. The Tudors always had trouble with aphids. I remember saying to Mary, Queen of Scots, that she ought to change her muckspreader . . .'

Bernice's laugh was cut off by the jumpy leader of the black-uniformed guards. 'Shut up!' he shouted, brandishing his revolver. 'You're to remain silent until we decide how to dispose of you.'

The captives obeyed and sat staring bleakly at the row of hedges in front of them for a few minutes. Bernice realized that the Doctor had been right and that the colonnade they were sitting in seemed out of place in its ordinariness as part of such a spectacular garden.

'It's no good!' the Doctor shouted suddenly. 'I can't just sit here and do nothing about it!' He stood up and, before the guards could stop him, lunged for the opposite hedge with his shears. One of them stepped forward to stop him. The Doctor stuck out a casual leg and tripped him over as he got to work. The others stopped still in amazement. Half a minute later, he had traced the upright rectangular outline of something Bernice recognized instantly.

An outraged shriek came from the direction of the house. Bernice turned to see a very small elderly woman stumbling over the front lawn towards them. She wore a simple black dress that clung to her scrawny figure perfectly. Her hair, which was sculpted in a bouffant style, had been dyed black. Her features were sharp, strange and full of character under several layers of heavily applied make-up. 'Stop him, you idiots!' she cried out to the bemused guards.

They rushed to obey, bringing the enthusiastic Doctor to a final halt in a flurry of punches and kicks. He was dragged away from the hedge which now, incredibly for so short a time, was an exact scale replica of the police box exterior of the TARDIS.

'Who is this maniac?' the tiny woman wailed in heavily accented and, Bernice thought, heavily affected tones. 'Why has he been allowed to desecrate my beautiful shrub?'

'Desecration?' the Doctor snorted. 'I've done you an enormous favour and not even charged you.'

The woman stalked over to him and stared him in the face for a while. Bernice thought she looked like a small but very tough bird. Her eyes were thin slits that even heavy mascara could not accentuate. She looked the Doctor up and down and then considered the hedge. At last she nodded, almost reluctantly.

'You are right, it is good, I think you say, a mystery box. But I do not think you came here to perform free topiary, no?'

'We came here in the belief that you could help us find a missing friend,' Bernice said honestly. 'We are looking for somebody called Madam Guralza.'

The woman turned her terrifying stare to Bernice. A tense moment passed and then she started to laugh. 'You do not know me? You really do not know me?'

'I'm afraid we're new to the area,' Bernice tried to explain.

Guralza clapped her hands together and laughed again. 'Oh, my dear, you cannot fool me, you are new to our world. I have not met offworlders for many years. It was very different in my youth, Olleril was then almost cosmopolitan.' To Bernice's astonishment she took her by the hand and started to lead her in the direction of the house.

'You've decided to trust us, then?' asked the Doctor, disengaging himself from the grip of the bemused guardsmen. 'Your friends here were shooting at us just now.'

Their host giggled girlishly. 'They are foolish boys, eh. Oh, I know the odd ways of the offworlder. Now, please, come with me and we will talk about this friend of yours.'

In his sanctum aboard the *Gargantuan*, the Supreme One was dabbing at his lips with a handkerchief. He arranged his knife and fork with precision on his clean plate. The meal, best end of Slaag in a Frestan cheese sauce, had been most agreeable. He let out a contented burp and glanced at the small gold watch that adorned his slender wrist. He had several appointments in the city to keep before Tragedy Day. Things had to be kept looking normal in every detail. Afterwards, of course, they would be very different.

He called up the security unit. 'This is the Supreme One. Please have my skimsub ready for departure in ten minutes.'

'As you order, Commander.'

'Oh, and how are the Slaags doing?' the Supreme One enquired casually.

'The settlement has been cleared,' the security leader reported. 'The Slaags will have picked off any strays shortly.'

The Supreme One nodded happily. He broke the connection and began to gather his things together for the journey home. The clearance of the island was almost complete, then. One less thing to concern himself about. It was good.

Forgwyn and Ace stood on the large rock at the edge of the settlement and looked down at what remained of the tribe's tents. The reinforced canvasses were almost all that was left. The wooden poles and struts had been eaten up along with everything else. Dark brown pools of foul-smelling mucus had been left behind by the creatures.

'There's no blood or bone,' Ace said. 'You wouldn't know anybody had been here if it wasn't for the smell.' Her palm was cupped over her nostrils to cover the stench. She looked over at Forgwyn and noted his expression, again as calm as hers. He must have seen a lot of death, she reasoned.

'It was those creatures, then, like the one you saw?' he suggested. 'I wonder how they hunt.'

Ace considered. 'I didn't see nostrils or eyes, just antennae. I reckon they work by sensing movement. With luck, if we lie low, the two of us shouldn't bother them now they're full.'

Forgwyn clambered down from the rock and turned his head away from her. 'If they reach the ship . . .' he said, 'I hope Meredith can hold them off.'

'She got any weapons?' asked Ace brightly.

Forgwyn grimaced. 'Oh, plenty.'

'Then she should be all right,' said Ace, clapping a hand on his shoulder. 'It's us we've got to worry about.'

The boy looked at her, his face now troubled. 'There's something important you should know,' he said. 'My mother's pregnant. Very pregnant. I've got a brother on the way. He may have arrived by now.'

Ace frowned. 'How far is the ship?'

Forgwyn pointed straight ahead. 'About another four hours' walk that way, I reckon.'

'Let's move, then.' Ace started off, avoiding the muck left behind by the monsters. She realized that Forgwyn was not behind her and turned. He was staring to their left, squinting to see something in the distance. Ace followed his gaze.

The island was almost flat. About a mile away on the horizon was a thin grey line that appeared at first to be stationary. She looked closer and saw that it was moving forwards slowly in the direction they were taking. It was a column of the creatures, possibly fifty of them. The noise of their gnashing teeth, an eerie, echoing chitter, was carried over by the wind.

Ace bit her lip. 'Did you say your ship was four hours away?'

Forgwyn nodded. 'About. There's another big heap of rocks on the way. Those things must be going the long way to avoid getting stuck.'

Ace was impressed. It made a change to be paired up with somebody intelligent on her travels. 'Then we've got the advantage,' she said. 'How fast can you move?'

On the third floor of Madam Guralza's palatial residence, the Doctor and Bernice were enjoying a buffet of finger sandwiches and chilled wine. The furnishings were opulent without crossing the line into vulgarity. The walls of the spacious lounge they occupied were covered almost completely by black and white publicity pictures from their host's film career. Nearly all depicted her in vampish poses, arms flung out and head thrown back. As the

Doctor explained the essentials of their arrival on Olleril, skipping over the difficult details such as the exact nature of the TARDIS, Bernice glanced quickly and often between the stills on the walls and Guralza. She remained a strikingly attractive woman in old age.

A bell rang and Guralza straightened up. Jalone entered with a sheaf of papers. 'Your signature is required on these agreements, Madam,' he said, handing her the first half.

She took a marble-effect fountain pen from the gold desk at her side, provided the necessary signatures in a flurry of flourishes and curlicues, and handed them back to her servant.

'And these,' he went on, handing her the rest, 'require the signature of the benefits overseer for the 900 area.'

Bernice and the Doctor watched as Guralza thought for a second and then etched a cramped and smudged name that was not her own on the remainder of the sheets. Jalone nodded perfunctorily and left the room with the documents tucked under his arm.

'Forgive me,' Guralza said, tucking herself back into a comfortable position. 'Organized crime, being bad form, cannot stop for tea. You were telling me of your troubles?'

'Yes, well,' the Doctor concluded, momentarily lost for words, 'as I was saying, apart from an old guidebook we've had no allies in Empire City until now.'

'You came here for Friday, Tragedy Day, yes?' Guralza asked. 'I have not attended for many years, although my friends inform me that it remains as tasteless and gaudy an occasion as ever.'

'We arrived inadvertently,' Bernice explained. 'Three travellers with no particular place to go.'

The old woman laid a friendly hand on her knee. 'And what is your opinion of our great city? Tell me, honestly, dear, I will not be offended.'

Bernice pursed her lips. 'I find it . . . disturbing. Ever since we arrived, I've felt something unpleasant was about to happen. And I'm usually the optimist of our small party.'

Guralza gave an exaggerated shrug and puffed on her twenty-eighth cigarette of the day. The corners of her mouth turned down. 'My offworld friends,' she said, standing, 'come with me to the window.'

The Doctor and Bernice followed her to the window, where she threw out an arm in a wildly extravagant gesture and spat, 'See! The cordon!' The high wall towered over a row of empty houses in the near distance. 'I came here from Fresta, fifty-seven years ago, a young girl with nothing but a suitcase and my dreams. The people of the outer city, they take me in, they give me food and shelter and good advice. My old benefactor,' she stopped to wipe away the trace of a tear, 'he provides me with the money to learn Empirican and train in my art. These are good people.

'And they are treated so badly. Two Big Wars and much death and devastation. Is it surprising they should turn to crime? I think not. You treat a person like an animal, he will take after the animal. You put him in a cage, makes him even worse.'

'And yet you remain here?' the Doctor prompted her. 'A citizen of your wealth is unusual in these parts.'

Madam Guralza struck another passionate attitude, hand clasped to her heart. The Doctor coughed as she exhaled a lungful of acrid smoke in his face. 'I balance the economy. What little I take, I give back in a better way. It is good business. Who else, friend, will help these people? My money goes to run classes, or provide bread and soup for the hungry. I am not like the dogs of Central, with their scented soap and expense accounts, who turn their eyes away but for one day of the year!'

Bernice joined them at the window. 'You enjoy wealth here, nevertheless. This place is like a fortress.'

'Oh, girl, you think I want it to be so? Do I appear so naive?' cried Guralza, throwing up her hands. 'I am a part of things here as much as any other, I know. The powers above me tolerate my works. The gangs and the police let me do what I will. I am no threat to them. But if I can make better the lives of just a few, then I must. I say only

80

that I do what I can, when I can.' She tapped a lengthy growth of ash from her cigarette into one of the many trays that dotted the lounge and returned to the huge padded sofa she had risen from.

Bernice threw the Doctor a meaningful glance, pointed to her watch and mouthed, 'Ace.' He wiped his hands on a napkin and nodded.

'Madam Guralza,' he said. 'Please don't think us ungrateful of your hospitality, but as we have explained, we have to reach Central if we stand a chance of finding our friend.'

She smiled. 'What makes you think, Doctor, that things will be any easier there?'

'I have a way with authority figures,' he said confidently. 'The City Council may listen . . .'

Guralza whooped. 'The City Council! The City Council! Oh, that old guidebook! It really is no ally! You have a surprise coming, the both of you.'

'You will help us through, then?' Bernice asked.

'Oh, of course,' she said casually with a smile that was suddenly demure and sincere. She pressed a buzzer on the table next to her and Jalone entered. 'Jalone, take the Doctor upstairs and find him ten thou and two all-zones access wafers.'

The butler nodded and extended a gloved hand. 'If you'd like to come with me, sir?'

The Doctor turned to Guralza and bowed. Bernice was amused at this show of politeness. She had forgotten his ability to get along with almost anybody. He left the room with Jalone.

Guralza offered Bernice a cigarette. She declined. The old woman stared at her for a few seconds and pronounced, 'Benny, my dear, you have what in the old days people used to call star quality.'

Bernice smiled. 'Thank you.'

Guralza nodded passionately. 'Yes, my girl, it's true. And the Doctor as well. You make a good team. I see you in one of the old bug pictures, you the brainy daughter, he the nutty old inventor.'

At a loss for what to say, Bernice asked, 'Do you still appear in films?'

Guralza hissed and shook her head emphatically. 'Nowadays it is a pleasure not to be asked. It is all bottoms and sex or big bugs that are put on after they finish the shoot. Rubbish. Nobody wants for the performance or the glamour. And the television,' she threw up her hands again and groaned, 'oh, you have never seen such dollop. This *Captain Spaceship*, ach, it is nonsense.'

As the two women talked, Bernice decided that the Doctor's theory about the social framework of Olleril had to be correct. The duplication of twentieth-century Earth culture, thousands of years in the past for Guralza, was almost exact.

They met the Doctor ten minutes later. He was standing outside the front entrance of Guralza's house, tapping his feet against one of the pillars supporting the mantel of the porch.

'Do I look distinguished enough?' he enquired of the women, puffing out his chest.

'Faintly ridiculous, in fact,' was Bernice's judgement, 'but only because I know you. And besides, why should you want to?'

He handed her two plastic cards. There was a magnetic strip on the back of each. The first bore the signature of Councillor Metin Kenniter, the second Dulcia Joliff. Both were marked FULL ACCESS TO ALL ZONES R123456.

'Are these real people?' Bernice asked Guralza. 'What happened to them?'

Guralza shrugged. 'I do not ask these questions. If you are wise you will not either. The wafers simply came into my possession. And now I give them to you.'

The Doctor stepped forward. 'Guralza, I cannot thank you enough,' he said. 'Without your assistance we might never have reached Central.'

Their host smiled graciously and said, 'You are too kind. Particularly as we have yet to discuss terms.'

The Doctor exchanged an anxious look with Bernice. 'Terms?'

'But of course,' Guralza insisted. 'We have a saying on the South Side. There ain't no such thing as a free tea. I believe it is the same elsewhere also.'

'We've hardly any money,' Bernice protested. 'We made that clear.'

'Money, puh!' Guralza lit another cigarette and said shrewdly, 'I have no need of it. No, I want a guarantee from you.'

Bernice sighed. 'Run it past us.'

The old woman walked slowly away from the porch and looked out over her garden. Dusk was approaching and the air was still and smoky. Engine noise, music, shouts and shots drifted over the wall.

'I am near to death. There is nothing here for me. I wish to leave here,' she said simply. 'I wish you to take me with you to the stars.'

The Doctor moved to her side. 'If that is your condition then we have no choice.' Bernice wondered if the Doctor was sincere in his assurance.

Guralza was obviously entertaining similar doubts. 'Another saying, my friend. There ain't no such thing as a verbal agreement.'

The Doctor spread his hands. 'It's all I can give. I don't like to carry cash and my nearest bank account is on the other side of Pantorus.'

Guralza shook her head. 'Uh-uh.' She pointed to his hand. 'The ring.'

His reaction was a surprise to Bernice. He frowned, smiled, slipped it from his finger and handed it to her. She nodded her thanks and held it up to the fading light. The blue gem glinted oddly.

'A strange stone, but enchanting,' Guralza said approvingly. 'Which of the planets does it hail from? I have heard of the merchants on Quique Forty who trade in jewels from the distant unions.'

'I'm afraid,' said the Doctor, with a smile to Bernice, 'that is one of my few remaining secrets.'

'And so it must remain,' agreed Guralza, putting a nic-otine-yellow fingertip melodramatically against his lips. 'It is mystery that keeps the public interested, nothing is more true.' She put the ring on.

'We must go,' said Bernice. 'Thank you again.'

Guralza snapped her fingers and Jalone stepped out from the house. 'Take the Doctor and Bernice to the back entrance and direct them to the access point on 765,' she ordered him.

'Very good, Madam,' he assented and led the travellers away.

The small, thin figure of Guralza watched them depart through the gathering night mists. She had been waiting for such an opportunity for years. Flights leaving Olleril were nowadays reserved almost exclusively for freight, packed into vacuum silos. Even if she could have char-tered a private ship, the press would undoubtedly have discovered her plans. She couldn't bear to think of the people of the South Side, her extended family, believing that she'd abandoned them. Even if that's what she intended, in truth.

No, she would fake her death in some glorious accident . . . no, an inspirational act of heroism! Whatever, it would enable her to slip away quietly with the Doctor and his friends and begin a new life on another world, away from the rotten pictures and rubbish television and poverty and snobbery, the sheer stupidity of life on Olleril. Somewhere there had to be a better place. She felt confi-dent of her escape, truly content for the first time in many years.

So why were her hands shaking like those of a small child?

It was something the girl Bernice had said earlier. Something that had resonated with her own thoughts. Something that was in the air, wherever you looked, in your dreams.

Ever since we arrived here, I've felt that something unpleasant was about to happen.

7

The Hotel

Meredith Morgan took the last of the painkillers from the medi-pack. Labour had begun a couple of hours before and now she could feel the baby pushing inside her. This one felt different to how Forgwyn had all those years ago. But then she was seventeen years older.

She recalled Forgwyn's fathercode and smiled. Intelligent, sensitive and attractive, the packet had claimed. The gene parlour had been almost too correct. He was a great kid, even if he was getting a bit too judgemental about her lifestyle. She'd selected a boy again for the second pregnancy, but this time had gone for a package described as tough and instinctive. The baby pushed again, reminding her of that choice.

She screamed up at the interior hull of the ship as the pain surged once more. Forgwyn had been gone four days now. That meant the deadline for the completion of her task on Olleril had passed. She tried not to think of what might happen to her as a result of reneging on her contract. The Friars had made the penalty for failure very clear.

The call from the access point came at the wrong moment for Jeff Shrubb of the city's top-selling daily, the *Clarion*. He would have described himself as a forthright political columnist. His detractors called him a sad relic of a long-gone imperial age and accused him of stirring up racism, sexism and homophobia. He was wrong and they were right.

His sagging, hairy body was immersed in the bath of

85

his apartment in central two docklands. He was watching the purple bubbles of the relaxing foam burst against the enamelled sides and flicking through one of the many books on military history that he had collected over the years. Some of the words were a bit difficult to understand but he nearly always caught the basic meaning. Visions of the glorious imperial past of his nation passed before his mind's eye. He liked to think about guns and soldiers and loud noises and mud and death because it made him feel strong and happy, like beating people up had when he was younger.

He groaned and barked, 'Accept.'

'Call from Mr Forke at Toplex Sanitation for you, sir,' said the operator. There was a crackle and then Forke's voice came through. A high-pitched tone in the background indicated that he had operated the scrambler, as was procedure for devotees of the Greatest Lodge.

'Mr Shrubb. O Hail Luminus. One of our scanners has picked up something odd on the access computer. The holder of wafer 6788767 has re-entered Central.'

'You daft pollick,' Shrubb snapped at the wall speaker in the gruff tones familiar to television viewers from his appearances on various panel games. 'I'm not a cagging computer myself. Who are you talking about?'

'Councillor Metin Kenniter,' said Forke.

Shrubb frowned. 'Hold,' he ordered and stepped from the bath. He pulled the plug and watched the bubbles gurgle away. It couldn't be Kenniter, of course. He had been disposed of three months ago, sent floating out to sea with a concrete slab around his neck and no arms. One of the gangs must have gotten hold of the wafer. It was nothing to worry about but there was no harm in checking.

He towelled himself dry, poured a fresh bajorum juice and returned to the call. 'Forke, this imposter, alone is he?'

'No, there's a Dulcia Joliff came through a few seconds later,' Forke replied. 'They've entered central six together.

If that is Dulcia Joliff, she's lost six stone and changed skin colour.'

Shrubb decided on a course of action. 'It sounds like someone's done a rush job. Could be Guralza. Stick a tracker on them, all right?'

'Right away, sir,' Forke confirmed. 'I could also authorize use of the ultra scanner if you wish.'

'Do it. Call me back in an hour. O Hail Luminus.'

'O Hail Luminus,' said Forke and broke off the call.

Shrubb tied the towel around his waist and walked through into the main lounge of his residence, which was decorated in Empirican flag wallpaper. His wife and their four-year-old son were watching Empire TV music and singing along with the simple lyrics of Fancy That's latest hit single.

His wife looked up as he entered. 'I thought you were in the bath,' she said. 'Work didn't call again?'

He nodded and sat down on the couch beside her. 'Jerry wants me in early tomorrow,' he lied. 'Problems with the ruddy layout computers now.'

'Oh, darling, not again,' she said, patting his bullet-shaped head. 'They seem to expect you to sort out everything. Still, things can't go wrong now, can they?'

Shrubb shrugged wearily. His wife was a looker but not very bright, which suited him perfectly. It was right for a woman. She believed, along with almost everybody else that knew him, that he was a forthright political columnist on the *Empire Clarion*. This was true enough, but she didn't know anything about his more important job as representative of the Greatest Lodge of Luminus. Nor did she appreciate the extent of his responsibility as Tragedy Day grew nearer. Afterwards, he thought to himself, her life would be so much better. Everybody's life would be better once the weak-kneed nancies and foreigners had gone to the wall.

The call tone sung out again. Mrs Shrubb said, 'I'll get it,' and made to answer it, but her husband stopped her and went to the speaker in the hall outside.

The caller was Forke. 'The security ultrascanner,' he

reported. 'We ran a check on those two imposters. The male has two hearts.'

Lorrayn had been a fan of Fancy That even before they'd had their first hit. She'd seen a postage-stamp-sized picture of them in one of the poster mags and fallen instantly in love with Danny, the small one. She'd collected every disc, every interview, every video and every mention in any magazine even if it was only really small. She wrote a letter to Danny every day. So far she'd only had one reply. It was a postcard of the whole band which said 'Lorrayn – stick with us – Danny' on the back in scrawly green crayon. Often she'd sit on her bed looking at the message, afraid to touch the card because he had.

The trouble was, there were loads of other girls who felt the same way. The group were always saying how much fan mail they got and their concerts were always sold out. They were always saying how lucky they were and how thankful they were to their fans. That was what separated them from other groups, thought Lorrayn, they really cared, not only about their fans but about things like the environment and animals. There was a lovely picture of Danny playing with a cat that she'd stuck on her wall.

People said that Lorrayn was strange to like Fancy That and not have a job and to follow them wherever they went. They said it was wrong that a girl of twenty-two should be obsessed by what they called a 'teen' band. What they didn't realize was that she was special, different to all the other fans. It was something she stressed in her letters, even though she was sure they weren't getting through. She was the one for Danny. They had been made for each other, it was as simple as that. The time had come to prove it.

This morning, Lorrayn had been supposed to go for a job interview with a bank in zone three. Her mum had persuaded her to agree to that. Just as Lorrayn was getting ready to go out, her friend Luka had phoned to say there was a rumour that Fancy That were back in Empire City after their tour of the independent states and that they were staying at the President Hotel in zone six. Lorrayn agreed to meet her and hung up. Her mum had come thumping down the stairs, shouting and screaming. The nosy old cow had been listening on the extension. She'd said that Lorrayn was going to the job interview or she would be thrown onto the streets, end of story. 'You're wasting the best years of your life,' she had cried. 'That rotten pop group is all you care about! At this time of year, too, you should be ashamed of yourself. Think of all those people outside the cordon who . . .'

But Lorrayn had heard enough caggy talk about Tragedy Day. She had slammed the door in her mum's face and stalked away. It was time, she had decided, to show everybody how special she was. Her friends, her family, the public at large, and most of all, Danny.

It was so easy to buy guns nowadays. You just went into the shop and handed over the cash. It was hidden under her coat now, the cold metal pressed against her stomach. The other girls all around her were screaming and wailing up at the hotel building. The noise and the heat and the crush all helped to stop her thinking properly. She wasn't sure what she was going to do, which was very exciting. This time tomorrow she might be dead or locked up or back home or anything. It all depended on what she did with the gun. She felt powerful for the first time ever.

'Would you excuse me, please?' an odd voice said behind her. She turned to see a weird little man and a snobby-looking woman pushing through the crowd towards the hotel entrance. She grabbed the woman's arm.

'Take me in with you!' she shouted. 'Take me in with you!'

The woman pulled her suede-jacketed arm back, gave her a condescending look and followed the man into the hotel past the bouncers. Patronizing bitch.

But the incident had given her an idea. Those two weirdos had got in because they didn't look like Fancy

That fans. Maybe it was time to use her age to her advantage.

She found a public loo in a square nearby, ran inside and quickly made her face up again, all posh. It was a good job about that interview, after all, because she was still wearing the long-sleeved blouse her mum had bought her for it instead of the Fancy That T-shirt she wore normally. She tried to make her hair look weird and studenty by putting blobs of soap in it and drying it in funny shapes under the hand dryer. After five minutes she looked in the mirror and congratulated herself.

Five minutes later she was even more chuffed. She'd *strolled* into the hotel past all those over-made-up little kids. Now all she had to do was find the boys.

That was easy, too. She took the elevator up floor by floor. On the tenth she saw two big bouncers standing in the corridor. She flashed them a room key she'd nicked from someone downstairs and sighed as if she didn't think much of staying mere doors away from the latest pop sensation.

Her heart was thumping and there were big patches of sweat under her arms, in spite of all the deodorant she'd put on that morning. There were male voices coming from around the corner – it sounded like – yes, it was Danny! She felt as if she was about to faint. She reached for the handle of the gun and turned the corner.

There he was, leaning against a wall drinking soda and talking to a guy with a notepad and pen. He looked taller than in the pictures.

'Er, right, next question. What have you got planned over the coming months?' asked the guy with the pad and pen.

'Well,' said Danny, 'more great videos, more great music, more great concerts . . .'

'Da . . .' Lorrayn croaked. 'Da . . . Danny . . .'

The two men looked at her. Danny is looking at me, thought Lorrayn. *He* is looking at *me*.

'Er, Carryl,' called Danny, looking worried. 'Carryl,' he called again.

'Da . . . nny . . .' Lorrayn said.

The bigger of the two big bouncers appeared. Lorrayn knew that if she let them lead her away she might never have the chance to do something with her life again. She would just be somebody in a bank.

She pulled out the gun and shot Danny three times. Each bullet did a strange thing to him. The first knocked him back and his hair fell off, like it was a wig. The second burst his stomach open but there was no blood, only a funny fizzing sound and a burning smell. The third blew his face off.

The last thing Lorrayn saw before she was shot dead by the bouncer was the complex maze of wires and circuits behind Danny's cute face.

The Doctor let himself into his spacious room, stretched his arms and flopped down onto the bed. He rubbed his eyes and stared up at the ceiling. He let himself imagine what Ace was up to. At least she'll be in her element, he thought, stuck in the middle of a war.

The phone next to the bed rang. He picked up the receiver. 'Hello?'

'Only me, Councillor,' said Bernice's voice. 'Plain little old Dulcia.'

'Have you got anything interesting to say? I was having a think,' protested the Doctor.

'Oh, I tried that once, made a hopeless mess of it. I thought you might like to know what I think of Central.'

The Doctor wandered over to the window of his room, which was on the twenty-third floor, and pulled open the curtains. This side of the building faced away from the cordon and he was afforded a magnificent view of the impressively faded splendour that characterized the architecture of the Central area. The effect had been spoiled somewhat by the addition of enormous blocks (of which the hotel, the Doctor ruminated, was one) that clashed oddly with the prevailing style. 'Go on, then.'

'Here are the marks of the Earth jury,' said Bernice.

'Nul points. That feeling I had when we first arrived in this city, it's getting worse.'

The Doctor frowned and rubbed his naked ring finger anxiously. 'I feel it too,' he admitted.

'A horrible, sweaty palms, waiting to go in and see the headmaster type of feeling,' continued Bernice. 'I haven't felt so jittery in years.'

'We'll talk at dinner,' the Doctor told her. 'I want to finish my think.'

'Fine,' said Bernice. 'Oh, and before I hang up, I found something amusing in my shower.'

'Yes?' the Doctor queried absently.

'A wig, of all things,' laughed Bernice. 'You'd think somebody would notice. I wonder if he'll come back for it.'

The Doctor's reaction was unexpectedly marked. 'A wig?' he said, suddenly serious. 'Chest or head?'

'As far as I can tell, not being an expert, a very ordinary hairpiece,' replied the bemused Bernice.

'Don't touch that wig,' the Doctor warned her. 'I want to see it. And don't let anybody take it away.'

'I absolutely refuse to ask,' said Bernice, 'but if that's what you want. See you at dinner.' She hung up.

The Doctor stared out at the evening sky. Events were moving too fast for him. His first obligation was to find Ace. After that, it would be sensible to go back to the TARDIS and try somewhere else. But he was intrigued.

The TARDIS, yes. It had given him such an awful amount of trouble recently. Perhaps he had been wrong to let it have its head. Perhaps its choice of Olleril had been a significant one. Perhaps it had been trying to communicate something to him.

Shrubb had made his excuses to his wife and hurried over to Toplex Sanitation. He enjoyed his rare visits to the Luminun base. It was bright and cool and efficient. Like the rest of the city would be in a few days.

Some of Forke's tracker agents had bugged the President Hotel's telephone network and the conversation between the strangers had been relayed to them instantaneously.

Shrubb removed his headset and frowned. 'Bloody offworlders. They are humanoids, though?' It was something. He hated to think of *mutants* getting through the passport controls.

Forke nodded. 'The security scanner gave her the all-clear. Her physiology is standard. But she did mention Earth.'

Shrubb sneered. 'Earth. The mother of all worlds.' He pressed a hand to his sweaty brow. 'Why would they have come so far? And why now?'

'You don't think they are here by accident?' asked Forke.

Shrubb poured himself a drink and swung his big feet up on Forke's desktop. 'At this time? Don't be a splot. You heard them discussing the hairpiece. They're on to the Celebroids already.'

'My trackers tell me that a Celebroid was badly damaged at the President earlier this evening, in what appears to be an unrelated incident,' Forke told him.

'You've blasted any witnesses?' Shrubb asked.

'Oh, of course, sir.'

'Then at least we don't have to worry about that,' Shrubb mused. He drained his glass and set it down. 'And what about the Devor operation?'

Forke indicated the desk where the operative assigned to Devor was working. 'Proceeding to schedule. The processor implant is giving us exactly what was needed.'

Shrubb caught a glimpse of Devor on the screen. He was in a plane of some kind. He sighed. 'Still, I've got no choice but to refer this matter to a higher authority.'

Forke gulped. 'You can't mean . . .?' he stammered. 'Surely, there's no need to disturb . . .?' He could not bring himself to complete the sentence.

'This close to Tragedy Day, there can be no question of the need,' Shrubb stated impressively. He liked to make stern pronouncements of this nature in front of people. He enjoyed the important feeling it gave him. It made him feel like a general. 'I must speak with the Supreme One. O Hail Luminus.' He nodded to Forke and left the chamber.

As the Slaags bounced noisily towards their place of feasting, their antennae quivered with delight. They had eaten most of the animals, and the humans left on the island were moving together. In their slavering anticipation of the blood glut to come, some of the Slaags bit at each other's leathery skin. They had learnt long ago that their own meat tasted foul and tough but it was so difficult to hold their hunger back. Others chewed on the vegetation that they passed and which was even less to their taste. They demanded and they deserved meat.

Meat to live.

The chittering cry of the creatures was even louder now. Ace and Forgwyn had barely exchanged words in the four hours they had been running. It was all they could do to keep moving.

Forgwyn cried, 'There!' He pointed to a black shape that was partly concealed by a line of large rocks in front of them. Ace grabbed him and hauled both of them painfully up the rise. She sneaked a look behind her. The hideous bouncing balls were only five minutes behind them.

'Meredith!' Forgwyn shouted down at the beached ship. Ace looked down and saw it in its entirety for the first time. It was jammed between two high ridges of rock. Despite the danger of the situation, she could not help feeling surprised and impressed.

'That's some ship you've got there,' she told Forgwyn but he was already knocking frantically on the main hatchway.

The ship was black with red markings. It was about the size of an upturned double-decker bus. It consisted of a central tube ending in a jutting prow and two enormous warp-stretch thrusters. For something that had supposedly dropped like a stone from the upper atmosphere it was

in good shape. Apart from a few scratches to the paintwork, Ace could see no obvious signs of damage. There
were no visible breaches. If Ace had not been so relieved
she might have wondered why something she had
expected to be like a family saloon planet-hopper
resembled instead a customized sniper attack craft. She
scrambled down to join Forgwyn.

He was tapping out an entry code on a small pad built
into the hatchway. He completed the code and waited.
The hatch remained shut. He cursed and slammed his fist
on the hatchway.

'Come on,' Ace urged him, glancing nervously up at
the top of the ridge. The terrifying screech of the monsters
seemed almost to be upon them.

Forgwyn tried again and the hatch whirred open with
agonizing slowness. 'Get in!' he cried. Ace threw herself
through and Forgwyn followed her in. The hatchway
closed.

The Slaags arrived moments later, the first hurling themselves gleefully over the ridge. They struck the metallic
hull of the ship with force and uttered resentful squeaks.
Where was the soft human flesh? They quivered and gibbered, senses combing the immediate area. The creatures
were moving inside this container. They would have to
open the container.

Swiftly, the Slaags arranged themselves over the ship
and began to gnaw fruitlessly at the strengthened jauxite
of the hull.

If the exterior of the ship looked well, the interior created
the opposite impression. Ace reasoned that the inner
quarters were designed to rotate during flight in an
approximation of planetary gravitic conditions. The shock
of impact had brought the loose fixtures and fittings crashing down. The storage lockers, cupboards and drawers
were open and empty. Equipment, curtains, bedding, posters, books and games were scattered about the main body
of the grey metallic cylinder, which was illuminated by a

string of weak argon lamps. At one end, the tube divided into two sections that had been made into bedrooms. Each was curtained off rather than sealed. At the other were the forward controls and scanners.

A woman's voice was making deep-throated gurgling noises from one of the alcoves. Forgwyn shouted, 'I'm back, I'm here,' and pushed through the curtain. Ace caught a brief glimpse of a middle-aged woman, slim and muscular, lying on a makeshift bed. She was naked, sweating, and obviously close to giving birth. The curtain swung back again.

A hollow thumping noise began. Ace realized that the creatures outside were bouncing up and down in frustration on the hull. She thanked fortune that the ship had not been breached in the crash.

'I brought back trouble,' she heard Forgwyn cooing to his mother behind the curtain.

'I thought you . . . were dead . . .' she croaked between spasms of pain.

Ace shouted, 'Forgwyn, could those things get in here?'

His head appeared around the curtain. 'Can you wait, she's about to . . .'

Ace frowned. 'Listen, if one of those things gets in here we're all dead.'

He shook his head. 'The outer coating is strengthened alloy. It survived the crash, it'll stand up to them.' He stopped to wipe the sweat from his brow. 'Ace,' he asked, suddenly looking rather pathetic, 'do you know how to deliver a baby?' His mother cried out from behind the curtain.

'As it happens, I don't,' she replied. 'I should just let nature take its course. We've got to get rid of those bugs, anyhow. Where are those weapons you said you had?'

He dragged out a large silver trunk from beneath a pile of junk and returned to his mother's side. Ace nodded her thanks and swung it open.

She gave a low whistle. Inside the trunk was a formidable range of firepower. She ran her hands admiringly along several of the items as she identified them. 'Giggaron grenades ... low-frequency ultra vibrascope ... an intelligence-seeking bullet program ...' Her grasp faltered as she brought out a heavy grey rifle with a revolving circular attachment clipped to the end. 'A Hiel rifle. Banned in nearly every civilized corner of the universe.' She turned to look at the curtained alcove. She could hear Forgwyn cooing words of reassurance to his mother. 'Just the thing for a family outing.'

She turned to examine the flight controls. Already she was thinking of ways to beat off the creatures outside. To electrify the hull and frazzle them was, she decided, her best idea. She flicked on what she guessed correctly was a scanner device.

The creatures outside, all sixty of them, were swarming at the entry hatch, each of them hissing and seething as their teeth scraped at the unyielding metal. She shuddered at the sight of their bloated, blubbery bodies rubbing against each other. The ship rocked as they jumped furiously against it.

She flicked off the screen and cast her eyes over the other controls. They appeared fairly standard, although some of the technology was beyond her understanding. One item in particular held her attention. It was a small pyramid made of red glass. She'd taken it for an ornament at first, but it was attached to the ship's flight program controls.

Ace looked closer. The pyramid was glowing. She blinked to clear her vision and looked again. For a moment she thought she'd caught an impression of the Doctor and the TARDIS; not an image, just a feeling about them. But there was nothing now. It must have been her imagination.

In the crowded dining room of the President Hotel, Bernice sat waiting for the Doctor at a small table next to a big window. Tired of the babble of the surrounding guests, she glanced down at the wide, clean, well-lit street below. Night had fallen and it was empty apart from three men of pensionable age, who were standing opposite the hotel. They were shouting up at the diners but their words could not penetrate the soundproofed glass. She squinted at the placards they were carrying. She made out RIGHTS NOT CHARITY and THE TRAGEDY IS OURS and ASYLUM FOR VIJJANS NOW.

A crowd of excited and beautiful young men and women were sat at the table next to her, laughing about who they had got off with at a party the week before. 'Wasn't it fancy dress?' squeaked one. 'You spent the whole night chatting up that girl,' squeaked another. 'She wasn't wearing a dress,' squeaked a third. They were each wearing a badge in the shape of a glistening black teardrop.

A young waiter was hovering at Bernice's elbow. 'Sorry, I'm waiting for my colleague,' she told him with a pleasant smile. 'Could you tell me who they are?' She indicated the old men. 'I'm a visitor to the city.'

The waiter sniffed haughtily. 'They're protesters, ma'am,' he explained. 'Old cags left over from decade six. I don't know why they bother.'

'Perhaps they feel our society needs changing,' said Bernice.

The waiter gave her an odd look and a smug smile. 'I don't think it's ever likely to change, do you? Would you like a drink while you're waiting?'

Bernice ordered something that looked inoffensive and settled back in her chair. The old men in the street were laughing and joking now. As people passed they attempted to hand out leaflets but hardly any were taken. A large open-topped car rattled past them. In it were another group of beautiful young people. They were also laughing. And just a few miles away was the cordon and beyond that the refugee camp.

For the first time since her teens, Bernice felt the urge to write bad poetry about how things just weren't fair.

'They don't serve Golden Roast in the independent states,' said the handsome actor, his eyebrow raised.

The Doctor scowled. He couldn't understand why a

simple video remote control unit was giving him so much trouble. No matter what combination of buttons he pressed he never seemed to reach the right channel on the large TV set in the corner of his hotel room. The viewing guide he'd found at his bedside stated in its listings section, concealed expertly between a glossy sandwich of cookery tips and true-life stories, that constant coverage of the City Council debating chamber was available on Channel 465. The Doctor had decided that this might prove instructive and attempted to tune in. His efforts had been rewarded only by a bewildering array of irrelevant items that were making his head spin. The preparations for this Tragedy Day charity festival thing, whatever it was, were taking up much of the airtime.

He stopped channel hopping at the sight of the square-jawed man he'd seen talking to the robot couple on their chat show. He was stepping from a private plane on a small airfield and walking over to the waiting cameras. A logo in the corner of the screen said SHOWBIZ GOSSIP – LIVE!

'How was your skiing, Howard?' called several voices.

'Just great,' he nodded, smiling. 'Just great.'

'Is it good to be back in the city?' they called as he walked to a private car.

He stopped, turned around and spread his arms wide. 'It's always good to be back in Empirica!' Flashbulbs popped about him. He got into the car and it began to drive off.

'Anything planned for Tragedy Day?' the voices shouted after the vehicle.

The actor leant out of the window and called, 'Wait and see! Wait and see!'

The Doctor changed channels a few more times. He located nothing of interest until the screen showed the robot couple, once again on their talk show. The Doctor paid particular attention to their hair, in an attempt to confirm a theory he had.

The couple's guest on this occasion was a boy of about twelve. He was dressed in an ill-fitting suit and tie and wore a pair of glasses. He had thick, straight, greasy hair, back-combed over his big head. His bearing was haughty and unpleasant.

'Crispin,' the male robot addressed him, trying too hard to be tactful, 'so you've got five degrees in advanced science by the age of twelve and you spend all of your time at home studying. I know many people might say that you're missing out on your childhood.'

Crispin shook his head. 'Not so, Robert, not so,' he replied in precocious, lisping tones that made the Doctor, a man not given to violence, wish for an opportunity to administer a clip around his ear. 'I've no wish to associate with other children. I don't understand them and I don't want to.'

'But surely,' said the female robot, leaning forward, 'you'd like to go to discos instead of being shut up in your room all the time?'

'No, not interested in discos,' said Crispin. The studio audience laughed nervously. The expression on the little boy's face remained still and superior.

The Doctor changed channels again. At last the identifier 465 flashed up in the corner of the screen. But what was going on here?

A bawling mob of people were arranged in tiered seating in a TV studio. A tall, lanky man (another robot, the Doctor noted from his movements) was leaping about with a microphone trying to speak to the people who were shouting the loudest. He stopped in front of a man with a red face.

'What the majority of people are agreed on is that we can't take even more immigrants in!' the man screamed into the microphone.

The harried robot leapt over to the other side of the noisy studio and thrust the microphone into the face of a young woman. 'What do you say to that, then, Powla? After you've heard what people have said here do you still think Vijjans should be allowed in to Empirica?' he said with condescension.

The woman tried to speak over the cries and shouts of

the mob. 'The truth is that there has been virtually no immigration to this country since the early . . .' Her words were lost under the shouts of the crowd.

Confused, the Doctor called room service. A porter arrived in seconds. 'There's something wrong with this set,' he explained. 'I can't get Channel 465.'

The porter looked at the screen, where the crowd had started to throw chairs at each other. 'That is Channel 465, sir,' he said.

The Doctor looked back at the screen. '*That* is the City Council debating chamber in session?'

The porter said, 'Yes.'

The Doctor sank down slowly onto the bed. On the screen a message flashed up: IMMIGRATION AMEND-MENT OF CITY COUNCIL PASSED BY DEBATING CHAMBER. NEXT: BENEFITS AMENDMENTS – INVALIDITY/MATERNITY.

'Why have you called me? You know how busy I am,' snapped the Supreme One from the speaker of Shrubb's communicator device.

Shrubb drew a deep breath. To displease the Supreme One was to invite death. But this matter was desperate. 'This is urgent,' he said. 'The Greatest Lodge of Luminus itself may be threatened.'

'Go on,' said the Supreme One wearily.

Shrubb told his master of the arrival of the mysterious alien with two hearts. The Supreme One listened attentively.

'Go to him,' he ordered. 'Speak with him and learn his purpose.'

'As you command, Supreme One. O Hail Luminus.'

'Shrubb,' the voice of the leader issued from the speaker once again, 'be discreet. Indulge this alien but do not reveal too many of our plans.'

'I obey, Commander,' said Shrubb dutifully. He pocke-ted his communicator and went to begin the task with which he had been entrusted.

* * *

'Humanoid,' the Supreme One said to himself, tapping a finger against his lips. 'But with two hearts . . .'

Now back in his residence in Empire City, he was enjoying a bedtime snack of milk and biscuits. He liked to dunk a biscuit into the milk and judge when it was the right time to pull it out before it got too soggy and dissolved. There were crumbs in his pyjamas which was irritating. He'd been hoping for a quiet night, too.

He put his snack to one side and picked up his personal computer terminal, the one he'd used to take over Luminus six years before. He searched diligently through the files accumulated over the centuries by the organization on alien forms of life. The result of his request for information on bivalve species both intrigued and disturbed him. Apart from a couple of monopod creatures and a drone race there was only one possibility.

'A Time Lord,' he said excitedly, his fingers drumming on the console before him. 'But they're forbidden to interfere.'

He asked for more information. The computer whirred for a few minutes and then gave him all it had, which wasn't much, on the mysterious Time Lords. One paragraph caught his eye.

All branches of the Order are to beware the renegade known as the Doctor. His activities on several of our planets have resulted in delays and even cancellations of control programs. He possesses his own time-space capsule, the TARDIS. His scientific skills are phenomenal. Standing orders re the Doctor: capture and control him and his TARDIS machine.

The Supreme One smiled. If the new arrival on Olleril was this Doctor, he could prove very useful to the great plan.

8

The Envoy

Bernice returned to her room at half past nine, singing to herself to keep her spirits up. The meal had been excellent even if the Doctor hadn't showed.

The phone was ringing. She picked up the receiver. 'Yes?'

'Only me,' said the Doctor. 'Where've you been? I've been trying to reach you for about an hour.'

'It really is just as well you've never married,' came Bernice's reply. 'I've been waiting for you downstairs. It's embarrassing to be stood up, do you know that? A girl's ego . . .'

'Listen, this is important,' he cut across her. 'Are you alone?'

'Only totally. Apart from the hairpiece of horror hotel, of course.'

'I've discovered something odd,' he continued. 'The City Council doesn't exist any more. Apparently the ruling party was re-elected constantly, by an extremely suspect system that was made to look eminently respectable. So they abolished the electoral system and privatised the administration.'

'So?'

'So the only say the people have here is a sort of televised slanging match, at the end of which the motion is always passed the way the administration wants it.'

'I've seen worse systems,' Bernice said, yawning. It had been a long day. 'We both have.'

'Yes, yes,' the Doctor said impatiently. 'But it tells us three important things. One, that if they can manage to

103

eliminate any real opposition and still keep things looking sweet and tidy, the Luminuns, the secret society, have the power to take more direct control than they do at present. In fact they have the power to do more or less anything they want.'

'So why haven't they done it? Taken more direct control?'

'That was my second point,' said the Doctor. 'It leads me once again into the curious question of this peculiar planet's strange society.'

'And point number three?' asked Bernice, kicking off her shoes and reclining on her warm, comfy bed. She yawned again.

'Ah,' said the Doctor, 'point three is, obviously, that it's going to be more difficult than we thought to find Ace, as the councillors don't – '

The line went suddenly dead. Bernice yawned a third time and rattled the hook. She was dialling room service when the full effects of the odourless vapour that was being pumped into her room finally reached her and her grip slackened.

'Bernice!' the Doctor called. 'Bernice!' He snarled and flung the telephone down. It rang immediately. 'Hello, Bernice?' he said eagerly, hoping to prove his suspicions wrong.

'Room service here, Mr Kenniter,' said a voice. 'There's a Mr Shrubb at main reception who would like to see you, sir.'

'Really?' said the Doctor. 'Tell him I'll be with him directly.'

He put the phone down and ran his fingers through his hair.

The Doctor emerged from the lift on the ground floor and looked around. A tall, bulky man in a suit and tie was waiting on one of the large sofas in the reception area. He was sweating profusely. He had narrow eyes and

104

resembled a pig. Piped music tinkled softly from small speakers in the ceiling.

The Doctor walked over confidently. 'You wished to speak to me?'

The man smiled, stood and extended one of his huge hairy hands. 'Councillor Kenniter. Jeff Shrubb, *Empire Clarion*.' His voice was too loud.

They shook hands. 'You will appreciate, I'm sure,' the Doctor said, taking the lead he had been given and sitting down opposite the man, 'that I can spare you only a few moments away from my work.'

'Oh, of course, sir,' Shrubb replied with a mocking smile. 'I've only really got the one question.'

The Doctor raised an eyebrow. 'Yes?'

'Yes. Tell me. Where did you come by your second heart?'

The Doctor sighed and sat back. He stared at his shoes for a moment, lost in thought. 'Where did you obtain surveillance equipment about two levels forward from the prevailing technology of this planet?'

Shrubb laughed. 'We're being honest with each other. That's good. I was afraid we might have to force the truth out of you. And I haven't got the time.'

'Oh?' remarked the Doctor. 'Something big planned?'

Shrubb swung his big hands wide. 'At this time of year, everyone in the city's got something big planned.' He produced a miniature listening device from an inside pocket and waved it meaningfully. 'Although, with your interest in our politics, I'm surprised you don't know that.'

'All that is really incidental,' the Doctor said airily, although his expression remained set. 'I'm naturally curious. My reason for coming here is a very simple one. I've lost a friend and I would very much like her back. With your resources that shouldn't be too difficult to arrange. And then we can cease to be a problem to each other.'

Shrubb nodded graciously. 'What's this about a lost friend?'

'Without going into particular detail,' the Doctor

explained, 'yesterday afternoon she found herself on a repatriation flight to a country I believe is known as Vijja.'

The journalist leant forward, suddenly anxious. 'Yesterday afternoon? To Vijja?'

The Doctor nodded. 'She was caught up with some people at the refugee camp.'

'Was she?' said Shrubb. He stood up. 'Will you please wait here, Mister . . .?'

'I'm the Doctor.'

'Doctor. I have to make a couple of calls.' He strode away briskly.

The Doctor leant back on the comfortable sofa, stretching and feeling rather pleased with himself. He had handled a difficult situation particularly well, he thought.

The Supreme One was enjoying a vivid dream about absolute power over all when the communicator peeped into life once again. He pulled off his night mask, gave an irritated tut, and switched on his bedside lamp. His eyes were still adjusting to the sudden glare as he fumbled for the answer button. 'Accept, accept.'

'O Hail Luminus. Sorry to disturb you, Commander, I know you value your sleep, but I have urgent information for you,' reported Shrubb.

The Supreme One straightened his pyjamas, cleared his throat and said, 'Proceed.'

'It appears that another offworlder, a female associate of the imposter with two hearts – calls himself the Doctor – went out on yesterday's flight to Avax.'

The Supreme One thought quickly. So this was the Doctor. And judging from his past record, he would probably already be plotting against them. They had to find out more about his contacts and plans. That would perhaps be best achieved by letting him think they weren't onto him.

By now the female offworlder was almost certainly a sticky pool of Slaag excreta, but there was a slim chance of her survival. If she was a colleague of the Time Lord, another scientist, her contribution might prove invaluable. It was time to call off the Slaags anyway.

'Very well, Shrubb,' he said. 'Tell this Doctor that his colleague will be located and returned to him as soon as possible.' He stopped himself and a sinister smile curled across his lips. 'No – there may be a better way. I wish to learn more about him and his purpose here. Much more. And to do that, we need to gain his confidence.

'I will arrange a high-speed heliflyer to be at the roof of the President Hotel in fifteen minutes. You will take the Doctor to Avax and pick up his friend yourself. This will serve as proof of our good intentions.'

'But Avax, sir,' Shrubb protested. 'It's secret to our own citizens, let alone interfering aliens. And I hear that the Slaags are loose . . .'

'The Slaags will be long gone, do not fret,' his superior soothed him. 'And if we reveal something to the Doctor, perhaps he will reveal something to us. Fifteen minutes.' He broke off the call, arranged for the heliflyer to be sent over, and then put himself through to the *Gargantuan*.

'Are there any survivors on the surface?' he asked the research leader.

'We were going to call you on this matter, Commander,' Gortlock replied. 'There are two survivors holed up in a spacecraft on the western coast.'

'A spacecraft?' spluttered the Supreme One. 'How did it get there without our knowing?'

Gortlock coughed nervously, his thoughts obviously full of the bloody demise of his predecessor. 'It's shielded, Commander,' he said. 'Even now it's not registering on our sensors. But we can see it on camera. We hadn't been scanning the west coast, we didn't think anything was there . . . we can hardly be blamed . . .'

'Very well, very well. Here are your orders. Call the Slaags back immediately.'

'I obey, Commander. And the spacecraft?'

'Leave it,' he ordered. 'I have a purpose in this that you will not question if you value your internal organs.'

107

He heard Gortlock's gulp and smiled. He liked to frighten people like that. 'Now carry out your tasks.'

The Supreme One tutted and tried to make himself comfortable between the sheets once again. There were biscuit crumbs everywhere but he tried to ignore the discomfort. Another alien visitation at such a crucial moment in the history of the planet could not be put down to coincidence. He was determined to find out what was going on. Particularly if it meant the problem of the psychic differential could be solved.

But first, to sleep. How he valued his four hours of total relaxation. He switched off the bedside lamp and closed his eyes. It was a measure of his confidence in his own infallibility that he was asleep within seconds and had returned to his dream about his favourite things; science and power.

The Slaags had lost patience with their attempts to penetrate the skin of the container but it was not in their nature to give up entirely. They had considered their options at length. Humans needed sustenance as much as themselves and there could not be very much inside the cylinder. They would wait for the humans to emerge and then feast. They sat quietly on the outer surface of the ship. The silence of their patience was broken only by an occasional squeak, belch or breakage of wind.

Forgwyn gripped his mother's hand hard. She screamed again, her face red and dripping with sweat. She had already taken all the available sedatives from the medi-pack. As far as he could tell, she was doing well in the circumstances.

She ran her hand across his cheek. 'Forgy, Forgy...' Her head turned deliriously from side to side. 'What day is it? How long have we been here? I can't fail them...'

'Don't worry,' Forgwyn told her with a confidence he did not, in truth, feel. 'Don't worry, things are going to be fine.'

'I can't fail them,' she gasped. 'Not the Friars, I can't fail *them*. They marked my soul . . .'

Forgwyn rubbed her hand reassuringly. He didn't like it when she talked about her job so openly, particularly not when there was a stranger around. It brought back really bad memories, of Saen and stuff.

He realized that Ace had pushed aside the curtain behind him. 'How's your Ma?' she asked.

'She'll be fine,' he replied, smiling up at her. 'What about those creatures?'

'We should be safe in here, like you said.' She bit her lip, as if unsure of saying something. Forgwyn recognized a conversational trick he often used himself. Without waiting for encouragement from him, she said, 'I had a look at your weapons cache.'

He looked down. 'It's not mine,' he said evenly. 'It all belongs to my mother.' He squeezed his mother's hand again and said, 'Meredith, this is Ace. She's a friend. Offworld, like us. Ace, this is my mother, Meredith.'

Ace didn't feel there was much point in acknowledging the introduction as the rules of normal conversation were being seriously compromised by the extraordinariness of the situation. She wasn't keen on all this gynaecological stuff. Instead, she got down on her haunches and said to Forgwyn, 'My mum's a hairdresser. She works in a salon called Rene's in the Broadway. In her bag she carries some curling tongs, a copy of *Take A Break* and some cosmetics. In her bag, your mum carries Giggaron grenades and a Hiel rifle. What does she do?'

She left the curtained alcove and returned to the main body of the ship. Forgwyn looked into his mother's dilated green eyes. Her face was contorted in agony. He wondered if any of her victims had screamed like that as she had plunged in the dagger or pulled the trigger.

Ace noted the cessation of the thumping noise as she returned to the controls of the ship. She flicked on the external scanner. Incredibly for what she had regarded as such tenacious beasts, the creatures were bouncing away from the ship and towards the sea nearby. They left behind a coating of slime as they wobbled away.

'Don't like that,' she said to herself. 'Happy little slime-balls give up and go home? I don't think so.'

This way, the signal called seductively. *This way, back to the sea, for meat. You know how much you need meat. It's good for you, builds you up, makes you strong.*

The Slaags' antennae twitched and their jaws snapped open and shut frenziedly as they hurried to meet the call of the signal. Soon, it promised, there would be so much meat, more than they could eat. A never-ending feast of blood and bone. And there would be much ripping, tearing, and sucking of the juices from warm living flesh.

They reached a clifftop and hurled themselves off into the sea in a tumultuous cascade of squeaks, whistlings and splashes.

The Doctor looked down at Empire City from the night sky. The central zones shone out a bright, tidy light. Outside the irregular loop of the cordon, the greater area of the city was in darkness. He thought of the owner of the small bar and the woman with dyed red hair and the man who pretended to be a pile of rubbish in a corner of the access point. They were all down there, going about another night.

He looked across at Shrubb, who was sifting through some important-looking documents that were covered in figures. The pilot of their luxury craft was in front of them, his hands steady on the guidance controls, his face impassive.

'How long to Vijja?' asked the Doctor, breaking a long silence. He had plenty of other questions to ask but had decided to play the situation by ear.

Shrubb put the documents to one side. 'We're not going to Vijja.'

The Doctor snarled, 'You gave your word.'

'Yes, I gave my word,' Shrubb went on. 'And the word of a member of the Greatest Lodge is his bond. We're going to collect your friend. She's on a small island two thousand miles away.'

'I've seen maps of this planet,' the Doctor said, his voice subdued and menacing. 'There is no such island.'

Shrubb nodded. 'There is no such island on the maps,' he said. 'Apart from rather special ones.'

'I see,' said the Doctor.'Special secret maps belonging to the special secret Greatest Lodge. May I ask what she's doing on this mystery island?'

'No, you may not.'

'Another secret. Don't you find all those special secret things boring after a while?'

'No,' said Shrubb and returned to his study of the documents.

The Doctor looked down again and saw the old dock-yards giving way to the ocean. He twiddled his thumbs, hummed and sighed. 'I would,' he said.

Shrubb looked up. 'You would what?'

'I would find it boring. Covering my tracks, lying all the time, saying one thing and meaning another. I'd find it very boring. Not to mention all those handshakes and rolled-up trousers and promising to obey the mighty pro-tractors or whatever.' He sniggered and shook his head. 'You must feel very foolish.'

'I certainly do not,' Shrubb said icily, playing directly into the Doctor's hands. 'The Greatest Lodge is above such trifles. Its ranks contain only the finest minds, the elite of our society. Its work is just and for the greater good. It holds back the curse that haunts the planet. It looks after the citizens and preserves the ideals of conflict and superiority.'

'To use an old Earth phrase, cobblers,' the Doctor snor-ted with derision. 'You may have fooled the people here, but to an outsider your activities are tatty and obvious.'

'You may have cause to repent your remarks, Doctor,' Shrubb threatened. 'Mockery of the Truths of Luminus is unwise.'

The Doctor beamed ridiculously. 'Oh, well, forget I said a word. I'm sure your club is great fun.' He looked down

111

at the sea again, his mind racing. So he was with one of the top-ranking members of the organization. Pumped full of propaganda, made to feel more important than he is. Seems impressive but has a weak, insecure personality. A thug with a typewriter, elevated to the status of a near dictator. The Doctor couldn't believe that Luminus was run along the lines of Shrubb's elementary philosophies of nationalism. That meant somebody further up was using him, encouraging him to believe what he wanted to believe.

The Doctor settled back to enjoy the journey.

Her examination of the weapons completed, Ace turned her attentions to the other oddments scattered about the capsule. Forgwyn's mother continued to wail and scream behind the curtain. Ace remained unmoved. If the woman was as tough as her armoury suggested, she'd get through the birth with no problems. Ace had seen documentaries where African tribeswomen just dropped their sprogs while they were working. Let these things sort themselves out, she thought.

She played a few of the games, enjoying the chance to brush up on her crisis-in-combat training, before she realized how tired she was. She stretched out next to the flight controls and found herself looking into the red pyramid again. She touched the smooth surface of the object and tried to remove it from the flight panel it was affixed to.

It felt as if she had plugged her hand directly into a power grid. She cried out as the pain seared along her arm and entered her head. Her vision clouded. Her view of the capsule interior faded out. For a second she saw a pit of flame. Watching over it was a cowled giant. From beneath his hood stared red eyes that pulsed in rhythm with her own terrified heartbeat.

Her fingers relaxed their grip on the red pyramid. She almost cartwheeled backwards onto the rug that was fortunately there to break her fall. The pain and the vision disappeared. She pulled herself up, swore and flexed her aching muscles. There was some defence mechanism built into that thing.

'Ace, it's coming! The baby's coming!' Forgwyn's head popped agitatedly around the corner of the curtain.

'Good, good,' she said. 'Just let it do what it wants to, I reckon. Here, what's that red thing on the – '

'No, I think there's something wrong,' he said, interrupting her. 'Are the feet supposed to come out first?'

The heliflyer was being guided to an exact destination on the island, the Doctor noted, by computer override from an outside source. The pilot was taking care of auxiliary systems while the craft itself sped over the dark, deserted surface of the island.

'Nearly there, I presume,' he said.

Shrubb grunted his confirmation. The heliflyer slowed and began to descend. The Doctor squinted through the window at his side and made out a cylindrical black shape in the darkness. It was wedged between some rocks not far away. He had not seen a ship like that for years. It was a luxury two-wing warp-stretch family saloon that had been lovingly customized. The pointed snout of the prow would have increased the velocity of the original unit by five magnitudes. Perhaps the owner was in the habit of needing to make quick getaways.

The flyer touched the surface. Shrubb nodded to the pilot, who pressed a button. The door on the Doctor's side of the passenger compartment swung up automatically, allowing him a gasp of fresh night air that was marred only slightly by a distant briny odour.

'I have your permission?' the Doctor asked Shrubb.

Shrubb waved a hand. 'Please, go ahead.'

The Doctor nodded civilly and jumped down from the flyer. Shrubb watched the alien moving, with that peculiar walk of his, towards the ship. Another figure was coming towards him.

'You took your time!' Ace, hands on hips, called playfully

to the Doctor. She looked him up and down as he got nearer.

'Your approval makes all the difference,' he greeted her, smiling. They held hands and he said, 'What have you been up to?'

'Bad stuff. I've got trouble at the moment, in fact. I was chuffed to see you getting out of that flyer, I can tell you.'

His eyes narrowed. 'What mischief have you created now, Ace?'

'Created nothing.' She jerked her thumb back at the grounded spacecraft. 'There's a woman in there giving birth. And I must have been bunking off the day they did midwifery at school.'

'Well, I shouldn't think even you could cause that kind of problem,' the Doctor said affectionately. He allowed her to lead him through the hatch and into the ship.

Inside, Meredith was now strangely quiet apart from a series of short gasps. The Doctor said, 'Goodness,' and pushed his way through to where she and Forgwyn were crouched in the makeshift sleeping quarters.

Ace attempted to perform introductions. 'Forgwyn, this is my best mate, the Doctor. Doctor, this is Forgwyn, and er, this is his mum.'

The Doctor smiled at Forgwyn. Without knowing why, the boy felt reassured immediately. The composure and authority of the intruder were overwhelming. He said, 'I think they call it a breech birth.'

'They do indeed,' the Doctor confirmed, taking off his jacket and rolling up his sleeves. 'Could you fetch me a bowl of hot water, a bar of soap and some clean towels, please?'

Forgwyn nodded and went to collect these items. When Ace was sure he was out of earshot she leant closer to the Doctor and whispered, 'There are some crass things going down on this island. A whole tribe of people's been wiped out. We reckon it's a weapons-testing area. Really sick. There are some bugs about, too, not big but nasty. And I'm not sure about these two, either . . .'

'Really, Ace, one thing at a time,' the Doctor shushed

her. 'I've got to concentrate, I haven't done one of these for a long time.' He wiggled his fingers like a concert pianist. 'Not since Genghis Khan, in fact.'

'You delivered Genghis Khan?'

'Yes, he was a very sweet baby. You never can tell. Ah, my equipment!' He took the bowl of water and the towels from Forgwyn as he returned and set to work.

'Meredith,' he said, 'please listen to me. I want you to relax and breathe deeply.'

Ace sighed. She was bursting with questions to ask the Doctor. And she still hadn't found out what that pyramid thing was.

The Supreme One, sleep period over, was now immersed in his personal ion-bombardment container. A session of rejuvenating ion bombardment was essential to his health and was the first thing on his daily routine. He reclined in the container, dressing gown hanging loosely from his thin frame. He was just beginning to feel the effects of the device when the communicator rang again. He groaned, switched off the unit and called, 'Accept. What is it now?'

'O Hail Luminus,' said Shrubb. 'I have reached Avax with the Doctor, Commander. He has met with his friend at some kind of offworld ship.'

'Observe him closely,' the Supreme One ordered. 'And those he meets with. Offer him the warmest hospitality. We must ascertain his purpose in coming to our world.'

'Very well, Commander. And when we return to the city?'

'Leave that to me. I have an idea in mind as we speak. We will discover more from the Doctor and his friends if they are permitted freedom of association and unrestricted access. Remember, watch him closely.'

Before he returned to the ion treatment, the Supreme One glanced at a wall clock. He consulted his work notes. The presence of the Doctor was both a boon and an irritant. The schedule had been planned to the last detail. The arrival of a random element of such significance in the last few days of the operation was unfortunate, to say the least. But his superior knowledge might be of use in the technical area.

With the final stages of the plan in mind, he reached for his communicator unit and dialled a complex code. The calling tone rang out for a full minute before the call was accepted. 'Who is that?' a male voice snapped. 'Do you know what the crusting time is? People are trying to cagging sleep!'

'Good morning, Howard,' the Supreme One greeted the star of *Captain Millennium*, wincing at the loutishness and the impertinence of his newest recruit to the Greatest Lodge. At least Shrubb retained an air of respect in their dealings.

The man on the end of the line gulped. 'Er, Commander,' he said. 'Er, O Hail, er, Luminus.'

'Hello, Howard,' the Supreme One said smoothly. 'Were you satisfied with our handling of your request re Mr Lipton?'

'Oh, yes. Very satisfied.'

'Good, good. Well, remember, if there's anything else you want doing, just ask.' The Supreme One almost choked on his words. But Devor was so necessary to the plan.

He dialled another code. 'Toplex Sanitation, Mr Forke speaking, how may I help you?'

'This is your Commander.'

'Supreme One! O Hail Luminus!' Forke's voice sounded extremely surprised. He was unused to direct dealings with the Supreme One.

'I have a task,' said his master, 'for your friend Sergeant Felder. I want him to trace the movements of this Doctor.'

'Don't look so worried,' Ace said to Forgwyn. They were waiting outside the alcove where the Doctor was delivering the baby. 'If anybody can do it, the Doctor can.'

Forgwyn tried to smile and feel relaxed. 'You travel with him, you said?'

'I do, yes.'

'Where are you from? The rim systems?'

'No. Roundabout.'

'Right. How old is the Doctor?'

'Why do you ask?'

Forgwyn shrugged. He was trying to make himself comfortable on the rug next to the flight controls. 'He seems really old and really young at the same time.'

'Yeah. Strange, isn't it?' She reached across to the weapons trunk and pulled out one of the Giggaron grenades. 'Bit like these.'

Forgwyn took it from her. 'All right,' he said, avoiding her eyes. 'My mother is a killer. She's been killing since she was my age. Killing anything anybody pays her enough to.'

Ace nodded. 'And what about you?'

'I'm trying to complete my studies,' he said. 'But we move about too much.'

'I bet,' said Ace. The boy looked so helpless and fragile. She wanted so much to reach out and touch him but he seemed to be putting up a kind of barrier. There were so many questions she could tell he didn't want to be asked. A lot like her aged seventeen. She laid a hand on his shoulder.

The Doctor called out suddenly, 'Ace! Forgwyn! It's a boy!'

'We know!' Ace shouted back. She and Forgwyn hurried through into the sleeping quarter. The Doctor smiled up at them. He had cut the umbilical cord and handed the tiny, wailing child up to its exhausted mother. She smiled and cried with relief. 'Thank you,' she whispered to the Doctor. 'Thank you so much.'

'All in a day's work,' he said, cleaning his hands in the water. Ace could see he was feeling rather pleased with himself. 'Now,' he said, 'we have to leave here, sooner than is really sensible. Forgwyn, would you please gather whatever things you and your mother need to bring?'

He nodded pleasantly and went off. The Doctor looked indulgently down at the mother and child and slipped back into his jacket. 'Where's Benny?' Ace asked him.

'She's safe and well, back in the city we came from.'

He gave her a meaningful look. 'Let's discuss matters on the way back, in private, yes?'

Forgwyn knew that his mother couldn't leave behind the tools of her trade. He picked up the heavy trunk of weaponry and weighed it next to his own, which he had jammed full of books, games and clothing for them both.

He took a look around the central cylinder of the ship. It had been his home for as long as he could remember. It was strange to think he might never see it again. He'd learnt to read here, bouncing on his mother's knee in the brief periods she could spare during her assignment on Kallak 56. He'd sat in here for hours looking at warp space on the main screen as she'd hurried to collect the payment that would provide his first year's schooling. The kids in his class had been impressed when they discovered he was the son of the woman who had killed the Prime Motivator of the Rullian confederacy. It meant he could do what he liked. Even the teachers had been afraid.

And it was in here that he had pleaded with Meredith not to kill Saen's parents. Perhaps it would be best to leave the past behind.

He decided then that he liked Ace and the Doctor, whoever and whatever they were. She was a bit gruff and over the top, but friendly enough and very capable. The Doctor appeared kind, wise, funny and quite unique. What Forgwyn's classmates back on Gholeria would have called a good bloke.

He was about to rejoin the others when he heard them talking in low tones on the other side of the curtain. He stopped to listen.

'What about the TARDIS?' Ace was whispering.

Forgwyn almost dropped the heavy cases. TARDIS!

'We'll worry about that later,' the Doctor replied. 'We've much to discuss, but it can wait until we've got these people to safety.'

'That's another thing,' Ace went on. 'That woman is a hired killer.'

'As you were once as an irregular soldier,' the Doctor replied smoothly.

'Yeah, as part of an army, in wars. But what's she doing here on this planet?'

Forgwyn decided it would be best to break up this conversation as soon as possible. He called through the curtain: 'I'm ready.'

The journey from the spacecraft to the waiting heliflyer was slow. Ace dressed Meredith and helped the Doctor to carry her over while Forgwyn tagged behind carrying the baby.

As they approached the flyer, Shrubb leaned out. 'Need any help there, Doctor?' he called smarmily.

'We can manage, thank you.'

Ace had taken an instant dislike to the chubby-faced stranger. 'Who have you been palling up with, Doctor? Is he something to do with the set-up here?' she asked belligerently.

'Patience,' he replied. 'Keep your head if you'd like to keep it. If you see what I mean.'

The Doctor and Ace climbed into the heliflyer. Meredith was made comfortable on a recliner in the passenger section. Ace took the baby from Forgwyn and he ran back to collect his cases from the ship.

'He seems a nice young lad,' the Doctor observed.

Ace yawned and made herself comfortable in her big padded seat. 'Yeah,' she said and drifted into sleep.

Forgwyn slipped back into the ship and picked up the cases. He glanced at the flight controls, where the pyramid of red glass continued to glow eerily. This was supposed to have been an easy and very lucrative task for his mother. She hadn't been able to resist the lure of a big-pay kill, even when eight months pregnant. If things had gone according to plan, they would be on the way back to Frinjel 87 to collect the payment now. Instead they were trapped on a distant planet and, although his mother didn't know it, involved in a most awkward situation.

You will take this device and track your prey, the Friars of Pangloss had said through the mouth of the mystic. *He is returning to the planet from which he took the red glass. You must retrieve it and bring us his TARDIS. If you fail, in this, we will take your soul. You must kill him.*

Kill the Time Lord.

He took the red pyramid from the console and stuffed it into the case.

The Friars returned to the shrine after a visit to the flame fields. They had gone to employ their powers to blow open new pits in the smoking earth. Golden liquid had rumbled noisily from freshly squeezed pores in the ground, bubbling over the nearest ranks of workers. The workers had mumbled their holy allegiances to drudgery and despair as the molten geysers claimed them for the core of almighty Pangloss. The few who had attempted escape had been herded back to their appointed destiny by Portellus's fork.

Obeisance was made to the Principles of Obedience, Servitude and Eternal Suffering, and the discussion began.

'I sense his living presence,' said Caphymus. 'The Time Lord remains alive. I can hear the babbling cacophony of his frivolous thoughts across the galaxies that divide us. I can see him as he lurches through another of his frivolous misadventures. And,' he lowered his voice nervously, 'the cursed fragment is still in his possession. What if the workers one day look up from their toil and see it has been torn from the Immortal Heart? What, then, will become of us?'

'This shall not happen. We shall retrieve the crystal,' Portellus said gravely.

'The human Meredith Morgan has failed us,' said Anonius. 'Thus her soul will spin in the Vesuvian vortices of Tophet. But what of the Time Lord? Has the time not yet come to break with precedent and manifest ourselves?'

'Not as yet,' said Portellus, wiping the blood from his fork on a rag. 'Whilst you were bathing this morning, I contacted another who will aid us in our purpose. This other will very soon reach the planet.'

Anonius and Caphymus exchanged a perturbed glance. Decisions were supposed to be taken by all three Friars.

'And may we know the identity of this new agent of yours, Portellus?'

He nodded. 'He is the one known as Ernest.'

9

The Preparations

Harry Landis was brushing away blood and broken glass from the floor at Yumm's. The early morning light was dim and the sky grey. Sometimes, at the height of summer with the suns high in the sky, Harry almost succeeded in convincing himself that his bar looked good. On mornings like these, when the weather outside matched the odour of stale beer and nicotine within, he came close to despair.

Somebody hammered at the door. Harry looked up nervously. At this hour it was unusual for anybody but him to be awake. He switched on the exterior camera. Three burly male figures dressed in immaculate blue uniforms were standing outside, weapons raised. Their leader, who possessed small, drugged eyes and a hard, angular face, raised his extended truncheon and hammered again on the door.

Almost without thinking, Harry went to the door and opened it. He didn't want to cause more trouble than was necessary. Occasionally gangs from either side of the law passed by looking for information on one of his customers. This was probably no different.

As the last of the bolts was drawn, the three policemen burst in. Harry was almost thrown back onto the floor by the force of their entry. The leader, who wore the tattoo of a broken dagger, barked, 'Two nights ago. These.' He thrust a crumpled photograph in Harry's face. It showed the blurred likenesses of the odd couple that had booked in on Tuesday night.

'They were here,' he said, trying not to look at the officers in case he offended them. 'But I've never seen

them before or since. They must have signed in though.'
He scrabbled for a thick ledger that sat on a ledge beneath
the bar and flicked through to the relevant page, his hands
shaking. 'Here. Mr and Mrs Smith. They took separate
rooms. That's really all I know. They left early yesterday
morning.'

The leader of the gang nodded slowly. 'They said
nothing to you?'

Harry shook his head fervently. 'Nothing. Er, the girl
drank ale, the guy just a glass of water.'

The leader chuckled and his fellow officers joined in.
Then he turned away from Harry and made for the door.
They followed.

Harry collapsed onto a barstool in relief. His body was
shaking from head to toe. He looked up as he heard the
leader say, 'I don't like this scummy little dive. Torch it.'

The two officers grinned and extended their truncheons.
Balls of fire shot from the tips. In seconds, the interior of
Yumm's was ablaze.

Harry ran forward. 'No!' he cried. 'No!'

One of the men strode forward and cracked him savagely over the head with the butt of his truncheon. Harry
fell to the floor, screaming. Blood poured from his head
and trickled over his broken face.

The policemen left the premises as the fire took hold.
They didn't see Harry crawling pathetically for the stairs
leading up to where his sick wife was sleeping. He coughed
once and died on the second step.

The supermodel woke up in a huge bed that was not her
own. The strong arm of Howard Devor was still wrapped
around her. She peeled it away carefully, provoking only
a mumbled protest from him. Then she retrieved her
clothes and her bag and tiptoed to the door, past the
shelves creaking with thick volumes that had never been
read past the first page. Before she left she took one last
glance at his snoring form. Millions of women, she
thought, would have gladly exchanged places with her last
night. It was just as well they didn't know what they were

missing. His sexual performances were as feeble as his television performances, if last night was anything to go by. He'd obviously been reading too many articles in the glossies and thought he'd been doing the right things, poor love. She slipped out of his apartment, shaking her head ruefully.

Devor woke half an hour later. He stared at the indentation in the sheets next to him for a while, and decided that the girl had been too impressed and awestruck by him (and, of course, his technique last night) to hang around. Which was a shame; she was a babe.

There were more important things to think about, anyhow. He was a member of the Greatest Lodge of Luminus, after all. The brain implant they had given him had made him even more intelligent. The things he was asked to do by them and their creepy leader were pretty weird sometimes but the career rewards were amazing. He now had total control over his show. Casting control, director control, script control and, he thought with a smile, producer control. He imagined George Lipton trying to cut it in the refugee camp and laughed out loud.

He washed and dressed and collected his post. He threw his fan mail down the chute and took the elevator down to the ground floor. A car from the studio was waiting for him. A woman on the other side of the street saw him and shouted, 'Morning, Captain!' He stuck a middle finger up at her and got into the car. Would he ever be free to walk the streets without the cretin's nudge or the idiot's wink? It was dreadful that an artist of his worth should have to be assailed constantly in this manner.

The car drove through the massing crowds hard at work on the preparations for their big day. Howard was reminded briefly of the Tragedy Days of his childhood. Everything had seemed much more exciting then, even if he had spent most of his time learning scripts for *Martha and Arthur* or studying with the network tutor.

The car turned into the media compound. Howard looked casually down at his watch. He was over two hours late for the shoot. Not that it mattered. They could hardly start without him.

He walked into the studio. A nervous boy approached him with his daily snack of freshly squeezed bajorum juice and thin ham slices in a granary bap. He took the plate without a word and examined it. 'Hey, you,' he called to the boy. 'This juice isn't freshly squeezed.'

'I'm sorry, Mr Devor,' the boy stammered. 'We were waiting for you, you see.'

'And now I'm here. You're fired.' He threw the plate at the boy and strutted on past the cameras. The technicians stood as he passed and hurried to their positions with worried looks on their faces.

A voluptuously attractive woman wrapped in white feathers and a crushed velvet stole appeared suddenly before Howard. They stopped and pecked each other on the cheek.

'Howie, darling,' the woman said, holding up the pink pages of the latest script revision, 'why are we wasting ourselves on this rubbish? With all our training and experience. I was promised a good script this week after the last disaster and what do I get? Guano, darling, pure guano.'

Howard moaned sympathetically, rubbed his co-star's arm and took the script from her. 'Show me, darling, show me.'

'It's here,' she said, pointing out a section heavily under-lined in black ink. 'Would Libida say that? I mean, would she, really? "Align destructo-thrusters at power factor five. Destroy *Space Ranger Six* and all aboard." When only last week we were kissing. It doesn't make sense, anybody can see that, I'm not wrong. You don't think I'm being unreasonable, do you?'

Howard shook his head. 'Of course not. I'll walk over to the script pool this afternoon and get the chimp that wrote it fired.'

The woman did a little dance of happiness. 'Oh, would you, Howard, would you? Sweetie. Why should we encourage amateurs, after all? It only makes for poor product. As an actress one *knows* it. I sometimes wonder why we don't write this ourselves.'

'That's not a bad idea,' Howard said. 'We'll discuss it over coffee.' They walked off together to the staff canteen for a break from shooting. The technicians observed their departure with amazement.

Bernice yawned herself awake. The room she found herself in was certainly not part of the President Hotel. She was surrounded by soft toys and black and white posters of attractive young men and women, all of whom appeared to be having a really good time. The walls were also covered by small postcards featuring animals in cute poses. The biggest poster in the room showed an artist's impression of a Vijjan woman. Underneath was written *If you do not respect the land you and your children will perish. The red glass cursed all.*

She realized that there was somebody else in the room with her. A sleeping person was concealed under a huge duvet on a bed next to the far wall. She crept over and ripped off the cover. Ace was revealed, curled up in a foetal ball. She opened tired eyes and smiled. 'Hi, Benny.'

Bernice sat down on the bed and took Ace's hand. 'I was worried. It's good to see you. Where's the Doctor?'

'Oh, just along the hall,' Ace replied, rubbing her eyes.

'And where are we?'

Ace swung herself off the bed. 'We're in this guy called Shrubb's house. This is his daughter's room, she's away at university.'

'I have a number of questions which I suspect may require long answers,' said Bernice.

She listened attentively as Ace related the story of the island, the weapons test on the tribe, the flesh-eating monsters, and of Forgwyn and his pregnant assassin mother. 'You have been busy,' she said. 'All the Doctor and I have done is meet a film star and book into a hotel.'

Ace nodded. 'He said. He's right, though. Yesterday night, when we got back here, I couldn't believe we weren't back in my time. It even smells the same.'

127

There was a knock at the door and the Doctor's voice said, 'Are you two girls decent?'

'Hardly ever,' Bernice answered as she opened the door.

'Very good,' he said, beaming ridiculously. 'Well, it's time we were off.'

'What, back to the TARDIS?' Bernice said doubtfully.

The Doctor snorted and shook his head. 'When there's so much more to discover here? Mr Shrubb has extended his hospitality to all three of us and our new friends.'

'Shrubb is a shifty git I wouldn't trust as far as I could throw,' Ace remarked. 'Can't we just go? Whatever's going on here isn't our quarrel, is it?'

The Doctor had entered the bedroom. He was staring at the large poster of the Vijjan woman. His fingers, Bernice noted, were rubbing anxiously at his ring finger, although outwardly he retained his composure. He read the words at the bottom of the picture and frowned. 'Memories,' he said, troubled. 'I feel I've forgotten something. Something important.'

'What, have you left the gas on in the TARDIS?' Ace said. She and Bernice laughed.

He turned to face them, his face set. 'It's important,' he said and walked out.

The smell of coffee and toast was drifting into the room. 'I'm starving,' Ace said. 'Let's go and cheer him up.'

Forgwyn's appetite remained unsated after four rounds of hot buttered toast provided by Shrubb's wife. He was now dressed in his best black denims and was watching the TV. Some young people and puppets dressed in brightly coloured clothes were rushing around very quickly and pretending to be wacky. The Doctor walked into the breakfast room.

'I'm not interrupting, am I?' the strange little man asked.

Forgwyn shook his head. 'No, no. Have some toast.' He indicated the pile before him.

The Doctor pulled up a seat and munched on a slice. 'How's your mother?'

Forgwyn was afraid to look into the Doctor's eyes. What if Time Lords could read minds? If the Friars of Pangloss were so bothered about him, the Doctor must be capable of anything, he decided, so it was best not to worry over details. 'Shrubb says both she and the baby are safe and well at the Empire TV Maternity Block. He pulled some strings to get them in. I'm going to see them later today.'

'Empire TV Maternity Block?' the Doctor said. 'Care for employees from the cradle to the grave.' He smiled and Forgwyn couldn't help smiling back. He couldn't believe the mess his mother had got him into. Why would anybody want such a sweet old guy dead?

He brushed a few toast crumbs from around his mouth and asked the Doctor casually, 'Are you leaving soon?'

'A few things to sort out yet,' the Doctor replied, spreading some marmalade. 'This planet fascinates me.'

'Dangerous, though,' Forgwyn went on, trying hard to sound matter-of-fact. 'This planet, I mean. I'd be off as soon as I could if I were you.'

The Doctor smiled again and said simply, 'You're not.'

Ace entered the room with Shrubb. Behind them in the hall, Forgwyn saw another woman, presumably their friend Benny, playing building bricks with Shrubb's little kid. 'Morning,' Ace greeted them.

'Sleep well, Doctor?' asked Shrubb.

'Yes, thank you,' the Doctor replied politely as he sipped at his coffee.

'You've got a good place here,' Ace said to Shrubb, picking up a round of toast. 'Pity about the poor zobs on the island, wasn't it?'

The Doctor sighed and applied a slight pressure on her wrist. She shook him off angrily. 'No, Doctor. You didn't see what happened.' She turned back to Shrubb, who remained relaxed, a smug grin splitting his porcine features. 'A whole race of people wiped out. And what for?'

'I'm told,' Shrubb replied evenly, 'that the extinction of the tribe was an oversight by our scientists.'

'Oh, well, that's all right, then,' Ace said sarcastically. 'The Great Lodge of Luminus would like to apologize for any inconvenience caused by your pointlessly violent death. We hope it didn't spoil your enjoyment of our weapons-testing programme too much.'

She snatched up some more toast and bolted through the door, leaving an uneasy silence behind her. The Doctor spread his arms wide and said, 'Youngsters nowadays. Working themselves up into a lather.'

'Depends how you look at it,' Shrubb said aggressively. 'If she understood more about us, she'd see why things have to be like this.'

'Oh, yes, I'm sure,' the Doctor agreed, nodding. 'I'd like to know more myself.'

Shrubb waved a hand dismissively. 'Later. We're anxious to make up for any bad experiences you may have had on Olleril. We thought the least we could do was show you some of the better things about our way of life.'

The Doctor slipped off his stool and smiled at Forgwyn. 'Sightseeing? I like sightseeing.' The boy laughed.

'You've arrived just before our great annual carnival,' Shrubb pointed out.

'Yes, Tragedy Day,' the Doctor said. 'It sounds fascinating. What's first?'

Bernice was adding the last of the bricks to her structure. 'There we are,' she said to Shrubb's son. The little boy had thick eyebrows like his father. 'A village. All the people go in to work and be friends and be happy.'

'Stupid,' said the little boy. He kicked the bricks over and ran off down the hall, laughing. 'Stupid lady.'

Bernice noticed Ace standing above her. 'This planet becomes less attractive by the minute,' she told the younger woman. 'Even the kids here are obnoxious.'

Ace grunted and handed her the toast. She took it and asked, 'What's up?'

'The Doctor. He's being as sweet as pie with Shrubb. I know its probably the right way to go about things. But he didn't see what I did.'

Bernice nodded sympathetically. 'I've felt really jumpy since we got here. He feels it too but he hasn't really shown it. He's just covering up what he feels, which is typical of him.'

'I suppose you're right,' Ace said, forcing a smile. 'Here, I've got to tell you something. I haven't mentioned it to the Doctor. On Forgwyn's ship there was this weird pyramid thing.'

'Yes?'

'Well, I touched it, right, and – '

The Doctor, Shrubb and Forgwyn emerged into the hall before Ace could continue. 'Ladies,' the Doctor said enthusiastically. 'We are going to have a day out. You three are going to, er, where was it, Forgwyn?'

'It's a huge amusement park called Funland,' Forgwyn said. 'Best rides on the planet, so Mr Shrubb tells me.'

'We could do with some fun, couldn't we, Ace?' Bernice said brightly, taking her friend's arm.

'I've forgotten the meaning of the word, Benny,' she replied.

'Good, good,' the Doctor said. 'Mr Shrubb and I are going to see some sights of political and historical significance.' He directed a meaningful glance at Bernice. 'I know that's more your line but I think best when I'm alone.'

'If that's all settled, there's a car waiting,' Shrubb said.

'I loved you, Millennium,' soliloquized the actress playing the part of the evil Libida, Queen of the Virenies. 'But love is not enough in a universe as evil as ours. O, that you could have shared in my conquest. But no, you spurned my offer, with your futile dreams of fairness and justice.' Her head dropped down dramatically. 'Align destructo-thrusters,' she barely whispered. Then she threw her head back to reveal glistening tears. 'Lieutenant, destroy Space Ranger Six and all aboard her.'

The director ordered a wrap. Devor stepped out from behind the cameras clapping. The technicians and floor crew started to clap too. 'Darling, you were marvellous,' he congratulated her. 'That speech was fantastic.'

She smiled through her tears. 'Did you think so, Howie?

Did you? I'm so pleased. It makes much more sense our way.'

'You're right,' he said. 'We understand these characters better than anyone else. It makes sense for us to write the show, too.' He wheeled about to face the director. 'Don't you think so?' The director nodded meekly.

'There, everybody agrees,' said Devor. 'Do you know, I think we're on the verge of a new era here. Old George was so inflexible, wasn't he?' He sniggered to himself.

The floor manager sidled over cautiously. 'Er, Howard,' she said, 'there's a kid on the set.'

'Well, get it off,' he replied.

'Er, no, you don't understand – '

Devor's attitude changed instantly. 'Oh, you mean a sick kid,' he sighed. 'Send it over, then. I suppose one more delay won't make much difference.'

'No, the kid isn't actually sick, Howard, it's just that the press office wants a picture of you together.'

'I see, a star kid? From movies?'

The floor manager fiddled anxiously with the pen on her clipboard. 'Not really, Howard, it's that child genius, little Crispin.'

Devor snorted derisively. 'The jumped-up little git with the specs and all those qualifications?'

She nodded. 'Yeah, that's the one. Apparently, you're his TV hero.'

Devor considered. Five months ago he would have no choice but to break the shoot for this kind of garbage. But a lot had happened since then. 'Tell the snotty-nosed little crust to jump in a rad pit, I've got a TV series to make,' he said.

'Not the sort of remark one associates with the stoic Captain Millennium,' an unpleasant voice echoed across the studio. Little Crispin strolled over arrogantly, shirt untucked on one side, greasy hair parted in the centre. 'And at this time of year, when we should all be thinking of others less fortunate than ourselves.'

Devor was momentarily rendered speechless. Unsurprisingly, it was a moment that soon passed. 'Get this evil

132

brat out of here before I do it myself!' he shouted to nobody in particular. He shook himself and strutted off in the direction of his trailer, a cluster of hangers-on at his heels.

The floor manager turned to the little boy. 'Sorry about that, he's having a difficult morning,' she apologized. 'He's got lots on at the moment.'

'As have we all,' the child replied. The floor manager flinched at the strange smile he gave before he turned and walked confidently from the set.

The car arranged by Shrubb was long and black. It was driven by two men in black suits who said little and listened a lot.

'I wish he wouldn't off-load us like this,' Ace complained as the journey from Shrubb's house in the zone two docklands got underway.

'I wouldn't worry,' Bernice said cheerily. 'I'm sure the Doctor has his reasons.' She leaned forward and closed the shutter that separated them from the drivers' compartment. 'Let the Doctor do what he wants,' she whispered.

Ace nodded. She sat back in an attempt to relax. 'I don't like hanging about.'

Forgwyn pointed at something outside the large windows of the vehicle. 'What's going on out there?'

The women looked where he had indicated. A large group of people were decorating one of the wide, clean streets with black bunting. Large papier mâché skeletons were being hung from each lamp-post, to the delight of a party of well-fed schoolchildren huddled below. There was an almost palpable feeling of excited expectation in the air.

'It must be for their carnival tomorrow,' said Bernice. 'Those images of death are very interesting from an anthropological point of view. On Earth there were similar figures used in carnivals in Mexico.'

Forgwyn nodded. 'The death figure employed as an archetype to expunge deep-rooted societal guilt or fear, you mean?'

'Or alternatively to emphasize the transience of the human condition as it is experienced by the individual,' Bernice commented with enthusiasm.

'Do you need a degree to join in this conversation or am I just thick?' said Ace with a sigh.

Bernice ignored her. 'You've studied social sciences?' she asked Forgwyn.

'A bit,' he said sheepishly. 'My mum used to leave me alone with my Auntie Doris's textbooks when I was a kid. She was doing a correspondence course with the Academia Temporalis.'

'Who's Auntie Doris?' Ace asked, keen to bring the debate back to what she considered a reasonable level.

'She was a friend of my mother's,' he replied. 'They worked together for years. Then Auntie Doris went off on her own and got vaporized by a Rutan suicide squad.'

'Do you mind if I ask how it feels to have an assassin for your mother?' Bernice asked as tactfully as she could.

Forgwyn shrugged. 'Everybody else does. I can't really answer because she's the only mother I've ever had, do you know what I mean?'

'Yes,' said Bernice.

'I mean, it could be worse. She doesn't tend to talk about it and neither do I.'

Bernice held a hand over her mouth. 'Point taken,' she said. 'I won't mention it again.'

Forgwyn laughed and returned his attention to the preparations the city was making for Tragedy Day. Almost every person and vehicle they passed was adorned with a badge in the shape of a glistening black teardrop. At the corner of nearly all of the streets stood a huge skeleton. Each was personified differently; in a suit and tie, as an Ollerine tribesperson or a weeping child. He reasoned that the people chose a costume or theme to represent a particular cause supported by their area. Shops displayed sugar skeletons surrounded by black balloons.

Occasionally the car passed huge electronic boards that were adorned with a symbol Forgwyn recognized from the Empirican currency Shrubb had provided him with.

They were probably designed to flash up the amount of money raised in each area.

The car travelled on to Funland.

Lerthin Square was the centre of the preparations for Tragedy Day. A large crowd was already massed outside the old City Council buildings, most of which were empty. The administration company that had taken over from the government had built itself plush new offices in Zone One with some of the money it couldn't spare for education and benefits payments.

A stage took up one side of the square. The Tragedy Day symbol, a weeping skeleton, loomed over the proceedings. A technical crew were carrying out sound, lighting and camera checks. It was from here, the oldest part of the city, that the official carnival headquarters would broadcast the latest updates to the people, interspersed with items of interest and pleas for money to be pledged.

In a far corner of the square a large black car stopped and Shrubb and the Doctor got out. They looked up at a large bronze statue of a stern-featured man in uniform.

'That is General Stillmun,' explained Shrubb proudly. 'He led the first imperial expedition to this planet and laid the foundations on which our great city was built.'

The Doctor tutted. 'You can tell a civic administration by its statuary,' he observed. 'This man killed thousands of innocent natives, you say, and he is represented as a hero.'

'This is a great work of art and cannot be disturbed,' Shrubb said defensively.

'It's a dreadful work of art,' the Doctor pointed out rudely. 'The hands are out of proportion and the nose is crooked.'

Shrubb was about to deliver a rebuke when he heard his name being called. He looked around and saw Robert Clifton pushing through the crowd towards him. 'It's good to see you,' the newcomer said brightly. 'I'm surprised you're not at the office.'

Shrubb carried out the necessary introductions. 'This

is the Doctor. Doctor, meet Robert Clifton. He will be presenting the television side of Tragedy Day tomorrow.'

'Pleased to meet you,' the robot said as it shook the Doctor's hand.

'We have met before,' the Doctor pointed out.

The robot shrugged and said, with a stunningly accurate duplication of human self-absorption, 'I meet so many people in my job. I forget.'

'I'm sure of it,' the Doctor said quietly.

'Anyway, I must get on,' Robert continued. 'Wendy and I have to go over our scripts again. Bye!' He walked off towards the stage.

The Doctor turned to Shrubb and said, 'The hair isn't very good.'

'I know,' said Shrubb. 'But only if you're looking for it.' He changed the subject. 'Shall we go somewhere else? Somewhere more modern?'

'They ought to hand out buckets when you come in here,' remarked Ace as another person dressed in a fluffy bunny costume waved over at her. 'I think I'm going to be sick.'

'I've never been to one of these places,' said Bernice, munching on a green frond of flavoured candyfloss, 'and I'm not going to let you spoil it for me.'

Ace chuckled. 'I'm surprised you and Forgwyn haven't analysed its exact social function by now.'

They were standing in a small cobbled area of Funland styled in a twee approximation of something like medieval architecture. Forgwyn joined them, ice-cream in hand, and they wandered past the restaurants to the ride area. The attractions, a startling variety of death-defying mechanisms, seemed to spread over a mile ahead of them. Tragedy Day was represented here by more skeleton figures. Parents pretended to be frightened as their offspring jumped around corners dressed in skull masks. Black bunting was strewn between the candy-coloured lamp-posts.

Bernice finished her candyfloss and fiddled in her pocket for the tokens she had purchased at the gate. 'I want a go on that! I definitely want a go on that!' she shouted, pointing at an arrangement of whirling, tilting seats titled garishly HYPERTHRILL 9000.

'Let me finish this,' Forgwyn said, wolfing down his ice-cream.

'You'll throw it all up again after going on that,' Ace remarked.

'You sound more and more like my mother, you know,' he said, handing her the stick. He and Bernice ran to get seats on the ride as its spin slowed gradually and the previous users clambered off shakily.

Ace watched as their seat started to whirl about. Bernice waved and stuck out her tongue on their second fly-past but she didn't respond. Watching other people enjoying themselves wasn't her idea of fun. She found herself a patch of grass nearby and sat down.

Five minutes later Forgwyn joined her. 'You should have gone on with us,' he said exuberantly. 'It was brilliant.'

Ace looked up. 'Have you noticed them?' she asked, pointing over her shoulder. Their drivers were standing in the crowd not far away. 'I wonder how long our leash is.'

'Don't worry about it,' he said nonchalantly.

'You sound like the Doctor.'

There was an awkward silence. Forgwyn said finally. 'You said your mum's a hairdresser, yes?'

Ace nodded. 'A hairdresser's assistant.'

There was another long silence. 'I've got something I think I should tell you,' Forgwyn said. 'It's about my mother.' He swallowed and pressed his hands together in a nervous gesture. 'The person she was hired to kill here.'

'Yeah?' prompted Ace, suddenly interested.

'I think it's the Doctor,' admitted Forgwyn. 'Is he a Time Lord?'

Ace sat up straight. 'Start from the beginning,' she said.

Forgwyn sighed. 'She got a call from a mystic,' he began, 'on Frinjel 87. He said he was a medium and was in contact with the Friars of Pangloss. They wanted to speak to her.'

'Hold on a second. The Friars of what?'

'Pangloss. It's a vast region of uncharted space quite near here. Olleril's the nearest inhabited planet.'

Ace nodded. 'Okay, go on.'

'The Friars spoke through this old guy, the mystic. When they did he had a different voice, really scary. They said to go to Olleril and kill the Time Lord. He took something of theirs once, I think. They knew that he was coming back, I don't know how. They're probably precognitive.'

'All right,' said Ace. 'What happened then?'

'They transmitted a device, a sort of red pyramid, into the old guy's hands. It would lead us to the Time Lord's TARDIS when we arrived on the planet. They were offering enough cash to retire on. Twenty million mazumas. It was silly money. Meredith was sure she could complete the job, give birth and get back to Frinjel in time for the rendezvous. Which was set for yesterday.

'Anyway, the ship went out of control, we crashed on the island and the rest you know.'

Ace put a reassuring arm around his shoulder. 'Don't worry about it. You're well out of that deal. Money isn't everything, you know.'

'I wish it was,' he said. 'There's honour as well. I've never seen my mother fail, Ace. She won't rest until the Doctor's dead.'

'But he practically saved her life,' Ace protested. 'You can take ingratitude too far, you know.'

Forgwyn lay back on the grass and stared up at the suns. 'Last year we were staying on Gholeria. We were put up in impressive quarters. Life was good. I felt settled. I was seeing this lad Saen at school, nothing serious.'

'Yeah?' Ace prompted.

'Mum was hired to pick off some underwriters at the Gholerian bank. She worked her way through them quickly. I wasn't paying much attention, though. Then I found out by accident that her next targets were Saen's parents. I asked her not to go through with it. She ignored me.'

Ace frowned. 'I've had to make choices like that before. She won't kill the Doctor.'

Forgwyn stood up as he saw Bernice coming back towards them, whooping with joy from the thrill of her latest ride. 'I just don't know. Because they said they'd marked her. And if she failed, then when she died, wherever she was, they could take her soul.'

'That sounds like a heap of doings to me,' remarked Ace.

Forgwyn shrugged. 'We've been together all these years, but I feel I don't know her. She might kill him.'

Ace shook her head. 'She won't. Because I'm not going to let her.'

The media compound dominated the centre of Zone One. The sound-stages, studios and backlots were surrounded by large office blocks and luxurious staff quarters. The car carrying Shrubb and the Doctor stopped beside a props store. The Doctor slipped out and looked around.

'The centre of our culture,' Shrubb said proudly. 'From here our society is entertained, informed and educated.'

'Yes, I've seen some of your television,' said the Doctor non-committally. 'This is where you shovel it from, I take it?'

Before Shrubb could reply, Howard Devor appeared around a corner with his entourage. 'I can see this set-up working very well,' he was saying. 'If I look after the scripts, casting, design and direction, you can all get on with more interesting things, can't you?'

'Howard!' Shrubb called out. 'Come and meet a new friend.'

The Doctor watched as Shrubb and Devor exchanged a complex-looking handshake. 'Doctor, this is Howard Devor, a famous fellow in these parts. Howard, this is the Doctor, a visitor to Olleril.'

The Doctor nodded a greeting. 'Delighted.' He looked carefully at the newcomer's hairline and then shook his head slowly.

'It's not often I get to meet an offworlder,' Devor said.

'In real life, anyway. I must be getting on, my schedule is as hectic as ever.' He and his cronies strolled off in the direction of the canteen.

'Am I right in thinking that Meredith Morgan and her baby are somewhere about here?' the Doctor asked Shrubb. 'Forgwyn said they were under the care of Empire TV.'

Shrubb nodded. 'The staff medical wing here offers the best care in the city. Just follow the signs.'

'You're not coming with me, then?' the Doctor enquired suspiciously.

'It may surprise you, Doctor, but I've got a job to do.' Shrubb pointed to a large block in the near distance that was marked with the symbol of the Empire Clarion. 'Duty calls.'

It was not a particular surprise to the Doctor that the leading Empirican newspaper and the leading Empirican television network shared offices. He knew also that Shrubb had no intention of leaving him unobserved and that his movements, reactions and everything he said or did were likely to be under the closest scrutiny. 'I'll see you later, then,' he said and walked briskly away.

As soon as the Doctor had turned the corner of the props store, Shrubb produced his communicator. He punched in a complex code and awaited the reply of his master. 'Commander,' he reported when the call had been accepted, 'the Doctor had given us little relevant information. I have decided to allow him unfettered access through the city. Perhaps his movements will betray him.'

The strange voice of the Supreme One replied, 'You have done good work for the nation, Shrubb, and you will soon be rewarded. This Doctor has done well not to betray himself. Perhaps it is time to take more direct action against him. I cannot allow the slightest variance in my designs at so crucial a time.'

Shrubb nodded. 'Tomorrow the glory of Luminus will return to total control,' he said enthusiastically. His eyes glazed over. 'O Hail Luminus!' This outburst had attracted the attention of a couple of passing extras. They looked over curiously before deciding that he was practising lines.

Shrubb coughed, straightened his tie and continued more calmly, 'And my new orders for the Doctor?'

'Do nothing, as yet,' replied the Supreme One. 'I have a mind to deal with him along with the other outstanding matter.' He chuckled. 'The processor implant has done its work. We need no longer indulge that fool Devor.'

Shrubb listened attentively to the words of the Supreme One. A smile crossed his thick lips as he contemplated the imminent demise of the egotistical actor.

The Supreme One finished giving his orders to Shrubb and broke off the call. The journalist was an ideal servant; loyal, repressed, fanatical. He decided to contact another, Sergeant Felder of the South Side Police.

'Nothing to report,' the sergeant's voice grunted gruffly across the airwaves. 'We've tracked their movements as ordered. They showed up at the refugee camp. Got thrown out. Booked into a bar. Tried to cross at Point 65. Then went to Guralza.'

'I long ago tired of that dreary woman,' the Supreme One said venomously. 'Find out whatever you can from her. Remember, discretion is no longer necessary. Tomorrow we have total control.'

'Yes, Commander,' said Felder and disconnected.

The car carrying the Supreme One through the streets of the central zones turned past Lerthin Square. The great intellect of Olleril peered through the tinted glass at the enormous weeping skeleton suspended over the stage. His normally reserved manner gave way briefly to a tingling anticipation. After years of preparation the moment was at hand.

Tomorrow, Tragedy Day. Tomorrow, total control.

The Doctor strolled confidently through the media compound. He had lost himself several times, on one occasion walking onto the set of a soap opera during recording. He had been pointed in the direction of the medical wing and was walking there now. Two minders walked a discreet distance behind him. He didn't even bother to register them.

He had decided that a long talk with Meredith was necessary. She seemed to be a formidable woman and he needed strong allies on this planet. He would tell her about himself in the hope that she would reveal more about herself. And then they could work together to work out what was going on. Besides, he liked babies.

He walked confidently in the direction of the medical wing.

10

The Abduction

The sound of gunfire from the garden distracted Guralza from the book she was reading. A riot had spilled over into the grounds, probably. The riot forecast had said mild, but when had that ever been accurate? Whatever the case, her staff could deal with it. She reclined on the *chaise longue* in her courtyard and returned to her reading. In a few days, she thought, she would be away from this dismal planet and its problems forever.

A rarely heard bell rang from a communicator perched on a nearby desk. The lovebirds that flew about the courtyard twittered in alarm. Angrily, Guralza stretched out an arm and accepted the call. 'Yes, Jalone?'

'Ma'am, it's Sergeant Felder's gang,' he reported. His voice had lost its customary air of calm. Behind it, Guralza heard shots and cries. 'They've stormed the building. We've had to fall back. I've – ' There was another shot. Jalone gasped. The communicator went dead.

Guralza cursed and stubbed out her cigarette calmly. She had been waiting for something like this for years. She was prepared for it. It was likely that the Doctor had been picked up by the authorities in Central. He was probably already dead.

She crossed over to a dresser built into one wall of the courtyard and opened the bottom drawer. The starched uniform of one of her female domestic staff was inside, perfectly folded. She changed into it slowly, keeping herself calm as the gunfire came nearer. She took a frilly white cap from the drawer and placed it over her head. Then she walked over to a particular chunk of jagged masonry in the opposite wall and moved it slightly. A concealed compartment swung open and she slipped through.

The black-uniformed staff of the house were no match for the strength, size and brutality of Sergeant Felder's gang. Guralza's men knew the grounds and the house better, but their respect became a weakness. The police moved without regard for the beauty of their surroundings. They smashed windows, set fire to trees and shrubs and moved inwards destructively. The bodies of the domestic staff were strewn on the patio that led up to the back entrance of the house. Felder's men swarmed inside, treading on the dying men, growling and grunting as they did.

One of those left outside to guard the wrecked garden, a young constable, watched as a maid appeared from around a corner. She looked scrawny and old, not worth taking back to the station for afters. He called out, 'You! Stop!'

The old maid continued walking. She walked slowly in the direction of the garden. She seemed to be crying.

'You! Stop!' he called again and let off a warning shot.

The woman reacted. She turned around and he saw that she was carrying a small side-arm. She fired at him and missed. He fired back and hit her. She fell, her bones cracking as her frail body thumped down.

The guard wandered over and looked down at the body of the old woman. A big red hole opened over her stomach. Blood was pouring from her lips and she was making a gurgling sound. He bent down curiously and took the side-arm from her. There was a valuable-looking ring on her hand so he took that too. As he stood up he thought he heard her say something about the stars but he couldn't be sure. He slipped the ring into his pocket.

He was about to return to guard duty when he saw Felder himself coming out of the house. The sergeant did not look pleased.

'Search again!' he screamed at his men. 'She has to be

144

here somewhere!' He strode angrily in the direction of the guard. 'Seen anything, constable?'

The younger man showed him the pistol. 'Took this from her, Sergeant,' he reported, gesturing to the dead maid. Felder turned the weapon over in his hands. 'Could be an antique, I reckon,' his junior said helpfully.

Felder looked more closely at the dead body. 'Cag!' he screamed at the constable. 'That's Guralza!'

The constable felt the blood draining from his face. 'Er, Sergeant, I didn't, I mean, I – '

Felder shot him with the antique pistol and watched the body collapse next to that of Guralza. 'Don't you watch the movies, crust?' he sneered down at the young man. Then he went through the belongings of both corpses. He pocketed the blue gemstone ring he found in the constable's pocket. It might be valuable.

He took one last look at the burning garden before turning back to the house to reassess the situation. The fire had reached an oddly shaped hedge that resembled a tall box. It was picked away in seconds.

The Doctor had bluffed his way into the maternity wing of the Empire TV medical complex and was walking confidently through the corridors of the seventh floor. A nurse had given him directions to Meredith's room in the belief that he was the happy father. His minders followed on at a discreet distance.

He found the private room he was looking for at last and knocked on the door. There was no reply, so he poked his nose around the door.

Mother and baby were fast asleep. The Doctor looked down at them and smiled benevolently. He wondered whether to wake Meredith. Her presence on the planet remained an enigma to him, after all, and the more information he received the better. He couldn't bring himself to disturb her. He had other plans to attend to.

He shut the door of the private room and strolled over to a nearby lift. His minders got in with him and the doors closed.

'Lovely spell of weather we're having, don't you think?' he asked them cheerfully.

The minders said nothing. The Doctor realized that he had to get rid of them if he was going to learn anything of value on the trip he had planned. He looked around the lift for something to help him and had an idea.

'Do either of you gentlemen smoke?' he asked his minders. He hoped he had the terminology right. 'I'm gasping.'

Fortunately, one of the minders did. He reached into his jacket and produced a cigarette. The Doctor took it eagerly and fumbled in the pockets of his jacket. 'Ah,' he said, 'I don't suppose you would have a light?'

The minder produced a box of matches. The Doctor nodded his thanks and made to light the cigarette in his mouth. He struck a match and then dropped it on the floor of the lift. 'Fire!' he shouted hysterically, leaping up and down, although the offending match did little more than smoulder disappointingly. 'Fire!'

The minders watched, perplexed, as the Doctor took down the small axe on the wall and smashed the glass covering the fire extinguisher. Instead of directing the jet at the spent match he sprayed them both until they were covered in sticky white foam. The men attempted to grab him as he passed, but the Doctor had sensibly covered their eyes first of all.

The lift door slid open and the Doctor sprang out onto the ground floor of the medical wing. The door closed behind him and he walked confidently for the exit.

A large and formidable-looking matron loomed around a corner. She fixed the Doctor with a terrifying stare and boomed, 'No smoking in the medical wing, please, sir.'

The Doctor realized that the cigarette was still drooping, unlit, from his mouth. He spat it into a nearby wastepaper bin and said apologetically, 'Quite right too. Filthy habit.'

'You have failed us, Meredith Morgan,' the first voice accused.

146

'The Time Lord still lives,' said the second.

'The Holy Principles of Pangloss cannot sanction your titubation in this matter,' the third voice thundered.

The three voices pronounced as one in an array of condemnation: *'Yea, by unholy Abaddon, your dying day will see your soul absorbed by Pangloss!'*

Meredith woke from what she knew was more than a nightmare. The door of her room burst open and somebody walked in. The baby started to cry.

'Hello, Ace,' she said weakly and let her head fall back on her sweat-soaked pillow. 'Knock next time. Somebody walks in like that, I go for my gun.'

Ace looked at the woman strangely, then walked around her bed and peered into the cot. 'He looks comfy,' she remarked. 'What are you going to call him?'

'We decided, Forgwyn and me,' she replied, 'on Malinchen. But now I've seen him and it doesn't suit him.'

'You're right. He looks tough, a real fighter.'

'I'm sure he's a perfect angel,' said Bernice as she entered the room. She leant over the cot and made silly noises to the wailing child. Ace caught her glance and shook her head meaningfully. So, thought Bernice, the Doctor hasn't been here.

'How are they looking after you?' Meredith asked Forgwyn as he came to her bedside and took her hand. 'You're eating well, I hope.'

'Yes, yes,' Forgwyn said quickly, embarrassed in front of the two women. 'This planet's a mess, though. I want to get away from here as soon as we can.'

Meredith frowned. 'Forg, I've a job to do here, remember?'

Bernice and Ace looked over anxiously. 'Don't worry about that now,' Forgwyn said soothingly. 'You relax.'

She reached up and ruffled his hair. 'I never relax, you know that,' she said. She looked around curiously and asked, 'Where's your friend, the Doctor?'

Ace tensed. 'Why do you ask?'

Meredith smiled. 'I want to say thank you,' she said.

147

'And he seems like a smart man. I think we could be friends.'

Robert Clifton was going over the script for tomorrow's item on misery makeovers when there was an urgent tapping on the door of his personal trailer. He threw the papers down angrily and jerked the door open. He'd expected to see one of the technical staff but the person standing outside was a short man with a deeply lined face.

'Hello,' said the stranger. 'Remember me?'

'No, I don't,' snapped Robert. It was probably, he decided, an autograph hunter or some other sad specimen. Unless he was being stalked by a deranged member of the public. He tried to close the door but the short man had put his foot in.

'You wouldn't,' he said, inviting himself in.

Robert backed away nervously. He'd heard how celebrities could meet their ends at the hands of crazed fanatics. The weirdo probably thought he had been receiving messages through the TV or something. 'What do you want?' he asked.

'Your co-operation,' said the short man. He ruffled in his pocket and produced a conker tied to the end of a piece of string. He swung it slowly before Robert's eyes. 'I want you to look at this as it spins,' he said gently.

Robert snorted. Now he had the measure of this freak. 'Would you please leave, now,' he said confidently. 'The talent contest is already... fully... subscribed...' His eyes rolled and he collapsed.

The Doctor pocketed his makeshift pendulum and grinned. So the personality matrix of the robots was sophisticated enough to hypnotize, as he had gambled. Now for a proper examination. It was irritating that he didn't have the right equipment. He would just have to make do.

The Doctor took out his penknife. He knelt down and sliced Robert Clifton's forehead open. He held one end of the plastic skin and peeled it away from the face. A metallic skull was revealed. Two eyes and a voicebox were connected to the eye-sockets and mouth areas. Wires threaded through a tangle of densely packed circuitry. The Doctor wrenched at the skull and it came away in his hand. Beneath was a flashing unit about the size of a potato.

He took it out and turned it over in his hands. 'An electronic brain,' he said admiringly. 'Very sophisticated. Personality matrix, motor functions, reasoning intelligence.' He slipped it into his pocket.

Shrubb sat behind a large desk in his private office at the Empire Clarion. He sighed and put his toy soldiers back in their box. He probably wouldn't have time to play with them for a while.

The newsdesks above babbled reassuringly through the air-conditioning of the block. The payments deficit was up, a city manager had been caught with an actress, benefits payments were to be re-examined in view of the clampdown on public spending. All these things seemed so important today. Tomorrow they would not be. In the last few months he had found it hard to restrain himself from hinting in his editorials that the day of judgement was about to come for all the subversive elements, the deviants, the foreigners. They would be the first to go. A healthier nation would emerge, master of the planet once more.

He had been waiting months for what was about to happen. Of all the preparations for Tragedy Day it was this that would give him the most satisfaction.

There was a knock at the door. Without bothering to wait for an answer, Howard Devor walked in, now in full costume as the Captain. 'I hope you called me here for a good reason,' he snapped. 'I don't think you newspaper people realize the tight schedules we in television work to.' Without waiting to be asked he sat down opposite Shrubb and poured himself a rakki from the drinks trolley.

'I'm sorry,' Shrubb said. 'But I have a message for you, Howard. From the Supreme One.'

Devor frowned and sipped at his drink. 'Now that is a good reason. The Supreme One is a good friend of mine.'

'He's waiting to speak to you now on the security channel,' said Shrubb. He indicated a large speaker set into one wall of the office. 'So whenever you're ready.'

Devor finished his drink slowly and settled the empty glass on the desktop. 'I think I'm just about ready now.'

'Good,' said Shrubb. He smirked and called out, 'Mr Devor is ready to speak to you now, Commander.'

The actor swung his chair to face the speaker. 'O Hail Luminus,' he said perfunctorily. There was no reply. 'Commander?' he prompted. There was still no response. 'Commander?'

He turned back to Shrubb. 'There must be a fault on the communicator. Can't you do anything prop – ' he attempted to say, but the newspaper editor had already fired the tranquillizer dart. He gasped for air and fell backwards over the chair.

Shrubb glistened with sweaty satisfaction. He put away the dart gun and said, 'Commander, Devor is ready for shipment as per your instructions.'

'Excellent,' said the strange voice of the Supreme One from the speaker. 'The test on that worthless fool is over and my scientists can begin to collate the results. Our engagements here in the city are complete. We will return shortly to the *Gargantuan* with Devor and the Doctor.'

Shrubb felt for the dart gun. 'You wish me to bring you the Doctor?' he said eagerly. His nostrils flared. He had been waiting years to do things like this. 'He has spoken ill of our Lodge and I would like to see him suffer at my hand. He smells of deviance and subversion.'

'Later, later,' the Supreme One promised. 'I have operatives moving to collect the Doctor as we speak.'

The Doctor was pushing through the crowds at Lerthin Square. His aim was to make his way to Shrubb's house, collect Ace and Bernice, and then sneak back to the TARDIS for a proper look at the robot brain. He had to learn more about the Luminuns and their plans, and this seemed as good a way as any to make a start.

Rain clouds were gathering in the late afternoon sky.

Despite the trappings of celebration and carnival the atmosphere of the city remained as despondent as ever.

A large man with a sour expression collided with the Doctor in the crush. The long thin point of the man's umbrella dug into his side. He pushed past impatiently and reached the edge of the square at last.

He stopped to catch his breath and leant against the statue of General Stillmun. His limbs felt weak and his mouth felt dry. As his legs gave way, the Doctor's head flopped upwards. A big raindrop splashed into one of his eyes. The last thing he saw before he lost consciousness was the inscription carved into the base of the statue.

STILLMUN OF LUMINUS
THE RED GLASS OF OLLERIL CURSED HIS
SOUL

The Doctor remembered something important at this point. But his brain had already closed down as the drug took hold, and the thought was lost.

11

The Dancefloor

Two minders followed Bernice as she left Shrubb's house after a satisfying evening meal prepared by his domestic staff. Shrubb himself had been absent, detained on business, a common enough state of affairs according to his wife.

Another long black car pulled up in the pleasant, tree-lined street. Ace got out and waved over at her. 'Mother and baby are doing fine,' she reported. 'After you left I checked with the nurses. Turns out the Doctor has been round there today. I told them he wasn't to see Meredith again without contacting us first.'

'That's sorted out, then,' Bernice remarked. 'For the moment, at least. Where's young Forg?'

'Gone out clubbing,' Ace replied. 'I left him to it, I'm knackered. Where are you off to?'

Bernice pointed ahead. 'There's a big fireworks display in a park over there. I like fireworks a lot. I thought they might cheer me up. Coming?'

Ace shrugged. 'Why not?' The two women walked on together.

The dance music on Olleril was surprisingly good, Forgwyn had found. He had been directed by friendly strangers to Globule, a club in Zone Three that had the best reputation for a good time. He had left his guard outside and now he was walking around the club's cavernous, throbbing interior. The upbeat electronic music could not dispel the atmosphere of despondency that characterized the city. Elaborate Tragedy Day skeletons and masks decorated the glowing red walls.

He noticed several other offworlders, humanoid mostly, mixed in with the crowd. Their presence made him feel slightly more comfortable. The local clientele, no matter how young or attractive, were endowed with the blanked-out quality he had come to associate with people on Olleril.

His circuit of the club completed, Forgwyn bought himself a drink and sat down on a clammy leather sofa. Directly opposite him was one of the dancefloors. Some of the others he had seen were half filled already, but this one was curiously empty. It was shiny and black and looked special somehow. He stared at it, sipping his drink and getting bored.

He wanted to get away from Olleril as soon as he could. If he could persuade Meredith to forget about her contract with the Friars there was a chance they could go with the Doctor. Ace had explained to him about the exact workings of the TARDIS. Now he was stuck in a grotty nightclub on a grotty planet. Still, he decided, it was better than being nearly gassed or eaten by mutants.

That dancefloor, he thought to himself, is waiting for somebody cool to step onto it. Somebody who can show the dumb pollicks on this planet how to enjoy themselves and stop hassling each other and putting each other down. How to have a good time. He put his drink down and walked over.

Forgwyn danced on the black dancefloor and a crowd gathered around him. He looked up occasionally and noticed the gawping group growing. Their eyes glinted with excitement. They looked alive for the first time that night. Nobody joined him and after a couple of minutes he became unnerved and embarrassed by the staring. He left the dancefloor and moved towards the bar. The crowd parted to let him pass. He was reminded of the tribe's adoration of him. This was weird.

He reached the bar. The barman looked at him

strangely and handed him a bottle of strong, ice-cold beer, waving away Forgwyn's attempts to buy it.

A tall blond boy of about Forgwyn's age walked over. He was pretty but Forgwyn knew he could never fancy anybody from Olleril. 'That was chipper,' said the boy admiringly. 'I've never seen anybody go that long.'

Forgwyn smiled and said, 'I don't understand you.' He pointed to the earpieces of his interpreter to indicate his offworld origins.

The boy laughed. 'You don't know, do you?'

'You're right, I don't,' said Forgwyn, who was getting irritated again.

'We call it the dancefloor of destruction,' the boy explained. 'There's a thousand to one chance of it surging with anti-matter at any moment.'

Forgwyn took a long swig from the bottle. He stopped himself from fainting and attempted to look as if he didn't care. 'Is that legal?' he asked curiously.

The blond boy laughed. 'Nothing worth doing is legal on Olleril,' he said. He looked Forgwyn up and down and walked away.

The Doctor returned slowly to consciousness. He tried to sit up and found that he was strapped down on a hard surface. He was in total darkness. He slumped back. The Doctor had experienced similar intimidation from captors before and had developed a technique for provoking a reaction.

'I'm a blue toothbrush, you're a pink toothbrush,' he sang loudly, taking note of the echoes of his voice. They told him that he was in a small metallic room. An anguished groan came from the darkness to his left. 'It's not that bad,' the Doctor protested.

'What's ... what's happening?' the cracked voice said. 'Where am I? Who are you?'

'Well, in short order,' the Doctor said breezily, 'something unpleasant. Somewhere unpleasant. Somebody extremely clever who's going to solve all our problems. Maybe.'

'I know your voice,' said the stranger. 'You're that friend of Shrubb's . . .'

'I am the Doctor, yes. And you, if I'm not mistaken, are Howard Devor?'

Before Devor could confirm this, the door of the room they were in slid open slowly with a low hum. A shaft of light from a corridor outside revealed Shrubb and two guards.

'Good evening, gentlemen,' he said. He had taken off his jacket and tie and was wearing a blood-red apron. A silver apple, the symbol of Luminus, was embroidered on it.

'I like your pinny,' the Doctor observed. 'Did you sew it yourself? You must lend me the pattern.'

Shrubb walked across to the Doctor and slapped him savagely around the jaw. 'I need no longer indulge your infantile flippancy.'

The Doctor smiled. 'I see you're one of those boring maniacs who starts to use unnecessary adjectives when he gets to a position of power.'

'Shrubb,' Devor snapped. 'What the crust is going on? Have you flipped your top?'

Shrubb smiled. 'I have never been more sane, I assure you.' He gestured to the guards. 'Take Mr Devor to the study room.'

The guards pushed Devor's trolley towards the door. 'As a devotee of the Greatest Lodge of Luminus, I command you to release me immediately!' Devor screamed up at them.

'Devotee?' sneered Shrubb. 'You are a pawn, a plaything in our purpose. We tolerated you when it suited us.'

'I warn you, Shrubb,' Devor rambled, 'I have the ear of the Supreme One himself. He will be displeased if you do not obey me!'

'Oh, close your mouth for once, you puffed-up poser,' Shrubb said with relish. The trolley and the protesting actor disappeared around the corner. He turned back to the Doctor. 'I have come to speak with you.'

'Speak away,' said the Doctor.

'You are shortly to undergo what we call the thought duplication process,' Shrubb said. He clicked his pudgy fingers and the area of the room surrounding the Doctor was illuminated suddenly in a pool of murky yellow light.

The Doctor looked up. Suspended above him was a large item of scientific apparatus. At the centre of the device, which was rectangular and covered in knobs and switches, was a glowing eye.

'If you co-operate,' Shrubb continued, 'the process will be painless and swift.' He dropped his voice to a whisper. 'If you do not tell us what we want to know, it will be painful and protracted.'

The Doctor appeared unbowed. 'It rather depends what you want to know,' he said.

'Why did you come here, Doctor?' asked Shrubb, 'and where is your spacecraft? The Supreme One tells me it's called the TARDIS. Where is it? Where is the TARDIS?'

The Doctor shook his head. 'I'm sorry, I really have no idea what you're talking about. I came here on a freighter from Quique a month ago.'

'You're lying, Doctor,' Shrubb said menacingly. 'The pain will destroy your mind if you refuse to tell us.'

'I doubt it. And I'd very much like to meet your Supreme One, incidentally. I prefer organ grinders to monkeys.'

Shrubb sighed. 'Do not attempt to change the subject. For the last time, I order you to reveal the location of the TARDIS!'

The Doctor closed his eyes and faked a yawn. 'Oh, go and shout at somebody else. I'm bored and my head hurts.'

'Very well, Doctor.' Shrubb made for the door. He turned at the threshold. 'Remember, I gave you the choice.' He left the room and the door slid shut. The room returned to darkness.

The Doctor kept his eyes shut. He was summoning up the reserves of psychic energy he would need for the coming ordeal. All the same, he wasn't really worried. He had undergone similar processes before and had escaped unscathed. The Potentate of the Medusoids had actually run out of mind extractors in his attempts to –

The glowing eye of the machine hummed with power. The Doctor's eyes opened wide and he spasmed as wave after wave of agony seared through his defenceless body. Each thought, each memory, every characteristic was wrenched from his screaming mind. He struggled desperately to block off the deeper sections of his identity. He took little comfort from the realization that the process was incapable of copying his mind completely. It was rather like trying to pour an ocean through a funnel.

Bernice and Ace watched as a firework burst green shoots of crackling flame over the crowded park.

'I'm off back to the house,' Ace announced. 'I want to see if the Doctor's back.'

Bernice stopped her. 'Wait a second,' she said, 'and I'll join you.' She closed her eyes and crossed her fingers.

'What's your problem?' Ace asked, bemused by the strange behaviour of her friend.

'I'm making a wish,' Bernice told her. She continued wishing in silence for a few moments. Then she opened her eyes and smiled broadly. 'Let's go, then.'

They walked along, not talking for a few moments. The fireworks continued to boom in the night sky. The mirrored blocks of the financial sector reflected vivid streaks of red and green. 'What did you wish, then?' Ace asked eventually.

'Oh, vaguely,' Bernice replied, 'I wished that tomorrow, the people of Olleril would solve their problems and learn to live in peace together.'

'Some hope,' said Ace. 'They've got big problems. Problems you can't solve in a day.'

'I know,' said Bernice, 'but it's a nice thought, isn't it?'

Forgwyn was waiting in the line to collect his coat from the cloakroom at Globule when he heard one of the club's bouncers shouting at somebody trying to get in.

'Club rules, mate. No weapons on the premises.'

Forgwyn looked over curiously. The strangely accented voice of the person trying to gain entrance, whose appearance was blocked by a glowing screen, said, 'Let me through, lad. I drop my eight-guns for nay one, d'you hear my words, you great wet lettuce!'

'I'm telling you, mate,' the red-faced bouncer went on, shaking his huge fists. 'It's management policy, no weapons!'

'Ah, get knotted,' the strange voice shouted. Forgwyn watched bemused as a long slim hairy leg swiped the bouncer and brought him crashing to the ground. Then its owner appeared from behind the screen and crawled into the club.

Forgwyn recognized the unmistakable aspect of Ernie 'Eight-Legs' McCartney, the most feared assassin in the Seventh Quadrant and his mother's major rival for commissions. The giant arachnid adjusted his stetson primly and swept past the astonished teenager. Many of the locals had obviously never seen a spider mutant before. They screamed and ran for cover as Ernie crept over to the bar. The woman on duty at the counter saw him and fainted.

'Ee, lass, don't take on,' Ernie said with a sigh. He rolled his protruding eyestalks in a gesture of exasperation. 'What does a man-jack have to do to get himself a drink round here?'

With a complicated movement of his legs, he slipped one of his fearsome-looking weapons from its holster, aimed it at one of the bottles of spirits hanging over the bar and fired. The perfectly aimed bullet sent the bottle spinning into his grasp. He chewed the end off with powerful teeth and gulped down the liquid within.

Forgwyn, along with the other clubgoers at Globule, had seen enough. The stampede for the exit followed instantly. Expensive fur coats and skin handbags went unclaimed in the cloakroom as their owners poured out from the club in terror.

The gigantic laboratory was an area of the *Gargantuan*

158

that Shrubb's duties did not often take him to. He disliked the company of the research team, many of whom seemed more devoted to their work than to the true cause of Luminus. Many of them hadn't been on the surface for years and were pale and unhealthy-looking. Each wore a white coat and a plastic identity badge bearing the silver apple of Luminus. The laboratory was packed with advanced equipment, the nature of most of it a mystery to Shrubb, for whom machines were only as important as the people that controlled them.

A red light flashed on the duplicator control panel and a buzzer sounded. A screen monitoring the process room showed the Doctor slumped unconscious after his ordeal. 'The process is completed,' Gortlock, leader of the Luminuns' research team, told Shrubb. He leant forward and said into a speaker, 'Security, take the body of the Doctor to cryo-storage.' He turned to Shrubb. 'The Doctor's mind is yours.'

'Excellent,' said Shrubb. He appreciated the sensation of giving important orders. 'Activate a Celebroid immediately. Despite the Doctor's alien physiognomy, a standard model will suffice as a base for the external details.'

Gortlock nodded. He pressed a button on the duplicator panel and a long spool of black plastic slid from a small slot. Shrubb took it and crossed over to the duplication cubicle, a tall yellow booth with a heavy metal door. He slid the plastic strip into a slot in its side. A small screen flashed into life.

SUBJECT: THE DOCTOR
IDENT: ALIEN RENEGADE
SELECT NUMBER OF COPIES REQUIRED

Shrubb pressed a button marked with the number one and a whirring and clanking noise came from within the booth. A few moments later a chime sounded.

'The Celebroid is primed for use,' said Gortlock. 'Shall I activate now?'

Shrubb considered. 'At present we need it for one function only. Bring it up to first level usage, factual retrieval. Don't activate the personality circuits.'

Gortlock nodded. He entered the sequence of instructions on the cubicle panel and then swung open the heavy metal door. 'Doctor,' he called into the darkness within. 'Doctor, come out and speak to us.'

The copy walked stiffly from the booth. Not for the first time, Shrubb marvelled at the superior technology of Luminus. The duplication was exact, down to the last detail of the clothing. The features were still. 'Hello, I am the Doctor,' the copy said flatly.

Shrubb straightened himself up. 'Doctor,' he said, 'tell me, why did you come to Olleril? Are you plotting against Luminus?'

'I was just passing,' said the copy. 'And I haven't had time to plot.'

Shrubb frowned. At first stage, a Celebroid should not be able to lie. He decided to try another question. 'Where is your TARDIS?'

The copy said nothing. Shrubb asked again. 'Doctor, your TARDIS. What is its location?'

There was no response. Gortlock frowned and asked it, 'What is twenty-three times fifty, Doctor?'

'Eleven hundred and fifty,' the Celebroid replied with its customary lack of enthusiasm.

Shrubb turned angrily to Gortlock. 'What has gone wrong?'

The scientist ran his fingers nervously through his hair. 'Memory degradation occurs in a Celebroid only after prolonged usage. I can suggest only that the Doctor's original has shielded certain areas of his mind from the duplicator.'

'Is that possible?'

'It could be. We have never tried to duplicate an alien before.'

Shrubb slammed his fist down on the nearest workbench. 'This is unacceptable, Gortlock. The Supreme One himself has requested this information.'

The voice of his commander came from a speaker next

to the booth. 'I did indeed.' Shrubb's red face blanched. He knew that the Supreme One had cameras positioned around the *Gargantuan* and that he must have seen the humiliating results of the duplication process.

'I did as you instructed, Commander,' he babbled. 'It was Gortlock who carried out the process.'

'I followed standard procedure,' Gortlock bleated.

'Cease this squabbling,' the Supreme One ordered. 'You are devotees of Luminus. Such behaviour is unnecessary and undignified. I witnessed the Doctor's defiance earlier. I expected him to resist. But we must have the TARDIS by tomorrow night. It could be damaged if it remains in the city during the construction programme.' He coughed. 'We will have to operate a contingency plan.'

'Yes, Commander?' asked Shrubb eagerly. He liked the sound of this.

'Gortlock, time the Celebroid's personality circuits to activate at exactly seven hundred hours tomorrow,' the voice instructed. 'Arrange with Security to have it transported to Shrubb's residence on the mainland. Implant a cover memory for yesterday and introduce an impulse to locate the TARDIS. When you have completed your task, I want you to return to the study room and prepare Devor.'

'I obey,' the scientist said and went to begin his task.

Shrubb looked up at the camera. 'But master,' he pointed out, 'the information is not in the Celebroid's mind print, the Doctor has shielded it.'

In his sanctum, deep in the bowels of the *Gargantuan*, the Supreme One looked down at Shrubb's face, distorted by the scanner relay. Under normal circumstances the man was an ideal servant, if a little too excitable. As Tragedy Day approached he was becoming almost manic at the prospect of power. 'You would suggest,' he said, 'a different approach?'

'The Doctor,' said Shrubb. 'We must use the means at our disposal to wrench the truth from him.'

'He would die rather than reveal his secrets to an

enemy,' the Supreme One said dismissively. 'Do not concern yourself, Shrubb, I have other plans for the Doctor. And the copy will lead us to the TARDIS.' He watched Shrubb struggling to understand the complexity of his scheme.

'You're going to use it on the other aliens?' the journalist said slowly.

'Exactly. They would not reveal the truth to us, at least not without the persuasion we have no time for. But they will lead the Celebroid to the TARDIS.'

'That's very clever, Commander.'

'I know it is.'

Shrubb smiled. The Supreme One coughed and continued. 'And there is another matter concerning the Doctor I wish to address. It concerns his scientific knowledge as an alien and our problem with the psychotronic differential.'

Empire TV's many channels were saving money again by rerunning shows at night from the schedule of the previous day. The cliff-hanger to *Whittaker's Harbour* saw Lophie receiving the disastrous news that her father was coming out of prison. *Martha and Arthur* was next, one of the weaker episodes in which Junior, played by the young Howard Devor, was followed home by a dog and hid it in his room.

The television signals pulsed through the night air of Empire City as they had done for many years. In Shrubb's house, Bernice and Ace were talking. Sergeant Felder and his gang were cruising the streets in a crime wagon, stopping occasionally to beat up somebody wearing the wrong clothes or who had the wrong colour skin. Forgwyn was walking back to Zone Two, thinking about the arrival of Ernie McCartney on Olleril. Harry Landis's neighbours were searching his charred body for money after emptying his cellar. Ernie was booking into the President Hotel and explaining that he didn't need a bed as he would be weaving his own. The evening meal was being dropped over the heads of the Vijjans in the refugee camp. Meredith and her baby were safe in the maternity wing of the media compound. In the floodlit Lerthin Square, the technical team was going for another check. The citizens of the central zones slept soundly in their comfortable beds. Many of them dreamt of previous Tragedy Days and the fun they had had and the money they had raised and the good they believed they had done. Life nowadays was so depressing and awful for so many people and they felt they had to do something.

Outside their homes, the empty streets were lined with rows of weeping paper skeletons. They swayed in the slight breeze blowing from the north.

12

The Ally

The Doctor's mind returned to his body after a flit around
the ether necessitated by the severity of the duplication
process. He took a deep breath and found his lungs drawing on freezing air with an unreasonably high oxygen
content. He spluttered and tried to open his eyes. They
were stuck down with ice. He was just able to move his
hands. They touched a panel that was above his body. As
he had suspected, somebody had attempted to freeze him
in a cryogenic unit. They had not reckoned on his constitution. He concentrated, gathered all his strength, and
then jerked his entire self upwards. The panel was
knocked away. He drew on the cold air outside the casket
and life returned slowly to his frozen muscles. A few
moments later he succeeded in opening his eyes.

He was inside a vast room that contained several
hundred coffins identical to the one he had just escaped
from. Silver pipes containing coolant gases snaked around
the bays of caskets. The bright whiteness and low tempera-
ture was almost overwhelming. He rubbed his arms and
legs once again and then stood up and peered at the next
cabinet along. The covering panel was frosted over and
stuck down. The Doctor produced his hankie, blew on it
and scrubbed at a small area of the glass. The frost
cleared and the face of a handsome young man was
revealed. Around his neck was a white plastic collar which
read DANNY – FANCY THAT. The Doctor checked his
own throat and pulled off the similar collar which had
been placed there. It identified him as THE DOCTOR –
ALIEN RENEGADE.

He threw the collar away. He estimated that there were three or four hundred caskets in the chamber. Three or four hundred famous people, replaced by exact duplicates and kept frozen by the Luminuns. And somewhere there was a duplicate of him.

He was searching for an exit from the chamber when he heard a distant mewing sound. The Doctor realized that he was listening to the weeping of a child.

He followed the noise to a line of caskets on the other side of the vault. He listened closely and tracked it finally to one of the ghastly white coffins in particular. He wrenched the lid off and looked down at the small startled boy lying within. His face was covered in ice and his spectacles were frosted over. His clothes were crumpled and torn and there were bruises across his forehead. When he saw the Doctor he began to wail even louder.

The Doctor shushed him. 'Don't worry,' he reassured the youngster. 'I'm not going to hurt you.'

The boy extended a frail white hand. 'Please sir,' he whimpered, 'please, sir, help me.'

Not far away, Gortlock was returning to the laboratory, having dispatched the Celebroid copy of the Doctor to Empire City. An aide hurried up to him.

'All systems are prepared, sir,' he reported. 'The psychotronic links are ready to receive the final subject.'

Gortlock smiled. Everything was running according to schedule, the careful preparations of years performed precisely. 'The signal transmitters are aligned?'

The aide nodded. 'The boosters are tuned to the psychic frequency as instructed.'

'Good,' said Gortlock. 'Keep it that way. The final subject will be handed over to you shortly.' He walked through to the study room adjoining the laboratory.

Howard Devor was inside, strapped to a datalyzer couch. A complex array of sensors were attached to his supine form. The sophisticated computers that lined the walls of the study room whirred and clicked busily as data

165

poured from the unconscious actor. Gortlock noted with irritation that Shrubb was still hanging around.

'There's no need for you to remain here,' Gortlock told him. 'The research team is quite capable of attending to this task. There must be security matters to attend to?'

'I've been ordered by the Supreme One himself to oversee this stage of the project,' Shrubb snapped. 'Would you like to take the matter up with him?'

Gortlock frowned and bit his lip. What did Shrubb know anyway? A surface agent, a pen pusher, suddenly down here giving orders. Was this what things were going to be like from tonight? He was thinking of something to say to wipe the smug smile from Shrubb's ugly face when Devor's eyes fluttered open.

'The Supreme One, yes,' he rambled drowsily. 'I'm a personal friend of the Supreme One . . .'

Shrubb leaned over him and smirked. Gortlock recoiled from the journalist's sadistic enthusiasm. 'You fool, Devor. You really believed it all, didn't you?'

'I have kissed the silver apple,' Devor protested desperately. 'I am one of the inner circle. I have the power to destroy you!'

'Not so.' Shrubb gripped Devor's square jaw. 'Your power extended only as far as your own back lot. Do you really think we would let a worm like you enter Luminus?'

'I exiled George Lipton, I'll do the same to you,' Devor attempted to say.

Shrubb spat in the actor's eye. 'George Lipton! That middle-aged non-entity was missed by no one. Your futile acts of arrogance were all part of our plan.'

He gestured to the computer banks chattering behind him. 'Remember that implant we gave you?' he inquired slyly.

Devor nodded. 'To increase my brain energy, yes. And it worked, yes, I felt it working . . .'

Shrubb shook his head. 'Not so. It is a brain monitor. It recorded your thoughts as we gave you power.'

He held up the reams of printout that were spewing from the overheated machines. 'And here it all is. When our machines have cross-checked and collated the data, we will have what we need.

'And then,' he concluded, 'you will perform one last function for us.'

Devor struggled to free himself from the datalyzer. Gortlock waved an attendant forward and an anaesthetic was administered. The actor fell silent.

Shrubb struggled to regain his composure. He wiped his mouth and took deep breaths. 'I must rest in my cabin,' he said. 'See that Devor is taken to the generator as soon as the implant is exhausted.' He stumbled from the study room without a backward glance.

Ernie McCartney yawned as the early morning sun shone through the curtains of his room on the tenth floor of the President Hotel. He stretched out a leg, dialled room service and ordered a full breakfast.

There was a lot of noise in the street outside. He crept over to the window and looked down. A large group of humans were gathered in the street. Many of them carried collecting tins which they were shaking up and down rhythmically. Others waved huge banners displaying pictures of starving or wounded children. Another group was blowing black whistles and paper skeletons were strapped to their backs. He shook his head in bewilderment. Humans were a peculiar lot and no mistake.

There was a knock on the door. He shouted, 'Come in,' and a young lady entered. She was pulling a trolley and her back was towards him. 'Will you be wanting tea or coffee with your breakfast, sir?' she asked automatically.

'Tea, lass, strong black tea,' he said emphatically.

She poured him a cup as requested and turned to hand it to him. She saw him, screamed twice, and ran from the room. 'I don't credit this,' Ernie said despairingly, pulling his pyjamas closer around his hairy chest. 'Has she not seen a bloke dressing before?'

He examined the trolley and found toast, fried eggs and bacon, all of which he gulped down in seconds. He chewed open the lid of the tea urn and drained the contents. Then he dressed himself in his best leathers, slung on his eight guns, popped on his stetson and felt inside his pocket. He produced a pyramid of jagged red glass. The old bloke on Frinjel 87 had told him it would lead to this TARDIS doings. A glow throbbed deep inside it. The trace indicated that the TARDIS was not far away, somewhere on the other side of the city.

'Right, Time Lord,' he said to himself, 'Ernie McCartney's on his way!'

Bernice pulled herself into a woolly jumper that belonged to Shrubb's absent daughter. She turned to Forgwyn. 'I'm not too sharp of a morning. Tell me again. This Ernie McCartney person – '

'No, this Ernie McCartney arachnid mutant,' he corrected her.

'Pardon me. This, er, creature is the most, er, the most – '

'The most feared assassin in the Seventh Quadrant,' he completed gloomily.

'Right. And he must be here to kill the Doctor. It would be too much of a coincidence otherwise.'

Forgwyn nodded. Bernice sat down at her dressing table. 'Oh blimey,' she said. She combed her hair slowly. 'Oh blimey,' she said again.

'You don't seem very surprised,' Forgwyn observed.

'My dear, I've lost the capacity to be surprised over the last couple of years,' she told him. 'I could pretend. *Oh my goodness! Kill the Doctor?* But what would be the point?'

Ace walked into the bedroom, towelling her hair dry from the shower. 'Morning, chums.'

'Ace, last night Forgwyn saw a giant spider in a night-club who almost definitely wants to kill the Doctor,' Bernice told her. 'And hurry up and drink that coffee before it goes cold.'

As unsurprised as Bernice, Ace picked up the steaming mug and sipped. 'You make a lovely cup of coffee, Bernice,' she said.

'Don't mention it,' said the archaeologist.

'Sure you haven't been at the local ouzo, mate?' Ace asked Forgwyn.

'No I haven't,' he insisted. 'You don't seem to be taking this very seriously. Ernie "Eight-Legs" McCartney is dangerous.'

Bernice finished her couture, stood up and stretched. 'So are we. I suppose we'd better find the Doctor, then.'

'No need,' said Ace between sips of coffee. 'Just seen him on the stairs.'

The Doctor sat in the breakfast room munching on a piece of toast. This really was a most agreeable planet, he decided. He would have to come back one day. But now it was time to move on. If only he could remember where he'd parked the TARDIS. He leant back in his chair and wondered where his capricious time machine might take him next.

The door opened and his young companions Ace and Bernice walked in, followed by that young fellow Forgwyn. 'Good morning,' he said cheerily.

'You look happy,' Ace said suspiciously. 'What have you been up to?'

'Oh, this and that. Mostly that,' he joked weakly. 'Saw a few sights. Met a few civic dignitaries, shook a few hands. Rather a dull day, actually.'

'We've been worried about you, Doctor,' said Bernice. 'You're in more danger than I think you realize.'

'Go on,' he said.

'There are two top-class offworld assassins on Olleril with orders to kill you,' she told him.

'And one of them's my mother, Meredith,' Forgwyn admitted, shamefaced.

'Oh,' the Doctor remarked. 'I wonder what I've done to offend them?'

Forgwyn sat opposite him. 'You stole a piece of red glass from the Friars of Pangloss, hundreds of years ago.'

The Doctor frowned and searched his memories. There were so many of them, that was the problem, all jumbled up and confused. Recent events he could see quite clearly in his mind's eye. Before that everything was mixed up and strange, as if there wasn't room in his head to hold everything properly. He was sure he hadn't felt like that before.

He shook his head. 'I don't think I did,' he said. 'I don't think I've ever met these Friars of Pangloss.' He stood up and smiled. 'Not to worry. It's another good reason for going back to the TARDIS.'

Ace's suspicion increased. 'Going back to the TARDIS?'

'Yes,' he replied. 'Why not? I've seen enough of this planet.' He noted her doubtful expression. 'You wanted to go back yesterday,' he reminded her.

'Yeah, I did,' she agreed. 'But you didn't. What about the Luminuns? Don't you want to find out what they're up to?'

The Doctor snorted. 'The Luminuns?' he said disparagingly. 'Just another clapped-out cult. The universe is full of them. I say let's go for a holiday. We need a rest. Zeraticus 2 is good at this time of the epoch, I believe.' He walked out eagerly.

The Doctor felt in his pocket and produced a crumpled paper bag. 'Here you are,' he told the small, frost-covered boy. 'Have an aniseed ball.' The little fellow smiled and took the sweet. Then he started to cry again.

The Doctor patted him awkwardly on the shoulder and tried to quieten him. 'Please be as quiet as you can,' he whispered. 'We don't want to be found, do we?'

They had escaped from the cryo-storage chamber, where the Doctor's ball of twine had come in handy for fusing the security systems. A corridor outside had led them to the small room they were hiding in now. It was adjacent to a row of primed escape pods which reinforced a theory the Doctor had.

Occasionally people passed by outside. Some carried weapons which the Doctor had noted were several centuries ahead of the technology used in the city.

He asked the boy his name. 'Crispin,' he replied. 'Haven't you heard of me? I'm often on the television.'

The Doctor shook his head. 'I travel a lot,' he explained. Then he looked closer at the greasy hair and glasses of his new friend. 'Although I do seem to recognize you.' He searched his memory. 'Yes, of course. I saw you on television a couple of nights ago.'

The boy started to weep again. 'That can't be right,' he wailed. 'I've been here for months and months, stuck inside that horrid coffin thing. I thought I'd never get out.'

The Doctor tried to comfort him. 'There, there. I think a fault had developed in the system and you were woken up. You'll be quite safe as long as you do what I tell you. Do you understand?'

The small face nodded tearfully. 'What do we have to do?'

'I need to find out more about this place,' the Doctor said. 'Let's explore. But you must keep quiet.' Crispin nodded his understanding.

They continued down the corridor and descended two flights of stairs without seeing anybody. The functional whiteness of the cryogenic area gave way to a darker metallic decor on the lower levels. The walls throbbed with engine noise.

The Doctor crossed over to what appeared to be a viewing port set into a wall. 'Good grief,' he exclaimed.

Crispin hovered at his side. 'What is it?'

'We're underwater,' said the Doctor. He stared through the porthole at the busy marine life of the ocean depths. 'And we're moving.' He rubbed his chin thoughtfully. 'Yes, we're on a submarine. It must be enormous.'

The sound of footsteps sent them both scuttling for cover. The Doctor dragged Crispin under a nearby walkway and watched a group of white-coated men walk by. They wore visors and carried a large piece of cutting equipment. 'I wonder where they're going with that,' the Doctor said.

'It's a laser torch, isn't it?' Crispin whispered helpfully.

The Doctor nodded and emerged from cover. 'Let's see

what they're up to.' He followed the scientists at a sensible distance.

A few corners later, he and Crispin came to what appeared to be some kind of blasting chamber. A large area of the deck had been cleared to accommodate the customized spacecraft belonging to Forgwyn and Meredith. A swarm of scientists surrounded it, taking readings and making tests using a variety of instruments. The laser torch was being lined up on the hull.

Crispin gasped. 'What is it?' he asked. 'It looks like something from *Captain Millennium*. Is it a spaceship?'

The Doctor nodded. 'Yes, and it belongs to friends of mine.'

'You're from another planet?' exclaimed the boy. 'Wow!'

But the Doctor had seen enough and did not want to remain in such a crowded area. 'Come along,' he told the boy. 'There must be a control centre somewhere aboard this thing. Let's find it.'

Although it was only eight o'clock in the morning, the Tragedy Day totalizers were already passing the three million credot mark. The Tragedy Day marathon, this year in aid of food parcels for Vijja and medical care for the outer city, passed through the taped-off streets of zone six to the excitement of the crowds watching from the pavement. Costumed fun runs and bed pushes in aid of terminally ill children were the focus of the fun in zone four, while celebrity kidnappings and an open-air music festival designed to raise cash for life-support units occupied the revellers in zone three.

The streets of zone one were filling up with decorated floats for the central parade. It would start at midday at the offices of the admin company and finish at five exactly when it reached Lerthin Square.

By 8:30, ninety-nine per cent of the Central city's accumulated guilt had been exorcised. Nought point oh-oh-oh-oh-oh-oh-one per cent of the Central city's wealth had been redistributed. The companies sponsoring the various events had received free advertising to the value of thirty-five million credots.

A very small but very sophisticated piece of technology zoomed over the heads of the crowds gathered in zone two. It was a camera disguised as a fly. It had been programmed to follow a beacon attached to a particular Celebroid. It transmitted the location of the robot instantaneously to the offices of Toplex Sanitation.

Forke and a couple of his operatives were watching the images from the tracker camera. So far the party they were observing had wandered about vaguely, moving backwards and forwards and getting nowhere.

One of the Luminuns was wearing headphones. 'They're talking again, sir,' he told Forke.

'Put them on the main speaker,' Forke ordered. The voices of the Celebroid and the Doctor's companions were relayed to the control chamber.

'Doctor, we've been along here before,' said the voice of the younger woman.

'Do you know, I think you're right,' Forke heard the Celebroid say. There was an uncomfortable pause, then it said, 'I've forgotten where we left it.'

'You've never forgotten before,' said the older woman. There was another uncomfortable pause.

'I know this city quite well now,' said the teenage male. 'Where do you have to go?'

Forke leant forward eagerly. This was what his masters were waiting to hear. 'Back through the cordon,' said the older woman, 'and then through the South Side until we reach the refugee camp.'

Forgwyn took a street map from his inside pocket. He pointed out the necessary route. 'We're here,' he said, pointing to zone two. 'What we need to do is go to zone four and cross the cordon.'

The Doctor took the map from him. 'Thank you. But you needn't bother coming to see us off.'

Forgwyn gulped. His face was flushed with disappointment. 'But I can't miss the TARDIS,' he protested. 'I've been looking forward to it.'

The Doctor frowned. 'Very well then,' he said. 'But a quick look is all.'

Forgwyn thanked him and they walked on, heading towards a subcar terminal that could take them to Zone Four. Bernice took the Doctor's arm as they pushed through the excited crowds, who were watching a complex dance routine performed by figures in skull masks.

'Interesting,' she said. 'It reminds me, Doctor, of our bewildering experiences on the planet Rhoos.'

He stopped and looked at her, bewildered. 'Where?'

'Don't you remember? Rhoos, the planet of volcanoes.'

The Doctor smiled and nodded. 'Ah yes, Rhoos, of course. Yes.' He murmured something and his face creased with puzzlement.

Bernice withdrew her arm from his. Her suspicions were confirmed. Something was very wrong with the Doctor. The planet Rhoos did not exist.

Ernie's car was the most expensive available from the top dealer in the Seventh Quadrant. It had brought him all the way from Frinjel 87 and off at the correct hyper exit, all on the one tank. It was class.

He drove through the streets of Zone Four, two legs on the wheel, two on the pedals, two holding open his street map and two passing mouthwards his morning snack of dead fly biscuits. Passage through the crowds was painfully slow. He was due back on Frinjel 87 to collect his reward in two days. He couldn't afford to waste time.

He wound down the window and shouted out, 'Will you lot of daft ha'p'orths get out of me ruddy way!'

The humans crossing the street fled from his gesticulating legs and scurried out of the path of the car. Ernie drove on. He shivered slightly. He didn't like to admit it to himself, being a feared assassin and all that, but sometimes humans scared him, not so much when they were still but when they scuttled about like that, very quickly.

He told himself not to be so daft and returned to the

matter in hand. He would very soon reach the access point that led to the area the map called the South Side. From there it should be easy enough to find the TARDIS and kill the Time Lord.

'Look, Doctor,' Crispin called helpfully. He pointed to a map that was mounted near a corridor junction. 'That must be the craft that we're inside.'

The Doctor inspected the map. 'You're right, I think.' He squinted to make sense of the coloured labels and corresponding key. 'We're up on level fourteen, which is right next to the main laboratory.' He turned to the left. 'Let's take a look. This way.'

Crispin tugged on the tails of his jacket. 'No, Doctor,' he said, with a slight tone of impatience. 'It must be this way.' He pointed in the opposite direction.

The Doctor consulted the map again. 'Yes, yes, of course, you're right.' He smiled down at his young friend. 'I was forgetting. You're the one with all the qualifications.'

The boy smiled as they walked along. 'But then, you're a doctor. What planet are you from?' he asked in wonder. 'Why are you here? Where's your spaceship?'

'I'm here by accident,' the Doctor said. 'Trust the TARDIS to land me in trouble.'

'What's the TARDIS?'

'Never mind that,' the Doctor whispered. He put a finger to his lips and gestured to a huge door marked LABORATORY in large red letters at the end of the corridor ahead of them. 'I want to see what's in there. It could be dangerous and I don't want to involve you.'

Crispin stuck his nose up precociously. 'I'm capable of looking after myself, you know.'

The Doctor sighed. 'As long as you understand the risks.' He sneaked forward and pushed open the door. Crispin followed.

The laboratory was easily twice the size of the cryo-storage chamber. The Doctor marvelled at the diversity of the projects and the complexity of the equipment.

Most of the systems, he realized with distaste, were weapons-related. Gas canisters and grenades were stacked next to instruments of torture. A large section was occupied by a sealed-off unit containing the creatures Ace had described to him, floating in fluid like pickled onions. The scientists on duty had not noticed the intruders. They were gathered outside a door marked STUDY ROOM with their backs to the main entrance.

Crispin crept over to a desk and picked up the papers that had been scattered there. 'What do you think these are?' he asked the Doctor.

'Let me see.' He examined the papers. Attached to them was a diagram of a device that was labelled TRAGEDY DAY – SPECIAL PROJECT. He flicked from the diagram back to the notes anxiously. 'What are they playing at?' he said quietly.

'What is it, Doctor?' asked Crispin.

The Doctor handed him the notes back. 'See for yourself. The Luminuns have constructed a psychotronic generator of incredible power.'

'A psychotronic generator?' queried Crispin. 'I've studied those in theory.'

'Yes, yes,' the Doctor snapped irritably, snatching back the plans. 'It generates waves of psychic energy. But I've never seen one as large as this before.'

'What will it do?' Crispin asked, worried.

The Doctor folded up the plan and put it in his pocket. 'Blanket a large area of the planet with a psychic signal, possibly hypnotic.' He snorted. 'They're not as clever as they think they are, though. They'll lose half their output using this system.'

Crispin nodded. 'Because of the psychotronic differential, yes, I noticed that. But how could they stop that?'

The Doctor was glad of an opportunity to talk science with somebody who understood. 'It's simple,' he said. 'Can't see why they haven't seen it themselves. All they have to do is attach something like a Triton T80 to the links.'

176

'A Triton T80,' said Crispin slowly. 'I suppose you could construct such a device, Doctor?'

'Of course I could,' he said breezily.

Crispin's childish smile disappeared. He straightened himself up, took off his cracked glasses and replaced them with an identical pair that were undamaged. His expression was set.

'Thank you, Doctor,' he said loudly. 'That's what I wanted to know.'

A guard stepped from behind a filing cabinet. His blaster was aimed at the Doctor. The Doctor's face dropped. A small but important part of his reasoning clicked over in his mind and he put a hand to his head. 'Oh, crumbs,' he said.

The scientists at the far end of the laboratory turned. Their leader, a short, fussy-looking man identified by his badge as Gortlock, ran forward. He stared at the Doctor and Crispin in astonishment.

'What's going on here?' he asked the guard. 'Take these two back to cryo-storage immediately.'

The guard remained still. 'I said return them to cryo-storage!' Gortlock shouted. 'The Supreme One will punish you if you do not obey me.'

Crispin stepped forward. 'Don't bother, Gortlock,' he said in his high, strange, nasal voice. 'I am the Supreme One.'

13

The Gunfight

The officer in command of the refugee camp squeezed through the entry hatch to storage bay forty. His subordinate indicated the tall blue box in the corner. 'That's it, sir.'

'You tried busting it open?'

'Yes, sir. No joy, sir.'

The officer lifted his wrist communicator to his mouth and dialled the special number he had been given. 'Mr Forke. I have it. It's a tall blue box.'

'Excellent,' Forke's voice filtered back. 'Have it transported to Sector 3B of the docks. My team are waiting there to receive it.'

'Right away, sir.'

'And I've another job for you,' Forke went on. 'Four offworlders, two males and two females, are approaching the camp. Bring them to the docks along with the box.'

The officer broke the connection and turned to his junior. 'Right, get this thing loaded up. And send team four out to the check-point with orders to bring in the offworlders.'

Forke leant back in his chair, content. The plan of the Supreme One to capture the TARDIS had been a complete success. All that had to be done now was to transport it to the *Gargantuan*. For this service he had been promised great rewards, perhaps even deputy controllership of the South Side. The moment of control was only hours away. He felt for the immunizer plate at the nape of his neck and smiled.

'Sir,' said one of the trackers. 'The vehicle containing the Celebroid and the others is approaching the exclusion zone now.'

Meredith swallowed her medication dutifully and smiled as the matron left her room. The noise from the crowds outside had woken her at six in the morning. She had propped herself up on some pillows to watch the television and found herself confronted by endless coverage of the parades and the concerts and the special events.

'Sadly, neither Robert nor Howard Devor can be with us today,' Wendy Clifton chattered on inanely from the stage at Lerthin Square. 'They've both gone down with a bug. Ahhh. What a way to spend Tragedy Day! But never mind, because at 11.20 we'll be joined by Fancy That and at 11.45 the managing director of the admin company, Maurice Taylor, will be bringing us his special Tragedy Day message along with the cast of *Whittaker's Harbour*. But now it's time to go over to Charlie on the riotboard. Has that earlier disturbance in Zone Six cleared up yet?'

Meredith realized that she had had enough. More importantly she had a job to do. She got out of bed, stretched, and pulled out the suitcase that Forgwyn had packed for her. Nestling between her coveralls and fatigues was the red pyramid supplied by the Friars. She took it out and concentrated, as they had instructed her. The glow surged up from the depths, brighter and stronger than it had been before. The TARDIS, and therefore the Time Lord, were somewhere in the city nearby. She still had a chance to complete the job.

She dug deeper into the rolled-up jumble of clothing. From the pocket of one of her summer dresses she produced a slim, functional-looking blaster. Then she dressed herself quickly in a lightweight armour suit, tucked the weapon and the pyramid into the waistband, and took a last look at her baby. His smooth, chubby face smiled up at her.

'Don't worry, little one,' she cooed down at the cot. 'Mamma will be back soon.'

* * *

After crossing the cordon to the South Side, Bernice had hired one of the open-topped buggies that seemed popular with the young people of the city. Ace had insisted on driving, with Bernice as map reader. The Doctor and Forgwyn chatted in the back seats.

'Do you believe him?' Bernice asked Ace. 'About his reasons for going back?'

''Course I don't,' Ace replied. 'I'm not that stupid. He's up to something. Let him get on with it, I say.'

Bernice nodded. 'Hmm,' she said. She glanced over her shoulder.

'Bernice was telling me you've been to a place where fiction became reality,' Forgwyn was asking, wide-eyed. 'What was it like?'

The Doctor shrugged. 'Very interesting, really,' he said and coughed. 'I can't remember too much about it though, strangely.'

Bernice turned back to Ace. 'I'd agree with you. If that was the Doctor and not a rough approximation.'

Ace pulled the brake handle and pulled the buggy over to the side of the road. She looked Bernice in the eye. 'One of those doubles?'

The Doctor leant forward. 'Why have we stopped?' he asked. 'I'm keen to get on.'

'Oh, I was just telling Ace,' Bernice said breezily, 'about your promise to Madam Guralza.'

'And I thought I'd stop to ask you,' said Ace, picking up her cue, 'if you wanted me to pick her up and claim your ring back.'

The Doctor blinked several times and nodded uneasily. 'Well, don't worry, Ace,' he said. 'Forget about that, we're going on holiday, remember?'

Ace nodded and started the engine. 'You're right, Doctor. Silly of me, wasn't it?' He nodded again and sat back.

The buggy drove on towards the camp and the docks. The two women sat in silence for a few moments. Then Ace said, 'You're right. Whatever that is, it isn't him.'

'They can get the appearance right,' said Bernice. 'But

the character is wrong. You do realize,' she went on, 'that we've told that thing where to find the TARDIS?'

Ace nodded. 'Yeah. Which means that we've probably told the Luminuns where to find the TARDIS.'

'Which means that they've probably got the TARDIS,' Bernice pointed out.

'Which means that they're probably waiting for us up ahead,' Ace completed. 'Which means I was probably right to nick these from Forgwyn's mum.' She took her left hand from the wheel, felt inside her jacket and tossed Bernice two slim laser pistols.

Ernie's frustratingly slow progress through the carnival crowds had heightened his level of aggression. As his car passed through the access point, he drummed two of his legs on the dashboard. 'Come on, come on,' he muttered impatiently under his breath as the vehicle in front of him stalled yet again. 'Move, you wally, move!'

The owner of the car in front got out and, with irritating slowness, propped up the bonnet. He looked inside and shook his head.

Ernie had had enough. He wound down his window and shouted, 'Eh, you! Get a flamin' shift on, some of us have work to go to!'

The owner looked up, caught sight of Ernie's angry face, and ran screaming down the tunnel. Ernie shook his head. 'What a bunch of splots,' he said. There was only one way to deal with the problem now. He unholstered his mattershift disrupter and fired at the car. Its physical structure dispersed instantly, leaving a patch of black soot. Ernie grunted with satisfaction, put away the weapon and drove on.

He glanced down at the pyramid tracker. The Time Lord must be very close now.

The Doctor had been marched through the dark, throbbing corridors of the submarine to a large door. Stencilled on it were big red letters that said PSYCHOTRONIC GENERATOR.

'I wonder what you've got in there,' he said.

Shrubb stepped forward, hand raised to deliver another brutal blow. 'I'll beat – '

Crispin held up a warning hand. 'Please. I've brought the Doctor here to talk to him, not bludgeon him.'

'Thank you,' said the Doctor.

Crispin waved aside his words of gratitude. 'Think nothing of it, Doctor. Now, let's go in, shall we?'

One of the guards escorting them pulled a large red lever on the wall and the doors slid open slowly. The small party walked through.

A huge device dominated the far end of the chamber beyond. It stood over thirty metres tall, was dull green in colour and consisted of several sections of bulging, doughnut-shaped technology laid on top of one another. It was encased in a scaffolding tower which more white-coated technicians were standing on to tend to various panels built into its sides. The apparatus hummed and whirred to itself. Occasionally it emitted a low growl and a hiss of steam, as if somehow it had become aware of its own importance.

But the aspect of the design that drew the attention of the Doctor's experienced eye was at the base. Built flush into the machine were eight upright human-shaped alcoves. All but one was occupied by an unconscious upright human. Each had been fitted with a silver dome that rested on their heads. Attached to the domes were wires that trailed up to a central junction box that winked with red and blue lights.

The Doctor looked more closely at the humans. There were four men and three women. All but one of them, a woman, were in late middle age. They were dressed in white one-piece coveralls.

Crispin was watching his reactions. The Doctor nodded and said, 'It's an impressive system.'

The boy nodded. 'That you can improve.'

'Given the right facilities, yes.' He wandered nonchalantly over to the device and stared up at the top. 'But

I'd like to know exactly what this thing is being used for before I begin.'

Shrubb lurched forward again. 'You've no right to know.'

The Doctor sighed and sat down on a workbench. 'Can't you send him away?' he asked Crispin. 'Or at least take him for a walk or something to calm him down?'

'Mister Shrubb is one of my most trusted advisers,' Crispin said icily, 'and will be treated with respect at all times.' He turned to Shrubb. 'Check with the mainland regarding the Celebroid.'

Shrubb nodded stiffly and left the chamber. 'Oh, good,' the Doctor said brightly. 'Perhaps now we can have a proper chat.' He stood up and took another look at the generator.

'Now,' he said, 'I'd like you to tell me about Luminus.'

Crispin moved to stand beside him. 'We've been around for centuries. Possibly millennia. Luminus exists. That is all you need to be told.'

The Doctor shook his head. 'I'm afraid it isn't. You must have aims, objectives.'

'We exist,' Crispin continued slowly. The Doctor sensed the growing anger of the little boy at having his orders questioned. 'We exist to control by whatever means necessary.'

'But why?' the Doctor protested. 'You must have some sort of philosophy. Religious, political, economic.'

Crispin shook his head. 'It is enough to know that we exist to control. Our philosophy is whatever allows us that control in the given circumstances.'

The Doctor was beginning to lose patience himself. He indicated the generator. 'You control Olleril anyway,' he pointed out. 'Why do you need this? What is it for?'

'Improved efficiency,' Crispin said simply. 'Despite the hopes of our ancestors, the operation here has proved itself inefficient. I have devised a superior means of control.'

'It was their operation to recreate a culture that died out

thousands of years ago in another galaxy. Why twentieth-century Earth?'

'My predecessors,' explained Crispin, 'considered it an eminently suitable model for control. History was shaped to bring us to this moment. Coercive capitalism with benefits for many and a manageable level of poverty. I disagree. It is costly and wasteful. I intend to make adjustments and create a new society. Starting with Empire City.'

'Do you have to be so tight-lipped?' the Doctor said. 'I presume that the psychic wave pattern is formed from the brain activity of those seven, yes?' He indicated the people linked into the machine. 'Who are they?'

Crispin took a deep breath and began. 'Thirty years ago, the most popular television programme in Empire City was *Martha and Arthur.*'

The Doctor frowned. 'What has that got to do with anything?'

'A great deal, Doctor. Martha and Arthur were an ordinary suburban couple. They had two children, Junior and Betsy. Next door lived funny old Mr and Mrs Rogers. The series ran for nine seasons. A record run.'

'I still can't see the relevance.'

Crispin walked over to the base of the machine and indicated the seven linked up to it. 'I believe *Martha and Arthur* to be the ideal model for control at this moment in the history of the city.' He looked down at the sleeping faces and smiled. 'Here they are. The original cast. Martha, Arthur, Betsy, funny old Mr and Mrs Rogers from next door.'

The Doctor pointed to the two weary-looking men laid out in the adjoining alcoves. 'What about those two?'

'Scriptwriter and director,' Crispin explained. 'The creative talent that inspired the series. With these talents I shall forge a new destiny for this planet and its people.'

The Doctor shook his head in bewilderment. 'You intend to generate a psychic-wave emission based around an old television series?'

'Oh yes,' said Crispin proudly. 'And Tragedy Day, so symptomatic of the old order, a jamboree of hopelessness in the guise of good works, seemed a good day to implement it. Tonight, everybody in the city will take on one of these characters. What free will they had shall be swept aside. The people will not question but obey. This is my model for total control.'

'And what will you do with this control when you get it?' asked the Doctor, fascinated.

'Restructure, reorganize, rebuild,' Crispin replied matter-of-factly. 'The city is overpopulated and there will have to be a culling. Our workforce of robot duplicates will perform such tasks. They will then move out to subjugate the rest of the planet.'

The Doctor could listen no longer. His disbelief erupted into anger. 'This is monstrous. You're like a deranged child.' He stopped himself. 'You *are* a deranged child. How were you allowed to get this far?'

Crispin smiled smugly. 'Merit, Doctor. Merit. Anybody could have done what I have done. I simply made full use of the opportunities presented to me, set myself targets and achieved them. I am the Supreme One of Luminus.'

'You are a freak,' the Doctor ranted, trying to create some sort of reaction from the boy. 'A child of your age should be out kicking a ball, not sat inside a submarine planning to take over the world. Don't you want to play with other children? Go to discos?'

Crispin remained unperturbed. 'No, not interested in discos. And I find the company of children unpleasant.' He sighed. 'I would appreciate it, Doctor, if you wouldn't raise your voice. I believe that people who lose their temper during a debate are basically immature and conceding their defeat.'

The Doctor bit his tongue and stamped his foot. Once again he found himself longing to administer a little violent correction, which was most unlike him.

'Now,' Crispin went on, 'you will, I'm sure, have noticed the empty alcove at the base of the machine. This is for Junior, as played by Howard Devor. I'd like you to come with me to my sanctum. There we will witness his absorption into the psychotronic net. And then you will begin construction of the component you described to us.'

The buggy turned onto the long, wide bridge that led from the outer streets of the South Side to the refugee camp. As Ace and Bernice had expected, a line of ten armed men, dressed in the black uniforms and visors used in the camp, were waiting for them at the checkpoint. Parked behind them were two vehicles. One was an empty truck. The other was a haulage vehicle. Strapped onto its back was the TARDIS.

Ace slowed the buggy and gripped the hilt of the pistol in her hand. It felt good to have a weapon again. She smiled and glanced over at Bernice. The older woman turned to Forgwyn and the false Doctor.

'Right, lads,' she said. 'I suggest you get under cover. There are some people in front of the TARDIS. Some armed people.'

The robot frowned. 'I'm sure there's an amicable way of solving this dispute,' he said and hopped down from the buggy. He waved at the line of guards. 'Excuse me. That belongs to me.'

An amplified voice came from ahead. 'Lay down your weapons and move forward with your arms raised.'

The false Doctor shrugged and turned back to his companions in the buggy. 'I think we'd better do as they say,' he said.

'No chance,' said Ace dangerously. She and Bernice climbed from the buggy and took cover behind the rear wheels. Forgwyn followed them. He flinched as one of the guards let out a warning shot and gestured his men to move forwards. They advanced slowly.

'Are you sure you know what you're doing?' he asked Bernice nervously.

'Of course not,' she said indignantly.

The guards continued their advance. 'Step into the open or we will fire,' said the amplified voice.

'There's really no need, we're quite harmless,' the false Doctor protested, holding his hands up. 'Come out, Ace,' he shouted over at the buggy. 'You'll only cause more trouble.'

Ace took a deep breath and readied herself. She flicked the safety catch off the pistol and set the power control built into the hilt to blue for stun. She watched as Bernice did the same. 'You take the right side,' she whispered over. Bernice nodded and crawled over to the right side of the buggy.

Ace made her move. She leapt from cover and fired twice, bringing down the man on the far left of the advancing group. The guards returned fire instantly, sending the false Doctor scurrying for cover at the back of the buggy.

'Ace, what are you doing?' he screamed.

'Save your breath!' she shouted, springing out again to deliver another round of stun bolts. Although her shots went wild, she was pleased to see that her opponents had broken their formation and were spreading out across the bridge. She also realized that the weapons the men were using were drug guns. So they were wanted alive.

Bernice shot down another couple of the men. Her reflexes were not as quick as Ace's and she narrowly avoided being hit by the drug pellets that were fired as her head popped up. She rolled back onto the tarmac and smiled up at Forgwyn. 'You wouldn't like to have a go, would you?' she asked him, offering the pistol.

'No, I wouldn't,' he said emphatically. 'Ethical reasons.'

The false Doctor nodded. 'Very sensible, too.'

Ace whooped with glee as she brought down more of the guards. There were now only four left. 'We're almost there,' she called to the others. 'Get ready to run for the TARDIS.'

The pyramid was now almost completely aglow. The hairs on Ernie's face stood up excitedly. The kill was in sight. As he turned the car onto the bridge that led off the South Side (which he had found dirty and disgusting, typical of non-arachnid races) he checked his weapons one last time and lit a cigarette. This would help both to calm his nerves and to make him look even tougher.

There was already some kind of fracas going on ahead. Four humans were crouched behind a buggy. Two of them, females, were shooting down uniformed men who were advancing on them. One of the females was a great shot. The two males with them were cowering, their heads lowered. One of them looked up briefly.

Ernie saw all that he needed to. The instincts with which nature had provided his arachnid forefathers told him that the male in the pale clothing was the Time Lord. And the blue box thing strapped to the vehicle further up ahead was his TARDIS. The kill was his. And then the cash. What he wouldn't do with the cash.

There were now only three guards left standing. Ace heard one shout an order but she couldn't make out the exact words. She sensed one of the men moving back towards the TARDIS.

She was making ready to come out of cover and finish things off when Forgwyn tapped her shoulder. 'Ace, there's someone coming up behind us.'

She looked back. A bright red vehicle resembling a sports car was drawing up behind them. She squinted to make out the driver. Behind the windscreen she caught a glimpse of lots of hair and lots of slithery movement.

'Ah, yes,' the false Doctor said confidently. 'That would be, er, let me see, an arachnid mutant. Possible origins, er . . .'

'The Acteon group?' suggested Bernice.

'More likely the Seventh Quadrant,' remarked Forgwyn. 'That's Ernie McCartney!' He threw himself flat on the tarmac. Because it seemed logical in that moment of panic to copy him, Bernice did so. The false Doctor stared into space, very confused.

Ace watched amazed as the door of the sports car burst open and Ernie McCartney sprang out. In every way he resembled a house spider, except that he was two metres wide and wore a studded leather jacket and a pair (or rather, she decided, an octet) of leather trousers. A broad-brimmed stetson was jammed on top of his head. Each of his legs displayed a holster and a different weapon.

He moved incredibly quickly. As he advanced, the two guards approaching the buggy fired their drug guns at him. He laughed and brought both of them down with quick blasts from two of his weapons.

Ace stood up slowly as the creature advanced. She had learnt to be comfortable with all forms of sentient life, but there was something about the creeping motion of the spider that made her shiver.

'Well done, mate,' she said amicably. She noted that Ernie was chewing on an unlit cigarette.

'Which one of you lot is the Time Lord?' he demanded in a full-blooded Yorkshire accent. Ace reeled. This was one for the memoirs.

The false Doctor stepped forward. His face was still and determined. Ace wondered for a moment if this really was a duplicate, so convincing was the dignity of that familiar expression. 'I am the one you seek,' he said. 'What do you want with me?'

Ernie chewed on the cigarette. 'Give me the red glass,' he drawled.

The false Doctor's brow creased. 'Red glass? Red glass?'

'Some friends of mine,' Ernie went on. 'They'd like it back. Belongs to them, see. So hand it over.'

The copy shuffled uncomfortably. 'Well,' it said eventually, 'if I have got it, it's not on my person, so I suppose it must be in my TARDIS there.' He pointed to the police box.

At that moment the vehicle beneath it moved. Ace watched as the last survivor of her attack drove straight towards them at full speed. The van swerved to avoid the buggy and Ernie's car and then sped off in the direction of the city.

Both Ace and Ernie attempted to put out its tyres and missed. The reassuring blue shape of the TARDIS receded into the distance.

'Quickly,' said the false Doctor. 'We must get after it.'

Before he could reach the buggy Ernie had shot him twice. He staggered about, a look of astonishment on his face, and collapsed in the road.

Ernie chuckled gleefully. 'One dead Time Lord,' he said to himself, rubbing his legs together happily. He crawled back into the sports car and drove off in the direction the van carrying the TARDIS had taken.

There was a sudden silence. The wind had snatched away the sounds of the city. Forgwyn uncurled himself from behind the buggy and looked about at the bodies of the stunned security men. Bernice and Ace were walking slowly over to the side of the bridge, against which the Doctor had collapsed. His head was lolling back at an odd angle and blue fluid was gushing from his lips. The bullet-holes opened by Ernie McCartney in his chest revealed not blood but sparking circuitry. Dead, the Doctor resembled a smashed doll.

'He was an android,' Forgwyn said, walking over to the two women. 'An android all along.'

'In fact no,' Bernice said coolly. She reached forward and pulled the robot's hair off. 'Not very well made, are they?' She tucked it away in an inside pocket. 'I think I'll keep it in case I ever go bald.'

Ace grinned. 'Just a bad copy. We spotted it a mile off.'

Bernice harrumphed. '*I* spotted it a mile off, thank you. The Doctor doesn't make promises lightly. And he certainly doesn't break them. He would never have tried to leave without Guralza.'

'Accept no imitation, that's what I say,' said Ace, giving the burnt-out robot a final kick. 'We want the original.'

To their astonishment the robot attempted to speak. 'Ace ... Bernice,' it wheezed almost inaudibly. 'I think I'm ... going to ... be sick ...'

'It's weird,' said Forgwyn. 'The personality matrix must be completely integrated. It believes itself to be the Doctor. Creepy. Makes me go existential all over.'

'Help me,' it said finally. 'I think I'm ... me, I feel like me ... if this is what being me feels like ... I need a lie-

190

down . . .' Its voicebox whirred and its jaw dropped open. The false Doctor was dead.

'What's the difference between a real personality and a created one, if the created one is endowed with a belief in its autonomous existence?' Bernice asked nobody in particular.

'Have you read Druver's *Artificial Intelligences: The Moral Dilemma*?' Forgwyn asked her. 'There's this really good bit, right, where Druver's saying that for an intelligence to be truly aware, it must . . .'

'Why don't you two shut the frag up?' Ace shouted. The others watched bewildered as she threw her laser pistol over the side of the bridge.

'I think we needed that,' Bernice observed.

Ace pointed ahead of them. 'Against that lot we'd need a Hiel rifle to stand any chance.' A large black personnel carrier was approaching. Before it had stopped the back doors were flung open and a large number of armed men climbed out.

'I think you're right,' Bernice said. She threw her pistol over the bridge and raised her hands. 'I know what, let's surrender.'

'This, Doctor, is what makes the human race so unique. The capacity to make foolish mistakes. The Stupidity Factor,' Crispin said proudly. Between his thin white finger and thumb he held an almost invisible piece of silver wire, of about five inches in length. One of the many screens in the darkened inner sanctum flickered and the wire caught the glint and sparkled strangely. 'A range of emotional responses captured by our scientists during the irresistible rise of Howard Devor.'

The Doctor looked around the sanctum disapprovingly. In contrast to the pristine whiteness of the upper corridors and the functional bolts and rivets of the lower decks, it was a cold, damp place. Each of the screens that covered one wall displayed a different image from, he guessed, the hundreds of television stations broadcasting around Olleril. The other walls were lined with ranks of sturdy-looking filing cabinets. The drawers of the cabinets were labelled with pieces of pink or blue card. The floor was carpeted a sickly purple, over which a smaller rug had been laid; the tassles at either end had been combed perfectly straight.

He returned his attention to the matter in Crispin's hand. 'For your robots, I assume. You've had problems recreating such responses in them?'

Crispin nodded and handed the Stupidity Factor back to a hovering aide, who replaced it immediately in a heavy silver carrying case. 'Most human characteristics transfer easily into the personality matrix. Foolishness was, until now, one of the very few that eluded us.'

'And without it your copies lacked essential human qualities? A sort of intuitive illogic?' queried the Doctor.

'Yes. Qualities that may be necessary in future tasks. Devor was the obvious choice for a subject to extract it from. We encouraged his conceit. It was a harrowing experience.'

The Doctor's attention was caught by an image on one of the screens. It showed Devor being wheeled into the vault they had just come from. His unconscious body, now swaddled in white robes, was propped up in the empty alcove at the base of the generator. A team of scientists led by Gortlock worked quickly, fitting the silver dome to his head and connecting up the wires to the junction box.

'The final moments,' Crispin said eagerly.

'Let's see what's on the other side,' said the Doctor. He crossed over to the screens and sat down disrespectfully in the chair before them. He shook his head and tutted. 'You'll get square eyes, you know.'

He picked up the slim remote control unit lying on the console before him and increased the volume on the Empire TV news channel. The robotic Wendy Clifton was talking to a thin-lipped man in a grey suit whose blandness rendered him almost indescribable.

'And your final words to the nation, Mr Taylor?' asked Wendy.

The bland man smiled. 'I'd like to wish everybody a very

192

enjoyable Tragedy Day and remind them that, despite the unfortunate increases in food charges, energy charges and the charge overheads charge that the admin company has been forced very reluctantly to make, recovery is with us.'

The Doctor grunted. 'Another of your robot puppets. In office but not in power.'

'Not at all,' said Crispin. 'Maurice Taylor is all too human. One of the drawbacks with the old system was that I needed people like him. I made a very good back-seat driver. But no more.' He leant forward, took the remote control unit from the Doctor's hand and reduced the volume.

'Now, stand up,' he ordered. 'Nobody sits in my television chair.'

The Doctor leapt to his feet. 'I'm so sorry,' he said. 'I didn't realize it was your *television* chair.' Before Crispin or one of his attendant guards could stop him, the Doctor had hopped over to the nearest of the filing cabinets and pulled the top drawer open. Stacked neatly inside were a pile of small metal triangles. The first one was labelled *Captain Millennium – Season Three, Episode Fifteen (23'14")*. 'A collector, eh?' He looked through the stack of cassettes. 'You're missing episode twenty-three.'

'It disappeared last week,' Crispin said evenly. 'I'm having a copy made.'

The Doctor put the cassettes back in position and slammed the drawer shut. 'Good thing, too. There's no point in having a collection if there's something missing, is there?'

Crispin frowned.

Something else had caught the Doctor's attention. It was a closed bookcase that was lit internally with a soft blue light. Inside was a dusty heap of books. He squinted to make out the titles along the fraying spines. '*The Collins Guide to the Twentieth Century* . . . *One of Us, Hugo Young* . . . *The Manufacture of Consent* . . . *The Smash Hits Yearbook* . . . ' He looked up. 'The ancient records, I presume, from which your organization constructed its society?'

193

Crispin decided to change the subject. 'The other aliens, from the ship. What is your connection with them?'

The Doctor replied, 'No connection at all. I only met them the day before yesterday.'

Crispin nodded. 'I believe you. At first I suspected a plot, but you have shown yourself to be far too disorganized and flippant for that.'

'Oh, thank you,' said the Doctor, as if he had been paid a compliment.

'Now, Doctor,' said Crispin, 'the Triton T80. The laboratory is waiting. Devor is linked in. It's time you started work.'

The Doctor shuffled his feet and looked at the floor. 'What if I say I've decided I don't want to help you?'

A bleeper sounded. Crispin took a small communicator from his pocket and thumbed the answer button. 'Accept.'

'I've just spoken to Forke, Commander,' said Shrubb's voice. 'The Doctor's TARDIS is on its way. Three of the other aliens – the two women and the younger male – are also being brought in.'

'Well done,' said Crispin. 'Inform Forke that his status is to be upgraded.' He broke off the call. 'Well, Doctor. Do I have to threaten your friends to make you co-operate?'

The Doctor shook his head. 'No. You don't. But you will. So show me the laboratory.'

The Friars had promised Ernie twenty million mazumas in used sovereigns for this kill. As his car sped along the roadway after the van carrying the TARDIS he allowed himself a few moments to imagine what he could do with twenty million mazumas. First off, he'd buy a planet for a new home, one of the luxury Grade Sixes on the fringes of the Seventh Quadrant. Half a million purchase price, then another million to atmosphorm it just right. Polar caps, one scenic to impress guests, sloping and wooded for skiing, and the other he could use to keep cold things in. You can never have too big a fridge, he decided. A wide equatorial belt with purply green sky and matching sunsets. And of course a continent composed entirely of tunnels and caves where he could set up home. Stock it up with lots of the latest videocomp gadgets to impress his mates and the ladies. It would be grand.

His day-dreams were interrupted by a series of high-pitched wailing noises. A few dingy police vehicles were gaining on him from behind. The nearest came so close he was forced to avoid it by swerving onto the hard shoulder. The van disappeared behind an overtaking lorry.

Furious, Ernie wound his window down, extended the leg carrying his imploding-slug gun and fired at the police vehicles as they drew up. They collapsed in on themselves with a squelching sound, leaving behind sticky, smoking black patches of metal, plastic and flesh.

Ernie drove off again, imploding a couple of the vehicles in front of him and driving over the remains of their owners. He saw the van turn off down a road sign-posted as leading to the harbour.

He put on an extra turn of speed, zooming around the twists and turns of the road as it snaked down to the waiting grey sea. The sports car rattled up and down. 'I knew that suspension needed seeing to,' Ernie growled as his head and upper legs bumped against the ceiling.

The abandoned docks came into view. The few vehicles that were moored there were decrepit. He guessed that this area was used mainly by black marketeers.

The TARDIS was being loaded off the van by a scurrying team of black-uniformed guards. Ernie took another look at the alien structure. He knew that it was supposed to be a time-space capsule, but it looked like nothing more than an old wooden hut. He couldn't risk destroying it by opening fire. He watched as it was carried over to one of two vehicles that appeared to be underwater skimmers of advanced design. The skimmers were only large enough to contain a two-man crew, but their engines were enormous, clinging to their mottled orange and green sides. Their hulls were decorated with the symbol of a silver apple.

As soon as the TARDIS was lowered inside, the hatch

195

on the top of the first skimmer slid shut and it submerged itself. With an eruption of bubbles it careered off.

Ernie glanced down at the red pyramid and smiled. The chase was not over yet. He flicked open the glove compartment of his car and a small control unit popped out with a bleep. On it were four buttons. Each was marked with a different symbol. Ernie selected the one marked with an elegantly depicted fish.

The windows of the car closed instantly and fins sprouted from its side. The radio aerial retracted. Ernie flicked on the detector shield.

The mouths of the guards at the harbour dropped open in astonishment as the red sports car flew into the water after the skimmer carrying the TARDIS.

Bernice, Ace and Forgwyn had been pushed into the back of a van that was now being driven very fast in the direction the TARDIS had been taken. Two sullen guards sat with them, dart guns poised.

Ace broke the uncomfortable silence. 'A spider with a Yorkshire accent. I've seen everything now.'

'Not necessarily Yorkshire,' Bernice remarked. 'Variations in localized atmospheric pressure can create similar speech patterns in locations galaxies apart. Take the Doctor. When I – '

One of the guards nudged her. 'Silence!'

Ace shrugged. 'Shirty,' she said. Bernice burst into giggles. The guard pointed the tip of his dart gun in her direction. 'I said silence!'

Bernice sat back. She was unsettled by their situation and to comfort herself she took Forgwyn's hand. He looked at her in surprise. 'Don't worry, I haven't got designs on you. Besides, I wouldn't be so obvious. I just need somebody nice to grip.'

Forgwyn said, 'I've been in messes like this before. Kidnaps and that sort of thing. Meredith's usually about to get me out.'

'Not much chance of that,' said Ace. 'She'll be flat on her back cooing at the sproglet.'

The van swerved suddenly. Gunfire rattled outside. A window smashed. A man cried out. Pungent ozone was released into the atmosphere. The van veered crazily for a few seconds and juddered to a halt.

One of the guards in the back kicked the rear doors open and jumped out. He was shot down instantly in the street outside.

Meredith appeared, blaster raised. The remaining guard lunged for Ace, intending to use her as a hostage or a shield. He had barely moved when Meredith killed him, the blaster bolt taking him in the heart.

Meredith smiled and nodded. 'Forgy!' she exclaimed. 'I thought you might be around here somewhere. Tell me what you've been up to.'

'Mum, you're so embarrassing,' said her son. 'Can't you ever take a rest?'

'Well, I'm glad she hasn't,' said Ace, jumping from the van and clapping Meredith on the back. 'That shot . . .' She shook her head and whistled.

'I surprised myself,' Meredith admitted. She pointed to the nearby dock area and the bodies of the men lying around it. 'I'm getting too old for this.'

'I know how you feel,' Ace said, grinning.

Meredith smiled without humour. 'Do you?'

Bernice jumped down from the van. 'Come on, the TARDIS.'

Ace kicked her in the shin and swore. Forgwyn sighed. 'Whoopsy,' said Bernice.

Meredith's face registered confusion and then sudden understanding. 'The TARDIS is yours,' she thought aloud slowly. 'Which means that the Doctor is the Time Lord. The hit. The kill.' Her gun arm dropped and she shook her head. Her handsome face took on the appearance of a much older woman.

She reached over and ruffled her son's hair. 'Oh, Forgy, what have I got us into this time?'

He rested his head on her shoulder. 'Another thing. Eight-legged Ernie's here on the same job.'

She bristled. 'Competition. Well, he can take the job.'

She weighed the gun in her hand. 'I can't kill the man who saved my life and the life of my child.'

Forgwyn flung his arms around her. 'You understand why I couldn't tell you; I couldn't take the chance.' His eyes reddened slightly. 'Not after what happened to Saen's parents.'

'Of course I understand,' she said gently. 'But things are different this time. Now, where's the Doctor? I want to thank him.'

'He's wherever the TARDIS went,' said Ace. 'It was being driven here.'

Meredith fumbled in the waistband of her body armour and brought out the glowing red pyramid. The light inside flickered as she angled it towards the sea.

'A TARDIS detector,' Bernice observed. 'I'd like to take a look at that later. I'm fond of crystals.'

Ace shook her head. 'I wouldn't,' she said. 'So long as it works it's fine by me.' She examined the vehicles lined up along the dockside. One of them was different to the others. It was camouflaged orange and green and bore the symbol of Luminus. The two-man crew lay over the docking hatch where Meredith's blaster bolts had found them.

'That looks like my kind of conveyance,' she said. 'Who's coming for a dip?'

14

The Hours

Crispin sat in his television chair. The midday news was being transmitted. The final midday news. He increased the volume and closed his eyes.

Concern is mounting for the three pot-holers missing since the weekend in the rad pits of the East Side ... Trade and Industry manager Joan Cale has welcomed this month's seasonally adjusted production and export figures cautiously ... tributes are flooding in from the world of entertainment following the sudden death of comedian Triss Laughline ... in the central zones, Tragedy Day celebrations are in full swing, with only five hours to go before the parade reaches Lerthin Square ... '

Five hours, thought Crispin. Five hours until the moment of total control. When all of those lives become mine. And all this before his thirteenth birthday. It was a good start.

He took another look around the chamber. He was surrounded by his favourite things. His books and videos and computers and viewing unit made him feel safe and secure. In one corner was his personal computer, the one he had used to take over Luminus. His predecessors had been rather lax, leaving themselves wide open like that. All it had taken to assume control of their entire computer net had been a slalom through four thousand shifting protection programs. He had held their organization to ransom, threatening to send a destructive pulse through their command circuits unless he was made leader. While they debated his ultimatum, Crispin had read through their files and decided that he wanted in.

In his first three months as Supreme One, he had improved the efficiency of the Olleril operation by fifteen per cent. The leaders of Luminus were pleased and arranged a meeting. Their shock at his identity hadn't lasted long; Crispin had destroyed them and taken over the *Gargantuan* within hours. He then hid away, surrounding himself with pigheaded guards. Shrubb was one of the few other adults who had seen him and lived, and he was easy enough to keep under control.

Shrubb entered the sanctum without knocking, a presumption that Crispin found annoying. 'Commander,' he blurted breathlessly, 'I've just heard from Forke on the mainland. The Doctor's friends have escaped.'

'Five hours,' Crispin whispered. His oddly shaped head, pale face and glasses appeared stranger than ever in the blue light from the screens. 'In five hours, what will it matter? They will become part of the psychotronic net along with all the other inferior citizens. We can deal with them at our leisure. They will be our playthings.'

Shrubb shuffled uneasily. 'There are complications, Supreme One. They've stolen one of the skimsubs from the docks.'

Crispin raised an eyebrow and smiled an unpleasant smile. 'Then they are coming here anyway. Guide it in on remote.'

'I've already given that order, Commander. A squad of guards has been posted at the entry hatches.'

Crispin stood up. 'Well done. Now, let us visit the Doctor and see how his work is coming along. The component must be completed before five.'

Shrubb frowned. 'Why don't you fit the Doctor with an immunizer and allow him more time?' He felt for his own immunizer on the back of his neck.

'I regret,' Crispin explained, 'that the generator will have to be inactive when the device is fitted. There is no other way.'

He stopped at the door of the sanctum. 'And when the signal is sent, I want the Doctor to be as helpless as the rest. He will then admit us to his TARDIS. And a new age of Luminus can begin.'

'Let's take a look at the totalizer!' shrieked Wendy Clifton. The crowds in the square cheered themselves heartily as the neon board displayed a figure of two hundred and thirty-five million credots.

Wendy smiled, put her microphone between her hands, and clapped the audience. 'And we're still only just over halfway through the day!' she continued. 'Let's remind ourselves, shall we, of one of the many causes that the money that you're pledging is going to. Earlier this week, Robert and I visited the refugee camp on the South Side of the city. And I can tell you, it's not a very nice place. Let's see what we saw there. Coming up now. Here it is.'

She turned her head to the large screen above the stage and watched as the recorded insert was shown. 'Here we have, er, Frinna,' said Robert as a Vijjan was brought forward, 'one of the many sultry young Vijjan girls . . .'

Tragedy Day continued.

The Doctor's jacket was folded neatly over the back of one the many uncomfortable metal chairs in the laboratory. He was sat at a bench nearby, working on the construction of the Triton T80, an eyeglass in his left eye, a screwdriver in his right hand. His deeply lined features were bathed in the eerie green glow that came from the bubbling Slaag fermentation tank. The bench was covered in components that had been brought up from the *Gargantuan's* technical stores. A cheese sandwich sat untouched on one corner. The Doctor had demanded it, mostly to inconvenience his captors, and promptly forgotten it as he set to work.

The thin figure of Gortlock hovered about, his path taking him occasionally over to where the Doctor was working. He looked closely at the complex maze of circuitry that was being formed.

Without moving, the Doctor said, 'You would make a very bad store detective.'

Gortlock stiffened. 'I have been instructed by the Supreme One to observe you in your work.'

The Doctor popped the eyeglass from his eye and caught it in his free hand. 'Afraid I might try something, eh? Throw a spanner in the works?'

'We have no reason to trust you.'

'I'd say you've no reason to trust anybody. Least of all the Supreme One.' He fixed Gortlock with a stare that made the scientist's legs wobble. 'A child. No more than a child. Is it any wonder that he hid himself from the rank and file?'

'I have complete faith in the Supreme One,' Gortlock said.

The Doctor leant forward. 'You fear him. That is something very different.'

Gortlock turned away. 'I am a devotee of the cause of Luminus,' he said, as if repeating a ceremonial oath. 'May the red glass curse my soul if I disobey.' He walked off.

The Doctor grinned and popped the eyeglass back in. Then he popped it out again and his brow creased over.

May the red glass curse my soul.

He stood up and sat down again, nibbled anxiously at the sandwich and stared into nothingness for several seconds. He remembered the inscription at the base of the statue and the poster in Shrubb's daughter's room.

May the red glass curse my soul.

It felt, he thought, rather as if a clean, crisp white page of his memory was filling up with bold black words. Line after line slotted in. He saw once more the lively, intelligent faces of the villagers and the valley that made their homes so strong against the elements. He heard himself say, *No, thank you. I have a pipe of my own.*

'Of course,' he muttered to himself, 'I should have realized. This planet. The red glass. The curse. What can it all mean to them, I wonder?'

His ruminations were interrupted by the arrival of Crispin and Shrubb. The Doctor returned his concerns regarding the red glass to the back of his mind and greeted them brightly. 'Good afternoon, gentlemen. You'll be pleased to hear that the Triton T80 will be complete in another couple of hours. And then,' he added inflammatorily, 'you can act out your fantasy as you wish.'

As the Doctor had expected, Shrubb's face flushed. 'An hour under the vibrometer will cure your impudence!' he threatened. A pulse throbbed rapidly over his bloodshot left eye.

The Doctor shrugged. 'Whenever you're ready.' He gestured over his shoulder to the glowing tank. 'I'm finding it difficult to concentrate as it is with those things glaring at me.'

Crispin walked over casually and tapped the thick plasti-glass of the tank. The beasts within reacted to the vibration and swarmed over, rows of viciously sharp teeth snapping obscenely between lipless mouths.

'They're blind, Doctor,' Crispin explained. 'They react to movement. So you needn't worry about them looking at you.' As he spoke the creatures, enraged by the thwarted prospect of a likely snack, started to rip at each other's flesh. The bright green suspension fluid was stained by squirting gouts of purple blood.

'Oh dear,' Crispin said. He picked up the Doctor's cheese sandwich from the desk and inserted it, engraved china plate and all, through a small opening in the wall next to the tank. He pressed an adjacent button and a shutter slid over the opening. A clunk came from the machinery inside and the sandwich and plate floated into the nutrient juices. Both were devoured frenziedly in seconds.

Realizing that he was supposed to be impressed and alarmed, which in truth he was, the Doctor observed facetiously, 'An innocent sandwich. It didn't stand a chance.'

Crispin decided to ignore the remark. He waved a hand airily. 'The Slaags are a weapon, Doctor. The ultimate living weapon. I built them from genotypes I found in two species from the Agrave hinterlands; the Sline lizard, the Aaglon shark. Hence Slaag. The results of their clearance of the island of Avax, as witnessed and so nearly experienced by your friend Ace, suggest that they would be capable of eating their way through an area the size of Empire City, should I ever find it necessary, in under two days.'

The Doctor frowned. 'They are twisted abominations,' he said, his voice betraying his anger at this abuse of science. A scraping sound came from the tank as the Slaags struggled for possession of the last scrap of the plate. One of them was ripped apart by the others. As its body slid horribly down the Doctor glimpsed a tiny yellow brain and inflated digestive organs wrapped in tight grey coils of inflamed intestine. 'What have you created?'

'They hunger, Doctor,' said Crispin. His watery green eyes remained unmoved as the Slaags tore frenziedly at the remains of their dead brother. 'They exist to eat. As soon as they eat they begin to excrete. They can never be satisfied.'

'Monstrous,' the Doctor muttered. His face crumpled with compassion. 'Living creatures . . .'

'For a man of science, Doctor, you talk like a sentimental fool,' Shrubb said melodramatically and unhelpfully. He walked over to a nearby cold storage unit that looked uncannily like a household freezer and removed a large joint of animal. He sent it into the tank, the shutter slicing it neatly through. The Slaags abandoned the body of their own kind and sank their teeth eagerly into its fatty texture.

'As you can see, they prefer meat,' Crispin pointed out. 'Now, Doctor, return to your work. And do not attempt sabotage or delay. I know of your ways.'

The Doctor's curiosity was aroused by this statement. He was not often recognized. 'You do?'

Shrubb grinned arrogantly. 'Luminus is aware of all things.'

For the first time, the Doctor noted a grain of impatience in Crispin's treatment of his second. 'Please,' he admonished Shrubb, and returned his attention to the Doctor, unable to resist the chance to gloat.

'Our computer records miss very little, Doctor. And Luminus is a very big organization. Your presence has been noted on several previous occasions, interfering in the affairs of our sister worlds.'

'Really?' said the Doctor.

'For example,' continued Crispin, 'the planet Argos.'

The Doctor nodded grimly, recalling the details of the experience. 'Where I averted a catalogue of disasters, yes,' he said. 'But Argos is three or four galaxies away. And those events happened, what, centuries ago.'

Crispin nodded and said, 'As I said, ours is a very big organization, Doctor. I control only this branch. How many planets have you travelled to, I wonder? Over what unimaginable lengths of time?' He clasped his hands together over his chest and said, 'And on how many occasions, as you blundered around on your wayward missions of mercy, have you really been dancing to our tune?'

The Doctor held his gaze for a long moment, digesting the implications of the suggestion. Then he said, 'Claptrap. Absolute claptrap. Half-baked psychological trickery may spellbind uptight fools like him,' he indicated Shrubb, 'but you'll have to do better than that if you want to impress me.

'Besides,' he cried suddenly, arms flinging wide at the stacks of equipment and the rows of experiments around him, his temper running ahead of him again, 'what is this all for? This control of yours. Why bother? Why not leave people alone, let them sort themselves out? What is the final point of all this power?'

Shrubb answered, again, the Doctor thought, rather like a schoolboy repeating a passage from an exercise book. 'We are born diseased. Where there is light, there is dark. Where there is goodness, there is evil. Where there is purity, there must also be a dark and wanton side. The majority, the mass of the human race must be kept in check, Doctor. There must be discipline if civilization is to survive. The alternative is anarchy, chaos, disorder. There must be a hierarchy. There must be an elite. There must be control.'

Crispin stood beside him, smiling sweetly. 'There you

have it,' he said. 'Simply put, but there's nothing there I particularly disagree with.'

'I bet you don't,' said the Doctor. He decided to discover some more while they were in the mood for explanations. 'And what of this red glass I've heard about? Is it some sort of symbol?'

Shrubb evidently enjoyed repeating the edicts of the imperial past. His mouth opened wide, revealing an unhealthy-looking grey tongue. 'The red glass cursed the disorder of the old Ollerines. They passed it to a stranger and believed themselves saved, but the might of Luminus crushed them. The red glass cursed this world and its people.' His voice grew ever louder, until the Doctor felt rather like a private on a parade ground. 'The red glass is the symbol of the enslavement to duty that each man must endure!'

'And what,' asked the Doctor, trying perhaps too hard to sound casual, 'if it should return?'

'It will not return while we control,' Shrubb chanted sternly.

'Indeed,' said Crispin quietly. 'These superstitions are, of course, not admissible to a rationalist such as myself. But we have made sure that the citizens are familiar with them. It increases their doubt, and doubt makes them good followers. There will always be leaders and followers. And I know which of the two I prefer being.'

He left the laboratory. Shrubb, his face now completely red, followed him out. He wiped flecks of saliva from his chin with an embroidered handkerchief.

The Doctor sighed. He had encountered many species in his centuries of travelling, but none levelled his spirits more than human beings with attitudes like that. Pushing the thought aside, he returned his attention to the component.

'Control, yes,' he murmured. 'But how much control?'

The sleek red shape of Ernie's vehicle slid gracefully through the depths of the ocean, surprising the variety of unusually shaped species that flourished there. A shoal of glowing fish scattered as the meteorite-scarred fins zoomed by on a trail that was leading deeper and deeper down.

Inside, Ernie checked his wing-mirror sensors. His instincts were again proved correct. There was another craft behind him, and it appeared to be identical to the skimmer in front. Whatever its origin it wouldn't have seen him, anyway, what with his detector shield up. He wondered whether to slow down, hide behind a large rock and then blast it as it came by. But that would delay his progress and the pursuit of the TARDIS was more important.

The pressure gauge informed him that he was now almost at the bottom of the ocean. The upper layers of pollution had faded along with the light. His headlamps showed the life of the sea bed; daintily waving fronds of bright yellow and green; fat-headed fish with wide saucer bodies and rheumy eyes; clumps of sparkling weed that clung to the windscreen as he drove through them.

'Ee, it's a spooked old planet, is this one,' he observed to himself. The glow from the red pyramid flared for a moment as if in agreement.

The dashboard computer pinged repeatedly. Ernie fumbled for the readout display switch, anxious to find out anything his vehicle's in-built intelligence desired to share with him.

The autosystems took over for a second, allowing Ernie to relax his grip on the wheel. He shook his legs to relieve the accumulated tension of the last few hours and watched as the windscreen clouded over with computerized displays. Thin white lines of animation snaked together to map out the oncoming terrain. His own position was marked on the display as a small blue blip at the foot of a winding gorge that led between a range of undersea mountains. Just ahead of him was the skimmer carrying the TARDIS; just behind him was its sister ship. And on the other side of the range was something that Ernie described to himself in indelicate terms as, 'A bloody great whopper. Will you look at the size of that. Roger me sideways and call me Mary . . .'

He shook his hairy head and gave a low whistle of admiration. Then he checked the display once more. The path he was following was leading him directly to the thing, whatever it was. And whatever the thing was, it was about two miles wide. Which was indeed big.

Ernie prepared himself to board and crossed his legs for good luck. He'd never been very good at three-point turns.

The hands of the intricately carved metal clock that dominated the buildings around Lerthin Square crept round to one and a single chime sounded loudly. On any other day the chime would have been heard as far as the financial sector. But today was Tragedy Day, and in addition to the cheers and cries of jubilation generated by the crowds, Fancy That had just taken to the stage.

'Hey,' mimed Markus as the other boys danced energetically behind him, 'you'll take everything I have, my soul, my pride, my dignity . . .'

The giant skull that towered above him seemed to nod its paper head mournfully in time to the bass-enhanced beat.

'Is the baby going to be all right?' Forgwyn asked his mother as the skimsub they had stolen raced through the ocean.

She pushed a strand of hair from her face and sighed. 'They'll look after him,' she said guiltily, 'at the hospital. They're good people.'

Forgwyn nodded uneasily and looked over to the other side of the cramped vehicle, where Ace and Benny were hunched over the auto-nav controls. 'Any luck?' he called.

Bernice looked up. 'Not so far. The overrides are there, we think, they'd have to be, but the locking equipment is fiendishly clever.' She stood up and dusted her hands down. 'Too clever for me, anyway.'

'So we're going where they want us,' Meredith observed. 'We might as well have surrendered.'

Ace's voice came from the mass of circuitry she had stuck her head into. 'If I can break this last defence code we'll be free, don't worry.'

'Free to go where they want us,' Forgwyn said.

'Yes, but at least we'll be doing it ourselves,' said Bernice, 'which will do wonders for my battered ego. What a day. Captured, escaped, captured again, escaped again. I should have stayed in bed, I was having a really good dream about fudge cake and the collapse of Roman imperialism.'

Forgwyn guessed that she was trying to keep his spirits up. He smiled for her benefit and thought, *Wow, what a woman.*

'I don't like this,' he confessed. 'I thought I could handle most situations, but this . . .'

Bernice nodded. 'We're out of our depth.'

Meredith had joined Ace at the controls of the craft. 'There's something registering on the sonar,' she said worriedly.

'Yeah, don't worry, it's just the skimmer we're following,' Ace called up reassuringly.

'No, it's a separate trace,' Meredith insisted. 'It's huge.'

Ace popped her head up and the others hurried over to the sonar screen. The readings confirmed Meredith's diagnosis. The object that they were being led towards was enormous.

'Perhaps it's some kind of marine creature,' Forgwyn suggested.

'If it is,' said Bernice, 'we're about to find out what it feels like to be a maggot on the end of a hook.' She smote herself across the forehead. 'I can't believe I just said that.'

The Doctor's hands worked almost of their own accord on the construction of the Triton T80 as his mind sifted fruitlessly through its cobwebbed recesses for memories of his previous visit to Olleril. Only fragments remained accessible. He realized that he had edited out the rest, although there was just a chance he might have jotted something down in one of his old Time Logs. He needed to get back to the TARDIS to check, and there was little likelihood of that in the regrettable circumstances he found himself in at present. And then there was the matter of the red glass itself. He was fairly certain that he hadn't destroyed it or thrown it away; in fact he had vague recollections of submitting it to tests. But he had no recall of the results or of its current whereabouts in the dusty labyrinth of his time-space craft.

What was it exactly? What was the nature of its power? Where did it originate? Had all the problems that had befallen the planet since his last visit been a result of its malefic influence?

He pushed the questions aside and continued working.

The mouth of the creature lowered slowly and the first skimsub slid into its gullet. Ernie, watching from a safe distance, marvelled at its enormous size. Its ghastly glowing eyes and upright fins gave it a look of startled ferocity. Of course it could not be a real marine beast. He checked his sensors and confirmed his suspicions. The thing was a cunningly camouflaged submarine of advanced design. Life readings indicated a crew of at least a thousand humans.

The mouth was already swinging shut. Ernie revved his motor and drove forward at full speed. Darkness engulfed the car as it passed over the lips. A sensor check revealed that he was being sucked through in the wake of the skimsub towards a metal tank of prodigious proportions. It was inevitable that he would be noticed soon. He checked his weapons individually and prepared himself. Smash and grab, he decided, was the best policy in this instance.

It was two o'clock. The parade marched through the streets of Zone Three, whistles blowing and banners flying. Small children were lifted up onto the shoulders of their parents. They wondered about the old people who were standing on street corners, shouting and stamping angrily at the fun-lovers. Who were they? Their parents answered that they were grey-haired spoil-sports with wrong-headed, funny old ideas that everyone knew were silly and outdated. The children nodded because they knew it was important to agree.

Bernice covered her face with her hands. 'Tell me I didn't really see that.'

The others remained silent for several moments, reacting in their individual ways to the sight of the monster that lay waiting for them on the other side of the mountains. ''Fraid you did,' Ace said quietly.

'We're heading straight for it,' Forgwyn observed.

Bernice looked up. 'The Doctor has to be somewhere aboard. That's something.'

Ace opened a locker above the control deck and pulled down three rifles of the type used by the Luminun guards. She tossed one each to Bernice and Forgwyn and then appraised her own. 'Mezon mini-cartridges. About fifty rounds in there, I reckon.' She looked at Forgwyn. 'See, I can be useful.'

He put the weapon down. 'I don't know how to use them and I don't intend to start learning now.'

'I think he's right,' said Bernice. 'They'll probably throw us in the same cell as the Doctor. Why not let them?'

Meredith answered for Ace. 'You're assuming too much. They may want us in there to take us to pieces for all you know.' She held up her own blaster. 'I'll lead. I'm the best shot, this is our best gun. It saw me fine on Margatrox against the Fuzis.'

Ace nodded eagerly. 'Recharging, isn't it?'

Bernice let her head drop. Forgwyn patted her shoulder gently. 'Let them get on with it,' he suggested. 'I know what my mother's like when she gets started.'

The first skimsub and Ernie's car passed slowly through the mouth of the *Gargantuan*, magnetic beams pulling

211

them toward one of a series of large tanks. As soon as both were inside a door clanged shut behind them automatically. A mechanism moved and the water inside the tank began to gurgle noisily away.

The moment after the last of the water had drained away, Ernie sprang from his car, weapons raised. He scuttled over to the skimsub. The hatch was already being pushed open from inside. The face of the first crewmember registered terror and alarm. Ernie blasted him away. His colleague appeared and Ernie dealt with him similarly.

Ernie chuckled and crawled over eagerly to his prize, the waiting TARDIS. He put the first of his legs on the lowest rung of the ladder leading to the entry hatch.

Shots rang out from above. Ernie flung himself flat on the floor and peeped up under the brim of his hat. More guards were running onto a balcony that ringed the tank and firing indiscriminately down. Despite the swiftness of his reactions, one of the shots had caught Ernie in the thorax. He twisted himself about to assess the damage. Fortunately he had suffered only a flesh wound. Black blood dripped from the injury.

The guards started to climb down the stairway from the balcony. Ernie considered his options. Injured, he could not take them all. Nearby was the mechanism through which the water had drained, a wide hole criss-crossed by a steel grid. He might just be able to squeeze through. There was a chance.

He gathered his thoughts as quickly as possible and then hurried over and through the hole. Mezon bolts buzzed about him but the guards were too late. Ernie had escaped into the pipes.

Crispin drummed the fingers of one hand impatiently on his desk. The *Martha and Arthur* impulse was about to be sent. He congratulated himself on his plan yet again. Tonight would see a return to decent, core values. Family values. He turned the word over in his mind. Family.

His overcrowded memory threw up an odd image, faded and scratchy. He was cuddled between something warm

and he felt safe and happy and protected. The warm thing
was alive. It had four arms and two heads and did everything for him. It fed him, clothed him, took him to the
toilet and taught him about all kinds of things.

He shook himself. Weak-kneed stupidity. He had to
stand on his own two feet. That was what life was all
about, helping yourself. Dependency was soft and silly
and ultimately wicked.

But the memory kept coming back. And in it, he was
laughing and the cuddling creature was laughing. And on
the TV screen in front of them was *Martha and Arthur*.

Shrubb's face appeared on a screen in the sanctum.
'Commander, another offworlder, a mutant of some kind,
has boarded the *Gargantuan*,' he reported from the entry
hatch. 'It's gone down into the pipes.'

Crispin thought for a moment. 'Has it now?' He glanced
at the other screens that displayed interior sections of the
vessel. The Doctor was still working under the unsubtle
eye of Gortlock, the Slaag tank bubbling behind him.

'Shrubb,' he said, 'it's not with the Doctor, this thing?'

'No, sir.'

'Well, we can't have it running about in the works. We
must dispose of it.'

'But, Commander,' Shrubb protested, 'the workings are
too narrow for us to traverse.'

Crispin nodded. 'Precisely. This gives me the opportunity to carry out a test I've been meaning to try for
some time.'

The Triton T80 appeared to be almost complete. Its complex innards had been covered in a grey rectangular
casing, from which two switches protruded. The Doctor
had labelled them ON and OFF in fibre-tip pen.

Gortlock could account for every one of the items the
Doctor had used in the assembly of the device, but
the scientific principles behind his combination of them
was by turns baffling and inspirational. The alien appeared
to work with almost no regard to the simplest laws of
physics and yet everything he did made sense. Gortlock's

pockets contained reams of hastily scribbled notes he had made on the Doctor's techniques. They would revolutionize the technology of Luminus.

'There you have it,' said the Doctor. 'And I hope you make good use of it.'

Gortlock picked up the device. It was surprisingly heavy. He inspected the terminal links at its base. The Doctor had aligned them perfectly for integration into the psychic-wave suppressors of the psychotronic generator. 'I will deliver it to the Supreme One personally,' he said, thinking of the honour of being present at such a crucial moment of history. He waved a guard forward to keep an eye on the Doctor and turned to leave the laboratory.

Shrubb was standing in the doorway. 'I'll take that.'

Gortlock's eyes narrowed. 'I have been on this vessel for thirteen years,' he said.

Shrubb snatched the Triton T80 from him and handed it to a guard. 'Take it to the generator with instructions for immediate installation.' The guard hurried out. Shrubb returned his disdainful attentions to Gortlock. 'I place you under arrest. Guards, take him to the brig.'

Gortlock lunged forward and grabbed Shrubb by his shirt collar. 'You haven't the authority,' he snarled. 'Who do you think – '

The protests of the scientist were silenced as Shrubb, demonstrating a high level of physical strength, punched him in the stomach, twisted his arms behind his back, kicked him in the shins and pushed him toward the Slaag tank. He wrenched one of Gortlock's hands out and forced it towards the open feeding hatch.

'No,' Gortlock pleaded, his eyes wide with terror. 'No, Shrubb, please no . . .'

Shrubb's bloated features reformed with grotesque enjoyment of the man's fear. 'You will obey me now?'

Gortlock nodded again and again. 'Yes, yes, I'll do anything, anything you say . . .'

Shrubb's grin spread wider. 'Deviant,' he spat. 'You are not fit to join the elite.'

He thrust Gortlock's clenched fist into the hatchway

and pressed the button next to it. Somehow aware of the commotion outside their plasti-glass world, the Slaags were bouncing about excitedly, jaws snapping. The Doctor struggled frantically with his guards, desperate to prevent what was about to happen.

The metal hatchway slid shut, slicing Gortlock's right hand off in a simple guillotine motion. He screamed and collapsed instantly. Shrubb laughed as the scientist was carried from the laboratory by shocked colleagues. The thin veneer of politeness and charm apparent in his earlier dealings in the city had disappeared completely. Foam trickled over his juddering lower lip. His starched white shirt was spattered with Gortlock's blood.

The Doctor cast his eyes down as the Slaags feasted on the hand, their bloated bodies bumping against the side of the tank. 'There must be control if civilization is to survive,' he commented sardonically.

Shrubb raised his fist and struck the Doctor across the face twice. 'Soft-hearted alien scum!'

'No!' boomed the voice of Crispin from above. 'Shrubb, stop this! You overreach yourself! Return to your task!'

The journalist calmed himself slowly, taking deep breaths and clenching and unclenching his fists. He pointed to the nearest scientist, one of a crowd that had gathered to observe the demise of their leader.

'You,' he ordered. 'Bring a container. We are going to remove a Slaag.'

The young scientist hurried to obey. Shrubb turned to the Doctor. 'Another test.'

The Doctor gasped for air. 'You're ... insane,' he managed to say.

'Take him to the sanctum,' Shrubb instructed.

A giant airship hovered over Empire City. Its silvery bulk rippled in the wind. The glistening black teardrop of Tragedy Day was embossed on its underside. Crowds in the central zones looked up from their revelry as it passed, and waved. The time was three o'clock.

* * *

215

The drainage process was completed and the door leading to entry hatch number fourteen of the *Gargantuan* swung open slowly. The ten guards sent by Shrubb to bring in the Doctor's companions ran through onto the balcony beyond, mezon rifles charged and raised.

Meredith and Ace burst from cover beneath the skimsub. Ace took three of the guards with the first five rounds from her weapon and then flung herself back into cover. Meredith, muttering and cursing like an old woman untangling knitting, swept the bolts from her blaster around the balcony. She anticipated every move the guards made. Their shots went wild, missing her by inches as she leapt from side to side, firing all the while. Ace observed her technique with a mixture of elation and envy.

Bernice's head popped up from the entry port of the skimsub. 'Finished?' she enquired sombrely.

Ace and Meredith were already climbing the ladder leading to the balcony. Ace called back, 'If you're coming, come on!'

Bernice turned the mezon rifle around in her hands. 'You go on,' she told Ace. 'Do what you're best at. And I'll do what I'm best at.' She watched as Ace followed Meredith from the tank.

Forgwyn appeared at her side. 'What are you best at?'

She swung her legs over the side of the skimsub and started to climb down. 'Writing treatises,' she replied, holding out a hand to help him out. 'Not much chance of doing that here so let's explore. I've never been inside a thing like this before.'

Ernie crawled along the pipes, squeezing himself through the tighter passages by holding his breath and folding his legs together. He was moving towards the loud throb of the submarine's engines. The vaguest of plans to effect some sabotage and force these underwater weirdos to give him the TARDIS was forming in his mind. It was not Ernie's style to make meticulously detailed preparations and he was feeling out of sorts as it was, with his injury slowing him down.

Perfect night vision was the asset most useful to him now. The wheels, clamps and hatchways that he slid past now and again indicated that these channels were used as part of some sort of coolant system. If they started to heat up, there were exit ports every few turnings that he could use to escape. In all, he thought, despite his earlier disappointments, he wasn't doing too badly.

A strange squeak and a rustling noise came from the darkness behind him.

Ernie stopped for a moment and trained his senses in that direction.

Silence.

He shrugged his shoulders as comfortably as he could in the enclosed space and sighed to himself. 'You're frightening yourself, you daft beggar,' he muttered. 'Probably only a loose fitting.' He moved on.

A minute later he stopped again. Something else. A pungent odour. Sort of fishy. And more of the distant scraping. Squeaking. Slobbering.

Snapping.

Ernie uncoiled his matter-imploder leg and pointed it behind him. Several of his other legs he employed to fumble with a locking wheel above him. He reasoned that it was an exit port.

He had reasoned incorrectly. The wheel clicked and scalding steam poured from the vent it had opened. Ernie convulsed and yelped. He hurried off down the pipe, blood still trickling from his wound. The steam hissed in, blinding him and disorientating his other senses.

'Ahh, McCartney,' he chided himself as he limped multiply on. 'You haven't the sense you were born with . . .'

The odd noises behind him grew louder as whatever was making them grew nearer. And whatever it was, it wasn't a loose fitting. He put on speed, turning randomly from junction to junction in an attempt to confuse his pursuer. He could hear it clearly now, its horrible clicking and squeaking only a few metres behind him. He ran along pipes, up pipes, down pipes, through choking clouds of boiling steam. Whichever way he turned it followed him, keeping to his path as if it knew where he was going before he did.

An acute pain shot through Ernie's abdomen as he collided with a spike-ended lever that dangled unsafely from the locking mechanism it had been attached to. He screamed. He felt his precious life juices gushing out of him and let his head fall back, prepared for death. His dreams of wealth returned. He bit his tongue with the pain. To be so close . . .

No. He might be dead but he wasn't going alone. He would take this smelly rotten beast with him, along with as much of the submarine as he could. He dragged one of his legs from beneath his shattered body and aimed the matter imploder back down the pipe.

The creature was on him before he could fire, bouncing out of the hissing blackness, its mouth open wide. It crunched the matter imploder and the leg that was holding it off with its first bite. Ernie lost consciousness.

The Slaag found the eight-legged assassin extremely tasty. There was an abundance of thick blood and hairy flesh in the snack, and the crunchy metal of the weapons made for an excellent contrast of flavours. Perhaps some of the internal organs were slightly tart for the Slaag's personal taste, but after all, meat was meat.

A couple of minutes later, the Slaag heard the signal calling it back to the tank for some more food. It jumped back hungrily, spreading what had been Ernie McCartney over the pipes as it went.

The locking wheel Ernie had tampered with was the first of a series that maintained the structure of the sub's mid-section. His interference had weakened the structure slightly.

Crispin ran his hand over the battered blue box. He felt the humming vibration of the latent energies contained within and shivered in anticipation.

The door of the sanctum slid open and the Doctor was brought in. His face lit up at the sight of the TARDIS. 'Ah. My property, I think.'

'Not any longer, Doctor,' said Crispin quietly. He crossed over to a control console and pressed a sequence of switches. A thin green funnel of laser light spun itself around the police box. The swirling vortex emitted a piercing screech.

'A simple protective force-fence,' Crispin explained. 'In case you had any notion of escaping.'

The Doctor spread his arms wide and donned an outraged expression, as if to say *Who, me?*

His opponent poured two glasses of orange squash, diluted them and handed him one. 'We have things to discuss,' he said in a businesslike manner. He glanced at his watch. 'In an hour and ten minutes, Doctor, the psychotronic generator will begin transmission of the *Martha and Arthur* impulse. Without an immunizer, you will be as helpless to resist as the other inferiors.'

'Er, yes, it had occurred to me,' the Doctor said, sipping at his squash.

'Your mind,' Crispin went on, 'will be open to me. You may resist at first, but you cannot shield yourself forever. I will pluck the secrets of the TARDIS from your defence-less psyche. Your personality will become that of an insensible drone. Your abilities will become just another available resource.'

He sat in his television chair and started to swivel slightly from side to side. 'I can offer you an alternative.'

The Doctor snorted. 'Some sort of partnership, I presume?' He shook his head. 'Domination isn't to my taste, I'm afraid to say.'

Crispin drained his squash and set the empty glass on the top of the console. He sighed. 'I thought you might say something like that,' he said. 'Remember, I offered.'

'Oh, I'll remember,' the Doctor said affably. He turned to the door. 'Er, can I go now?'

'No,' the boy replied. 'I want you to be here when the impulse is sent and the Third Great Age of Luminus begins.'

'Stuff your Great Age, I need a rest,' the Doctor said rudely.

Crispin stood. A gleam glass entered his eyes. 'Your wanderings brought the TARDIS to me, Doctor,' he began. 'It is my destiny to control it. I shall sweep through the millennia, through the galaxies.' His breaking voice switched from high to low pitch and back again as his mania increased.

'I shall bring control to thousands of worlds. With the Stupidity Factor, I shall create armies of Celebroids in my image. They shall construct more Celebroids, more TARDISes. The empire of Crispin will expand until the entire universe is in my thrall! *Ecce iterum Crispinus*!'

There was an uncomfortable silence in the sanctum but for the throb of the *Gargantuan's* engines and the whine of the force-fence. The Doctor thought he had better do something to break it. 'I can list several hundred practical reasons for not attempting to do that,' he said.

Crispin looked down at him and started to laugh. His laugh was a high girlish snigger. 'You sad, predictable old fool, Doctor,' he said, 'flying around in your pathetic box. What a pitiful existence you have led. Who really cares whether you live or die but me?'

The Doctor had had very few dealings with children in his long life, but some aspects of the undeveloped personality he had seen many times in people much older than Crispin. Petty spite was one of them. He decided to address it on its own terms. 'Who cares about you, you mean?' he said, smirking. 'I bet I've got more friends than you have. What do you do all day except sit in here with only the goggle box for company. It's no wonder nobody likes you.'

Crispin's face was red. The Doctor was certain he saw tears glistening in the boy's eyes. He had to continue if he wanted to save the planet. 'You're a failure, Crispin, underneath it all,' he goaded. 'A failure as a human being.'

The sanctum door opened and Shrubb strode in. The Doctor cursed his bad luck as the moment was lost. Crispin had closed his eyes and was taking deep breaths.

'Commander, good news,' Shrubb began.

Crispin held up a hand. He continued to breathe deeply

for a few moments and then opened his eyes. His supercilious aura had returned intact. 'Yes?'

Shrubb smirked. 'The Slaag has returned from the pipes, Supreme One,' he reported. 'The mutant is dead.'

He glanced at the Doctor. 'Shall I take him to the vibrometer?'

Crispin shook his head and said. 'Oh no. He must witness our triumph.'

At four o'clock it was one of the traditions of Tragedy Day for the Father Family to pass by Lerthin Square. They were the descendants of the first civilian colonists on Olleril. In more auspicious times they had been accustomed to travelling the streets of the city in horse-drawn carriages. Now they cycled sadly by on folding bikes, recognized only by a handful of flag-waving enthusiasts.

Bernice and Forgwyn walked nonchalantly through the throbbing, humming corridors of the submarine. Their presence was unremarked upon by the uniformed members of personnel who hurried past on official-looking matters, as if they were too engrossed in important business to concern themselves with anything outside it.

'You'd think somebody would have tumbled us by now,' said Forgwyn.

Bernice shook her head. 'They have complete confidence in their security, I think.' She pulled Forgwyn into a corner as a man came into view ahead. He was carrying a clipboard.

'What's the matter?' Forgwyn whispered.

'Nothing,' she replied. 'But we need to find out more about what's going on. I want them to notice me. I've a theory and it needs testing.'

She stepped from cover and extended a friendly hand. The approaching man stopped and looked at her, very confused.

'You're . . .' he stammered. 'You're a woman.'

Bernice looked herself up and down. 'Yes, you're right, I am.' She smiled at Forgwyn. 'Theory confirmed.'

The man started to back over to a communicator panel affixed to a nearby wall. Bernice stalked him slowly, a sardonic smile playing across her lips.

'Women are not permitted aboard this vessel,' the man continued. 'I must report this to Security.' He reached for the call button.

Bernice caught him on the jaw with her best right hook. He slumped against the wall. The clipboard fell from his grasp. Bernice dusted her hands down, picked up the clipboard and tossed it to Forgwyn. 'Well?'

He flicked through the printout paper. 'Production estimates,' he read out. 'Projected figures for industrial sector, Frestan States. Report on the commission on the extraction of sunbeams from cucumbers. Increasing the infant mortality rate in Vijja.' He nodded. 'Looks like they do control everything. Science, politics, wars, everything. Super fascists. Or super communists. Or super anarchists.'

'I think "mad bastards" sums them up quite nicely,' said Bernice. She bit her lip and tried to cool her temper.

The sound of running booted feet came from further along the corridor. Two passing guards had noticed the supine figure of the unfortunate technician and had raised their mezon rifles in the direction of the intruders.

Another Luminun technician was caught by the blasts from Meredith's blaster. He fell forwards, blood trickling from his mouth. Behind him was revealed a glowing map of the *Gargantuan*.

Ace stepped nimbly over the body and scanned the diagram. She pointed to a red spot marked on the lower levels of the huge craft. 'That's us,' she said. 'And that's the control, something called the sanctum.' She traced the route between the two points.

Meredith blasted down more guards who had come running up to investigate. The men were knocked backwards along the corridor, holes punctured in their chests. 'Hurry it, girl,' Meredith urged Ace.

'It's this way,' the younger woman replied. She pointed

to a lift, the doors of which were sliding open. Meredith fired again, killing the three occupants.

Ace followed her inside and the door slid shut. As the lift moved slowly up the shaft, she looked across at Meredith. Her craggy, embittered features looked wearier than ever. Her eyes were alert but somehow blank at the same time. The joints on the hand gripping the blaster were white.

'Today's nothing,' she stated, obviously aware of Ace's unspoken thoughts. 'I killed fifty-nine in two hours on Phlanji. Walked into a building at nine. Walked out of it at eleven. Bought Forgwyn a new buggy and some toys with the proceeds.'

In her years as a soldier, and during her travels with the Doctor, Ace had seen many examples of combat psychosis. She had learnt to identify the signs in herself, and, she hoped, suppress them. What worried her about Meredith was that, unlike those battle-scarred veterans, she was tired but still completely in control.

She looked down at the surprised, dead faces of the men Meredith had just killed. None of them had been armed.

Lerthin Square resounded to the clamour of the crowds as they welcomed the front of the parade, which was led by an authentic Frestan brass band, shiny slides pomping in and out. The totalizer updated itself in a grand flurry of figures. People jumped and whooped and kissed each other. Even the rain that began to patter on their heads didn't matter to them. It was good to be alive.

Wendy Clifton moved to the front of the stage. She dabbed at her eyes as if tears were forming there, which of course they weren't, and said falteringly, 'Well, it's nearly five o'clock, and we've already gone over our target of four hundred million credots . . .'

The Doctor ran over to Bernice as she and Forgwyn were brought into the sanctum. They hugged each other and he ruffled her hair. 'Benny, I thought they might have harmed you,' he said, his face crumpled with relief.

'It's all right,' she said brightly. 'Don't worry, I'm fine.' She stared at him quizzically. 'You are you, aren't you?'

He grinned and tugged at his hair. 'Yes, I know I am.'

Forgwyn was staring incredulously at Crispin, who was watching the reunion from his television chair. 'Who are you?' was the only thing he could think of to say.

The Doctor stepped forward. 'Bernice, Forgwyn,' he said, 'allow me to introduce the Supreme One of Luminus.'

Crispin nodded sagely.

Bernice laughed. 'You are joking.'

Shrubb growled. 'Show respect for your new master!'

Bernice laughed again. 'You're not joking, are you?' She cast her eyes to the carpeted floor and whispered, 'Oh my God.'

There was a strange silence in the sanctum. Bernice became aware of a large digital display on one of the many screens behind Crispin. It was ticking down with a measured and orderly electronic beep. It had reached 145.

She tugged the Doctor's sleeve urgently. 'When that countdown reaches zero . . .'

He nodded. 'Something very bad is going to happen, yes.'

Forgwyn asked nervously, 'What are we going to do, Doctor?'

'There is nothing you can do,' Crispin proclaimed. 'At five o'clock, I shall assume total control.'

The countdown had reached 106.

'I'd like to say thank you to all the companies and individuals who have helped to make today the most successful Tragedy Day so far,' Wendy chittered away as the parade marched in, swelling the numbers in Lerthin Square and its neighbouring districts up to several hundred thousand. 'Sugarmart, the Shinty Brothers organization, National Fuels . . .'

The countdown had reached 45.

The reinforced steel of the sanctum door split in two and four blaster bolts shot through. One of them caught Shrubb in the arm. He was thrown back by the force of impact and collapsed in a heap next to the shielded TARDIS.

Meredith burst through the smoking gap in the doors. The four guards in the sanctum were dispatched in a blur of shots, cries and smoke. The countdown ticked away in the background, reaching 30. A look of alarm crossed Crispin's face. Ace entered, her face red and soaked in sweat.

'. . . Luke Trading, Quickblend coffee, Windrome the confectioners . . .'

'Help me,' the Doctor cried, dashing for the controls.

The countdown reached 20.

Meredith stepped forward. She raised the blaster and looked him in the eye. 'A job's a job,' she said simply. 'Sorry.'

Forgwyn leapt forward. 'No!'

The Doctor looked down at the smoking tip of the weapon.

The countdown reached 15.

'. . . Linkun Bank, Dannur frozen foods . . .'

'You don't really want to pull that trigger,' the Doctor said softly. 'You don't need to. You don't have to.'

Meredith closed her eyes and prepared to fire.

Crispin shot her four times in the heart, the pencil-thin beams of green light shooting from the small gun he had produced from his inside pocket. Her knuckles relaxed and the blaster fell. She dropped on top of it. Forgwyn ran to her side.

The countdown reached 5.

The Doctor put his arms around his two companions and they put their heads together.

Crispin settled back down in his television chair.

'It's five o' clock!' shouted Wendy Clifton.

The scream erupted from the mouths of the crowd, constant and high-pitched. They put their hands to the sides of their heads. There were several heart attacks and many of the victims died instantly.

The psychotronic signal took effect throughout Empire City. Cars and trains crashed as their owners took up the scream. Dogs yelped crazily and started to scratch at themselves. Cats screeched and ran through the streets filled with swaying, screaming humans.

The nation sank to its knees, tears streaming from its eyes. Rich and poor alike found their noses on the tarmac, their minds blank, their nerve endings scraped by a psychic vibration unlike anything experienced before. Their identities were lost.

The scream continued until it became a low, continuous wail, blotting out the noise of the fires and explosions and crashes that were its consequence and the rumble of thunder that threatened overhead.

In Lerthin Square, Wendy Clifton, Fancy That and the cast of *Whittaker's Harbour* stood immobile on the stage, robotic faces set in their final expression. A warm smile.

Then the screaming stopped.

And the laughter began.

Portellus lifted his right hand to silence the other Friars. His gnarled fingers were the size of oaks.

'Brothers. Our agents are lost to us. Their essences have been effaced from the mortal plane.'

Caphymus straightened his chasuble and wrung his hands fussily. 'Your efforts to bring down this interfering Time Lord have come to naught, then,' he said.

'Put plainly, you have failed,' Anonius pronounced bluntly.

'You were not slow in concurring with my artful strategies,' Portellus reminded him. He lowered his voice and cast a meaningful glance at the high windows of the shrine, through which the workers could be seen, toiling in the gorge of the western mountain. 'I consider it unwise to dispute in a place so open. Remind yourselves, Brothers, of our great powers and our great responsibilities to almighty Pangloss.'

He turned to the Bibles and bowed his head in reverence. The others did the same.

'You speak with wisdom as ever, Portellus,' grovelled Caphymus, fanning his face as a gust of smoke belched up from the brimstone foundations of the shrine.

'Nevertheless,' spoke Anonius, 'I would presume to discuss what action we must take if the Time Lord is not to evade our dominion.'

Portellus put a hand to his head. 'Presumption is a flaw to which I am now long accustomed.' He crossed to the throne on the far side of the shrine. Its arms were decorated with encrusted red crystal. He sat for the first time in fourteen hundred years.

The sky over Pangloss split with a crack and the flame pits flared. The red crystals in the shrine lost their shimmer.

Caphymus swallowed. 'Direct influence?' he queried nervously. 'A manifestation?'

Portellus nodded.

Caphymus gulped. 'But over such a distance?'

'As brother Anonius delights in pointing out, there is no other course left open to us.' Portellus pushed the cowl back from his head and commanded them to sit.

Anonius' lips upturned with the merest hint of a satisfied smile. He sat in the second throne and the power grew stronger.

Caphymus remained standing. He looked through the window at the psychic vortex that had cracked the clouds apart. The last time they had travelled an equivalent distance through it he had almost lost his mind for lack of concentration. Now they were set to travel even further, beyond Pangloss itself.

'Will you obey me, Caphymus?' Portellus snapped. 'Or must I despatch you to the deepest abyss of fiery Phlegethon?'

Caphymus squeaked and hurried to take up his seat.

The geomantic vortex plucked the linked minds of the Friars of Pangloss from their bodies and hurled them into the maelstrom where insanity is the only reality. It battered at their defences, keen to guzzle these puny morsels from the universes of thought. They were protected by centuries of mental training and exercise. It was their single-mindedness and lack of imagination that saw them through the void. They twisted it to their purpose as only true Masters can.

They commanded it to allow their spirits entry to the planet known as Olleril. And, howling its protests and agonies all the while, it obeyed them.

15

The Laughter

'Junior, what is Mrs Rogers going to think about you taking her laundry?'

'Aw, Mom, I had to! Y'see, there was this bear – '

Laughter.

'A bear? In the city? And this floor! It looks like you've dragged a football team across there!'

Laughter.

'C'mon, Junior, you'd best own up.'

'Leave it to me, Betsy, I'm the oldest.'

Laughter.

The people of Empire City acted out the first new episode of *Martha and Arthur* to be made in almost twenty years. The lines echoed up from both sides of the cordon. The gruff tones of Arthur, Martha's placating zaniness, the kids' endearing gaffes.

Forke's unconditioned voice reverberated above the script. 'Able-bodied children and able-bodied adults aged eighteen to thirty-five, return to your dwellings. Other citizens are to remain in the open and await further instructions.'

Still gibbering inanely, two million married couples and six million children obeyed. They stumbled blindly through the streets to their residences. Older people remained in the streets, their Tragedy Day banners and streamers left forgotten on the floor.

The streamlining of Empirican society was about to begin.

'C'mon, Junior, you'd best own up,' said Ace.

'Leave it to me, Betsy, I'm the oldest,' said Forgwyn.

'When I look at you now,' said Bernice, 'I can see why I married your father.'

The Doctor's ears pricked up. He turned from the imaginary newspaper he had been reading. 'Oh, really? What's that?'

Crispin walked between the four aliens. He waved a hand over the Doctor's bemused face. He did not react.

'Perfect,' said Crispin. 'Total control.' His shoulders slumped and he took off his glasses and wiped his brow. It had been close, but his plan had succeeded. Empire City was his.

A handful of guards were stepping through the buckled entrance to the smoke-filled sanctum. 'Take these aliens to the brig,' he ordered them, 'and remove these.' He indicated the bodies of Meredith and the guards she had killed. The guards hurried to obey. The Doctor and his companions were led away, unprotesting. 'Oh, no, here comes Mrs Rogers,' Bernice was saying.

A groan came from the corner of the sanctum. Shrubb pulled himself up. He rubbed at his left arm where the blaster bolt had taken him and looked about, confused. 'The generator?'

Crispin pointed to one of the screens. It displayed Devor and the cast and crew of *Martha and Arthur*, now linked into the machine. Their lips were twitching and their bodies jerked about in their restraints. 'The signal is operative,' said Crispin. He looked up at Shrubb. 'No thanks to you and your guards. Those intruders came within inches of destroying all we have worked for.'

Shrubb loosened his collar. 'I simply followed your orders,' he said. He suddenly realized how much bigger than Crispin he was.

'Your interpretation of them was bizarre. Two women, Shrubb. Two women strolled in here. We are not holding a tea party. Are we?'

'No, Commander,' Shrubb said reluctantly.

Crispin waved a hand dismissively. 'Go, then. Go on. Begin the work you've been waiting for. But do it well.'

Shrubb strutted from the sanctum. Crispin collapsed in his television chair and rested his large head in his hands. 'I may have to dispose of you, old friend,' he whispered.

Shrubb stopped off at his cabin on his way to the ops room. He washed and changed, taking care not to aggravate the wound on his left arm. He could get it treated later. There was no real pain, only discomfort. And he wasn't going to let it stop his enjoyment of the task ahead of him.

He sauntered into the ops room, a slim file tucked under his arm. A technician showed him to the communications console. Forke was already waiting on the other end of the line. 'First stage completed, sir. Citizens in Band A are returning to their residences.'

Shrubb nodded. 'Good, good.' He took out a sheaf of handwritten notes from the file. 'That's the under thirty-fives, yes?'

'Yes, sir.'

Shrubb's stumpy fingers moved around his rough map of Empire City. 'I don't see why we need wait any longer. Send in the 'dozers on the South Side, as agreed. And activate the Celebroids. Recognition pattern six. Anything over thirty-five into the camps. Also Vijjans. In fact any foreigners or offworlders. That should take off,' he counted on his fingers, 'about sixteen million. And prepare the dancefloor.'

'Right away, sir,' said Forke.

Shrubb looked up at the large screen suspended over the ops room. It showed the citizens of Empire shambling about. He had never understood Crispin's insistence on all this *Martha and Arthur* business. But the boss was the boss and in a couple of months everything would be running smoothly. The weird frills were of no importance, really. What was about to happen was good old-fashioned discipline.

Oh, and there was one other thing he had forgotten to remember to forget. He reset his watch. The old world was dead. The date was zero.

* * *

The Celebroids that were stored in the warehouses around the offices of Toplex Sanitation responded to their activation signal and jerked into life. The personality matrices of the copies were unnecessary for this breed. Their faces were lifeless and blank. They climbed up into their designated positions on the vehicles stored alongside them. The bulldozers and crushers and flatteners rolled out.

The Celebroids destroyed everything in their path. Schools, apartments, cinemas, churches, bars. Block after block was levelled. Clouds of choking brick-dust blew around the oblivious citizens as structures toppled and girders clattered down. The humans that got in the way were simply rolled over.

In an hour the South Side had been demolished.

Larger vehicles followed on behind. More Celebroids worked without tiring to clear away the debris left by the first wave. Whenever a large enough space was cleared they moved in, slotting together the candy-striped walls, doors and roofs of the new houses. A patch of bright green turf was laid before each, and then the furniture and personal possessions of the characters were unpacked and installed. The Celebroids were a workforce of alarming efficiency and speed. A row of six houses took an average of twenty-five minutes to construct. Three houses for Martha and Arthur and three for their neighbours, the Rogers. Every row was identical.

At the same time, the population of the central zones was being streamlined. The Celebroids that had been programmed with the personality matrices of the famous stalked eerily through the muttering crowds. Any citizen that did not meet the recognition criteria was knocked out with a chop to the neck.

The robotic duplicates of Wendy Clifton and Fancy That climbed from the stage in Lerthin Square and advanced. Their arms swung back and forth as they dealt blows to the old men of the band that had led the parade. The bodies of the old and the foreign and the alien and the

232

not quite right collected in heaps, ready to be transported and disposed of.

A group of Luminuns were detailed to Globule. The dancefloor of destruction, the ultimate pose for the nihilistic youth of Empire City, was being prepared for an even more sinister purpose.

The brig of the *Gargantuan* was a dark and unwelcoming place. The several cells and torture chambers had been placed very close to the engines, and the noise of the grinding turbines and pulleys that propelled the vessel through the water echoed through the thin metal walls. On a normal day, it counterpointed the drawn-out screams of the Luminuns who had displeased the Supreme One in some way. But this evening a different kind of interrogation was taking place.

The Doctor and his three companions had been tied to upright pillars. Beams of bright green light were shining onto their upturned faces. A low burble of electronic activity indicated that a mental probe device had been activated. The muffled voice of the Chief Interrogator spoke from the shadows.

'You will open the doors of the TARDIS,' it said.

'A talent contest? What use would I be in a talent contest?' the Doctor murmured as Arthur.

'Oh, Arthur, you could show the judges that old trick you used to play on the girls at the prom,' giggled Bernice as Martha.

'You will open the door of the TARDIS,' the voice repeated.

'Hold on a sec. Dad, you used to go to the prom?' asked Ace as Betsy.

'Bet you were a real wow dancer, Dad,' teased Forgwyn as Junior.

The door of the brig slid open and Crispin entered. He snapped his fingers and the room brightened instantly and the probe was switched off. The Chief Interrogator put down his microphone and shrugged.

'Commander, the Doctor has shielded his mind too well, as you predicted,' he reported.

Crispin waved a hand dismissively. 'He will break,' he said confidently. 'And the others?'

The Chief Interrogator shook his head, puzzled. 'It's as if he'd extended the shield. None of them respond to orders.'

Crispin nodded. He stared at the older woman for a while and noted the almost imperceptible lines of strain around her eyes. She might be the first to crack, he decided. There was something about her that intrigued him. He couldn't think what.

He turned back to the Chief Interrogator. 'The strain on the Doctor's mind must be enormous. Continue the questioning. We will weaken him. It may take weeks, but I will have the TARDIS. O Hail Luminus.' He clicked his heels smartly together and marched out.

Crispin yawned as he made his way back through the corridors to the sanctum. He needed some food and a long sleep.

You're a failure, Crispin, said a familiar voice in his mind. *Underneath it all. A failure as a human being.* He pulled himself upright. Why should the Doctor's ridiculous ramblings bother him?

He stopped to peer out through one of the portholes. A fish shaped like an upturned tea-tray swam by. Its large eyes blinked at him, its antennae twitched and its mouth opened and closed a few times. Crispin laughed. What a funny fish. Then he shook himself and walked on. He was wasting time thinking such ridiculous things when there was so much work to be done.

He decided to work out the revised production costs of the reconstruction programme taking place in the city. That was a sensible thing to do. The figures totted up in his head, but he kept losing concentration. It was the tiredness, of course. He really had pushed himself to the limit. But there was something else. He kept thinking of the eyes of the Doctor's friend, the older woman.

234

Bernice was her name, wasn't it? Bernice. She had dark hair that was cut in a fringe and a smile that looked clever and funny. Her eyes were deep blue. Blue like the sea. And her hair was black like space. Bernice. He hadn't realized it at the time, but when he had been standing next to her just now in the brig he had noticed something in the normally flat air of the submarine. It wasn't a smell, more of a feeling that she gave out. It made the tips of his fingers tingle.

He had reached the sanctum. He nodded to the guard on duty at the now repaired doors and hurried to his cabin.

He flopped onto the bed and stared up at the ceiling. As the *Gargantuan* rocked gently from side to side, he considered his great achievements happily. The world was being reshaped as he had decided it. It was something to be proud of. Nobody else could do what he had done. He deserved a rest.

He took off his glasses and fell asleep.

The flying spy cameras enabled Shrubb to select any area of the city for a visual check. He had watched as the Celebroids built the long series of new houses on the South Side. The suns were setting now, and the identical avenues seemed beautiful to him in the fading light. Some of the people were moving in already. The city yawned as Arthur declared his intention to go to bed.

Shrubb yawned as well. Things were progressing smoothly but he found he couldn't relax. More and more sweat seeped from him as the hours passed. He was watching his childhood dreams coming true. He'd been waiting for this day all his life.

He called up a camera that was hovering inside the refugee camp. The lazy scum inside were bunched together, their stupid Vijjan faces mouthing words they couldn't hope to understand. It was a shame, thought Shrubb, that the skiving little cags wouldn't really know what was happening as they were culled. His face flushed and his pulse stepped up its pace as he imagined them screaming and running from death on the dancefloor. He would like to see that, yes.

He flicked his tongue out to moisten his lips. His eyes felt heavy and he realized he couldn't move his injured left arm. He hefted up his right and ran his fingers through his hair.

His hair moved under his hand.

Shrubb kept his hand on his head for what seemed to him like a long time. Then he excused himself from the ops room and staggered back through the corridors to his cabin.

What was her name again? *Bernice.*

She leant forward and kissed him on the lips. It was a long, wet kiss. She almost swooned in his strong arms. He brushed his face against her neck. It was warm and soft and smooth. She smelled of girls. It was the most wonderful smell in the universe, he decided. And girls were the most wonderful things in the universe.

'I love you, Crispin,' she said passionately. 'Nobody can love me like you can. You're the man for me. Love me now.'

He slid his hand over her soft . . .

He woke up and stared at the dull grey metal ceiling of his cabin. His skin tingled and his muscles felt stretched and strange. He looked at his bedside clock. It was eight-thirty in the morning.

He knew he had lots to do but he still felt tired. He curled up under the sheets and closed his eyes. He wanted to dream about Bernice again. She was beautiful.

Five minutes later there was a knock at the door. 'Come in, then,' he shouted.

An aide shuffled in carrying a file. 'The morning reports, sir.'

'Leave them and get out,' Crispin ordered without opening his eyes. As soon as he heard the door close, he rubbed the sleep from his eyes and got out of bed. There was a large mirror on the other side of the room. He squinted into it and saw a boy of twelve with horrible greasy hair who was wearing a suit that was several sizes too big for him and made him look stupid. The boy was ugly and his body looked the wrong shape and his head was too big. Girls would never fancy anybody that looked like that.

He wanted to tell somebody about these strong and important feelings. But he remembered that he didn't have any proper friends to talk to, only people that were scared of him, and robots.

No wonder nobody likes you, said that irritating voice in his head again. But what did the Doctor know?

He wanted to kill the stupid boy in the mirror, with his big head and ugly face and computer qualifications and clever plans. He hated his room and his clothes and the submarine and everything. He wished he had never been born.

He fell back on the bed again. Only Bernice would understand. People would say she was too old for him but he didn't care. She was the most fascinating thing in creation and he knew he loved her more than he could ever love anybody or anything else. He wanted to go out with her to discos and parties and restaurants. He would be able to talk to her about really special and secret things and they would kiss all night long and eat breakfast in bed and read the morning papers. They would watch the moons eclipse the suns and call each other silly names.

But the morning reports had still to be read. He reached down and picked them up. The Tragedy Day operation had been a great success. The signal from the psychotronic generator was holding steady. The neighbouring nations were, as planned, too busy with their own problems to interfere. Many dwelling units had been built. And just under a million citizens had already been collected for disposal on the dancefloor.

Crispin flung the report across the room and buried his face in his pillow. A million people. A million lives. He started to weep.

'What have I done?' he cried.

16

The Explosions

The door of the cryo-storage chamber hissed open and Shrubb walked in. He looked tired and his clothes were crumpled. He couldn't get his hair to look right. It flopped over his left temple, making him look strangely lopsided.

He tottered jerkily along the rows of white coffins and peered at the frozen celebrities inside. He recognized the faces of each well-known personality. His memory, he realized, must have been programmed perfectly. Crispin had done a good job. He had never doubted his own organic existence before last night.

He stopped at a particular cabinet. He had found himself. The chubby cheeks and the loutish sneer of Jeff Shrubb, political columnist of the *Empire Clarion*, stared up at him through layers of encrusted ice.

Confusion filled his mind. He put a hand to the left side of his chest and felt nothing.

'No heart,' he moaned. 'No . . .'

That confirmed it. He could eat, drink, sleep, dream and think. But he was a Celebroid, a machine.

He was determined to survive. He thought quickly. It was probable that only Crispin knew of his robotic origins. With the generator up and running, the boy was now dispensable anyway. It was time to get rid of him, and all the other humans. Was his race not superior?

But there was one more thing to do before he left. He reached down and pulled the coolant pipe from its socket at the the base of his original's cryo-coffin. He watched as the ice began to melt. Jeff Shrubb would be dead within minutes, his body rotted beyond recognition.

Jeff Shrubb checked the charge in the hand-gun concealed in the inside pocket of his jacket. Then he left the cryo-storage chamber.

Crispin had changed his mind three times in the journey from the sanctum to the ops room. He couldn't decide what to do. Everything was mixed up in his mind. Half of him said that he ought to carry on with what he'd planned and the other half said it was wrong and that he should stop the whole thing now before it went too far. He felt strange all over and really angry. He wanted to stamp and shout because things were so unfair. Why had he got all these responsibilities? Why couldn't he just be with Bernice all the time? Not that she would fancy him anyway.

He entered the ops room and the men on duty looked up from their consoles. They bowed. 'O Hail Luminus,' they chorused.

Crispin looked around at the computers and control systems. He understood the workings of each one down to the last nanoprocessor. Computers had fascinated him for as long as he could remember. That was why he had been taken away from Mum and Dad and sent to the special school. He had been five years old then.

He hadn't thought about Mum and Dad for years. He thought he had forgotten them. A clear picture of them suddenly popped into his head, waving and looking sad as he was driven off. They were crying, as if they cared about him.

'Commander, is anything wrong?' asked one of the men on duty.

Crispin shook his head, but he felt very strange inside. His heart was pumping fast against his ribcage and his eyes felt like they were going to pop out of his head. On the big screen he could see long rows of streets filled with identical families of Marthas and Arthurs. A smaller screen showed people being herded up by the Celebroids from the newly constructed death camps across to the dancefloor of destruction. It was just as he had planned.

The whole thing was pointless, he decided. The Doctor had been right. He had made a terrible mess of his life. He had no friends. He had been directly responsible for the deaths of millions of people. Worst of all, he just hadn't cared.

'Listen,' he blurted. The men looked up at him, puzzled by his behaviour. 'Listen,' he repeated. 'I want you to switch off the generator and reverse the signal. The operation is cancelled.'

The Luminuns stopped what they were doing and a hush fell over the ops room. Nobody moved or spoke. 'Well, didn't you hear what I said?' Crispin snapped unpleasantly. He kicked the senior operative in the shin. 'Go on, do it, or I'll feed you to the Slaags!'

The men did not obey. Crispin realized that they were afraid that this was some sort of trick or test he was playing on them. 'I mean it!' he screeched.

The senior operative said, 'Commence shutdown procedures.'

Crispin ran from the ops room in tears. He collapsed sobbing against a wall in the corridor outside and banged his head against it. 'I don't deserve to live,' he wailed. 'I'm evil, I'm so evil . . .'

Without any warning there was a tremendous explosion from somewhere deep inside the *Gargantuan*. The lights went out, leaving the corridor in pitch blackness. The vessel lurched and a burning smell wafted by. Men were screaming somewhere nearby.

Crispin was terrified. He was thrown from side to side and bounced up and down. There was a loud and protracted creaking sound and the red emergency lighting flickered on. He pulled himself up and staggered back through the door of the ops room.

Inside was chaos. Several of the instrument panels had caught fire and alarms were sounding. The big screen had gone blank. Operatives were rushing for the door. They stopped when they saw Crispin on the threshold. 'What is going on?' he asked.

'The generator,' explained one man. 'A power surge. It's gone up!'

Crispin's mood changed instantly. 'Incompetents!' he screamed. 'Return to your posts. Contact the generator room. Get the signal back on line!'

'But Commander, you ordered . . .'

'Do it!' He watched as they hurried back to their positions. The submarine jolted again and they were all thrown to the floor. Another console exploded.

Hot tears trickled down Crispin's cheeks. He ran his fingers through his hair. He was more confused than ever. All the equipment in the generator had been checked many times. The Doctor's Triton T80 could not have caused a power surge on such a scale. That meant there had been a failure in some other area. The one big achievement of his life, his grand plan. He hadn't even got that right. Everything was going wrong.

He ran off through the dimly lit corridors.

The psychotronic frequency cleared over Empire City. The carrier wave of the *Martha and Arthur* impulse dissipated and the people woke to find themselves in very changed surroundings. The citizens of the South Side stumbled from their ugly new houses. They felt tired and hungry and confused.

The Celebroids froze into mannequin poses. The construction work stopped instantly. Silence fell over the city.

The people were free.

But the long line of rejected citizens continued to walk through the doors of Globule and onto the fizzing, crackling dancefloor of destruction. They were used to queueing. It had become a way of life. Did it matter what was waiting at the end?

The valve opened by Ernie McCartney had weakened the structure of the *Gargantuan* considerably. The craft scraped its prows against a series of giant corals and the hull was torn open.

* * *

241

As the signal lost its power, the Doctor blinked rapidly and sneezed three times. He wiggled his fingers. 'I'm alive,' he told himself and beamed broadly. 'I'm definitely alive.' He tried to move and looked down at the restraints securing him. 'Although I appear to be tied to a post.'

'Doctor,' Ace's voice groaned from the darkness nearby. 'Doctor, what's going on? What's that noise in my head?'

The Doctor frowned and looked up at the revolving green eye of the mental probe device. 'Oh, that. Don't worry, Ace, it's just a low-level brain disrupter.'

He heard her groans of discomfort. 'It's screwing up my head . . .'

The vessel moved again and the lights came on. The Doctor saw that their interrogator had been knocked out and was lying over the control panel. His hand had knocked one of the power switches on the probe control. The green eye started to flare brighter.

'Oh dear,' said the Doctor. 'Oh dear.' He looked over at Bernice and Forgwyn, who were slumped against the posts they had been tied to. 'It's just as well they're unconscious, I suppose.'

'Why?' Ace grunted. She closed her eyes as the hum of the probe increased with the brightness. There was no answer. 'Why? Doctor?'

'The power's increasing, I'm afraid,' the Doctor replied. He closed his eyes. 'Ace, try to relax and clear your mind.'

'Some hope,' she cried. 'It's going to . . . kill me . . . Can't you get free?'

'No,' he replied. 'Now do exactly as I tell you. Have you ever been to Bognor?'

She gasped with pain. 'What are you talking about?'

'Bognor, on the south coast. Delightful place. Went there once, or was it twice? Fell asleep on the beach and the tide came in. Very embarrassing.'

Ace realized that the Doctor was trying to distract her mind from the disrupter. 'What happened?' she asked through gritted teeth. The Doctor's voice seemed distant and strained.

'I was washed up at Hove,' he replied. 'But not before I'd had a nasty experience with a jellyfish.'

Ace's head dropped. She felt like she was about to be sick. 'And?' the Doctor prompted her. 'Ace? And?'

'And!' she shouted.

'Then I bought myself some fish and chips and sat on the prom. Took ages to dry myself out . . .'

'It's not working, Doctor!' Ace cried. She screamed as the green eye spun faster and faster over her head. 'It's not working!'

'Hold on, Ace!' he urged her. His face was twisted up with the effort of resisting the probe. 'Hold on!'

Howard Devor opened his eyes. His head was throbbing. He'd been having a dream about *Martha and Arthur*, of all things. It had seemed very real. Now there was a terrible thumping noise nearby. He couldn't see anything. He was lying on some sort of couch, which was very uncomfortable. He sat up. The floor lurched and he was thrown off. He banged his knees against a sharp corner of something in the turbulent darkness that surrounded him. He could hear running feet and alarms and the stomach-turning creak of rending metal.

He pulled himself up and staggered forward, arms outstretched to feel for any obstructions. The floor swayed again and he fell forward onto what felt very much like a dead body. His hand brushed against a long metal tube. A weapon.

He might need that. He slipped it from the grip of the dead man and stumbled on. There was light coming from somewhere ahead.

Still only semi-conscious, Howard was thinking even less clearly than usual. His memory of recent events was a jumbled-up mess of conflicting images. One thing he was certain of. Shrubb had abducted him and tried to use him in a plot to overthrow the Supreme One. Now he was free he had to find Shrubb and kill him. Then he would be a hero, probably go up in the organization. The

Supreme One might even allow him to become the new second in command.

The Doctor twisted his head round and opened one eye a tiny fraction. Ace had lost her battle against the probe. Her head had flopped down onto her chest and her eyes were wide open and terrifyingly blank.

He clenched his jaw as the hum of the machine became even louder. It was essential that he kept his wits about him.

'Doctor!' a familiar nasal voice called. 'Doctor! Wake up!'

The Doctor opened his bleary eyes and received a confused image of a distraught-looking Crispin. He nodded to the control panel. 'Switch it off!' he yelled. 'Switch it off!'

Crispin hurried to the panel, and reversed the power setting of the probe. Its frenzied whirling came slowly to a halt and the green light winked out. The brig was illuminated only by a dim red emergency light. The Doctor looked down at Crispin. 'Having problems?'

'A power surge,' accused the small boy. 'Your machine.'

The Doctor shook his head. 'I did exactly what you asked me to,' he said. 'I can hardly be blamed for botching the initial calculations.'

Crispin bridled. 'It's not fair. My calculations were correct in every detail!'

'Rubbish. Your power requirements were colossal. You can't . . .' He tried to illustrate his point with his hands but he was still tied up. He coughed. 'Er, would you mind?'

Crispin turned a switch on the control panel and the restraints on the Doctor and his companions sprang back. Ace, Bernice and Forgwyn tumbled to the floor. The Doctor went to check their life signs.

'Yes?' Crispin said impatiently. 'You were saying. About the calculations.'

'Well, psychotronics really isn't my field,' the Doctor explained as he slapped Bernice gently to wake her. 'But even I know that you can't generate a field of that size without an ever-increasing power source. The longer you operated it, the more power it swallowed. My Triton T80 merely hurried things along. The end result had to be what we abstract theoreticians call "kerbang".'

'That was the very effect I had intended you to eliminate,' pointed out Crispin.

The Doctor scowled. 'The power differential could never be bridged. You were working from a false premise. It's what comes of not putting your workings in the margin. And now we're all in the same pickle.'

Bernice sat up and smiled. 'Hello, Doctor,' she said warmly. 'Where are we again? I forget.'

'We're on a sinking submarine belonging to a secret cult bent on global domination,' he reminded her.

She nodded. 'Oh yes. How are we going to get off it, then? Swim?'

He shook his head. 'You've forgotten something else. The TARDIS is here.'

They were knocked down again by another lurch on the part of the submarine. When they lifted their heads they saw Crispin lying in a heap on the floor, crying.

'I don't believe this,' said Bernice.

'Nobody cares,' Crispin wailed. 'Nobody in the world cares.' He sobbed hysterically, yelping like a wounded puppy.

The Doctor bent down and picked the boy up roughly by the scruff of his neck. '*I* care,' he shouted. He was shaking with anger. '*I* care about the damage you've done. I said it would all end in tears.'

Bernice grabbed Crispin by the ear. 'Elementary parenting, Doctor. Very good. Somebody should have done this years ago.'

Crispin struggled. His tear-stained face was bright red. 'Leave me alone! Just leave me alone!'

The Doctor was suddenly pushed out of the way from behind. Forgwyn had woken and seen Crispin. He leapt for the younger boy's throat. 'You killed her!' he shouted. 'You killed my mother!'

Bernice pulled him off and pushed him back. 'Hold on, hold on.' She looked into Forgwyn's big tearful dark eyes. 'Meredith was going to kill the Doctor. She lied to us.'

Forgwyn's shoulders slumped and his head fell. 'I'm sorry, Bernice,' he said in a broken voice. 'It's just, I don't know. I don't know what to think. What to feel.'

She smiled. 'Your anger. Save it. We're going to have to fight to get out of here and we're going to have to work together.' She pointed to Ace. 'Wake her.'

She turned back to the Doctor. 'So which way to the TARDIS?'

He looked at Crispin. 'It's not as easy as all that. There are several hundred innocent people aboard this thing. Frozen in cryo-storage. We have to evacuate them.'

'The celebrities?' Crispin's jaw dropped. 'They're not important. We must get out of here.'

The Doctor shook him again. 'You are going to take us to the cryo-storage chamber. The escape shuttles are on the same level, if I remember correctly. You are going to help me wake them and get them off this ship, do you hear me?'

Crispin gulped and nodded his large head. The Doctor turned to Forgwyn. At his side, Ace was slowly coming round. 'Take her to the sanctum,' he ordered. 'And wait for me by the TARDIS. Big blue box. Yes?'

Forgwyn nodded. 'Right, Doctor.'

The Doctor pushed Crispin through the door of the brig. Bernice waved once to Forgwyn and followed them.

The darkened corridors of the *Gargantuan* were packed with shouting, screaming, running men. Howard Devor pushed through the panicking crowds as if sleep-walking. If the lights had been on, somebody might have seen the half-dazed expression on his face and the mezon rifle in his hand and decided that he was quite possibly a dangerous liability in the circumstances. But the lights were not on.

For the same reason, Howard was unaware that he had walked through a metal door marked LABORATORY. The emergency lighting was better maintained in this section. He looked around the large, empty room at the variety of weaponry and equipment. There was enough here to make him rich. He would never have to act again. Why, just one of those compression grenades stacked in the corner would fetch a handsome price on the open market, four million credots at least. He moved towards the pile.

'What the crust are *you* doing here?' said a gruff voice from the shadows.

Howard turned and raised his weapon. His blurred vision swept around the laboratory and settled finally on the barrel-shaped silhouette of Shrubb. He was standing in front of a tank that was glowing bright green.

The mezon bolt from Howard's rifle went wild. Before he could fire another, Shrubb had unholstered his own gun and pulled the trigger. A hot hole was torn open in Howard's chest. The rifle fell from his hand and clattered on the floor. He swayed and fell on his front like an overstacked bookcase.

He heard Shrubb's footsteps coming closer. The strong, sweaty hand of the journalist clasped Howard's head and lifted it from the floor.

'I've wanted to kill you for so long,' he spat in the actor's face. 'I wanted to make it last.' He held a small piece of wire up to Howard's eyes. 'Here's what I came back for. The Stupidity Factor. Your one great service to Luminus.'

'Luminus,' gasped Howard. 'Yes, I'm a devotee of Luminus . . .'

Shrubb laughed and dropped the actor's head. It thumped on the metal floor. He walked out of the laboratory, still laughing.

A few moments later, Howard lifted his head again. He could hear a tumultuous round of applause. Multitudes surrounded him, chanting his name. His face was on the front page of every glossy magazine. He was the biggest star the planet had ever seen.

No, it was more than that. Entire firmaments were bowing to him. Galaxies saluted him. The universe itself proclaimed his total superiority over all things. He was the ultimate being, incandescent, unique, unmatchable.

Howard Devor knew he was going to cheat death. It was impossible that he could ever die. He was immortal.

With his new-found strength, he slid himself forward and reached for the rifle. His finger curled around the trigger. He tried to lift it up.

He died. He pulled the trigger. The mezon bolt struck the pile of compression grenades by his side. They scattered in all directions.

The *Gargantuan* chose this moment to hit bottom. The free-standing consoles of the laboratory were sent flying along with Howard's lifeless body. One of the grenades rolled, rattled and bounced its way further than the others. It was dented by the impact and the safety primer in its tip clicked off.

Three seconds later it detonated. The laboratory was lit brightly for a second. Then came the eruption. It melted the matter around it. The flesh of Howard's twisted body was seared away. An alarm started to bleat loudly.

The reinforced plasti-glass of the glowing green tank had been designed by Crispin to resist almost any disturbance. He had not foreseen the consequences of mezon atoms colliding with compression charges. A hissing ball of superheated energy coalesced in the centre of the laboratory. Forked tendrils at its shifting edges brushed out as it grew ever larger.

The tank shattered and the Slaags bounced out into the *Gargantuan*. Several of them were caught in the spreading fireball. They popped and spattered foul-smelling innards about. The rest learnt by their example and formed themselves into a line. One at a time they hurled themselves over the raging pool of heat and then scampered through the open doors of the lab and into the corridors beyond.

Bernice picked herself up from the floor. Her stomach was heaving and she was beginning to regret having selected heels from the TARDIS wardrobe. She was covered in bruises and her clothes were torn.

On the other side of the cryo-storage chamber Crispin was working on the revival panel. 'Hurry up, hurry up,' the Doctor was urging him. 'Any signs of change as yet?' he called over.

Bernice peered into the nearest coffin. In the emergency lights it was difficult to tell, but the ring of ice around the occupant did seem to be thawing slowly. 'I think so,' she replied. 'But it's too slow.'

The Doctor grunted and again told Crispin to work faster. 'I'm going as quick as I can,' grumbled the boy. 'The safety checks take time to clear.'

Bernice's attentions were caught by a row of monitor screens on a panel set into a wall close to her. She fiddled with the definition controls and managed to enhance the images with an infra-red facility.

She put a hand to her mouth. 'Oh God,' she cried out. 'Oh God, no.'

The Doctor heard her. 'Benny?' he queried, concerned.

'Doctor, you have a choice. Which do you want first, the bad news or the utterly appalling news?'

'Tell me,' said the Doctor, kindly and firmly.

She shuddered. 'We've been holed. Water is coming in through the mid-sections. And,' she swallowed, 'the creatures that Ace told me about, from the island. They're here, moving about.'

Crispin left the revival panel. His jaw started to judder with terror. 'No,' he muttered. 'No, no, no, no, no!' He ran for the door but the Doctor grabbed him and hauled him back.

'Slaags above, water below. How long have we got?' he demanded. 'Crispin!'

Crispin struggled frantically. 'We've got to get out of here, they'll tear us to pieces!'

The Doctor slapped him across the face and yelled. 'You're going nowhere until we get these people evacuated. How long, Crispin?'

He blinked rapidly and put a hand to his cheek. Nobody had ever had the nerve to hit him before. 'Ten, perhaps fifteen minutes. We can slow them down if we close the hatchways between sections. It'll keep us afloat longer, too.'

Bernice laid a hand on the Doctor's arm. 'Ace and Forgwyn.'

The Doctor consulted his pocket watch. 'They should be back at the TARDIS by now.'

'But if they're not?'

'It's a chance we have to take,' he said firmly. 'Close the hatchways,' he ordered Crispin and relaxed his grip.

Crispin punched in a security code on the revival panel and a section slid back to reveal a series of small buttons marked EMERGENCY. He pushed them all in turn.

'Now get back to waking this lot up,' the Doctor shouted. 'Override the safety checks. Get them up now.'

'Doctor,' Bernice asked him. 'With the hatchways closed, how are we going to reach the sanctum?'

'We'll worry about that later,' he told her, but his frown suggested that he was worrying about it now.

The Slaags surged through the crowded corridors in a wave of glee. The human meat tasted good. There was enough for all.

They devoured all that they could find and moved on, splitting up in search of precious food.

Forgwyn led the still-dazed Ace through a tilted corridor that was supposed to lead to another lift. The first they'd tried had stopped, fortunately not between levels, and opened its doors onto the living quarters. He reckoned that if they kept going down they would be all right.

Ace suddenly collapsed. Forgwyn attempted to hoist her up. 'Come on, come on!' he shouted at her.

She pulled herself up. 'Leave me,' she instructed him. 'Leave me here, I'm slowing you down.' She smiled. 'I never knew I could be such a hero.'

'I never knew I could either,' said Forgwyn. He pulled her forward into the darkness again.

The Slaag burst from the ventilator shaft above their heads. Its side had been ripped open somewhere on its

250

journey through the ship and it was evidently in an even less accommodating mood than was customary for members of its species. A piece of bloody meat that Forgwyn didn't want to think about was clamped between its slavering jaws.

There was a flurry of action. Forgwyn threw Ace forward to relative safety and ran back along the corridor to draw off the Slaag. He pulled open the door of one of the cabins and flung himself in. It was small, tidy and undecorated. He searched through the drawers of the bedside table. As he had hoped, there was a gun.

The Slaag smashed the flimsy wooden door off its hinges and bounced in. Forgwyn fired a gun for the first time in his life. His two shots succeeded in wounding the monster. It fell to the bed, gurgling and squeaking. Purple blood spurted from its leathery body.

Forgwyn skirted the bed and emerged into the corridor. He ran forward.

But Ace had gone.

His head turned from side to side as he looked up and down the corridor. 'Ace!' he called. 'Ace!' There was no reply. She had either wandered off somewhere, or somebody or something had taken her.

He ran up the corridor, calling her name in the near darkness. And then he saw the hatchway in front of him starting to close, blocking him off from the lift. He bent down and rolled himself under it.

Breathing heavily, he stood up. The lift door was in front of him. He eyed the call button with trepidation. If it did not respond he was doomed. He stuck out his thumb and pressed it.

It lit up and a moment later the doors opened. He took one last look around him and went inside. The doors closed.

On one of the screens in the cryo-storage chamber, Bernice saw a group of engineers fleeing from three Slaags. The humans hammered on the sealed hatchway that prevented their escape. The Slaags caught up with them and started to feast. She gagged and turned away.

The real Robert Clifton sat up in his coffin. He raised a questioning eyebrow and coughed. 'Excuse me, young lady,' he asked Bernice, 'can you tell me exactly what is going on in this place?'

'No questions,' she said briskly. 'Just follow them.' She indicated Fancy That, the cast of *Whittaker's Harbour* and numerous other celebrities who were being led by the Doctor to the escape shuttles along the corridor outside. Clifton nodded and joined the line.

Crispin sidled over to her. 'We must go,' he said. 'The hatchways won't hold the Slaags for long. We can use one of the shuttles.'

Bernice shook her head. 'We're going back to the TARDIS.'

A strange look came into the boy's eyes behind his cracked glasses. 'Bernice,' he said falteringly, 'let the Doctor go back to the TARDIS. Come with me in a shuttle.'

She was astonished. 'What do you mean?'

His head dropped. 'You see, I ... Oh, I can't bring myself to say it.'

'Try opening your mouth and formulating words,' suggested Bernice.

He stared at her. 'I love you.'

She put a hand to her head. 'Oh,' she said.

'Oh, come on, let's go, together,' he urged breathlessly.

'Not possible, I'm afraid,' said the Doctor as he returned to the chamber. 'There was no time to show them how to operate the controls of the escape shuttles. I had to activate the lot by remote.'

'So we've got no choice,' Bernice observed.

'Indeed not,' he said. 'I suggest that we head for the sanctum using the service shaft at the end of this section.'

'It might be flooded,' Crispin protested.

The Doctor sighed. 'Yes, it might be. It might also be infested with Slaags. Shall we find out?'

The fireball swallowed the laboratory and blossomed outwards. It melted away hazard shields and blast doors. It crept up stairs and down inspection gratings. The crew-members caught up in its passing were consumed in its core. The centre of the *Gargantuan* started to collapse.

The Doctor, Bernice and Crispin raced through the corridors of the lowest level. The water was up to their knees and the air was filled with choking black smoke. The emergency lights were crackling and fading one by one. Bernice put her hands to her ears to block out the sounds of screaming men, rending metal and roaring water.

She lost her footing and fell over. Her mouth filled with freezing water and she felt herself starting to panic. With an effort she pushed herself up and waded on. She could just discern the Doctor ahead of her.

'We've made it!' she heard him cry. 'This is the sanctum!'

She collapsed against the doors, soaking and shivering. The Doctor smiled at her and patted her on the back. 'Well done,' he said and then leant closer to her. 'Bernice,' he asked curiously, 'do you enjoy doing this sort of thing?'

She spat out a mouthful of water. 'I'm used to it by now.'

'That wasn't what I asked you.'

She shrugged and replied, 'Do you?'

He nodded. 'Yes,' he said. 'It's exciting.'

'Well, as long as you're happy,' she said breathlessly.

Crispin stumbled up. He activated the key code on the wall and the doors slid open. They leapt through and the doors closed.

'Oh no,' said Bernice as she looked around the sanctum. The TARDIS was not in evidence. 'It was here, wasn't it?'

'Yes,' snarled the Doctor, who was beginning to look as if he wasn't enjoying himself any more. He hopped up and down in frustration. 'Where is the blasted thing?'

Crispin ran over to his beloved television screens. 'The

entry hatches are near here,' he told them. 'I have an emergency escape chute.'

'Yes, I thought you might have,' observed the Doctor. The ceiling creaked ominously.

'Where are the others?' asked Bernice. 'They wouldn't have taken the TARDIS, would they?'

The Doctor shook his head. 'Impossible. Ace would never do such a thing.'

'So where is she?' Bernice shouted.

'There!' exclaimed Crispin. He pointed to one of the screens, which showed the nearest of the entry hatches. The unconscious Ace was being loaded into the back of Ernie McCartney's sports car by one of the guards. The TARDIS was already inside, lying lengthways on the back seat. 'What is going on in there?'

He was answered by a hiss of compressed air as the escape chute on the other side of the sanctum wheezed open and Shrubb stepped through. He was dribbling and his eyes were rolling. He growled and grunted and finally managed to form words.

'You ... little ... cackbag,' he addressed Crispin. 'I'm glad you're here. I want to see you die.'

Crispin sniffed superciliously. 'I don't think you realize what you're saying, Shrubb.'

Shrubb pulled off his slipping hairpiece and threw it to the floor contemptuously. 'Oh, I understand perfectly,' he said. 'I understand that I am superior. I understand that the Celebroid race shall break from its shackles to conquer this world and a million others. I understand that with the TARDIS I shall become supreme ruler of the universe!' He cackled. 'And all the pinko pansy foreigners will be first against the wall.'

'Most impressive,' Crispin remarked dourly.

The two remaining guards ran in through the escape chute. 'The girl and the box have been loaded aboard the alien craft, sir,' reported one.

'Good,' said Shrubb and shot both men dead.

'Why did you do that?' asked the Doctor fiercely.

Shrubb chuckled. 'All organic life is worthless, Doctor. The Celebroids are the superior race.'

Crispin shook his head. 'Fool. Yes, you are a Celebroid. But did you ever stop to wonder why I had allowed you to work as my deputy?'

Shrubb lowered his mezon rifle. 'What is this trickery?'

Crispin smiled. 'Your original was exactly what I'd been looking for. One step up on the evolutionary ladder from a bulldog and not much brighter. Loyal, obedient and hard-working. But after a while he began to develop a desire to usurp me. So I made you. Because I can destroy you.

Shrubb sneered. 'How? What's to stop me killing you all now?'

'This,' said Crispin and pressed a button on his console.

Shrubb's rifle slipped from his grasp and his arms jerked upwards. His eyes opened wide and a weird electronic bleeping came from his slavering mouth. His neck swivelled in its socket and then his head fell off. It clattered bumpily across the floor before coming to rest at the toe of Crispin's left slip-on.

'I shall be . . . Supreme One . . .' the head said.

Crispin kicked it across the sanctum and returned his attention to the escape chute. 'We must go now, Doctor, the ship is breaking up.' He indicated a glowing map of the damaged vessel. 'Sections five to twelve are already destroyed.'

'We can't go without Forgwyn,' Bernice insisted.

A frantic banging and shouting came from behind the doors. 'Let me in! Let me in!' they heard Forgwyn screaming.

The Doctor reached for the door control but Crispin pushed his hand away. 'If we open that door we're as good as dead,' he shouted. 'The water will flood in here!'

The Doctor knocked him aside angrily and activated the doors. Forgwyn and several hundred gallons of water entered. The *Gargantuan* shook and he was thrown to the floor. Bernice rushed to help him up. He fell into her arms. 'Benny, I lost Ace,' he wailed.

'It's all right, we've found her,' she told him.

'Right, let's go!' the Doctor shouted over the roar of the water. He turned to the escape chute, but Crispin was blocking the way with a gun in his hand.

'What are you doing?' cried the Doctor. 'There's no time for any of this!'

Crispin's face was twisted by confused emotions. He looked tired, scared, angry and sad all at once. 'Bernice is coming with me,' he said. 'I don't care about the rest of you.'

The Doctor threw his hands up in the air. 'What are you talking about, Crispin?'

'I love her,' the boy blurted. 'And she doesn't really like you, anyway. I can tell.'

The Doctor frowned. 'Crispin, drop that gun and let us pass!'

Crispin shook his head and wiped his running nose with his free hand. 'You can't stop me. I know I've made mistakes but I'm going to make a fresh start.' His finger tightened on the trigger. 'And if you don't step back, I'll kill you. Do you really want to be just another body in a heap of bodies?'

That had never been one of the Doctor's ambitions, but before he could inform Crispin so, the creaking ceiling finally crashed down. The four living occupants of the sanctum were showered with jagged-edged chunks of metal. The Doctor, Benny and Forgwyn had the sense to throw themselves into the water and hope for the best. Crispin remained standing. It was his final mistake.

When the dust had cleared the Doctor stood up. He made sure that both of his friends were still alive and then half-walked, half-swam over to the escape chute. Crispin's small, smashed frame lay between a sandwich of concrete blocks. His glasses had been pulled off.

The Doctor worked to free him from the wreckage but the blocks were too heavy. Bernice tugged at his arm. 'Come on, Doctor!' she urged him. The water was now up to their waists.

'He was only a child,' the Doctor said sadly. 'He could have done so much good.'

Bernice pulled him away and took his hand. The water was rising all the time. Forgwyn held her other hand and they rode the current into the escape chute together. It sucked them down to the entry hatch where the sports car was waiting.

A few moments later, the sanctum was submerged completely.

Bernice ran her fingers along the banks of weaponry controls. 'I don't know what any of these do or how they work,' she confessed to the Doctor, who was huddled in the back seat with Ace, Forgwyn and the TARDIS. 'They're meant to be operated by a creature with eight arms.'

The Doctor leant forward. 'Well, press them all in order,' he suggested. 'We can't get in any worse a mess.'

Something thumped onto the windscreen of the car. It was a Slaag. Many more of the ravenous creatures settled on the windows, teeth extended to gnaw through at the meal waiting within. The squeaking, thumping and flapping of the monsters nearly caused Bernice to lose control. She fought hard to contain her terror and revulsion.

Forgwyn called, 'Benny! Get us moving!'

She pressed her foot down on the accelerator pedal and pushed down four of the weaponry controls. The Slaags were repelled as the car surged forward erratically. Bright blue beams shot from the headlamps and blasted a sizeable chunk in the outer wall of the hatch.

The car left the gaping mouth of the *Gargantuan*, which they could see now was lying wedged between two huge rocks. It was listing to one side. Its mid-sections had caved inwards. A molten glow from within illuminated the large flat fish that lived in these lowest waters, which were schooling away from the crumbling wreck.

The Doctor hunched himself forward over the seat-rest and examined the sensor units. 'Forgwyn, what do you make of these?' he asked.

Forgwyn, who was shaking and shivering next to Ace, propped himself up and took a look. A thin red line was snaking up on the sensor display. 'It's a power build-up. I don't know the scale Ernie was using, but it looks big.'

The Doctor nodded and turned to Bernice. 'Take us up to full power,' he instructed her. 'The sub's about to blow.'

Bernice bit her lip and switched on the auxiliary thrusters of the car. She wondered if Ernie had possessed a higher tolerance to changes in gravity than humans. Full power could mean annihilation if he had.

She pushed the pedal down and they zoomed up through the deeps.

The *Gargantuan* bellowed its defiance for the last time and upturned. The few remaining crewmembers were crushed as the corridors mangled around them. The Slaags gibbered angrily in their last moments of life. The screens in the sanctum flickered and died. The smashed body of little Crispin, the Supreme One of Luminus, rested in darkness for a second.

Then the rumble of the fireball grew suddenly louder and the headquarters of the organization that had controlled the lives of millions of people on Olleril for centuries was destroyed in an explosion that tugged at faultlines on the other side of the planet.

The car carrying the Doctor and his friends rode the shockwave. The turbulence roused Ace. 'Have I missed all the fun again?' she asked.

'It looks that way,' Bernice told her. She ran her hands through her hair. She couldn't remember feeling more exhausted in her life. 'Doctor, this mystery tour of yours hasn't been a total success. Can we decide where to go next, please?'

He didn't answer. Bernice looked over her shoulder at him. He was staring into a pyramid of red crystal that had been jolted about and come to rest in his hand. It was identical to the one Meredith had used.

'The Friars must have given that to Ernie,' Forgwyn said helpfully.

The Doctor looked alarmed. 'The Friars?' he exclaimed. 'Oh dear. Forgwyn, would I be correct in thinking that Olleril is on the far rim of the Pristatrek galaxy?'

Forgwyn nodded. 'Yes. It borders on the void with Pangloss.'

The Doctor sank back in his chair, the pyramid still cupped in his palms. 'I'd drop that if I was you, Doc,' Ace advised. 'Gave me a nasty shock when I picked one up.'

'I can't,' he said solemnly. 'It's got me where it wants me.' Ace moved to brush it away but he stopped her. 'Don't, Ace. The energies in this thing could kill you.'

'What have these Friars got against you, Doctor?' asked Bernice. 'Honestly.'

'It seems I picked a fight with them, inadvertently, a very long time ago,' he explained. 'And they're among the worst people I can think of to pick a fight with.' He shuddered as the crystal grew brighter until it lit up the car. The others shielded their eyes.

'If I don't get back,' they heard him say, 'take the TARDIS. Meet you outside the ...'

But whatever plans the Doctor was about to make would never be known. The red light flared and then died. When Bernice opened her eyes again, he and the TARDIS had disappeared.

17

The Battle

On the day after Tragedy Day, Empire City began a slow process of recovery. The areas beyond the cordon had been almost totally converted into row after row of quaint, candy-striped wooden houses. The citizens weren't complaining too much, though. The sanitation and electrical facilities were all functional, and there was plenty of food in the cupboards. But there was much fear and confusion, particularly as Empire TV had stopped broadcasting and there was nobody to advise them on what to do or how to think or feel about what had happened to them. For the most part, people remained indoors and waited for something to happen.

The first wave of construction robots had halted on the fringes of the central zones. The damage done to the up-market areas had been far greater. The trappings of the carnival were scattered about between heaps of rubble from collapsed buildings. Adults hurried to help each other, sharing food and trying to work out what had happened to them. Children chased each other through shattered precincts, unaware just yet how much their lives of comfort and security had changed overnight.

In zone three, the queue to the dancefloor of destruction was growing. It attracted more and more citizens. A queue was reassuring, a link to the old world, the way things had been before this sudden strange change.

People were going into the nightclub, but nobody was coming out.

Bernice found Forgwyn on what had been one of the main streets of Zone Three. He had set up a makeshift stall and was passing out tins of food to a line of former financiers.

'I made contact with Quique,' she told him. 'They haven't signed an aid treaty with Olleril, but they're going to divert an explorer shuttle to pick you and the baby up. It'll take two weeks.'

He frowned. 'Aren't you and Ace coming with me?'

'We're going to wait for the Doctor.' She noted Forgwyn's doubtful expression. 'He'll be back, I'm certain.'

'You don't know the Friars,' Forgwyn said. 'Or the powers they control.'

'And you don't know the Doctor,' she pointed out.

Forgwyn handed out the last of the tins and took her aside. 'Look, Benny,' he said, 'I know why you're pissed off with me. But I had no idea that Meredith was going to try and kill him.'

She raised an eyebrow. 'No?'

'No. She brought me up, yes, but there was so much we didn't know about each other. I really thought she'd seen sense. And the way she died . . .' He sat on a large stone and rested his head on his hands. 'I sort of expected it. That was the way she saw life. Guns, corporations, deals, wars, violence.'

Bernice sat next to him. 'And how do you see life?'

He smiled. 'Differently.'

They hugged. Then Forgwyn asked, 'How's Ace today?'

'Last I saw her she was sitting up and cooing over your brother,' she said. 'They'll both be out of hospital later today. They need as many free beds as they can.'

'Did I hear my name mentioned?' they heard Ace say. She was walking towards them across the rubble. The baby was in her hands and she was feeding it with a bottle. She'd acquired a fetching white hat and a new pair of mirrored sunglasses from somewhere and was looking healthier than ever.

She handed the baby to Forgwyn. 'Here's bro.'

'Any sign of the Doctor?' asked Bernice.

'None,' Ace said simply. 'But he'll be back. Oh, and I've found us a place to kip tonight. One of the nurses says we can stay over at hers as long as we like.' She took off her glasses and looked around at the ruins of the city. 'I guess this is what it takes to restore the community spirit.'

Bernice gave her a friendly nudge. 'So cynical for one so young,' she said playfully. 'Think positive. The Doctor only just stopped Crispin, you know. Another few hours and millions would have died.'

Ace nodded. 'A mad kid,' she said. 'Yeah, I suppose he would have gotten away with it if it hadn't been for us meddling adults.'

'Eh?'

'Nothing.' Ace put her glasses back on as the clouds parted and brilliant rays shone from the suns. She took a deep breath. The air seemed to be clearer than it had been. 'Yeah,' she admitted, 'these people have got a chance now. Without the Luminuns, they might be able to make something out of this crummy planet.'

The sudden heat made the baby cry. 'Oh God, I think it's leaking,' said Forgwyn helplessly. 'Can we go somewhere to change it?'

Bernice spread her hands wide. 'Where? Does privacy really matter any more?' She took the child from him. 'There,' she said. 'Your brother's got a lot of learning to do, hasn't he?'

A man ran up to them. He was dressed in filthy grey rags. His jaw juddered as he wheezed to draw breath. Bernice recognized him as the man who had helped her and the Doctor at the access point a few days before.

She stopped him and tried to calm him down. 'Here, rest a moment. What's wrong?'

He pointed behind him and wiped his mouth. 'I've seen 'em,' he gasped. 'Lining up . . . lining up to die . . .'

'What's that?' asked Ace.

'The dancehall, they call it . . . but they're going in there and not coming out . . .'

Ace shook her head. 'He's rambling.'

'No he isn't,' said Forgwyn. 'He must mean that club I went to.'

The old man nodded enthusiastically. 'The killer disco?' queried Bernice. 'But the Celebroids are finished. Why are people going in?'

Ace sighed. ''Cause they don't know any better, that's why,' she said. 'We'd better get over there.'

Warm dewdrops fell on the Doctor's forehead. After a couple of minutes, he decided to open his eyes and find out where they were dropping from. It turned out to be a very large tree, one of three whose thick and tangled branches shaded him from the rays of a giant red sun. He looked about and discovered that his head was propped between deeply imbedded roots. The earth they clutched at was warm and crumbly, and wisps of smoke issued occasionally from it.

He loosened his collar and tucked his cravat in a pocket. The air entering his lungs was hot and heavy and as he sat up he subjected it to analysis with a scientifically curious sniff. Less oxygen than he would have preferred and a concentration of sulphur that was unpleasant and unhealthy. He held a finger up and then licked it. It tasted of volcanoes.

That was reasonable enough, he supposed, because he could see a range of what looked like volcanic mountains in the distance. Their peaks were visible through clouds of grey ash and the sky above them was a deep purple belt of contamination. On top of the highest mountain sat a large structure. It was a grotesque shape and was listing precariously to one side. The barren land between the Doctor and the mountains was completely flat and he estimated that they could have been anything up to thirty miles from him.

His attention returned to the immediate area as a crisp crunching sound indicated that people were approaching. He hid behind the nearest tree and watched.

He mistook them for a hunting party at first, but as they came closer he saw that the object they were hefting on their shoulders was not an animal but a smoking cauldron, a kind of vat. Their clothes were tattered and patched and their eyes were turned to the ground. They were the most miserable-looking people the Doctor had seen in some while. They were mumbling and grunting, and as they passed his hiding place, the Doctor picked up some of their words.

'. . . in obeyance and eternal gratitude to the Holy Principles . . . protect us in our worthlessness from your wrath . . . we dedicate our futile existence to the greater punishment . . . may the Friars strike us and string us up and pluck our hearts from our breasts if we think of evil-doing and disobedience . . . or if we dare to look on ourselves as beings greater than what we are, which is lower than dust . . . we are cursed, cursed, cursed . . .'

The Doctor decided that they were unlikely to prove a threat to his safety and stepped from cover. 'Good evening,' he greeted them, walking into their path. 'I'm looking for a tall blue box. Have you seen it anywhere?'

Looks of alarm crossed the set faces of the workers but they kept their eyes fixed to the ground and trudged on. 'Protect us from those who would talk to us as if we were more than the base and dung-loving insects that we are,' he heard them chant. 'We shall listen not to their false words and will keep true faith in ourselves, for we are as scabs on the backside . . .'

The Doctor watched them go. 'Some self-esteem needed there,' he diagnosed. He scurried back into hiding as another figure appeared. The newcomer was a short, fat, bearded man. His head was shaven and he was dressed in a leather jerkin and carried a curled whip in one hand.

'Move on there!' he ordered the straggling vat carriers. 'You don't want me to tell the Friars you've been keeping them waiting, do you?' He cracked the whip and the workers lowered their heads even lower. They disappeared behind a cloud of smoke that belched from one of the fissures in the ashy soil.

The Doctor walked over to the fissure and peered curiously down at it. Pieces of grit were blown into his eyes and he rubbed them clear. Then he followed the party at a discreet distance. He had no wish to be caught up in their affairs. Not yet, anyway.

The Friars watched the Doctor. 'He will very shortly reach his box,' Caphymus whispered.

'Indeed,' said Portellus. 'And then we shall extract his members from their sockets and hurl them to the four corners of the cosmosphere.'

The Doctor noticed that his trousers had worn away at the knees, a consequence of his journey from Olleril. He wasn't sure how he had been transported. His recollection was of a bumpy ride through some sort of mental vortex. 'A tunnel of pure thought,' he mused. 'That'd shatter a few cherished theories. When I get back perhaps I'll write a paper on it.'

He stopped as something interesting came into view. The vat carriers and their overseer had reached a channel of scorching hot liquid that bubbled and seethed ferociously. They upended the vat and its contents flowed out into the stream. The vat contained the same fluid.

Other groups of mumbling miseries were doing much the same thing. After the vats had been tipped empty, the overseers cracked their whips and urged them back to work. 'Get moving, scum!'

The workers stumbled off in search of more sources of fluid. 'Although we work badly and slowly we beg to be rewarded with life,' they intoned. 'Not that we are worthy of life. And help us to dedicate ourselves to the service of mighty Pangloss . . .'

The Doctor's eyes followed the course of the stream. It snaked away towards the mountains, where it appeared to broaden and became faster-flowing. Also in that direction he saw a settlement. It was small and grubby and its dwellings were stunted and wooden. A queue of workers had formed in the centre. They clutched small wooden bowls which were filled by the overseers with single dollops of something thick and stodgy.

'Yuk, semolina,' the Doctor remarked. 'Barbaric.'

He was about to move on when he caught sight of a very familiar object. The TARDIS, tall and blue and handsomely box-like as ever, stood only feet away. It had been obscured by the billowing gusts of smoke.

He hopped over to it and took the key from his pocket. Then a thought occurred to him. He leaned against the box and sighed. 'Doctor,' he told himself. 'That would have been very silly.'

'You will open the door,' a voice said.

The Doctor looked around. The workers had long since moved away and there was nobody about.

'Time traveller, you will open the box,' the voice repeated. 'Obey our will or face oblivion in the depths of Cocytus!'

The Doctor looked around again. But he was alone, apart from the three trees that he had found himself under. He frowned. Surely they had been further away than that earlier?

The middle tree moved. Its branches uncurled themselves from the tangle and it twisted and shook. A soot-coated bird cawed with alarm and flew out, its wings flapping. The Doctor stepped back as the tree wrapped itself impossibly into a new shape. The other trees followed its example. The Doctor was confronted by three giant hooded, cowled figures.

He clapped his hands slowly. 'I like it,' he said.

'Do not attempt to humour us,' the tallest Friar said. 'You are closer to death, Time Lord, than you have ever been.' He struck out an arm and a bolt of ectoplasmic energy flew from the tips of his long, gnarled fingers. It landed in front of the Doctor and burst. Two huge wolves, slavering and growling, appeared from inside. The Doctor leapt back but they were on him, tearing at his jacket and pushing him over. His vision was filled by their gaping jaws and dripping fangs.

He felt the giant footsteps of the Friars moving closer. 'You will open the box and give us the red glass,' they ordered him.

'I can hardly do that with these things on top of me,'

266

he shouted back at them. The wolves backed off slowly and disappeared. The Doctor sat up and brushed himself down. 'Thank you.'

'Obey us or confront oblivion!' the leader of the Friars thundered. The Doctor knew from his studies of galactic folklore that this must be Portellus, one of the most feared of immortal beings. The Friar to his left would be Anonius, thin and wise, and the shorter Friar to his right Caphymus the timid. 'Ere long we will summon the hounds of Baal to shred your gizzard!'

The Doctor staggered over to the TARDIS. He noted the scorchmarks around the lock and smiled. Now he knew why they had kept him alive. He turned to look at the Friars. 'Naughty, naughty. You've been trying to get it open without asking.'

The air shook and the stream of lava bubbled in response to the growing fury of the Friars. The Doctor shook his head and tutted. 'Don't get steamed up on my account,' he advised. 'The defence prisms are very sophisticated.' He patted the door of the TARDIS affectionately. 'There, there, old thing, were the nasty men trying to hurt you?'

'The red glass, Time Lord!'

The Doctor folded his arms. 'That's one thing I'm still not sure about. What is it exactly?'

Portellus stepped forward. 'You dare to claim ignorance of your wrongdoing?'

The Doctor thought quickly. 'I not only dare,' he shouted up, 'I proclaim my innocence from knowing transgression of your holy principles. I merely picked the thing up and took it away with me.'

'Yes, but why, eh?' sneered Caphymus.

The Doctor shrugged. 'I was curious. It looked interesting and I wanted to take a look at it. Why, is there anything special about it?'

Anonius chuckled. 'We know that you were the outside contact for the rebels of the Quantern group.'

'It's news to me,' the Doctor muttered, but the Friars were now in full flow.

'You were passed the glass by the last of the rebels and disappeared for centuries,' Anonius continued. 'But we were ever watchful for your return. Even then, the portents warned us that you were a disruptive force. We knew that you would attempt to use the red glass against us.'

'Now give it to us,' Portellus ordered.

The Doctor decided to risk playing for a little more time in the hope of gaining the information he needed so desperately. 'Forgive me,' he began, 'but you control an entire galaxy by the sheer force of mental power.'

Caphymus bristled. 'Our minds can bend raw matter to our will.' He pointed to the low-hanging sun. 'Even the star that burns in the eye of mighty Pangloss we have tethered with our powers.'

'Yes, yes,' the Doctor acknowledged primly, 'and very nice it is too. A vast galactic empire, built upon a foundation of fear and slavery. So why, I find myself asking, are you concerned with one little chunk of crystal?'

'You know why!' Portellus screeched. 'It contains the curse that binds our Union. That which holds the slaves in lowly vassalage. Fourteen centuries ago our powers were weakened as we fought to contain a solar fireball. Those craven-hearted outlings plotted against us, tainting our own control system and making off with the red glass from the Immortal Heart.'

'I see now,' the Doctor said. 'Your telepathic powers are spread thinly throughout your empire. And while you were looking the other way, so to speak, your enemies nipped in and procured the instrument of your power.'

Caphymus shuffled uneasily. 'We destroyed them as we destroy all those that presume to oppose us,' he snarled. 'Now give us the fragment.'

The Doctor thought back to the workers he had seen. They still believed themselves to be cursed, although the red glass had been missing for nearly seven hundred years. They obviously didn't know it had been taken; and its absence hadn't had much of an effect on their lives. What exactly were its properties?

He shook his head. 'I give you what you want and then

you kill me, slowly and horribly. That doesn't sound like too much of a deal. What's in it for me?'

The Friars were not used to having their orders questioned. They twisted and swayed and fumed with anger. 'You will obey us!'

'I have a better suggestion,' said the Doctor. 'I pop into the TARDIS and fetch you the red glass and then you let me go.'

The sky darkened and forks of lightning crackled about the Doctor.

'I'll take that as no,' he said. 'Well, then, I'll throw in the TARDIS as well. You can have it, a fully functioning time-space machine.' He squinted up at the giants. 'Although heaven knows how you'll get in without bumping your heads.'

'We intend to take the TARDIS anyway,' Portellus proclaimed. 'What difference will sparing your worthless life make? Prepare to be embraced by death!'

The Doctor rubbed his hands. 'I'll provide you with lessons in its operation. Warp-matrix engineering isn't just a question of saying a few magic words, you know. And besides,' he leant nonchalantly against the police box, 'there are the defence systems. The TARDIS will have to be reprogrammed to recognize you as its new owners. Otherwise . . .'

'Otherwise?' Portellus prompted loudly.

The Doctor smiled sweetly. 'It will expel you into the space-time vortex,' he lied. 'And clever as you undoubtedly are, I don't suppose even you could survive out there for very long.'

There was silence for a few seconds as the Friars engaged in a frantic telepathic conference. The Doctor took the opportunity offered by this lull to examine his opponents more closely. They were surrounded, he now noted, by a shifting green aura. He reasoned that their presence here was a manifestation of some sort and that their real physical selves were elsewhere, no doubt for reasons of security. They were probably afraid of manifesting outside Pangloss for the same reason, he decided.

269

Their powers were not without their limits. Hence their decision to employ Meredith Morgan and Ernie McCartney in the first instance rather than risk themselves, as they had finally been forced to.

He swept his eyes over the darkening skyline again and fixed his gaze on the misshapen structure that clung to the highest mountain. That seemed a likely place for the Friars to live.

Anonius spoke. 'We have decided,' he said with the oily malice of a creature unused to lying to cover its true motives, 'that your bargain is a satisfactory one. You may enter your TARDIS and make the necessary preparations.'

Caphymus lifted a warning hand. 'But be warned. Do not attempt to exit our dominion.'

Portellus nodded. 'You will find that impossible. We have placed a spell of entrapment about your craft. Try to break it and you may destroy yourself.'

The Doctor nodded enthusiastically. 'Good, good. Well, if that's all settled, I'll get started.' He pushed open the door of the TARDIS and leapt inside.

As soon as the door was closed, Portellus clapped his great hands together. 'These matters transpire better than I could devise,' he said.

Caphymus giggled. 'The little time traveller dances well to our tune.'

'I admire your confidence in the connection,' Anonius said gravely. 'He may yet stay in his grubby box for ages, and die for honour.'

Portellus shook his head. 'Not this Time Lord. He cannot be still or close his yapping mouth for one minute. He may work some trick in vain, but doubt not that we have him. The red glass will be displayed before the workers once again and our Union will go on.'

The Doctor observed this exchange on the TARDIS scanner. 'Maniacs,' he observed. Then he lost his balance and collapsed across the console. The effort of will it had taken to face up to the Friars had been enormous. He ran his

270

fingers through his hair and persuaded himself not to black out.

He carried out a basic systems check on the fault-tracer panel. 'A spell of entrapment, pah!' he snorted. The display showed an image of the TARDIS exterior cocooned in constantly shifting energy waves. 'A rudimentary matter envelope, more like.' He chewed a fingernail. 'Still, probably not a good idea to try and leave.'

The fault tracer began to scroll up a long list of all of the other malfunctioning systems, including itself, so the Doctor hit it and it fell silent. He staggered over to his uncomfortable armchair and sat down slowly.

A vague plan was forming in his mind. If he could work out the frequency on which the Friars' telepathic control operated he might be able to block it. It might help, he thought, to find the red glass he had taken all those years ago and work from that. But a search through the TARDIS for it could take years. 'And besides,' he admitted to himself, 'even if I managed it, all they'd have to do is change the frequency.' He sank lower into the chair, his exhausted face reflecting his inner despondency.

'I've got to do something.' He got up again and played with the scanner controls. The camera settled on the nearby settlement. The Doctor watched the beaten faces of the wretched workers as they choked down their slop. He thought of their lives, shovelling tar and lava from one place to another for no other reason than that it pleased their masters. And then he thought of the countless other inhabited worlds in the galaxy of Pangloss and the variety of creatures that would be trapped in similar drudgery: the victims of this mysterious curse that had reached out to ensnare Olleril as well. Whether he liked it or not, the long-dead rebels of Quantern had bequeathed him the task of defeating the Friars. But how was he to do it?

It was a matter of principle more than anything that prevented the Doctor from regular usage of the TARDIS databank. When pressed by his companions on his reluctance to access this vast store of accumulated information, he was apt to mumble aspersions as to the accuracy of the compilation. It would perhaps be truer to say that he resented its origins. The Doctor felt that consultation of the databank was a bit too much like running for help from the Time Lords.

In this instance he was left with little alternative. He turned on the computer and requested all it had on the Friars of Pangloss.

As it searched its files, he clicked his teeth. The screen went blank for a moment and then the legend PANG-LOSS, FRIARS OF appeared.

The Doctor speed-read the data. 'Area of extreme caution, etcetera, etcetera . . . origins uncertain, yes . . . mental powers enhanced by psychic reduplication . . .' He huffed. 'I know all that. Useless Gallifreyan archivists. Always looking the wrong way for the wrong thing.'

The screen beeped to signify the end of the data on the requested topic. The Doctor looked at the last footnote.

347. Interestingly, in her hypothesis of the relations between pan-universal constants, Lady Pandorastrumnelli-ahanfloriana supposed that psychic reduplication processes as used by the Friars of Pangloss would suffer severe dysfunction if exposed to areas (or substances pertaining to those areas) on the fringes of normal space (see entry – vacuum-charged environments) and/or unsimple spacial interfaces (see entry – parastatic fields).

The Doctor kissed the data bank. 'Wonderful Gallifreyan archivists,' he said.

A few minutes later, the Doctor made the final adjustments necessary to the navigation controls and put a troubled hand to his brow. The task he had asked the console to perform was a simple enough operation in itself. The problem was that he had no idea how his erratic craft would respond; it had been through a lot of scrapes recently.

He took a deep breath and opened the exterior doors. A shower of cinders blew into his face. He edged over and stuck his head out.

'Ready when you are,' he called up to the waiting Friars.

'Impertinent imp!' boomed Portellus. He spoke to the others. 'Brothers, we shall reduce this manifestation by the power of ten.'

The Doctor watched the Friars shrink to a height of about eight feet. The three hooded figures moved menacingly towards him, arms outstretched. Anonius laid his hand on the door of the TARDIS. 'Yes, this is good,' he purred. 'With this craft, distance shall no longer obstruct us.'

Caphymus nodded. 'We will seed our will throughout time and space. Our dominion will extend indefinitely.'

'Pangloss shall be all, and naught shall exist beyond it,' said Portellus. He knocked the Doctor aside and stepped into the TARDIS. Anonius and Caphymus followed him in. The Doctor picked himself up and turned to observe them at the console.

'The ancient wisdom of the Time Lords is barren, yet this spectacle impresses me,' Anonius said as he stroked the console. 'How is this trick of the proportions worked?'

'No trick, I assure you, gentlemen,' said the Doctor. He coughed politely. 'Er, would you mind taking your hand off there, please? It might be dangerous.' He pushed between them and pulled the lever that closed the doors.

'Here we are, then,' he said chirpily. 'The TARDIS is all yours. One previous careful owner. And a pleasure to drive.'

Caphymus had opened the inner door and extended his arm through the corridors. 'I fancy there to be a whole world in there,' he exclaimed.

'You will explain the principles to us,' ordered Portellus. 'And have a care to annotate your words exactly. Remember, we are unfamiliar with the path of pure,' he spat the next word distastefully, 'technology.'

The Doctor nodded. 'Quite, quite. Please observe closely as I fold back the zeta links and activate the lateral balance cones.' His hands worked feverishly over the controls in a sequence that the Friars could not have known was completely without effect. The Doctor had already preset the flight.

He reached for the dematerialization control. 'This is the master switch,' he explained. 'The journey begins.' He threw the lever.

The TARDIS shook furiously and the central column juddered into life. The Doctor was thrown to the floor. 'That shouldn't have happened,' he muttered to himself. He looked across at the scanner. It displayed a receding view of the flame pits of Pangloss. Crowds of dispirited workers could be seen darting about at the foot of the high mountain.

The Doctor stood up. 'No place like home,' he said under his breath. Then he spoke out loud. 'I hope you don't mind me asking,' he began.

Portellus turned to face him. 'What is this?'

'I was just wondering why you need to keep your planets so hot,' he went on. He gestured to the scanner, which now displayed an image of the inner planets of Pangloss, which were tumbling into the distance like red-hot coals.

'Heat is the foundation of our powers,' explained Caphymus. 'From it we derive the vast energies necessary to keep our system together.'

'Ah.' The Doctor nodded. The physics of the situation was becoming clearer to him. If the Friars' power thrived on the accumulation of decay through excessive friction then a reversal of basic scientific laws could indeed make things very tricky for them. He made a mental note to drop a line of congratulation to Lady Pandorastrumnellia-hanfloriana.

'Now, how do you steer this ship of Time?' Anonius asked.

The Doctor sniffed. 'I was just coming to that.' He pointed to a particular panel. 'This unit controls the alignment of the inner dimensional envelope of the TARDIS with exterior, that is real world, co-ordinates.' The Friars said nothing. 'Please stop me if I'm going too fast,' he urged them.

The Friars shuffled uneasily. 'Naturally, we follow these rudiments,' Caphymus said pompously. 'Continue.'

274

The Doctor nodded. 'Well, where would you like to go first?'

Anonius and Caphymus turned to Portellus. The senior Friar considered a moment, and then said, 'Why, the first place of life outside our domain. And that would be Olleril.'

The Doctor nodded and made a show of operating some other controls. A screen on the navigation panel bleeped into life suddenly and the words RANDOM SWEEP FUNCTION – UNSIMPLE SPACIAL INTERFACE – SEARCHING appeared on it. The Doctor switched it off quickly and crossed his fingers. There had to be a suitable area somewhere close. He couldn't keep the Friars fooled for long.

The queue shuffled slowly through the doors of Globule. The dispirited citizens weren't talking to each other. They looked down and walked a few paces forward every few minutes.

'They're like sheep,' Bernice observed. 'How are we going to stop this?'

Ace squared her shoulders. 'Easy.' She pushed into the shambling crowd, elbowing people aside to reach the front.

A man called out, 'There is a queue, you know!'

Ace sneered. 'Queues are for saps,' she called.

The queue surged angrily. Hands stretched out to grab Ace and the unity broke up. There was a stampede for the doors. Everybody ran at the same time and the entrance was blocked.

Bernice tapped Forgwyn on the shoulder. They nipped forward and squeezed through the mob, who were now beginning to turn on each other with cries of 'I was first!' and 'Stop pushing!'

Ace shoved her way through and went inside.

The last of the citizens who had passed through the doors were standing on the dancefloor, waiting for the next random surge. Bernice ran forward. She had an idea of how to handle this problem.

'That's your lot,' she called officiously. She sprang forward and barred the way. 'The queue will reform tomorrow at nine o'clock sharp.'

The citizens groaned and tutted and started to file out.

Forgwyn clapped Bernice on the shoulder. 'Well done. Now we'd better turn off the anti-matter field.'

Bernice held up a hand. 'Stop. Listen.'

Forgwyn didn't recognize the whirring, chuffing sound. But Bernice and Ace were both familiar with the grinding wail of materialization engines in operation.

'It's the Doctor!'

A small green light winked on the TARDIS console to indicate that the random sweep operation had been successful. The Doctor breathed a deep sigh of relief. 'Now,' he told the Friars, 'having achieved a perfect landing, the operator consults the exterior sensors.'

Portellus growled suspiciously. 'But you know where we are. The place called Olleril.'

'You can't be too careful,' the Doctor admonished him playfully as he studied the console readouts. 'From this, I can ensure that the base of the ship is firm, that the levels of radiation and atmospheric pollution are within my tolerance, and that any harmful . . .'

Anonius interrupted. 'The Friars will have little need of such information,' he said disdainfully.

Caphymus nodded. 'Our manifestations are powerful enough to withstand any local anomalies.' He prodded the Doctor with a skeletal finger and chuckled. 'Your constitution is weak, Time Lord.'

The Doctor brushed the sooty stain from his jacket. He said nothing and returned to the sensors. He was pleased to see that recently there had been a contained release of anti-matter in the immediate vicinity. There were traces of another brewing up slowly. The signs were hopeful.

He switched on the scanner and the shutters slid open. Outside appeared a large, dark, underground room. It was decorated with gaudy streamers and discarded skull masks.

Portellus stiffened. 'A shrine for unbelievers,' he said sternly. 'We must cleanse it and return it to a state of purity.'

Anonius inclined his head. 'Needs we must. Time Lord, open the doors!'

The Doctor nodded. 'Pleasure,' he said as he pulled the red lever.

Caphymus sidled up to him and whispered in his ear. 'And to show your faith in our bargain,' he said, 'you will leave the vessel first.'

The TARDIS stood solid and square in the centre of the dancefloor of destruction. Bernice stopped herself from running up to hammer on the doors. She turned to Ace and Forgwyn. 'We'll have to turn the thing off.'

Ace had found the DJ's console and was looking through the controls. 'There are tough operator key codes,' she surmised. 'It's going to take a while to crack them.'

'How long's a while?' asked Forgwyn, taking his brother from her.

Ace shrugged and began to work furiously on the controls. The array of safety checks was baffling. She forced herself to remain calm and started to work things through logically. Panicking wasn't going to help the Doctor.

'With luck,' Bernice said, 'he'll pick up the anti-matter trace on the sensors and stay inside.'

The door of the TARDIS opened and a green glow spilled out. Bernice knew instinctively that something was very wrong. She grabbed Forgwyn and they hid behind the bar.

The Doctor emerged from the TARDIS and looked around. 'All clear,' he shouted back in.

Forgwyn wriggled in Bernice's grip. 'We must warn him.'

She shook her head and pointed. Three hooded figures were stepping from the TARDIS. They were outlined by a shifting green aura and appeared slightly unreal and insubstantial. These were, she now realized, the dreaded Friars.

* * *

'The transfer is pleasing,' pronounced Portellus. 'You have now relinquished control of the TARDIS. Prepare to face death.'

The Doctor feigned surprise. 'Death? That wasn't part of the bargain!'

Caphymus strolled across the dancefloor and kicked the Doctor in the shin. 'Puny mortal. No creature betters the Friars of Pangloss.'

The Doctor took his opportunity to roll off the dancefloor. By now he had reasoned its function, if not its purpose. It was imperative that the Friars remained within its boundaries until the next surge.

He looked up. Anonius was shivering. 'This is far too cold a place,' he said. 'We must stoke its core to a frothing frenzy.'

The Doctor stood up. 'No, you mustn't!' he cried. 'There are millions of people on this planet!'

Portellus sniffed. 'Millions? Then we shall issue forth a wasting blight to fell the excess mouths.'

Come on, come on! the Doctor urged the dancefloor. If just one of the Friars took a step over, the planet – perhaps the universe – was doomed. 'You don't understand what you're doing!' he shouted up at the giants.

'The process will be simple,' said Portellus with relish. He raised his arms and his twisted fingers reached upwards. 'I shall speak dark words to bring the two stars in close. The clouds shall boil and fire will burst from the earth and the sky.' He pointed to the Doctor. 'And you shall perish in the inferno!'

A blast of heat issued from the Friars, knocking the Doctor from his feet. Anonius and Caphymus folded their arms and began to chant. '*Let the stars be torn from their courses! Let the moons be dashed to dust! Let fire and blood consume this place and join it with Pangloss! Pangloss! Pangloss! Pangloss!*'

The Doctor shielded his streaming eyes from the increasing brightness surrounding the Friars. A gust of hot air was roaring in his ears. He tried to stand and was blown down again. The ground started to shake.

He felt someone tugging at his sleeve. It was Bernice. She shouted, 'Where the hell have you been?'

'Precisely!' he shouted back.

The juddering and shuddering increased. By now, the chanting had become a single low note that came from the open mouths of the two subordinate Friars. The Doctor glanced up. He saw that Portellus was growing slowly to his full height. He would smash through the nightclub's ceiling in another few minutes.

Ace was suddenly next to them. 'I've done it!' she shouted. 'I've switched it off!'

'Switched what off?' called the Doctor.

'The anti-matter surge!'

The Doctor grabbed her by the shoulders. 'You've switched it *off?*'

She nodded. 'Yeah, from up there.' She pointed to the DJ's console.

The Doctor cursed and tried to crawl over to it. He felt himself being dragged back by the Friars' telepathic powers. 'Oh no, little man,' he heard Portellus declare. 'You will remain here!'

He collapsed. Bernice shook him. 'Doctor!'

The Doctor forced himself to think. He looked behind him and saw Forgwyn and his wailing baby brother hunched beneath the DJ's console. An idea occurred to him.

'*Prepare to be consumed by fire, mortals!*' Portellus boomed. His laughter vibrated what was left of the air in the club.

The Doctor produced a sheet of paper and a stub of orange crayon from his pocket and scribbled a short note. Then he folded the paper five times and aimed it precisely. He counted to three and launched it.

The hot wind blew the paper plane into Forgwyn's face. He grabbed it and looked up, confused. He saw the Doctor waving frantically at the console controls and shouting something inaudible under the roar of the Friars' magic.

Forgwyn unfolded the plane. The Doctor had written

TURN THE FIELD BACK ON on it. The message was snatched out of his grasp. Sweat was pouring into his eyes. He kept a tight hold on the baby and stood up slowly, fighting every inch of the way.

A sudden gust blew him around the console. The controls were now in front of him. He had no idea which ones to operate.

'*DIE, WEAKLING HUMANS!*' came the voice of Portellus. '*YOU ARE HONOURED TO BE THE FIRST! THE AGE OF PANGLOSS IS NOW! PANGLOSS! PANGLOSS! PANGLOSS!*'

Forgwyn saw the baby's red, scrunched-up face. He remembered his mother's bravery at the birth. He remembered the Doctor's kindness and concern for people he didn't even know. He remembered Bernice's humour and intelligence, Ace's breathtaking talents and valour. He remembered what it had felt like to fall in love with Saen.

And he knew it was down to him to save everything.

He fell over the controls, pressing every possible switch with his free hand. His efforts were rewarded by a dazzling burst of light as the club's sound system activated and the Friars' grave chanting was interrupted by a blast of dance music.

'*FOOLISH BEINGS, YOU WRIGGLE LIKE WORMS ON THE END OF A TOASTING FORK! SUCH TRIVIAL INCANTATIONS CANNOT HARM US!*'

Forgwyn redoubled his efforts. Nothing seemed to be happening. In desperation he thumped the console with his fist and screamed with rage and frustration.

'*NO!*' cried Portellus. '*WHAT ... WHAT IS ... HAPPENING?*'

Forgwyn looked up. A strange warping effect was passing over the dancefloor. The Friars' power diminished instantly. Portellus began to shrink and the chanting stopped. The ground stopped shaking. The thump of the dance music continued.

'What is this?' Caphymus shrieked, alarmed. 'We are being repelled, my brothers! Our way is lost!'

'We must concentrate!' Anonius insisted practically. 'Concentrate, or we lose ourselves!'

Forgwyn rushed over to where the Doctor, Bernice and Ace were getting to their feet. 'Have I done the right thing?'

The women laughed and they hugged and kissed him. The Doctor gave him an affectionate punch on the shoulder and walked forward. The Friars were slowly disappearing.

'Help us, Doctor,' Portellus cried weakly. 'Help us . . . you know what will happen if we are lost . . .'

The Doctor shook his head. The others saw the look of infinite pity that filled his face. He appeared almost guilty. 'I cannot,' he told them. 'This is the end for you.'

'There is no end for ones such as we,' moaned Portellus. 'You must help us!'

'You stand for everything I have fought against,' the Doctor replied. 'All my life.' He turned away from them.

The others looked on as the Friars disappeared forever, leaving only a trail of green ectoplasm to show that they had ever been. A few moments later, that too had dissolved.

'Anti-matter,' Bernice said over the thump of the dance beat.

'Quite,' confirmed the Doctor. 'It repelled their manifestation here.'

'Sorry about switching it off,' said Ace.

The Doctor smiled. 'That's all right.'

'Won't they try to get back here?' asked Forgwyn.

The Doctor shook his head. 'Oh no. They won't be going anywhere. They'll be going nowhere. Their powers are finished. Which means that your mother,' he told Forgwyn, 'and the spider fellow can rest in peace.'

He stretched his arms. 'The Friars of Pangloss. They fell in a puddle right up to their middles and never went anywhere again.'

That said, he walked over to the DJ's console, switched the field off, walked back on to the dancefloor, patted the unscathed TARDIS and started to dance.

* * *

Their power broken, the Friars lost contact with each other as their minds returned to the forty-ninth plane. Caphymus went squealing off into the howling depths. Anonius clung to the passing consciousness of a Zhkjantex anemone in a desperate attempt to reincarnate himself, but without the Union of Three he lost his grip and was flung into eternity.

Portellus tumbled over and over, weeping and wailing. He knew he was doomed to wander these wastes, powerless and alone, for evermore. Formless nothingness stretched away on all sides. It was impossible for him to orientate without his Brothers.

The sentence had begun. It could have no end.

The earthquakes that shook the galaxy of Pangloss sent the workers scurrying back to their hovels. When they emerged several hours later, they found rapidly cooling suns in clearing skies.

A group of overseers herded a group of workers up the mountain to the shrine. The workers pushed the doors of the Holy of Holies open and shuffled forward miserably.

'Forgive us our pathetic intrusion,' said the bravest. 'We are as lice in your presence. We note that the flame pits are closing up, and knowing that this must be part of your great design, await your words on our failure to understand your magnificent works.'

There was no reply.

The grovelling continued for many hours. Still there was no answer.

Finally, the spokesman looked up. He was the first worker in millennia to lift his eyes from the ground.

The Immortal Heart did not contain the cursed crystal. It was gone. If, he wondered, it had ever existed.

He saw that the bodies of the Friars were without souls and ordered that they were to be taken to the nearest flame pit and thrown in before it closed.

18

The Outcome

Robert Clifton straightened his hair and coughed to remind everyone that he was the centre of attention. He was Acting Chair of a small meeting being held in one of the shattered blocks of the media compound. Somebody had cranked a generator into life and the room was lit by a small yellow lamp.

'Now then, everyone,' he addressed the ill-matched assortment of actors, producers, writers and technicians. 'We're all aware of the momentous events that have taken place on our planet in the last couple of days. In fact,' he looked down at his shoes and tried to look modest, 'some of us were directly involved. There has been considerable loss of life and much of our city has been damaged beyond repair or simply swept away. Wendy and I have called this meeting to discuss our response, as professional news-casters, to the crisis.' He turned to his sensible salmon-suited wife. 'Wendy, would you like to start the ball rolling?'

Wendy smiled and held up a typewritten sheet. 'Now,' she said, 'I haven't been able to get to a photocopier as of yet, none of them seem to be working, and much of this information has yet to be confirmed but, basically speaking, this is a list of the staff who sadly lost their lives in the Tragedy Day tragedy.'

Robert nodded. 'And thus will be unavailable for production, I think Wendy means to say.'

She frowned. 'Yes. So, if any of you have any casting ideas, we'll have to cross check with the list, okay?'

One of the writers spoke. 'Yeah, well, as a screenplay,

I see this as a four part mini-series and very much a human interest drama.'

Robert scribbled the suggestion on his notepad. 'Human interest drama. Hmmm.' He chewed the end of his pen. 'You see, one of the things that occurred to me is that we could go for this as more of an action piece.'

The writer nodded, changing his opinion instantly to match where the money looked as if it was going. 'With this alien Doctor and his friends as the heroes, uh-huh?'

Wendy sighed. 'Here we have a problem.' She consulted some more notes. 'Alien heroes are quite popular with the B3 audience group, but we're really looking at a market penetration in the A4 group upwards.'

Robert nodded. 'So we thought of maybe using more upmarket heroes.'

'People who are from Olleril, but were deeply involved in the events,' Wendy put in.

'Well, how about you two?' the writer suggested.

Robert and Wendy looked surprised. 'Us?' they said.

'Well, it's a possibility, Wendy,' said Robert, and went on, 'but what about other casting? For the Doctor we thought Amm Piering.'

The writer laughed. 'But he's a sex symbol,' he protested. 'I heard this Doctor was supposed to be a funny little scientist.'

Wendy sighed again. 'True enough. But a character like that doesn't really fit into what we have in mind. And as for the girls, we thought we'd make it more interesting by making their relationship with him into a sort of love triangle.'

Robert pointed with his pencil. 'So there's a bit of your human interest.'

The writer nodded enthusiastically, principles not only compromised but forgotten. 'Who are you going to have for Howard Devor?' he asked curiously. 'And what about Crispin?'

Wendy shifted uneasily in her seat. 'Another snag there, I'm afraid. The whole child genius aboard the submarine bit, we think, is a bit far-fetched.'

'I don't really think people can be expected to swallow that, really,' said Robert.

The writer recovered some of his daring. 'But, I mean, well, that actually happened. I would have thought all the stuff about Luminus and its plans was pretty important to the plot.'

Robert leaned forward. 'It's a matter of emphasis, really, isn't it? We thought it would be more dramatic to play up the – '

The door of the room burst open and the Doctor strode in angrily. Wendy stood to greet him. 'Oh, hello, Doctor. We were just discussing you.'

He frowned. 'I know. I've been listening outside the door.'

Wendy looked down guiltily. 'Ah. Well, our legal department will be in touch very shortly about the rights to your story, and we'll be offering very favourable terms . . .'

The Doctor scowled. 'Listen!' he shouted. The room fell quiet. A clamorous roaring and cheering could be heard in the distance.

Robert sneered. 'Oh, it's just a riot,' he said casually. 'I wondered how long it was going to take for things to get back to normal.'

The Doctor walked over and hauled Robert to his feet. 'It's not a riot,' he said furiously. 'It's an uprising. The cordon came down two hours ago.' He relinquished his grip and Robert fell back in the chair. There was now a look of genuine surprise on his face.

'I'm sure the police will be able to sort it out,' Wendy said confidently.

The Doctor snorted and scattered the papers she had placed on the table. 'Don't you understand? No police. No barriers. No economy. No money. No control.' He pocketed the list of fallen performers. 'And no television. I suggest you find a shovel and get out and make yourselves useful.'

With that, he turned and left the room. Nobody spoke for a while. And now it had been pointed out, the uprising sounded louder and closer and more jubilant than a riot.

'He's overreacting,' said Wendy. 'Isn't he?'

'That's what comes of putting all your eggs in one basket,' Bernice observed as she watched the statue of General Stillmun being toppled from its base in Lerthin Square. There was a tremendously loud cheer from the gathered thousands.

'There must be some Luminuns still about,' Forgwyn said.

'Without their base they aren't going to be much use,' said Ace.

The crowd surged forward again amiably.

Use of a detector had enabled the Doctor to find the red glass quicker than he could have hoped in the corridors of the TARDIS. He took it from his pocket and held it up to the light of the suns. He had already carried out a series of tests on it and the results had been very interesting.

He put it back in his pocket and looked down. He was perched on top of the inspection tower at the refugee camp. Beneath him was a mass of heads. Lives that had been changed. They were moving towards the exits and seemed happy and hopeful.

Tomorrow, he knew, things would look very different to the people of the city. Their task was not going to be an easy one. There were so many possibilities open to them. But now was a good time to celebrate.

The offices of Toplex Sanitation were ransacked by the angry mob. The advanced equipment was smashed to pieces as they moved through the block. They found the computer files that detailed the extent of Luminus involvement in many of the atrocities to have befallen the planet. Their anger increased.

There was a blastproof vault in the cellar of the building. When the door was eventually opened, the crowd were set upon by Forke and his operatives. The battle lasted half an hour. The weaponry of the Luminuns was more sophisticated, but the numbers and passion of the people overpowered them.

Forke fell in the first minutes of the battle.

The Doctor stood between a row of striped wooden houses. This place was where the home of Madam Guralza had stood. He looked again at the list of fallen media personnel he had taken from Wendy Clifton. Her name was on it.

'Another few hours and I could have saved you,' he whispered. In his other hand was his blue gemstone ring. He had rescued it from the body of a police officer, a man called Felder who had been hated by nearly everyone on the South Side.

Word passed around the city that evening that there was to be a public address outside the offices of the admin company. At eight o'clock sharp, Maurice Taylor walked onto the high balcony and tried to speak. Everybody laughed and chanted up that they weren't going to pay him any more business charge or personal charge or registration charge or charge overheads charge. Maurice's words were lost under the shouting, which was a shame as he was trying to say sorry and had intended to announce the admin company's closure of business.

Next on stage was the Doctor, whose initial discomfort at the ovation he received soon gave way to a pleasant feeling that made him realize that what everybody in the universe needs now and again is a big round of applause for doing what they do best.

He blew a football whistle into the microphone to calm the crowd. 'My friends,' he proclaimed at last, 'I am about to leave your planet. Thank you for having me.'

The people laughed.

'When I first arrived here,' he continued, 'only last Tuesday, it was a very different place. Oh, it may have looked about the same. But there was something in the air. Gloom, despondency, frustration and anger. The curse of Olleril.

'Your histories speak of the people who once lived here; the people your ancestors all but destroyed. Of how they and their world, and thus you in turn, were cursed by the mysterious red glass. Many of you, I know, believe in this superstition.' He pointed to the night sky, the stars now visible for the first time in seventy years. 'Up there, the Friars of Pangloss, rulers of the empire from which it had come, were waiting for the return of the stranger that had taken it. They needed it back in case their slaves discovered it had gone.'

He pulled the crystal from his pocket. 'Well, I have the red glass,' he said casually.

The crowd gasped.

'And I can report,' he went on, 'that it has never contained the slightest trace of power, supernatural or scientific. It is a chunk of very ordinary crystal.

'The curse of the red glass was the curse of fear and guilt. The Friars of Pangloss were afraid of losing control of their empire. They told their slaves they had been cursed by the red glass. And the slaves believed. When the glass came here, much the same thing happened. The natives feared it. The colonists took on that fear. Their descendants in Luminus used it to increase the insecurity of you people. Thus breeding more insecurity. What a friend of mine called tangible unease.'

He coughed and straightened his cravat. 'This was the response of the human species. You are afraid of your own abilities to live and work together successfully. You worry that you are a divided and intrinsically violent race. You refuse to believe that the things you often take for granted – authority, law, money – could be the things that are holding you back.'

He held up the red glass. 'And you put all of your fear and confusion into the story of this. I suggest you forget it and get on with things.' He threw it into the crowd.

'Luminus, in all its many guises, is gone, at least from this world, and it's up to you now,' he concluded. 'I may pop back in a few hundred years to see how you're doing. Remember, there are vast areas of unclaimed land outside the city. Why not get out there and see what you can do with it?' He turned to leave and then nipped back quickly. 'Oh, and by the way,' he suggested. 'I've found that co-operation and everybody pulling their weight can work wonders.'

He left the balcony.

Forgwyn said his goodbyes to them later that evening. He would have liked to walk them back to the TARDIS, but he'd promised to get back to the house he was staying in by midnight.

'I'll probably never see you again,' he said tearfully as he was hugged by Ace and Bernice.

'Just don't forget us,' said Bernice.

'Have a good trip and a good life,' Ace said.

He shook hands with the Doctor. 'Thanks for everything.'

The Doctor smiled. 'Thank you. But please don't go saving the universe again if you can possibly help it. That's *my* job.'

Forgwyn turned and walked away without looking back. There was a big lump in his throat and despite the atmosphere around him – a *real* carnival atmosphere, he noted – he felt disappointed. Recent events had been terrifying, yes, but they'd also been challenging and exciting. He wondered if the rest of his life was going to seem dull by comparison.

He got back to the nurse's house and checked to see that his tiny brother was sleeping well. Then he went downstairs to make himself a drink. The gas supply had been reconnected, which was a start.

There were some other people staying in the house and he could tell that many of them had been drinking. One of them came over to him. 'You were at Globule the other night, weren't you?' he was asked by a blond boy of about his age.

Forgwyn stared and nodded. He remembered the boy and remembered thinking that he couldn't fancy anybody

289

from Olleril. But Olleril had changed. And so, perhaps, had he.

The Doctor, Bernice and Ace were walking back to the TARDIS. One of the giant papier-mâché skeletons was slumped against a wall. Its mouth had dropped open. It looked surprised.

'No more Tragedy Days for you, mate,' Ace told it. 'With everyone in the same mess there's nobody to feel guilty about and nobody to beg from.'

'Quite,' said the Doctor. 'Most tragedies are avoidable. From now on there'll be no rich and no poor. It's a case of half a dozen of one and six of the other.'

'Don't you mean six of one and half a dozen of the other?' asked Bernice.

He frowned. 'That's what I just said.'

They entered the nightclub. 'Doctor,' Bernice said, 'can I perhaps make a small request?'

'Be my guest.'

'Is there any hope of us choosing our next destination? In life I prefer to know where I'm going.'

The Doctor chuckled and patted her on the shoulder. 'How very boring.'

Ace laughed. 'Besides, the state the TARDIS is in now we'll be lucky to get where we want to anyway.'

The Doctor put his hand to the peeling paintwork of the police box. 'Don't listen to a word of it, old thing,' he reassured it. 'They're only jealous of your place in my affections.'

He opened the doors and they went inside. A few moments later, to the accompaniment of a raucous bellowing and chuffing noise, the TARDIS left Olleril to its uncertain but hopeful destiny.

Already published:

291

CAT'S CRADLE: WARHEAD
Andrew Cartmel

The place is Earth. The time is the near future – all too near. As environmental destruction reaches the point of no return, multinational corporations scheme to buy immortality in a poisoned world. If Earth is to survive, somebody has to stop them.

ISBN 0 426 20367 4

CAT'S CRADLE: WITCH MARK
Andrew Hunt

A small village in Wales is visited by creatures of myth. Nearby, a coach crashes on the M40, killing all its passengers. Police can find no record of their existence. The Doctor and Ace arrive, searching for a cure for the TARDIS, and uncover a gateway to another world.

ISBN 0 426 20368 2

NIGHTSHADE
Mark Gatiss

When the Doctor brings Ace to the village of Crook Marsham in 1968, he seems unwilling to recognize that something sinister is going on. But the villagers are being killed, one by one, and everyone's past is coming back to haunt them – including the Doctor's.

ISBN 0 426 20376 3

LOVE AND WAR
Paul Cornell

Heaven: a planet rich in history where the Doctor comes to meet a new friend, and betray an old one; a place where people come to die, but where the dead don't always rest in peace. On Heaven, the Doctor finally loses Ace, but finds archaeologist Bernice Summerfield, a new companion whose destiny is inextricably linked with his.

ISBN 0 426 20385 2

TRANSIT
Ben Aaronovitch

It's the ultimate mass transit system, binding the planets of the solar system together. But something is living in the network, chewing its way to the very heart of the system and leaving a trail of death and mutation behind. Once again, the Doctor is all that stands between humanity and its own mistakes.

ISBN 0 426 20384 4

THE HIGHEST SCIENCE
Gareth Roberts

The Highest Science – a technology so dangerous it destroyed its creators. Many people have searched for it, but now Sheldukher, the most wanted criminal in the galaxy, believes he has found it. The Doctor and Bernice must battle to stop him on a planet where chance and coincidence have become far too powerful.

ISBN 0 426 20377 1

THE PIT
Neil Penswick

One of the Seven Planets is a nameless giant, quarantined against all intruders. But when the TARDIS materializes, it becomes clear that the planet is far from empty – and the Doctor begins to realize that the planet hides a terrible secret from the Time Lords' past.

ISBN 0 426 20378 X

DECEIT
Peter Darvill-Evans

Ace – three years older, wiser and tougher – is back. She is part of a group of Irregular Auxiliaries on an expedition to the planet Arcadia. They think they are hunting Daleks, but the Doctor knows better. He knows that the paradise planet hides a being far more powerful than the Daleks – and much more dangerous.

ISBN 0 426 20362 3

LUCIFER RISING
Jim Mortimore & Andy Lane

Reunited, the Doctor, Ace and Bernice travel to Lucifer, the site of a scientific expedition that they know will shortly cease to exist. Discovering why involves them in sabotage, murder and the resurrection of eons-old alien powers. Are there Angels on Lucifer? And what does it all have to do with Ace?

ISBN 0 426 20338 7

WHITE DARKNESS
David McIntee

The TARDIS crew, hoping for a rest, come to Haiti in 1915. But they find that the island is far from peaceful: revolution is brewing in the city; the dead are walking from the cemeteries; and, far underground, the ancient rulers of the galaxy are stirring in their sleep.

ISBN 0 426 20395 X

CONUNDRUM
Steve Lyons

A killer is stalking the streets of the village of Arandale. The victims are found each day, drained of blood. Someone has interfered with the Doctor's past again, and he's landed in a place he knows he once destroyed, from which it seems there can be no escape.

ISBN 0 426 20408 5

NO FUTURE
Paul Cornell

At last the Doctor comes face-to-face with the enemy who has been threatening him, leading him on a chase that has brought the TARDIS to London in 1976. There he finds that reality has been subtly changed and the country he once knew is rapidly descending into anarchy as an alien invasion force prepares to land . . .

ISBN 0 426 20409 3

TRAGEDY DAY
Gareth Roberts

When the TARDIS crew arrive on Olleril, they soon realise that all is not well. Assassins arrive to carry out a killing that may endanger the entire universe. A being known as the Supreme One tests horrific weapons. And a secret order of monks observes the growing chaos.

ISBN 0 426 20410 7

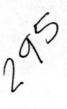

296

WHO ARE YOU?
Help us to find out what you want.
No stamp needed – free postage!

Name

Address

Town/County

Postcode

Home Tel No.

About Doctor Who Books

How did you acquire this book?
Buy ☐ Borrow ☐
Swap ☐

How often do you buy Doctor Who books?
1 or more every month ☐ 3 months ☐
6 months ☐ 12 months ☐

Roughly how many Doctor Who books have you read in total?

Would you like to receive a list of all past and forthcoming Doctor Who titles?
Yes ☐ No ☐

Would you like to be able to order the Doctor Who books you want by post?
Yes ☐ No ☐

Doctor Who Exclusives
We are intending to publish exclusive Doctor Who editions which may not be available from booksellers and available only by post.

Would you like to be mailed information about exclusive books?
Yes ☐ No ☐

About You

What other books do you read?

Other character-led books (which characters?) _____

Science Fiction	☐	Thriller/Adventure	☐
Horror	☐		

Non-fiction subject areas (please specify) _____

Male	☐	Female	☐

Age:

Under 18	☐	18–24	☐
25–34	☐	35+	☐

Married	☐	Single	☐
Divorced/Separated	☐		

Occupation _____

Household income:

Under £12,000	☐	£13,000–£20,000	☐
£20,000+	☐		

Credit Cards held:

Yes	☐	No	☐

Bank Cheque guarantee card:

Yes	☐	No	☐

Is your home:

Owned	☐	Rented	☐

What are your leisure interests? _____

Thank you for completing this questionnaire. Please tear it out carefully and return to: **Doctor Who Books, FREEPOST, London, W10 5BR** (no stamp required)